I0768583

CITY OF LIGHTS AND SKULLS

First Edition
First Printing, March 2025
Cover design by Seventhstar Art Services
Book design by Château Boho Books, LLC
This is a work of fiction. Names, characters, places, and incidents are either the product of the author's imagination or are used fictitiously, and any resemblance to persons living or dead, business establishments, events, or locales, is coincidental.
No artificial intelligence software was involved in the concept, writing, editing, design, or cover creation of this book.
Library of Congress Cataloging-in-Publication Data
Rose, Kathryn
City of Lights and Skulls/Kathryn Rose—First Edition
Summary: At the World Columbian Exposition in Chicago, 1893, two outsiders must work together to reveal the danger that threatens the city.
Hardcover ISBN – 979-8-9918827-0-5
Paperback ISBN – 979-8-9918827-1-2

Château Boho Books, LLC
Los Angeles, California, United States of America
www.chateaubohobooks.com

Printed in the United States of America

For Sarah

CONTENT WARNING

Death, violence, mutilation, kidnapping, firearms, weapons,
horror, profanity, one conversation implying self-harm.

CITY OF LIGHTS AND SKULLS

KATHRYN ROSE

"A tale born of others,
    Girls who lived before me.
    Their eyes had missed glamours,
    Warnings failed to slip free.

Bones made of pure iron,
    Their words dark like ore,
    And an army behind him,
    This devil folklore.

His grit old as time,
    He found a girl full of hate.
    In the pages that follow
    He'll chain her to a dark fate.

She'll hunger in silence
    For souls 'til she feeds
    Damned to do this for eons
    Until she's made to find sleep.

This island has hauntings.
    But there's one we must tell.
    Because girls might not know
    That they're dwelling in Hell."

—Excerpt from *"The Traveling Demon and the Peasant Girl"*
A Folktale of Chicago
By Anonymous

ACT I

CHAPTER 1

CHICAGO WINS—1893

A DINNER PARTY WAS IN FULL SWING BEHIND THE VERANDAH'S
gilded doors.

From the grounds within the estate of Mr. Rex Winston,
Fernando García Carolan listened to the music, its echoes
rendering the lonely backyard where he waited that much lone-
lier. Laughter and chatter wove through the melody, the kind that
came with money or celebration, or—if one were lucky—a
healthy mix of both.

Or so Fernando imagined. Or so Fernando hoped and
dreamed and wished for in a way he'd never dared to in Brooklyn. Because this was Chicago nearing the turn of the century.
The newly-minted greatest city in the American Midwest. The
very metropolis that had beaten his home of New York to host
the world on an international stage.

Saints be with me, Fernando prayed, more out of habit than
piety.

A stray copy of *The Chicago Tribune* from the farmer's wagon
on Fernando's cross-country trip was tucked in his pocket, a
prophetic edition from three years earlier whose front-page head-

line read, *CHICAGO WINS*. Beside it sat a letter from Fernando's father: heavy and carrying the look of something that contained hope in dollar signs.

Hope was never cheap.

Time crept by as Fernando waited for Mr. Winston to step away from the soirée to receive him. Each minute shrank Fernando's stature more and more, a ragamuffin boy whose black locks with their hint of curl were parted to the side in an attempt to distract from his work boots for the fairgrounds, ones that had served him well on his parents' construction site in Brooklyn.

Fernando wouldn't think about that now.

Mr. Winston's verandah was a garden of uniformly-cut shrubs and decadent white orchids that surrounded an eggshell-white, linen-clad table that had been setup for an impromptu tea by the housekeeper, Mrs. Grant. Two places were ready with embroidered white napkins, delicate china, and the smallest teacups Fernando had ever seen. A pot of hot black tea waited with steam billowing from the spout, and to its side sat a creamer and a dish of sparkling sugar cubes.

In the center stood a tower of cucumber sandwiches and white cakes. From where Fernando stood, he could smell the sweetness of the desserts, and suddenly hunger caught up with him. With a glance around the empty verandah, he inched closer to the table. Surely, no one would miss *one*.

With a careful footstep, he stretched his arm toward the cakes, and a finger brushed the frosting when—

"Skipping the sandwiches, I see," a voice called from the door. Fernando startled and yanked his hand away. His balance betrayed him, and he grabbed the edge of the table for support, jostling it until a splatter of Darjeeling spilled onto the linens.

Fernando's eyes widened in horror. He tore his gaze to the door. "Sorry. I'm so, so sorry."

"Forget it, my boy." Rex Winston strode onto the verandah in a black suit, his skin pale like overcast clouds. He was as tall as his voice was loud, though not as tall as Fernando remembered from the Sunday mornings in Brooklyn after Mass, when his mother would invite a man she perceived as both lonely and forgotten over for brunch. Now that Fernando had breached six feet in height, Mr. Winston seemed frailer, but just as staunch-faced as ever.

"It was a wise choice. The cucumbers render the bread soggy anyway. Toast is no match for a vegetable that's mostly water." Mr. Winston reached out in greeting a hand that occupied a familiar ring Fernando also remembered from childhood. An antique signet perhaps, it bore a stone skull in the band as though it'd been carved free of rock a thousand years before. Fernando recalled many Sunday mornings at the breakfast table staring at it, convinced it was alive.

Fernando told himself to forget the sharpness of those childhood memories, but it was impossible. Days after leaving home, New York's skyline was still branded onto Fernando's lids every time he shut his eyes—the shine of the rippling Atlantic, even more so. His mother's mantle in their Brooklyn apartment, painted shades of warm vanilla, adorned with pictures of the Holy Virgin and Child, and blessed with glass-bead rosaries—the only possessions she'd taken from Dublin when she'd moved to Barcelona at eighteen. His father's jokes—in Spanish and in English—and how his mother would laugh at them. Even the Spanish ones, which always swept past her while Fernando and his father understood them perfectly.

Fernando remembered how his mother smiled.

And then he remembered the words. Words in Spanish, words in English—whatever words he could yell at his parents the day of the accident. How three widows visited their Brooklyn home wearing white lace gloves that matched his mother's vanilla mantle because women of good standing wore white gloves when they couldn't afford black ones. The horror in Imogen Carolan's eyes when Juan had told her what'd happened, three new bodies in the Catholic cemetery with fresh soil not yet patted down. Why the structure had collapsed. Why Juan had looked away. Why their lives would change from eggs and bread and jam on the breakfast table to bread, and bread alone.

Days ago had quickly turned into a lifetime ago.

Fernando cleared his throat and shook Mr. Winston's hand. "Sir," he said in the voice of a gentleman. "I've interrupted your evening. Thank you for seeing me. Thank you very, very much."

"Interrupted nothing, I assure you." Mr. Winston smiled politely. His smiles felt practiced, unnatural, but Fernando wouldn't judge someone on that. "Dear boy, it's been quite a while." He slapped Fernando's strong shoulders. "Has it been ten years already? You're how old now?"

"Eighteen, sir."

"Eighteen." Mr. Winston's voice softened. "Mrs. Grant. Can you believe that?"

A woman in a starchy gray dress appeared at Fernando's side. Mrs. Grant's hair was wound around the back of her head into a chignon, its tightness perfectly matching her chilly disposition. With a glare at the spill on the tablecloth, she poured Fernando and Mr. Winston tea and called on her way out the door, "Not at all, sir."

"Eighteen," Mr. Winston repeated. "Have a seat. You've had a proper tea before, haven't you?"

"No, sir."

"Well, it's easy. Just drink it while it's hot and steer clear of discussions of politics. Then you'll be set to mingle with the folks in this city who spend their time swirling brandies."

"Yes, sir."

Mr. Winston searched the table for cream, and Fernando fished his father's letter out of his pocket. The letter felt even heavier now that Fernando was set to give it away, but he reminded himself that everything was already in place.

"Sir," Fernando began. "My father—"

Mr. Winston's eyes shot up—heavy and all-seeing under graying brows—and lifted his hand to receive the envelope. "Yes, that's right. Best to get all these details out of the way." The wrinkles around his eyes deepened with another forced smile.

Mr. Winston withdrew a silver letter opener from inside his pocket and lanced the seal. He pulled out a paper-wrapped wad of bills. Fernando gulped.

Jesus, Mary, and Joseph. Two people who swore they'd never speak to me again just bought me a new life.

Or at least a share of one as Rex Winston loaned him the rest.

Fernando's eyes brimmed with hot tears.

"This is enough for two weeks at any establishment in the city," Mr. Winston said thoughtfully as though his mind were more occupied with numbers than anything else. "It's good money—better than I expected when I spoke to your father, to be honest—but certainly not enough for an entire month."

He set the bills inside his jacket's inner pocket. The letter from Fernando's father he folded carefully into two squares as he made his way toward a fireplace in the corner of the verandah.

"No matter. Things will be taken care of. I've arranged work for you at one of the spectacles at the fairgrounds. At this… rounded structure they're rushing to finish. Months behind schedule, unfortunately. Bureaucracy—I tell you."

A burst of laughter in harmonious voices sounded from within the estate, and Fernando stared at the dark wood door, imagining the men behind it dressed in similar fashions to Mr. Winston: black silk and stiff white collars bejeweled with cufflinks of precious stones.

Mr. Winston gave a nod. "Once again, you interrupted nothing tonight."

Fernando managed a small smile.

"The contraption was named after the chap who designed it —George Ferris, I believe—and if you ask me, the blasted thing looks like a death trap. But a good start for anyone looking for opportunities in Chicago."

Mr. Winston spoke in a lighthearted voice, all the while preoccupied with the fire and how its flames ate up the letter.

"As arranged, I'm willing to pay the difference you'll need for several months' rent in exchange for a set percentage of your wages until your debt is paid off." Mr. Winston sat back in his chair. "I won't even charge you interest if you can make it up to me in three weeks' time. Now how's that for an opportunity, my boy? Don't get too used to it—deals like this one aren't usually so generous in the real world. Best you learn that sooner rather than later."

The letter singed until it turned to ash.

Fernando stared at the flames in the fireplace. He hadn't expected Mr. Winston to burn his father's letter.

"As for the fairgrounds, they've covered the lake with enough solid land to build a park. Railway tracks will converge, a divining point from east and west. Peristyles with an old classically-European shape—white columns and what have you. They've even built a giant pond in the middle with fountains. Trying to make the Parisians' new Eiffel Tower look bad, I surmise. The daily trek will be inconvenient, but not impossible."

Fernando stood, his tea now cold. "Getting there won't be a problem, sir. I'm eternally grateful. But I should leave. I don't wish to cause you any more trouble than I've already put you through."

"Sit," Mr. Winston replied, a wrinkled hand fiddling with the skull carving on his ring. Fernando couldn't deny how appropriate it was for Mr. Winston to have such a thing—the old man had always reminded him of a skeleton. Not in weight or size, but as though the sharpness of his demeanor needed perpetual enunciation. "You must be hungry. Famished, even. And I need a proper break from the talk in that other room. What with the Westinghouse nonsense now that General Electric's patent…" Mr. Winston trailed off, his face wincing as though a headache had just found him.

"General Electric," Fernando remarked. Such a name meant power. "That's Mr. Edison's company."

"Mmmm," Mr. Winston responded. "George Westinghouse is giddy with excitement that old fool Thomas lost the contract to light the fair. It's all anyone in high society will talk about. But the damn bulb patent conflict with Edison—a nightmare. Westinghouse will certainly concede, though. I'm sure of it. And then I'll have a good night's rest. Finally." He narrowed his gaze on Fernando. "Your eyes betray you, boy. If I didn't know any better, I'd think you were amazed by all this talk of electrical nonsense."

Fernando straightened in his chair. It was intrigue instead of amazement, if Fernando were perfectly honest, but the sharpness of Mr. Winston's words told him etiquette would insist he agree with his newfound patron. "Well. Mr. Edison did help create light in a different way, didn't he? My father read all about it. They've gotten electric streetlights in certain parts of Manhattan—"

"Bah!" Mr. Winston shuffled with annoyance like a distraught bird caught in the rain. "Harsh on the eyes and unnatural. That's what they are. Whenever those lights go on, that's when I retire to the sanctuary of home for the night."

Fernando couldn't bear the thought of agreeing, but he nodded nonetheless. "Of course, sir. Yes. Nonsense." His nails dug into the skin of his hands, and his fingers froze in place as he uttered the harmless white lie.

"Mr. Winston?" called Mrs. Grant from the doorway. Flickers

of candlelight from the dining room cast unruly shadows across the verandah. "Mayor Harrison has just arrived, sir."

Mr. Winston's gaze slid to the door. "Have him wait."

Mrs. Grant stiffened as though such an order were nearly impossible, and Fernando couldn't blame her.

Mr. Winston's eyes steadied on Fernando. "What else have you heard of this, boy? The lights, I mean."

Fernando sifted his thoughts. "They say the lights will change the way we live. Light whenever we please. They're already in use for illuminating subjects for photography—"

"Ha! Not when photographing me, they're not."

"But beyond that. No more fire or gas lamps. It's unbelievable, isn't it? To live in a world like that?" Fernando hoped his response came off as easy, but worry settled over him as he realized how tense it was just to think such a thing—and how his hands wouldn't budge from their intertwining clench.

Worry tugged at Mr. Winston's features. "Yes. Yes, it most certainly is."

Beads of sweat lined Fernando's forehead. He focused on the fireplace and told himself to relax, but his fingers had cemented together uncomfortably.

A gray moth fluttered through the verandah's window, landing straight on the table linens. "But for all of history, we've lived without such an innovation," Mr. Winston continued. "One that is peculiar, wasteful. Abominable."

A breath caught in Fernando's throat. He glanced at his hands, but the firelight or the falling sunshine or something else altogether was certainly playing tricks on him, and his heart stopped.

"Westinghouse and Edison were like bulls in this fight for the contract. Reckless instead of cautious. Stupid as they ignored how humanity has a tendency to do what it does best."

Fernando forced his fingers free and flexed them. Horror fell upon him as hands of bone now sat in his own lap. Each finger— one to ten, one to ten—like polished white stone with cracks at the joints.

Without warning, Mr. Winston's gloved fist came crashing down on the moth, flattening it against the diamond-white fabric.

Fernando's eyes shot to the table and then back again at his hands.

Which were now just as he'd always known them.

Fernando calmed any persistent nerves and called to his saints for whatever graces they could give. He stretched his fingers again, studying the skin he'd known his entire life. Each freckle, each scar, each ragged nail that had served him well over the past eighteen years.

Mr. Winston pressed the stain of the dead moth into the tablecloth. And then he looked up. Again with a practiced smile now more like the skull on his ring than ever.

"And that, Fernando, is squash a problem before it grows too big. Now, have your cake, dear boy."

Chapter 2

Legacy

The library at St. Joan's Academy for Girls was unlike any other library Clara Banks had come across in all her seventeen years. Filled with worn pages, polished oak shelves, and dimmed sunlight, the entire space was as long as it was dense, and it serpentined throughout the rest of the school like a hidden sanctuary for countless collections of books.

Books, Clara knew, that might include one of importance. A diamond in the rough. An heirloom. A legacy. A treasure given to St. Joan's by Clara's father quite some time before she had been admitted there.

Clara's kitten heels clacked quietly against the shining wood floors as she made her way toward the folklore section. Her eyes flicking toward every sound, she knew it would only take one stern word from the librarian Miss Betsy to Headmistress McGill to forever foil Clara's plans.

But the library was empty that morning. Its racks of romances and shelves of mysteries waited patiently.

Folklore sat on the top shelf of the eastern-most quarter between newspapers chronicling the beginning of Chicago and cities older. Clara read the embossed spines so ancient, she didn't dare brush a fingernail across them. She lifted to her toes, stretching for the shelf to no avail, and then fell to flat feet as she considered how to access the scores of folktales lined up and beckoning her.

A quick glance to the left, then to the right. "Aha," she whispered, a tuft of a word falling past her lips as she spied a ladder with wheels hinged to the shelves.

But before Clara could risk a step, another creak stilled her, and she sucked in a sharp breath. Classes were due to begin in only minutes, and no St. Joan's girl was to be inside the library unless with written permission from a teacher.

Clara did not have permission.

Pressing against an unsteady collection of Shakespeare and Milton, Clara squeezed her eyes shut, outlining the library in her mind as she imagined where the creak had come from—and who might have caused it.

It sounded again with heavy footsteps—ones Clara recognized from a day she'd had to retrieve a volume on Marie Antoinette for a history lesson. The library cart's wheel emitted a distinct chirp whenever it turned left as Miss Betsy sorted the books on loan back into their proper places. Miss Betsy's steps drew closer, and the grandfather clock against the library wall ticked in an ominously loud way now, as though it were a symbol in a play meant to foreshadow certain doom.

Please not this aisle, Clara prayed. *Who'd check out one of these blasted old folios anyway when every student here has gilded editions on their parents' bookshelves?*

Miss Betsy's cart coursed to a sharp stop one row away, and Clara peeked through the books. The older woman's silhouette peered through her glasses as she returned another volume to its proper spot. Clara straightened and stepped silently toward the end of the row.

A creak split the silence as the cart started up again, this time followed by some soft humming. As Miss Betsy pushed it into the next row, Clara slipped around and ducked underneath a shelf of gothic horror. She prayed somehow she could fade into the pages behind her as the clock ticked closer to the hour. Miss Betsy's singing continued. Only when some heavier volumes were returned did the cart carry on and Clara relax.

She rattled the ladder as quietly and inconspicuously as possible and slipped one foot onto the first step. An array of St. Joan's prized fairy tale editions sat on the top shelf, donated by alumna and philanthropists alike—anyone willing to foot the bill for first editions if it meant bronze placards nailed to the shelves for all to see.

Clara didn't have to search long to find what she was seeking.

"There you are." Her fingers graced the midnight fabric spine of a small novella, well-loved and faded from a lifetime of turned pages and inked words. "Why, hello."

She tipped it until it slid free from the rest of the surrounding stories, and her feet rushed to bring her back to safe and solid ground. Once she'd fully descended the ladder, Clara stole a handful of seconds she knew she couldn't afford to sit, draw her knees to her chest, and clutch the book to her heart.

"Finally," Clara whispered so softly she barely heard it herself. "Mother, I found it."

In the attic of her father's newly-purchased countryside estate had sat a long-forgotten crate of mementos from Bethany Banks's life. Amongst them had been a copy of a folktale known only in Chicago. Clara read the inscribed words on the book's dusty cover.

The Traveling Demon and the Peasant Girl.

The girls at St. Joan's were scheduled to study folklore in their literature class, and the story Clara's mother Bethany had told her time and time again had miraculously appeared on the syllabus. As familiar as bedtime and the shine of the moon, Clara could recite the entire one hundred-page novella perfectly—she'd even mastered its tricky iambic pentameter, a trick her mother had been more than pleased about. It'd been Bethany's favorite story, and the family copy had been a gift from Bethany's favorite aunt, Miranda.

And then donated to St. Joan's library because the very sight of his wife's possessions still devastated Jonathan Banks to his core.

Clara's heart hitched at that truth. On some days, she wondered if her father had donated this book to her all-girls private school for the connections, or if it had been charity by way of grief.

Regardless, the book was back in the hands of its rightful owner. Clara imagined the warmth of her mother's fingers as they crossed each page, an index finger slowly identifying each word as she read. Bethany Banks had never been terribly strong at reading—always mixing up letters or seeing them upside-down —but she'd helped Clara recognize each word as much as she could through a strange sadness Clara had never known her mother to be without.

Clara opened the book to the title page and read with surprise a faded inked inscription:

> To my dear niece Bethany.
> The second copy of this story should undoubtedly be yours.
> Love Aunt Miranda.

Clara tilted her head. *Second* copy? In the hundreds of times her mother held this book while reading to her, Clara had never noticed that before.

The paper dampened from the cold sweat in her palms, something that seemed to happen whenever Clara found herself amazed by the remnants of history. She peeled back the cover again until the spine cracked and ran her fingertips along the faint words.

The second copy of this story should undoubtedly be yours.

Second.

Clara switched back to the cover, where the story's title was embossed. Underneath it: *By Anonymous.*

The family story of Aunt Miranda was not as familiar as the story in Clara's hands, but what Clara did know was Miranda Carveth had been last seen in 1859, only weeks after this very precious book had been given to her favorite niece. For years, Miranda's memory had been tangible in the Bankses' house, and then their estate, a story that lingered and seemed to find its place in every room, from the parlor with the bright white curtains purchased from the Hudson's Bay Department Store on Jonathan Banks's failed business attempt in Toronto, to the high-windowed sunroom with a perpetual angle of light that illuminated the dust that danced with a grand piano beneath it. A question—a need to know why Miranda had vanished and what had happened to her—had burrowed inside Bethany for as long as Clara had known her mother. An enigma that had gone unsolved during Clara's short time at Curtis School.

But now, Clara was at St. Joan's Academy for Girls, on Bynum Island in Chicago.

The very spot Miranda had allegedly disappeared from, all those years ago.

Imagine that.

A slip of something yellow-tinged and frail tumbled from the back of the book, and Clara cringed as the realization that she'd accidentally torn a page free from something so old and precious washed over her like holy water to baptism. But upon second glance, no—she hadn't torn a page free. This was something quite different. Old, yes, but parchment from the desk of someone who could write in proper script and did so in a thick, heavy hand.

You know of this story as a folktale, my darling.
But it is so much more than that.
Do not disregard this warning. Monsters hide on Bynum Island.
I fear they'll take me next.

The curled tail of the last word spilled off the page and into oblivion. Clara flipped the parchment in her hand in case there might be any more strange words scribbled there—nothing.

A quick scoff escaped her. "How ridiculous." A lark perhaps. Clara cut her eyes to the right and then to the left like a child might during a game of hide-and-seek. She expected to see the other girls from St. Joan's laughing and giggling at the new girl from Curtis School. But no one was there.

Clara glanced back at the careful swoops and swirls of the penmanship. "Monsters," she uttered with a shake of her head. She'd given up on stories about monsters eons ago, though a spark of uncertainty filled her heart with wonder. She glanced at the folktale in her hand. Monsters lay there, too, in the pages thumbed and softened from nights filled with imaginations soaring beyond this real world. The spark urged Clara to take its hand and believe in something again, just like she had with her mother, when it had been so easy to believe there was magic surrounding them and that storybook adventures had once been real.

But that had been another time.

Clara cast away the spark and instantly it faded to ash.

Miss Betsy's cart slammed against the wall, and Clara jumped, a quick hand slipping the book into her skirt pocket. She spun around to the librarian standing in the early sunlight.

"You're late for class."

Clara winced and nodded an apology to Miss Betsy, and then she ran out the door, purposefully stealing a book that never should have belonged to anyone else to begin with.

CHAPTER 3

A GIFT TO THE ACADEMY

CLARA SLIPPED INSIDE HER HISTORY CLASSROOM AND SHUT THE door, and right away, the notion of monsters disappeared. With her hand still on the knob, she realized the entire room had suddenly gone far too quiet, and she glanced over her shoulder at Headmistress Florence McGill in front of the blackboard, hands clasped as she regarded Clara with a stern glance. Each of the girls in the class had already taken her seat.

Hot alarm flooded Clara as she realized she was the last to arrive.

"Thank the heavens Miss Banks has decided to grace us with her presence today. Any longer, and we would have been worried sick." Headmistress's eyebrows lifted in a way that channeled a proper amount of annoyance.

"Sorry, ma'am." Clara wove through the rows of cherry-wood desks until she found an empty seat by the window. The girls watched Clara, all of them identical in their uniforms of a white blouse with a gray bow to match a pleated skirt, the only color a few rebellious spots of red on the lips of some who'd managed to sneak rouge onto the school grounds. As she sat,

Clara shifted the small book with the yellowed note inside her pocket so the spine was free from digging into her thigh.

"To continue," Headmistress bellowed, commanding the girls' attention as her stern demeanor faded for one of sheer pride. "It is my privilege to introduce a gift that came to us at the behest of a generous former alumna some years ago." She removed her eyeglasses and used the sleeve of her dress to clean the lenses. There was a quick glance over to the far corner of the classroom and then a quick nod. "Yes, my dear girl. Please bring it forward. Third-years are now permitted to incorporate it into their studies."

Clara turned as a classmate named Stevie push a wheeled device covered with a dark woolen blanket toward Headmistress. Stevie whipped off the blanket, loosening a crop of dust that had settled over a shining three-foot-tall camera whose curved lens inspected each of the girls and reflected them back as glass ghouls.

The girls gasped and awed in delight, but it was only Clara who inched forward in her seat in sheer surprise. *An actual Kodak!*

"For any of our classes?" a girl asked from the first row. "Think of what we could do with it!" With each uttered word, the excitement in her voice grew.

Headmistress held up a finger, her eyeglasses cast aside on her desk. "It's the *school's*, Sally. If any of you think you can simply fiddle with this to your heart's content, you'll be back in second-year faster than you can say jackrabbit."

Stevie knelt in front of the camera, fiddling with its knobs and gears in a silent demonstration on how such a magnificent machine would work. Her hands dressed in crisp white gloves, she lifted the Kodak's great curved flash, aimed the dark lens at the girls in their seats, and ducked under the camera's velvet curtain.

"Ready," Stevie announced. "Smile for eternity, girls." Above her, the wall was lined with framed photographs of students from the past sitting exactly where they all sat now.

A crack split the air and a flash followed, and Clara rubbed her eyes as the classroom brightened and then slowly faded from a harsh shine into the dim classroom once again.

But with the flash's sudden burst, the book in Clara's pocket tumbled onto the floor with a thump, the yellowed note peeking out from amidst the pages. Her cheeks warmed as she felt the eyes of each girl on her as well as those of Headmistress, who set her glasses back upon her nose and stared at the small book.

"Last to arrive, first to steal from the library, Miss Banks?" Headmistress remarked.

Clara stumbled on her words. "No, ma'am," she tried as she forced herself to sit tall, her voice striving for strength. "I just—"

"Two months you've been at St. Joan's now, isn't that right, Clara? I imagine by now you've learned the library is off-limits to students outside of class hours unless they're granted clear permission. And I know it's the same rule at Curtis School, isn't it?"

Clara knew the question wasn't intended to be cruel, but she couldn't help but especially feel like she didn't belong just then. Around her, the girls stared, girls whose chance to attend the prestigious St. Joan's Academy for Girls had been determined long before their births. Destiny had a tendency to run through blood and lineage, Clara knew. Though there were exceptions to this rule, and she was certainly one of them.

"Sorry, ma'am," Clara replied, resigned to staring at the sharp lines of her desk. "I'll return the book to Miss Betsy immediately." A family heirloom, back in the hands of this private school. Clara detested the thought.

"No," Headmistress immediately replied, a softened voice sheer relief to Clara's nerves. "You might as well hold on to it." She spoke in a strict yet kind tone that had likely been forged from years of running a school for teenage girls. "After all, it's next on the academy's literature syllabus."

The silence that followed was hollow, a sort of silence that comes whenever the wheels spin wildly in someone's mind.

"Yes, ma'am," Clara whispered. She was tempted to remark upon her issues with the word 'academy' and how it implied such a contrast from 'school.' Especially since she'd come from a 'school' and it hadn't been immensely different from where she was now. The lessons weren't terribly unalike, but Clara had quickly learned where people came from determined whether they would attend a 'school' or an 'academy.'

And that was appalling, in Clara's humble opinion.

Headmistress beckoned Stevie, who right away set all of the Kodak's pieces back into place and covered it again with the blanket. "No one is to touch the camera without permission."

Stevie glared at a tall straight-haired girl at the front of the classroom. Behind Headmistress's back, she straightened both her thumbs and bended them in the girl's direction, mouthing *all thumbs*, to which the girl in question—Marta—scowled before returning to sketching an array of ships coursing across waves onto some parchment.

"But you girls are quite lucky. With the Columbian Exposition only weeks away, the eyes of the world are on Chicago. You'll have the perfect opportunity to capture history in the making." Headmistress met Clara's eyes. Soft gray balancing between kindness and discipline. "I'll expect great things from you." The statement was spoken to the class but directed at Clara.

It wasn't a surprise for Clara to hear of such high expectations. Curtis School had told Clara's father always to count on the same from his daughter. They'd agreed Clara was a natural when it came to history. Languages. Anything that examined the very essence of what it was to be human. Between the books she collected or retrieved and then stored in her father's newly-purchased estate in the countryside and the fascinating conversations she was able to have with her teachers, Clara needed to explore the complexity of humanity to its depths, dig as deeply as she could. She yearned to see how the same events in history would repeat themselves in every age.

A hand rose from the front of the classroom, and Clara glanced at Sally in the first row, the indisputable leader of a clique of girls Clara recognized but wasn't a part of. Sally straightened in her seat and tucked the simple ribbon holding her dark shoulder-length hair off her face. "Is it prudent to bring the Kodak to the fairgrounds on opening day, though? There will be thousands of people, and the camera might get damaged. Surely St. Joan's would have connections that would allow us to, perhaps, get a tour ahead of time?" Sally smiled sweetly. "For our education, naturally." Her tone was strong, and its cadence, elegant—expected from a girl who thrived in debate classes and educated the teachers at St. Joan's on the importance of including African-American writings in their curricula.

Clara's thoughts drifted back to the stolen book on her desk, the one that had *not* granted her the wrath of Headmistress McGill—a strange thing itself. With that, the note hadn't been discovered, and for some strange reason, Clara was relieved.

How on earth could she have considered taking it so seriously?

"Excellent point, Sally." Headmistress's shoes clacked across the classroom floor.

This was the place from which Miranda Carveth had disappeared. Had Miranda walked this very room? Had she seen the same trees and grass outside the window Clara sat by now?

"And there is someone in this classroom who could help us in that regard."

Clara rested her chin in her palm and hardened her gaze.

She had been given a unique opportunity—gifted with the perfect setting, the tools she required, the resources that would benefit her, and a clever mind. Everything she'd need to find out exactly what had happened to her mother's dearly beloved aunt.

Monsters hide on Bynum Island.

I fear they'll take me next.

Why would anyone write something so preposterous? Who would have done such a thing?

Headmistress McGill stopped in front of her desk, and Clara awoke from her thoughts and straightened in her seat. For a moment, she was distracted by the black leather gloves Headmistress always wore to ward off the chill in such an old school. But then Clara realized which elephant had just sauntered straight into their classroom.

For her father was Jonathan Banks, a business liaison to Mr. George Westinghouse, who'd just secured a very important contract for the World's Columbian Exposition.

Headmistress smiled. "In my days, we'd call this providence."

CHAPTER 4

THE MIDWAY TENT

The Midway Plaisance come nightfall was like stepping into a fairy tale Juan García Díaz might have told his son when his wife Imogen wasn't listening. Fairy tales steered awfully close to magic, after all, and there was no way on earth Fernando's devoutly Irish-Catholic mother would ever allow for such a thing to be celebrated in her home.

The tents lining the edges of the Midway just beneath the half-built Ferris Wheel were shades of pomegranate and fuchsia brightened a thousand times until simply looking at them hurt Fernando's eyes.

"Come on," a boy named Dodger beckoned Fernando. He was a tall white boy built like a bear with the keen sensibility of a lad who worked in Fernando's line of work, now dressed up in a tweed jacket—old but in good condition—that covered a clean gray button-down and matched his soot-gray trousers. Men working on the fairgrounds were aplenty in the apartment buildings on the west end of Chicago, and Dodger had quickly stumbled across Fernando after both of them had worked a fourteen-hour shift. Though Dodger's line of work was a little different from Fernando's.

"I'm manning the electricity at Machinery Hall," he'd told Fernando after hands had been shaken and pleasantries said. "The fountains, the lights—you name it. If Westinghouse's money is involved, I'm the brains operating it."

Fernando hadn't had much of a choice in whether to attend the typical festivities of a Thursday night on the Midway Plaisance: cards and booze with those who worked on the outskirts of civilization.

"You sure I'm allowed to be here?" Fernando asked as he followed Dodger toward the tent. "I wasn't exactly invited."

"*I* invited you," Dodger corrected. "Not a chance you're missing out. The boys from Donegal Castle hid loads of whiskey on the ship when they came to Chicago, and tonight they're cracking the bottles open. Not your poison? Rice wine from the Japanese Gardens. Lagerbier from the German Village. We've got it all."

The tent's flaps out front waved with the breeze and the song from inside, and Dodger and Fernando swept through to an earful of live fiddle music and staggering dances with kicking feet and little coordination. The smell of liquor permeated the air in a way that was hours from turning sour, but right now it was lovely and sweet, and Fernando breathed it in.

"Oy!" Antoine, the foreman from the Ferris Wheel, called as he stepped inside after them. A half-dozen people turned at the voice that sounded more like music than a command for attention. He tipped back his midnight-black bowler cap from his dark hair and pointed at a rather skinny lad at the head of the table. "Is that Frankie in my seat? You and I both know, buster, last week's winner at cards gets the throne!"

Ear-splitting laughter followed, Fernando the only one not in on the joke. There were cheers and waves of greetings, and as

Antoine slapped each hand raised toward his, Dodger led Fernando to an oak counter where there were spare crystal tumblers and a handle of shining whiskey.

Immediately, Fernando turned away from the crowd. "You didn't say Antoine would *be* here." He ducked his hand, pulling at his newsboy cap so the brim fell over his eyes. His own boss, there amongst a bunch of kids with booze and cards—not the vision of ambition Fernando yearned to present himself as.

Dodger glanced over his shoulder. "Who, Antoine? You think he gives a god damn? Shit, he's no older than we are."

"He's at least thirty."

"Nah, he just seems that way 'cause he's French. Antoine's nineteen."

"Dodge!" called Antoine, a French accent tinging his voice. He grinned, a blur of laughter in stark white threads that contrasted his dark skin. "My favorite unionizer! You must be here to win back the cash you lost last week!"

"Fuck no," Dodger replied curtly as he poured whiskey into three tumblers and handed one to Antoine. He shoved the third into Fernando's palm. Cold with sticky amber droplets spilling down the side. "I know when I'm beat," Dodger added. "But Fernando here might be interested in a hand or two." A wink.

In less than a jiffy, Antoine recognized Fernando. "Ah, the prodigal son from the east has decided to add more to his list of sins tonight."

Fernando frowned, unsure how Antoine could know about what had happened in Brooklyn. If that was what he'd even meant.

Then Antoine laughed. It was an easy way to laugh, like he'd been born to do it. "I'm only kidding. Come on. You deserve the ambrosia you have coming." He lifted his glass, and Dodger and Fernando followed suit. "To eves when we don't come home until dawn. To the memories from nights we'll yearn to forget."

Antoine eyed the crowd for anyone he might pursue once the drinks were drunk. "To the hearts we will break and to ours which might, too. To the folks we won't meet, or haven't met yet."

Dodger gave a quick nod. "I'll drink to that."

Fernando lifted his glass. "Hell of a toast."

"Practice makes perfect," Antoine replied.

Their glasses clinked, and they shot the whiskeys. Fernando's face fell into a wince as it burned his throat, and he imagined the room of suits at Mr. Winston's home. The soirée behind closed doors as he and Mr. Winston had made arrangements. How differently did folks drink regardless of status?

Antoine clapped his hands. "Cards! Fernando, you're next, but for now, I'm owed two dollars, and I plan to take more of these fools' money. Move it, Frankie."

Fernando lifted himself up onto a round stool at the counter. The table was cleared of glasses, and Antoine took a seat, rolling his sleeves with exaggerated drama. A few more Midway workers taunted Antoine jovially and found seats until there was a full table with a Queen of Hearts and a Jack of Spades sliding across the slick surface. The game was five-card draw, and Antoine had a rolled cigarette dangling from his lips and another glass of whiskey beside him, King of the Midway.

"Hey," Dodger said, elbowing Fernando. "That's Antoine's girl, Lily. She goes to St. Joan's." A pause. "Well, as of a few weeks ago, no longer Antoine's girl." His lips quirked with the feelings someone might have before daring to hold a girl's hand. "But they're still all right with each other," Dodger added, and then he cocked his head to the side. "Looks like she brought Marta. Don't worry—their fathers might be suits fit enough for the likes of The Cat's Whisker, but you'd never know it by the way they throw back whiskey. Come on."

A cloud of tobacco smoke bumped against the ceiling of the

tent, and Fernando followed Dodger through it, notes of laughter springing free from the pairs and trios of fair workers whose faces were in states of easy grins now that work had come to an end for the day. The patterns and fabrics of the clothing each person wore—as bright as they could find—were jewels in the dim candlelight. So bold that when Fernando and Dodger reached the back of the tent, where two girls were already slipping underneath, the girls' black velvet dressing gowns were nothing short of daringly different.

The first girl to straighten from the other side put on a big grin as she recognized Dodger. "Well, hello there, you!" she said in a cheerful voice as she tucked her curly blonde hair behind an ear. When Dodger moved in close, the girl slipped past him cheekily. "Ah, ah. Drink first. Antoine has the booze, right?"

"Just try to take it from him," Dodger answered. "Lily? Fernando."

The girl paused when she saw Fernando. "You're new," she declared, looking him up and down like he were a dress she might consider buying. "Where are you from?" She set a cigarette to her lips. It was already lit, and Fernando had no idea how she'd slipped it under the tent.

Fernando stuck his hands in his trouser pockets, uncomfortable by the attention, even with the ease of whiskey settling in his veins. "Brooklyn."

"New York? Oh, I *love* New York." She drawled out the word *love* in a way that was close to sarcasm but erred on the side of class. "Manhattan is one of the prettiest places in the world. My parents and I go there at least once a year. Never in the winter, mind you, because I really do believe New York has the coldest winters. Even more so than Chicago! That's because it's an island. You can't escape the water. It freezes, and that dreadful wind blows across the land with no mercy, and no wonder it's so easy to catch pneumonia!"

Fernando was not exactly sure if he should try to respond or just wait until the girl had tired herself out, but then another appeared behind Lily. She was much taller with long dark hair—straight while Lily's was curly—and seemed to study folks before engaging with them. And right now, her target was Fernando.

"She'll go on and on like this for hours unless you shut her up."

Lily turned to the girl. "So kind of you, Marta."

"Weren't you getting a drink?" Marta said, leaning on Lily's shoulders.

A spark of light fell over Lily's face. "I absolutely was." She sauntered away.

"Isn't New York kind of far to travel from for work?" Marta asked Fernando once Lily had left, with Dodger following.

Fernando glanced at her. "What?"

"New York," she said again, a magical cigarette appearing between her fingers. Just like Lily's. "The fair isn't going to be the big thing everyone says it is. It's only temporary. And after everything, all the glitz and glam of modern progress—" Marta made a gesture that feigned vomiting "—all of this rubbish is just going to collapse. None of the buildings were made to stand forever. Nothing is durable. Not even that standing disaster of a wheel waiting to fall over. My Sally and I have already made bets on when that'll happen." She gestured toward the outside of the tent, where the Ferris Wheel stood. "She's more optimistic than I am. Anyway, from what I heard, everything is going to turn back into the marsh it was only a few years ago. That's what my father says, and he works for *The Chicago Tribune*. There'll be no work for anyone who came to this city looking for a better life when that happens. Are you sure this was the best place for a job?"

The whiskey inside Fernando was warming his bones now, and he felt an unconquerable desire to speak the truth to a stranger. "Well, for now, it's got to be for someone who had nowhere else to go." The words anchored him in place, but it was a relief to finally admit it.

He'd chosen this life, he reminded himself. He'd said words that couldn't be unsaid, and then he'd left.

There's certainly work in San Francisco if nothing else, he reminded himself. An ace up his sleeve should he need it. A city with a cousin waiting for a telegram saying Chicago was a bust. Chicago was a failure.

You won't fail like they did.

Marta narrowed her eyes as though she were considering that excuse and then shrugged. "I guess I can't argue with that." She took another drag of her cigarette.

"That's a straight-flush!" Antoine shouted, the loud peppering of *"ha-ha-ha"* interjecting any objections to his win. "And I believe *you* owe me another bottle of that rice wine we drank two weeks ago. A deal is a deal, my friend."

Another boy clutched his head in his hands, his straight black hair over his fingers as he sat, hope vanquished. Then he straightened. "Give me another chance! Let me win back your wine!"

Antoine settled back in his chair, tipping it so he could rock back and forth. "That Bordeaux was a mistake, Yuki. I never should have offered it. I won it back fair and square, and there's not a chance on this cold Midwestern land I'm risking it again tonight." He lit another cigarette. "No deal."

Yuki sighed in exasperation. "*One* bottle of sake," he agreed, a pointed index finger emphasizing his agreement. Then he pushed away from the table. "And with that, I'm free of your ridiculous laughter." It wasn't a cruel statement—Fernando could tell Antoine and Yuki were friends. And to prove as such, Yuki reached over the table and offered his hand, and Antoine shook it congenially, more laughter leaking from his lips. "You play well," Yuki said with a nod. "*Too* well."

Antoine grinned. "You sure don't make it easy."

Fernando smiled as he watched. Many of his old friends from Brooklyn were from the same background as he was: New Yorkers, born and raised, most with immigrant parents, but not everyone. All had been Catholic, which had meant an array of inside jokes about the nuances of Easter Vigil and Christmas Mass, how the priests in their neighborhood had their own ways of consecrating the Eucharist, only noticed by kids no older than twenty, no younger than sixteen. His Brooklyn neighborhood had been home, but it'd also been just one little part of the country.

Here on the Midway, Fernando sat in a tiny tent with people who'd come from different parts of the world. Some spoke English, but most didn't. No matter—it was an exploration of cultures and finding the bridges between them. A hodgepodge of what was slowly becoming America, as Juan García Díaz had once told Fernando would inevitably come to pass: girls from private schools who'd been raised in Chicago, Antoine, a Black boy from France who, according to Dodger, enjoyed wandering the world more than he enjoyed standing still, kids from places like Tokyo and Cairo and the same Dublin that Fernando's mother had once hailed from.

Something magnificent, Fernando thought. Something he had never seen in his tiny Brooklyn neighborhood.

Fernando didn't know if it was the whiskey nudging these thoughts into his mind or if it was the peace of the moment, but oddly, right then, he didn't feel like he was without a home, or lost, or destined for failure, this American-born son of immigrants.

He felt like he belonged.

"Hey! Fernando!" Dodger called as he sat beside Antoine with Lily on the other side. Marta had wandered off, finding Yuki to sit with over two more whiskeys. "Get your ass over here and save us from Antoine's ramblings."

Fernando scoffed at the fan of playing cards lying in front of them. "Don't think so. That's a ploy to get my wages."

Antoine feigned horror at the thought and clutched his heart. "Fernando. That hurts. That truly cuts deeply into the bone."

Lily laughed beside him. "He's being ridiculous. Please, sit with us, Fernando! We won't play any games." As she spoke to him, Fernando watched as Dodger ever so indiscreetly inched his chair closer to Lily, and if she noticed, she made no show of it. "Perhaps you can shut Antoine up." She rolled her eyes. "Land sakes, monsters again."

Marta, across the room, lifted her head. "Again?" She mirrored Lily's eye-roll. "Honestly, Antoine, you're worse than my grandfather. We've heard this story a *thousand* times."

Antoine lifted a finger. "Better over-informed than caught off-guard."

"You sound like Sally," Marta retorted, a smile crossing her face as she twirled her black hair around one finger. "Is tonight a repeat of last week's soirée? Monsters from Europe and then monsters on Bynum Island?"

Antoine waved Marta off. "St. Joan's is a school of fairy tales, and your parents pay handsomely to send you there. Show me a girl who's seen what I've seen, and I'll listen to the folktale of Bynum Island a second time."

Fernando wandered over to a wobbly chair with one leg that was shorter than the rest. The entire table was surrounded by mismatched seats, including a barstool too fancy for a place on the Midway and an armchair Lily lounged in like a queen. Dodger slid another shot in front of Fernando, and he reached for it, his fingers cool on the glass as he twirled it against the wood. At Dodger's wink and beckon, Fernando silently toasted his saints, threw back the shot, and winced as the burn of it scalded his throat.

Then, "There's a story about monsters?" He didn't know why

he'd asked but took care to make sure his eyes weren't tricking him from the whiskey, letting him once again see pale bones where his hands should be. A trick of the eyes seemed to be common in this city, like the quiet clicking Fernando sometimes heard at night in his room, the chill from a window drawing his attention to the streets outside.

One night there'd been a lamplighter leaning a ladder against the iron post in the street, and Fernando had watched as the boy climbed it and set flame to the wick.

Wait, Fernando had thought as he'd inched closer to the glass of the window. *Wait, no.*

The boy hadn't been lighting anything, but switching on an electric lamp.

"Mr. Winston's greatest nightmare," Fernando had muttered as he'd pulled the thick curtains back for a better look. Cities throughout the United States were already using electric lights—Edison's General Electric bulbs, much to Westinghouse's disappointment, surely—but in Brooklyn, Fernando had never personally seen them. Now he had. The light's gleam was harsh, the painting of a vibrant flame frozen in time. The boy had swept up the ladder and back down in two blinks, and Fernando had shut the curtains, letting only a sliver of golden light sneak into the room.

That very scene had happened nightly in Chicago, until only last night, when something different had occurred instead.

Fernando forced his attention back to Antoine and clenched his fists.

Tonight, each finger was accounted for.

Lily glared. "Fernando, don't encourage him!" She rolled her eyes at Dodger, a love-struck puppy. He'd rested his elbows on his knees and was now cradling his chin as he stared. "You didn't warn him, Dodge? It really should be the first thing everyone learns about Antoine!" Playfully, she smacked at

Dodger's cheek in a way that was just as flirtatious as it was a way to touch him.

Dodger's mouth slackened in mock horror. "We've only just met! Besides, as though it'd do any good. If Antoine's going to tell that story a thousand times more, no one's going to stop that bastard!"

"Ah, ah," Antoine interrupted, wagging a finger in Dodger's direction. "Best not to turn up your nose. There's a proverb about not biting the hand that gives you drink."

"Don't bite the hand that *feeds* you," Dodger replied.

"Not in this tent." With a flick of his wrist, Antoine's empty whiskey tumbler flew in a perfect arc over his shoulder so he could catch it again. "Here, it's drink."

Lily leaned into Dodger, her gentle laughter dancing in his ear, which only created a stirring in Dodger's cheeks, like perhaps now Antoine was the last thing on both their minds.

"Fine, I'll bite the hand that gives me drink," Fernando interrupted. "What monsters?"

He ignored Lily and Dodger slumping in dramatic annoyance. Antoine leaned his elbows on the table, white sleeves rolled up to his forearms. In his hand were three playing cards, and he shuffled them between his fingers. Antoine's silence carried on for far too long—enough that Fernando knew he had the attention of nearly everyone at the table.

"You know where I come from, Fernando?" Antoine asked, his voice no louder than a faint whisper as his cigarette rolled between his lips.

"Paris."

"Paris," Antoine repeated. "I've been in Chicago for a few years now, but the last time I saw my home was with a new tower shadowing the streets and the Seine."

"The Eiffel Tower. Sure."

"From Paris's World's Fair." In one fast move, Antoine swiped up the rest of the deck, another quick shuffle tossing the cards from hand to hand. "In fact, I'm the only person here in Chicago to have worked at both."

Dodger cocked his head. "Not the *only* one. We figured that out last month at the Bavarian pub."

Antoine glanced sideways at Dodger. "The only one in construction. Not the suits." He sat taller. "Suits don't count. The only one whose blood and sweat helped build a fair from the ground up."

An interesting bit of trivia Fernando hadn't known. His mother and father hadn't followed the news of Paris's World's Fair, from what Fernando could remember during the year he was fourteen. At the very most, all he could recall was a Sunday morning when they'd been setting the table for breakfast after Mass and how Fernando's father made awed remarks to his mother about the sheer perfection in the architecture of Paris's new tower.

Fernando gave a nod to Antoine. "You worked on the Eiffel Tower?"

Antoine leaned back in his chair with his chin high. "Nothing like what you and I do on the Ferris Wheel sunrise to sundown. A hundred thousand men building the impossible. But as they say, *impossible is not French.*"

As he spoke, Lily leaned behind him, mouthing his words as though she'd heard Antoine say the same thing dozens of times. Dodger spat out a loud laugh, and Antoine spun in his seat just as Lily returned to hers, her big eyes round with guilt Antoine saw immediately.

"Enough, Lil," Antoine said, reaching for the glass of whiskey sitting in front of her. Lily's hand swiped for it, but Antoine was faster. "Don't forget, the first time you heard this story, I know for a fact you were petrified." He grinned at her, unaffected by any mockery as Lily sweetly smiled back. "Let me continue."

Antoine leaned over the table, closer to Fernando and drawing his attention from anything in the room. Antoine glanced at the cards in his hand, shuffling from his right hand to his left, and then back again.

"The darkest streets of Paris stank with rumors of it. Men and women at the feet of La Grande Dame swore it was everything from the dead rising from the catacombs to skeletons crawling from the ocean."

Antoine fanned a section of the cards in front of Fernando, beckoning him to choose one. Fernando hesitated then reached for one in the middle, tugging it free from the rest, and Antoine flipped it face-up onto the table.

Ace of Spades.

"I saw it once, and only once," Antoine continued. "The night before the first day of Paris's World's Fair. Passing the river, on my way home to my mother. There was a handful of men in black-and-white suits sipping their absinthe and spilling into the streets." He shuffled the cards again and gestured for Fernando to draw a second.

Fernando did.

Eight of Spades.

"Their silk ties must have cost as much as I was paid for ten weeks of work." Antoine palmed the cards and reached into his pocket for another cigarette. He lit it and inhaled. The wild smoke ribboned and curled from his lips as he set the cigarette on a glass ash tray and shuffled the cards again. "They laughed. The laughter was strange." His voice darkened, softened. There was no showmanship now, only a return to a memory perhaps Antoine longed to forget.

"The suits' laughter?" Fernando asked, any strength in his words somehow caught in his throat.

There had been scratches against Fernando's bedroom window the night before while Fernando's eyes had squeezed shut in a desperate attempt to fall asleep. *Fucking branches.* Back and forth, back and forth.

Antoine set the cigarette back between his lips and drew in again. "During the day, they were French men. No question about it. Through and through. But as they laughed, they spoke something else. Another language. All of them." Antoine freed himself from the dream and stared at Fernando. "Spanish."

Fernando fidgeted in his seat. "Probably business had called them to Spain at some point to—"

"No, you don't understand." Antoine fanned the cards again. "These men were *French*. I am so sure of it. I know enough of your father's language to understand what they were saying. They spoke of a prior home. Barcelona. They spoke of their true home, America—impossible, I maintain—but they swore they would steal and control the whole world for themselves. They said there was only a handful of years left before the hungry one would disappear. The one forever locked in place. Anchored, or something. Strange as it was eerie. And then they spoke of vengeance against someone called Eduardo."

A name for patriarchs in the García family, and once considered by Juan and Imogen before they settled on Fernando for their only son.

Fernando's heart thumped wildly in his chest.

There had been no wind the night before, no rattling of windows or low humming of a breeze born of the lake. Chicago had been silent. And yet, again, there it was: that long draw of tree branches against Fernando's window and the flicker of incandescent light behind it.

He silently ordered his heart to slow. He chose a card, and Antoine flipped it onto the table.

Eight of Hearts.

"Anyway," Antoine continued with a wave. "That wasn't the strangest part."

A darkness fell over the tent, the sounds and music of the soirée vanishing. Fernando was pulled to Antoine like there was a secret he'd soon know. One of importance. One that tied him to Chicago's fair and promised to explain why this city of the future had called to him. Lily and Dodger's smiles faded as an eeriness captured Antoine's audience.

Fernando's bedroom window was directly above his bed. The night before, Fernando had blinked himself awake and turned slowly toward the glass and the scratches that were growing long and desperate. Between dream and wake, he'd let his eyes adjust to the dull glow of the streetlights outside and forced them on the window, telling himself not to be afraid, though a part of him had wished for a rosary or a crucifix.

Antoine shuffled the deck again and offered the fan of cards to Fernando.

Fernando shook his head. "What was the strangest part?"

"Pick a card, Fernando."

"Is it all a trick?"

Antoine reset the cards on the table. One hand spread them in front of the three Fernando had already chosen. "They spoke about the future. About how the world would change. About how they could claim power and fortune and control through that change. If they were never stopped, never challenged. If they could slow progress for as long as possible."

Antoine waved his hands over the cards, another silent request for Fernando to choose. Fernando slipped free a card near the end, and Antoine flipped it over. Nine of Spades.

Antoine nodded. "Three Spades. My mother would have said there is a war awaiting you. Or perhaps one you've already run from."

Fernando stared at the cards and told himself not to think of the three men who'd died on his family's construction site less than a month before.

"Then again, there's also a Heart in the mix. That bodes well for you. Love is in your future."

Fernando's gaze lifted to Antoine's. "So who are the monsters, then?" He assured himself it was all a joke, a story. A fairy tale.

Antoine's lips quirked. "As I said, it was the laughter that said it all. The transformation of them. They laughed through moonlight and spirits, but not as men. Their faces faded, and their skin vanished. And then they were no longer human."

Fernando's first day in Chicago. His hands on his lap in Mr. Winston's home. The bones that had shone a dull white instead of skin.

The window the night before, and the outline of the branches that were too long and too bunched together to be what they should have been.

Antoine leaned in closer. "Go on, Fernando. Choose another card."

Fernando straightened. The tent fell into silence, and Lily and Dodger stared as Fernando shakily pulled free one last card and flipped it over.

King of Spades. An ugly card in a pristine set. This King was a skeleton, a sneering profile of a madman.

Antoine settled back into his seat. "You have a gift for finding Spades."

A chilly wind fluttered the tent and found Fernando's skin, stinging it with sharpness. Antoine's story no longer seemed so unbelievable. But then Dodger and Lily glanced over Fernando's shoulder, their eyes widening in perfect synchronization.

As Fernando had knelt on his bed the night before, moving toward the long twigs scratching at his bedroom window, a shudder of movement had suddenly appeared.

A pair of eyes.

Not eyes—*sockets*.

Black and deep and empty with not an iris to be seen.

A hand grabbed Fernando's arm and spun him around in his seat. He gasped, his blood cold. A face stared back at him. The flame of a candle illuminated a ghostlike growl. Fernando clambered up onto his chair.

Despite the rush of blood chilling his bones, he forced himself to stay in the present and forget the untrustworthy past. Because his bedroom curtain had resettled the night prior, and when it'd waved back again, it'd only been light, shining and static. No face. No sockets. No black eyes with a bone-white face holding them. It'd been the tricks of darkness, the flirtation of candlelight. The memory of those impossible skeletal hands while exhaustion from cross-continental travel had eaten at his bones. The loss of comfort from his mother's daily rosaries for Fernando's safety, and the guilt of a fallen Catholic boy telling him he was now being subjected to evil as punishment for not honoring his father or his mother.

Laughter followed in the tent, and Marta blew out the candle, her ghoulish grin turning into that of a girl's.

Lily's face filled with fury. "Marta! You just about terrified poor Fernando!"

Marta curled over, her hands clutching her stomach with laughter as Lily huffed her annoyance.

A shiver raced down Fernando's spine, and he ordered himself to calm down. "That's a pretty dark bedtime story," he said, a nervous laugh punctuating each syllable.

"The world is darker than you realize," Antoine said. "Might as well learn that now."

Fernando resettled in his seat. "Then why Chicago? If something…inhuman haunted Paris's World's Fair four years ago, why the hell would you come to the next one?"

Antoine shrugged. "If the money is good, I'll face a thousand monsters."

The mood lifted, and the music started up again.

Marta's hand landed on Fernando's shoulder. "I'm sorry. I couldn't resist," she said between giggles. "It's only because we've all heard Antoine go on and on about this a million times. Say, what was it that brought you to Chicago again?"

Fernando's eyes fell back on the cards in front of him, and it was enough to take a third shot of whiskey from Dodger.

CHAPTER 5

CREAKY WINDOWS

AT PRECISELY SIX O'CLOCK ON THURSDAY EVENING, A SHINING carriage picked up Clara at the foot bridge that connected Bynum Island to the rest of the city. The light dimmed over Chicago as the bumpy ride crossed the Midway Plaisance straight on to the fairgrounds, where Clara would meet her father—a Mr. Jonathan Banks—at an exclusive underground establishment by name of The Cat's Whisker. So elite a club, it moved weekly to perpetuate its reputation, despite the nuisance it would surely be to relocate an entire pub.

Money buys one out of nuisances.

From the carriage, Clara watched the land change into the cloud-white buildings of the forthcoming fair. As it'd been every Thursday since her transfer to St. Joan's, it was impossible to tell where she was, but still there was something about the landscape that made her think of the Kodak back at the school and how it might capture this scenery.

The carriage halted, and Clara stepped out. Decked out in her usual Thursday night wear of a proper gown—tonight, black chiffon with lace at the sleeves—and her unruly dark hair tucked behind her ears, she held her breath and let the concierge escort her inside The Cat's Whisker. She slipped through rows of white-linen tables crowned with glass tumblers of malt liquor and overcast with rich cigar smoke to a table near the back.

Clara smiled when she spotted her father. Banks sat tall at the candlelit table as he frowned intently at his menu even though Clara knew full well he would order the same meal he did every Thursday—halibut, nicely done, with lemon and buttered potatoes.

Banks glanced up. "Clara, dear." He rose and kissed her cheek before pulling out a chair for her. "Early tonight."

"Earlier than last week, you mean," Clara responded as she sat, a quick and silent wish crossing her mind that tonight would be as much of a return to the old days as possible. Before the death of Bethany Banks. Before Clara had left home for Bynum Island. Before a strange note that spoke of monsters. "Math this week is trigonometry. Not nearly as troublesome as finite mathematics."

Banks narrowed his eyes and pointed playfully. "You and I both know that's a lie. Show me a world in which I need to know anything about crises containing damn triangles, and I'll show you a world that has years to go in terms of progress."

Clara grinned. It was supper time again at the family table with her mother's songlike storytelling flitting throughout the kitchen. A warm tug of nostalgia embraced Clara's heart in a way that made her happy and sad at the same time.

The waiter arrived for their orders, and the evening descended into its usual conversation.

"How are the rest of your classes?"

"Fine."

"There weren't any lingering problems with the transfer, then?"

"Nothing too painful, thankfully. But even if there had been, it would have been more than worth it." Clara was thinking of the reclaimed folktale she'd unofficially deemed their family legacy but decided to offer a different explanation. "Third-years are permitted to use the school's Kodak."

"A Kodak? That's a hell of an instrument to teach young girls these days. But certainly a good thing." Banks took a sip from a tumbler, and Clara watched how that sip extended to a much bigger gulp. The whiskey newly-polished off, he sat back in his seat and shut his eyes for a moment, a wave of calm rushing over him.

A second glass tumbler shone beside it—empty with amber drops coating the edge. "You're tired," Clara said.

"The fair." It was the same answer as the previous week. And many weeks before. Ever since Clara's mother had passed, and even with the windfall that had been gifted to the Bankses afterward through savvy business connections, Jonathan Banks's tensions never seemed to lessen, as though money could not solve *every* one of life's problems.

A good and thorough discussion usually did the trick, though, even if only temporarily. Clara remembered the inscription written inside her mother's folktale. Her father had never known Miranda Carveth, but perhaps Clara's mother had once spoken at length about her aunt. Clara leaned forward, readying to ask. But before she could, the sound of glass shattering came from a nearby table crowded with sweaty drunk men, and Clara shot up in her seat.

"For the love of God," Banks swore. "Common decency, it seems, cannot be purchased for any amount."

Clara watched as waiters rushed to clean up the glass and drink, the culprits laughing with their smoky pipes cradled in their palms as they stumbled into each other, heavy hands clapping on backs. Eventually, the rowdiness turned to song, with a slew of men swaying back and forth.

"You can learn quite a bit from your father.
Who centuries before you carved himself a throne.
You should learn quite a bit from your father.
Until all that's left of you is bone."

"Apologies, Clara." Banks cleared his throat and straightened. Always the new money, never about to make the same commotions as these men who ruled Chicago and St. Louis and New York and Boston with iron fists strengthened with the finest liquor. "Perhaps some of them will get lost on their way to next week's location."

Clara knew her father would never suggest a different establishment for their weekly dinner because The Cat's Whisker was the unofficial social hub of all his colleagues. It would be in Banks's best interest not only to show off his bright and charming daughter but also be present for opportunities he might not get through Mr. Westinghouse, a man Clara had never met but had seen many sketches of in *The Chicago Tribune*.

For her father to have been granted an invitation to The Cat's Whisker had unquestionably changed their lives. A club *membership* would do so again in a way that was incomprehensible to Clara.

Though it still irked her that she couldn't put together any sort of pattern as to predict where the next location would be.

She graced her father with a smile. "It's all right." And then she decided to try. "How exactly do you know where to go each week, anyway?"

Banks whistled as though his daughter had asked for a queen's fortune. "You know I can't tell you that."

"Well, I'm allowed to be here, aren't I?"

"As a guest, Clara," her father replied in a tone that was disciplinary instead of cruel. "As the daughter of someone who has been given a chance for a better life. For both of us. Never you mind about the details."

Clara let it go with a shrug. In truth she didn't care about the ways these men lived their extracurriculars. Not when she could instead learn what had happened to Miranda Carveth. Especially with a clue lying on the nightstand beside Clara's tiny dormitory bed back on Bynum Island, one that called to her curiosity more than it should. Defying good table manners—at this point, she knew she was likely amongst the politest in the entire room anyway—Clara set her elbows on the table and clasped her hands together.

"Father," she said, her heart thudding with the thrill of mystery. "Mother never attended St. Joan's, did she?" Clara knew the answer.

Banks clutched his empty tumbler a little more tightly, and Clara saw how the memory of their prior status in society rattled him. "No," he admitted with a glance elsewhere inside the gilded pub. "But she'd have been thrilled to know you were."

It had been an attempt to steer the conversation back into the preferred direction, but with that statement, both daughter and father stilled. Clara searched her father for the features she'd subtly inherited: their thin pointed nose, the dark arched brows, the heart-shaped line of jaws. She told herself to focus on this instead of his eyes, because she could see how he was staring in a way one did when missing someone dearly.

Clara's gray eyes, just like her mother's.

Clara wished she could take back the question that'd led to this grief. "Thank you," she finally replied before clearing her throat. "Sometimes it feels like a dream to step through those hallways now."

This wasn't exactly true, but an embellishment that could create a natural path to Miranda, not to mention a way to remind herself she hadn't exactly been impressed by the elitism that came with attending St. Joan's. In Clara's humble opinion, Curtis School had been just as formative.

Clara took another breath. "I wonder if she ever wanted to attend herself."

Banks stared at his plate. "I'm not sure."

"Perhaps it could have been possible somehow if Great-Aunt Miranda hadn't gone missing."

Banks's heavy stare, crowned with fine lines and thick bags under them, found Clara again. "Let the dead rest in peace. They do not deserve the burden of hearing us lament in their memory."

So perhaps that's all he knows.

The waiters brought their food, and Clara ate it slowly, though she couldn't taste a bite.

Nightfall on Bynum Island was as lonely as day. Clara lay in her dormitory bed, her roommates Diana and Gabrielle already asleep. But the third roommate, Lily Garner, was nowhere to be seen.

In the first few weeks at St. Joan's—and to the knowledge of no teacher at St. Joan's—Lily had sneaked away almost nightly to the all-boys school, St. Francis Xavier Cabrini's, well off the island. Sometimes she would not return until dawn. Thankfully she was quiet about sneaking back inside.

"Sorry," Lily had whispered brashly the one night she'd woken Clara by crawling in through the window, white-blonde hair tangled and wild in a way that suggested she'd just visited a paramour. "These windows get creaky in the winter."

That night—and close to midnight—shadows danced along the walls from the evergreen trees outside Clara's window, but otherwise there was no movement. It was a strange sort of peace that gave her the chance to lie sleeplessly in a cocoon of blankets, though her thoughts raced with ideas of her mother's book and its inscription scrawled on the title page.

The window nudged open beside her bed with a slow moan, and Clara's eyes shot open. A chilly breeze followed. Lily had returned for the night.

Perhaps *for the night* wasn't entirely accurate, though.

A pair of girls whispered to each other as Clara sank more deeply into her pillows and squeezed her eyes shut.

"It's essentially spring, Lil. Why on earth would you need that ratty old sweater?"

"Because, Marta, it still feels like winter, for heaven's sake." Lily's words tumbled out in a tipsy way. "It'll only be a moment." She tiptoed across the creaking floor until she reached her closet.

Clothing hangers rattled as Lily sorted through rows of clothes. A moment later, those hangers clattered to the ground, just loudly enough for Gabrielle to turn on her back, breathing as though she might soon stir.

"Now you've done it," Marta scolded from the window. "Wake the entire island, why don't you? Shall I invite the entire fraternity of the Skulls while you're at it? Come on—hurry! Sally gets furious whenever we're late to the clubhouse, and we spent far too long on the Midway."

"Quiet yourself!" Lily retorted in a raspy whisper. "Don't draw attention! Girls go disappearing from this island. Even teachers! And frankly, I have no intention of becoming the next Miss Carveth, thank you very much."

Clara's eyes snapped open. *Miss Carveth?*

The sound of feet pattering across a wooden floor followed until the window closed with a soft thump.

After a pause, Clara crept to the window. Below, the girls in their black St. Joan's dressing gowns ran through the silvery field, and soon a prolonged whistle spliced the silence, quickly joined by other voices, and then more. As though there were hundreds of them all whistling the same song.

Even after they disappeared into the woods, Clara struggled to sleep. The possibility of ever breathing again was nothing more than a shattered dream. She knew options for nighttime mischief were limited on Bynum Island, and the most logical explanation was that Lily and her friends had gone to the fairgrounds to explore, or at the very least, St. Frances Xavier Cabrini's once again.

That can't be it, though, Clara thought.

Because Lily's friend Marta had said *clubhouse.*

And then there was that name she'd said along with it.

Clubhouses full of girls discussing disappearances on Bynum Island—including that of a teacher named Miss Carveth—were not something Clara wanted to ignore.

In only seconds, were she to slip away from the dorms and into the starlit night, a Bynum Island described in the folktale's yellowed note might lure her into something she never imagined possible.

There was only one way to find out.

She threw her blankets off and edged her feet into a pair of slippers. A black dressing gown embroidered with St. Joan's crest on the breast pocket lay at the foot of Clara's bed. She snatched it and threw it over her shoulders. Then Clara lifted the window Marta and Lily had just crawled through as high as it could go.

The cool night air bit at Clara's skin as she slipped out the window and into the moonlit woods.

Chapter 6

Bitterness

The winter breeze struck Clara's skin like icy silk scarves as she ran. Oak branches soft with their buds cut against her cheeks as she raced deeper into the woods. Lily had said girls disappeared from Bynum Island—just like the note, *just like the note*—and Clara couldn't help but wonder if she were tempting fate by following them into the unknown.

Shrieks filled the forest more and more the faster Clara ran from St. Joan's. She was certain she was near the grassy path that led toward the island's foot bridge, which would take any of the girls to Chicago proper, but the pattern of trees made Clara pause in step.

"No, this isn't right." She snapped around with the voices themselves. "Where the blazes did they go?"

A group of shadows drew her eyes to a space where the trees bent away from the sky to let in the moonlight, and Clara followed it for no reason other than a path of light outweighed one of darkness any day.

As her slippered feet crossed twigs and leaves, a different sort of movement drew Clara's attention to one of the trees, where she saw a girl with a shock of long red hair duck behind its branches.

Stevie Graham. The girl who'd demonstrated the Kodak in Headmistress's classroom. She sauntered away into the blackness, after the sounds of reverberating laughter.

Clara watched Stevie go, carrying a secret like night itself would eat it up and deny everything in the morning. The moon vanished behind a painting of wispy clouds, and darkness fell upon the woods. Clara's stomach flitted into a gale of butterflies that longed to fight whatever fear had stricken Clara's heart, but then Stevie vanished beyond the trees, the snapping of twigs tell-tale of where she was heading.

"Stevie!" Clara called as she pushed aside fear to follow. "Wait!" She ran.

The trees' branches swept across her face, wet leaves clinging to her skin like the trees were alive and reaching to hold Clara back. Up ahead, shadows transformed into a troop of girls, and though Clara couldn't make out any sign of Stevie amongst them, she recognized Sally Carter and saw it was definitely her clique alight with shrieks and mischief in the darkness. Clara stopped along the trail and took a breath before catching up to them. The girls were moving in a way that indicated something was happening.

Something probably not in compliance with the rules of the academy.

Clara lowered her eyes as she realized she was about to make her presence known to a pack of girls who hadn't invited her, but before she could return to the safety of the dormitories, a loud cackle erupted from the group as Sally recognized Clara.

"Is that *Miss Banks* I see?" she shouted in such a way that Clara was shocked no one came to see what all the commotion was about. "Girls, *Miss Banks* is in our midst!"

Lily was there, too, her blonde hair as untamed as ever. "Miss

Banks! Such an *interesting* specimen, the likes of which we've never seen before here at St. Joan's!" She pulled at the long woolen sleeves of a gray knit sweater slung lazily over her small frame. "Oh. Don't tell me I woke you. I did, didn't I?"

She'd have awakened the dead, Clara thought. "It's just that the windows creak, and——"

"Of course you did," Marta announced. "You were a mammoth in a china shop back there, forget any bulls. Apologies, Clara. Though if you're here to wring Lily's neck for her iron feet, I'd be more than happy to hold her still."

"You were speaking about a teacher——" Clara squeezed in.

"How dare you, Marta," Lily retorted over Clara's words. Lily's voice had a melodic strength to it as though in a prior life, she'd graced the stages of Europe as an opera soprano.

Clara thought it best to try another approach. "We're not supposed to be on the school grounds past curfew. What are you doing here?"

Silence. Then the girls crowded her, and instantly, Clara was hit with the aroma of spirits. Sweet and sharp and something else that reminded her of what she imagined a pirate ship would smell like.

Sally smiled. "Tell me, Clara. I've been dying to know ever since you transferred here. What was the first thing you noticed about St. Joan's? I don't mean to sound like you're an exhibition or anything, but truly. I'm curious. Was it the uniforms? I heard once from my cousin in Philadelphia that not all academies have the uniforms St. Joan's has."

Marta swung an arm around Clara's shoulders, the opaque shine of a pearl-crusted ring circling her left index finger. Clara was captivated—it was exactly the type of jewelry she'd wear, and as she stole a few quick glances at Sally and Lily, here were all of them wearing the same piece. "Don't listen to her, Clara.

We like you. We do. We get the sense you think we're all snobs, though, and that just isn't right. You don't even know us!"

Lily pulled Marta away. "I *told* you not to finish the damn bottle!"

As the conversation swayed away from her, Clara stepped back. "It's late, and if Headmistress were to find us here—"

"Hold on a moment," Sally ordered, a lifted hand stilling the entire group. "What brings you to this neck of the woods, Clara?"

There was another question veiled in Sally's words: *Why did you follow us?*

Clara searched for an excuse, and any courage brewing inside her to ask about Miranda Carveth was instantly dashed. "I saw Stevie in the woods and wanted to ask her more about the Kodak."

Sally didn't look convinced. "You're right. It *is* late. Well after midnight. Do you usually take moonlit strolls, Clara Banks?" She was the soberest of the troop, and none were inebriated enough to realize there might be a lie up the sleeve of Clara's dressing gown. Lily and Marta eyed her carefully.

Clara stammered, "I don't actually—"

"Do you know what I know of you, Clara?" Lily interrupted, creeping ever so closely to Clara but not reaching any higher than her chin. It didn't matter—Clara could have sworn Lily stood seven feet tall with the confidence she boasted. "I know you're new money. Your father is quite the talk of the town. Jonathan Banks, isn't that correct? Able to rise to the highest position just in time for the World's Columbian Exposition?"

Clara felt like a specimen despite Sally's promise. She wanted to be angry her entire life was being laid out for the sake of these girls' entertainment, but there was something about Lily's speech that rang more as curious than cruel.

"You were a legend at St. Joan's before you even stepped into its hallways, did you know that?" Lily added, her big eyes glossy mirrors in the dim light.

"Oh, yes, that's right!" Marta added. "Clara Banks, the very girl at Curtis School to get every male teacher on the entire humanities faculty into a ruckus over the legitimacy of the suffrage movement! Goodness, was Ms. Meyer ever hoping you'd take her history class!"

Clara opened her mouth to respond, but Sally stepped forward first.

"It *is* late." Sally glanced at the girls. "And further conversation out here in these woods doesn't work for us tonight, isn't that right, girls?"

Clara blinked at the strange statement.

Sally's smile was congenial. "Have a good night, Clara. Perhaps you could join us in the city one day for tea."

Clara ordered herself to speak the truth, that she wanted to learn what the girls knew of Miss Carveth, if it was *Miranda* Carveth as she'd hoped, but with their eyes on her and the cool night nipping at her skin, all she could manage was a nod. "Tea would be nice."

Marta and Lily pulled at Sally's arms, and Sally waved as she was drawn into the shadows for a few more hours of debauchery. "Then tea it is! The finest tea you've ever tasted, Clara!"

Suddenly the world was quiet again, the entire forest shrouded in black and white as the joy of the girls vanished like a dream. Clara's breathing slowed, but when a soft saccharine lullaby cut the silence, her heart sped up once again.

Clara followed the song until she found Stevie.

She was resting her head against a tree with her dress in the soil of a flower garden the botanical class had been tending to for a week now. Her bone-white shoes dug into the dirt, the heels digging up petunias and peonies the color of starlight.

"Learn quite a bit from your father. Centuries before you.

Carved himself a throne," she was singing. "Should learn quite a bit from your father. Until all that's left of you is…" She glanced at Clara. "Bone."

"Stevie, there you are." Clara approached the girl's side. Drunk as a church minister, just as Clara suspected. "Headmistress is going to be furious with you." She stared at the poor pile of dead flowers.

Stevie's eyes were two black spots in the night as she fought to maintain eye contact, and her red hair spilled to the side, the ends of a scarlet ribbon failing to hold her ponytail in place. "It was terrible."

"What was?"

"Lily and Marta's drink. It tasted sweet at first, like a licorice-y syrup—something your mother would give you for a cold. And then it tasted horrible."

Clara smiled. "Then why did you drink more?"

"It was the only thing that could get the aftertaste out of my mouth."

Clara offered Stevie a hand.

Stevie stared at it as though it were wobbling of its own accord. "What's that for?"

"Get up. Your friends aren't here anymore. I have no idea where they've gone."

Stevie scowled. "They're not my friends."

Clara dropped her hand. "Apparently not, if they let you drink such horrible spirits. Next time look for girls who dabble in champagne."

Stevie smiled. "*Champagne,*" she whispered, nearly a purr. "With chocolate cake. Bitter cake. Nothing terribly sweet when you've got bubbles made of sugar and bliss to go with it. That was always perfect. Do you have any of this?"

"Not with me tonight, unfortunately."

"That's a shame."

"Yes, it is." Clara stared through the trees and caught the echoes of more girlish laughter. "Where did they go, anyway?"

Stevie stared in the same direction. "Oh, who cares? Unless they cross the bridge, I'll just meet them at the clubhouse," she said with a wave. Refusing Clara's hand again, she stood up by herself, brushing soil off the white skirt Clara knew would be forever ruined.

Clara didn't know why the foot bridge would even matter, but something else piqued her interest. "Clubhouse?" she pressed. Marta had spoken of the very same earlier.

Stevie stumbled before righting herself. She squeezed her eyes shut as though attempting to regain equilibrium. "Yes, of course. The Alouettes' clubhouse."

Clara remembered a melody, a string of whistled notes. A French song for children.

Alouette, gentille alouette.

Alouette, je te plumerai.

"What are the Alouettes?" A hum of danger vibrated around Clara.

Stevie stared like she might have happened upon a field of ghosts. She set a hushing finger to her lips. "Your voice should be softer than that, little bird. Girls vanish from this island rather easily when they ask questions."

Clara frowned at the eeriness of Stevie's words, and a chill found her skin—from the spring night or a warning, she didn't know. Only that Stevie's words had drawn terribly close to a line of prose in *The Traveling Demon and the Peasant Girl.*

"Mind your words, little bird, and keep your voice very low. Questions might find you answers, none of which you'll want to know."

Eeriness aside, Clara thought it rather brilliant of Stevie to use what Lily had said about missing girls at St. Joan's as an allusion to an old dying story. Even if Stevie had inadvertently cast herself as the mischief-making sprite who taunted the peasant girl's village with clues about the traveling demon. The sprite had all but told the whole story to the peasant girl, but she inevitably turned out to be just as deadly as he was as she lured children toward danger.

Clara wanted to ask Stevie about whether she'd heard any tales of monsters on Bynum Island. But a chill found Clara at the sheer thought of it, and she pushed any inquisitiveness away.

"All right then," Clara reassured Stevie. "Here I am, as quiet as a mouse. What are the Alouettes?"

"Not *what—who*. For generations, they've been a group of girls in power. Invite only, and incredibly elite."

Clara knew any additional questions would have to be crafted carefully. "St. Joan's has a secret society?"

Stevie reset that finger to her lips. "Be quiet, little bird. Ou je te plumerai." Stevie yanked at Clara's hair once before dropping it.

Sally called from the distance. "Stevie! Hurry up!"

Panic wrung Clara's heart. There was no time. "Wait!" She shut her eyes and yelled after them, "Miss Carveth was my aunt!"

The entire forest went still until footsteps drew closer, closer. Without opening her eyes, Clara knew all of the girls in Sally Carter's clique were there again. When she finally relented, all Clara could see were four shadowy girls, their bright eyes shining.

"What did you say?" Sally asked.

Clara's throat went dry. "Miranda Carveth. She was my mother's aunt. And you said her name, Lily, in our bedroom. I heard you. It might have meant nothing to you, but she was everything to my mother, and if you know anything about her disappearance, please. I beg you. Please tell me." The words spilled out like the spread of wildfire, as fast as she could think them, but Clara didn't care. This was the moment that could make all the difference in the memory of her mother.

Sally stepped forward. "Your aunt was Miss Carveth?" Her

feet crunched the forest ground as she approached, and when she stepped into the moonlight splitting through the evergreen trees, Clara saw stark curiosity on Sally's face, and an afterthought of skepticism. Sally set her fists to her hips. "Prove it."

Clara opened her mouth, but what proof could she offer?

"Wait a moment," Marta said. Her hand slipped naturally into Sally's, their fingers closing over each other as Marta leaned close to Sally's ear. "She's telling the truth, Sal. My research on Miranda says she had a niece who ended up marrying a man named Banks." Marta narrowed her eyes on Clara. "What was your mother's name?"

"Bethany," Clara answered.

Marta nodded. "Bethany. Miss Clara Banks is telling the truth." The girls exchanged looks, and though Clara couldn't tell what they were thinking, she realized it was an unspoken language between Sally and Marta.

Sally's thumb brushed against Marta's hand, and then she nodded. "All right. Then it's simple. Clara, you absolutely must join the Alouettes."

CHAPTER 7

AN INVITATION

"JOIN?" CLARA WHISPERED AS THE FOUR GIRLS SURROUNDED HER. "You mean, you're inviting me to join your group?"

Sally's eyes shone in the light. "Stevie? Tell the girls there's about to be an initiation."

Stevie grinned, a Cheshire cat in the moonlight, and scampered away, the inebriated giggles of a girl still lush with booze accompanying her.

Clara's eyebrows rose. "Tonight?" Her skin crawled with goosebumps born of folklore and shadowy islands. "But you barely know me."

"We know you well enough," Sally replied. "Besides, what better way to become acquainted than by inviting you to join a lifelong sisterhood?"

Clara focused on Sally's voice as she tried to make sense of her words. "So it's real?" was all she could manage. "What Stevie said? There is a club on Bynum Island. A secret one."

"Stevie should have kept her mouth shut about the Alouettes. She isn't the leader. You figured that, though, right?" Lily pushed Clara's dark hair out of her face. "There. Now we can see you."

She smiled. It was a girl's smile. An innocent one. But Clara could see right through it.

"Who is the leader?" Clara asked.

The girls stared at Sally. "No more questions just yet," she said. "You're still not one of us. But tonight? You're getting a special treat, Clara Banks. If you pass one test tonight at the fairgrounds, you can join our club."

The Alouettes dragged Clara across Bynum Island's foot bridge toward the Midway Plaisance. It was now past midnight under a great full moon, and Clara imagined all sorts of starlit and fantastical possibilities the night might yield as the girls shrieked and pulled at her arms, the suspicious *"you'll see"* their only answer to Clara's question as to where they were going. She kept her eyes peeled for a palace in the middle of Chicago, a hidden one where all sorts of individuals in the city met to discuss Very Important and Secretive Things. But maybe the girls would instead bring her straight to the shores of Lake Michigan, just past the railway tracks, where she'd have to wade into the icy waves and sing a song of sixpence until her throat went raw.

Once they crossed over to the roads of Chicago proper and found the Midway, Clara nearly tripped over her slippered feet at how much the fairgrounds had transformed since only earlier that night. St. Joan's wasn't too far from the eastward-most point of the World's Columbian Exposition—perhaps twenty minutes by foot if a girl were in a hurry—but there was a drastic difference in how this part of the city looked before the tents arrived. And the colors. Before the magic that seemed to rise from the pathways and ask if she was brave enough to venture onward.

The Alouettes pulled her past every new kiosk, every stand, every village of Ireland or Germany with swords for battle and fencing on display, every advertisement that spoke of dances from places Clara had read about like Serbia or Persia, animals whose furs were masterful works of art, shows of magic from China that promised to dazzle or terrify or both. None of this was what her father had fretted over during their Thursday dinners. None of this belonged to Morgan, Ford, or Westinghouse. Or even the savior of the Westinghouse contract, Nikola Tesla. This was an entirely different sort of fair with no pavilions if they could fabricate a moveable circus instead.

"This way," Sally insisted, giving another playful tug at Clara's hand.

"What in the world are we doing here?" Clara asked again, exasperated.

Sally eyed each of the gas lamps lining the Midway. The girls kept their voices down in case of pestering guards once they'd reach the Court of Honor, but Sally answered Clara nonetheless. "You're not afraid of heights now, are you?"

Clara glanced ahead. In front of them sat a great big pond— too large to be considered a swimming pool. It was nearly the size of a pavilion itself. *The Grand Basin.* Clara's father had spoken of it many times. How there would be fountains to go off throughout the day. Lights that would rise above it and shine down like a thousand suns chasing the rippling waves. It looked like a sculpture Clara would find in an old book about Ancient Greece and their marble statues of the gods. A place of worship.

And behind it, there was a set of white columns dusted in night, but visible nonetheless.

A peristyle.

"No," was Clara's answer to Sally's question, the word passing her lips as soon as her sight rested on the breathtaking architecture separating the Grand Basin from Lake Michigan. "I'm not afraid of heights."

"Then you should have no problem."

Marta giggled as Lily offered something to Sally, but Clara couldn't quite see what it was in the darkness. When Sally lifted it into a beam of lamplight, Clara still couldn't identify it. A long cylinder, approximately the length of Clara's forearm, reached from Sally's fist, and Clara could tell it was hollow. She remembered the Fourth of July the summer before, and where she'd seen such an object.

"Is that a firework?"

Sally nodded with a beaming smile. "Light it."

Clara gestured toward the pool, the pavilions, the whole of Chicago. "Right here?"

Sally shook her head with a click of her tongue. "No, of course not." She searched eastward until her gaze landed upon something in the distance.

Clara followed Sally's line of vision past the water of the Grand Basin to the shining gold statue above the white columns of the peristyle. Clara's father had spoken of the Statue of the Republic, and how its hands lifted a torch and laurel toward the sky. At the top of the highest arch that served as a gateway to Lake Michigan was another collection of golden figures. Horses and horsemen, rearing together as though charging into battle.

Clara blinked. "Up there?" From the steps beside the Grand Basin, it was probably three stories. "Where's the stairwell to the top?"

Marta leaned in. "Off-limits tonight." She pointed to the arch. "Look closer."

Clara squinted in the dim light until an enormous extending ladder set against the columns came into view, reaching the first tier. Suddenly, Clara's eyes shot open. "You want me to climb that rickety old thing and set off a firework? I could fall! I could *kill* myself!"

"No one ever said it'd be easy to become an Alouette," Sally replied. Then she shrugged and held her hand out for the firework. "And no one will force you to try. But legends don't become legends because they've accomplished everyday things."

Clara clutched the firework until it was about to snap. "No more enigmas, Sally. No riddles. No mystery. Tell me exactly what this test is."

"Fine." Sally stared Clara down. "We, the Alouettes of St. Joan's Academy for Girls, want you to climb that ladder leaning against the peristyle until you reach the first tier. Find a way to get to the statue next. Once you've done so, set off the firecracker to prove you made it. Complete this task within the hour, and you'll become one of us tonight."

Clara could see the peristyle was intended to be a crossroads —the railways were nearby, and any boats coming in from Lake Michigan from different parts of the state would convene there. Jonathan Banks had told Clara this already, and the historian hoping to one day bud free had loved hearing every second of it.

But peristyles were real, tangible. They weren't meant to be metaphors. Clara *hated* metaphors. But there it was, a literature class playing out in Chicago. Symbols shone all around her in an experience that was designed to be unforgettable. Would this moment serve as one of the greatest memories she'd ever have if she lived to be one hundred?

A simple choice—yes or no—had the potential to bring her that much closer to finding out.

"Why should I join?" Clara asked, but there was no strength in her question. On the contrary, her exhaustion was nearly palpable. "Everyone at St. Joan's knows I'm nothing more than new money. Why would any of you want me as a member?"

Sally stepped closer. "What makes the Alouettes powerful is its sheer number of excellent girls. If there are only a few of us, everything falls apart."

Clara scoffed. "You make it sound like you're at war."

"Not all wars are fought with rifles."

The figurative language was exhausting. "Is it a prank, then? Maybe you want to make a fool out of the girl who came from nothing."

"No," Sally corrected. "That's not how the Alouettes work. And do not make comments regarding things you can't possibly imagine, Clara. You're new money, yes, but that doesn't mean your life is hard."

Clara didn't understand how Sally could ever feel, and Sally's allusion to Clara's privilege was indisputable.

But before Clara could answer, Sally spoke again. "This is a once-in-a-lifetime opportunity."

Clara stuffed the firework into the deep front pocket of her dressing gown and stepped away from the Alouettes. As her slippered feet crossed the path toward the Statue of the Republic, magic sang in the air. Around Clara stood buildings her father had told her of over dinners of lemony-baked halibut and buttered potatoes, once pictures in her head and now visions of greatness in front of her.

"Masterpieces. They're going to showcase the future of the world," her father's voice said loudly in her mind. *"Machinery, architecture, electricity, the liberal arts…the newest and brightest amongst us have come together to create an event that would rival even that damn tower that now looks upon Paris."*

The girls behind Clara had gone quiet, and all she heard now was her own stuttered breathing. She wasn't afraid of heights—not really—but it was quite different to look out a second-story window of her father's estate when compared to a ladder that stood three stories tall.

"Don't fall!" shrieked Lily in the background, her voice high-pitched enough that it echoed across the waves of Lake Michigan.

Clara knew if she turned, she'd lose courage. Sally's loud hushing of Lily followed, and from that point on, Clara knew the silence meant the Alouettes were watching.

Waiting.

Clara set her shaking hands to the ladder and braced herself for the ascent toward the stars.

The wood was soft and worn, like a thousand people had already climbed as high as it could go. The occasional jeer from the girls distracted from that first step of slippered toes on wood, but Clara ignored them. This was merely a ladder. And sturdy enough that when Clara took that next step, it didn't move.

Perhaps forty steps stood between Clara and the top, but she focused on how the night sky above Chicago looked the higher she climbed. Her stomach pressed against her lungs, but she would not turn back. She would do what no other Alouette had done before.

She pulled herself higher.

And took another step.

The ledge of the peristyle's railing was just as white-stoned as the rest of it. The ladder stayed strong, but the tension in Clara's bones shook her as she came parallel to the ledge and the safety of the promenade on the other side. She reached for the ledge separating the peristyle from certain death, and suddenly the ladder wobbled.

Clara gasped.

One wrong move would mean the end. But she gritted her teeth and reminded herself a girl was liable to die if she panicked. She grabbed hold of the railing, set her foot on the stone, and pulled herself free. Gripping the ledge with her arm and shifting her weight, Clara kicked the ladder until it nudged away from her.

Clara's eyes widened, and she swallowed a gasp once the wood slid across the railing and then tipped. It crashed against the ground, and she winced as the wood of it splintered loudly.

"Clara!" Sally screamed.

Clara dug her fingernails into the stone. She tilted herself over the edge, and with one long and easy breath, her feet fell to the peristyle. Abundant with relief, Clara smiled.

She shouted out to the Alouettes, "I made it!"

They shrieked in response, dark shadowy figures by the Grand Basin jumping up and down and clutching each other with excitement.

But it wasn't over yet. Clara faced the gold figures of horses and horsemen at the top. Three more stone tiers until she'd reach them, and the eyes of Romanesque statues stared her down as she found the next ladder—a smaller one.

Her father's deep voice rang as she climbed it. *"They want the fair to look old world and classical. But they also want progress. Quite the contradiction, isn't it?"*

The first tier had been the biggest hurdle. This one was easier. The echoes of the Alouettes' voices were no longer something Clara wanted to ignore but embrace. How they were watching her and admiring her courage. She needed them to witness this great feat, and even if Clara had no idea just how exactly she would get back down to solid ground, for now, it was much more important she reached the heavens first.

The third tier led her to the golden horses with soldiers reining them in. Clara dropped in front of them and ran a hand across the smoothness of each statue, palming the curves of a horse's mouth. The detailing was exquisite, and she wondered if the artist who'd created these gorgeous things had ever wept at the thought that no one else would ever see such mastery up close.

She looked upon the fairgrounds with Lake Michigan sparkling under the moonlight. A fog of darkness hugged Chicago, but there were flickers of flames from the lamps lining the streets, their glows ethereal and alive, fireflies in mid-flight. The Alouettes stood by the Grand Basin, and Clara saw only their outlines now—they hadn't left her. They hadn't abandoned her.

Now, the finale.

Clara did not smoke, so she did not have matches in her pockets. But she remembered from last year's science class that striking a blunt object could ignite a spark. She took the firework from her pocket and kissed her fingers once in prayer that what she'd learned in school would pay off in a practical way for once. She judged the correct end of the firework and braced herself for an explosion of fire and sparks, and then Clara scraped it against the rough stone beneath her feet and slammed it into the open grasp of a statue behind her. She ducked, hands clasped over her ears. A burst of light and a thousand crackles catapulted into the space around her, and when Clara dared to open her eyes again, the fizzing work of a mad genius cut into the sky.

Faint cheers followed from the Alouettes, and Clara grinned at her conquest, cheering back with abandon. She wanted to celebrate, and if she'd thought to bring champagne, she would have sprayed open the bottle and drunk the stars straight from a glass of it. She was on top of the world, she was filled with an energy she couldn't name, she was—

"What the fuck was—Hey! What are you doing up here?"

Chapter 8

The Girl on the Peristyle

The girl shrieked, startling Fernando back a few steps. As the scream faded into thin air, she ducked behind one of the statues.

"Whoever you are, I haven't done anything wrong!" she screamed from behind a concrete block hoisting a garish quartet of horses. "If you try to arrest me, there's not a chance in heaven or hell I'll go downtown to the police station, so you might as well leave me alone!"

Fernando caught sight of a shadow peeking out. The girl was hidden by night, but he could see her search the darkness, a handful of ringlets bobbing around her chin. He tapped up the brim of his newsboy cap—his mother had told him a thousand times that showing one's eyes was the most genuine sign of kindness—but remained where he was. He wished whiskey had the power to fortify instead of weaken but thanked his saints most of the booze from the Midway tent had left his system. Enough that only an hour before, he'd found his way to the top of the peristyle and stolen the night for himself and his own thoughts of Brooklyn. His hands settled onto his hips, and he gauged the sheer distance between where the girl had been standing and the ground below. His heart dropped at the thought of falling.

"Jesus, Mary, and Joseph," he swore. "Don't you know how *dangerous* it is to be up here? What if you'd fallen? How did you get to the top anyway?"

He knew he didn't sound angry as much as he sounded surprised, and with that, all authority melted away as the words sprang free. The girl peeked further around the statue, her eyes wide before they narrowed, like there was something curious about him speaking to her—or was it his very un-Chicago-like accent, forget the shock of seeing someone else on this peristyle in the middle of the night?

A wry chuckle escaped the girl's lips. "But it seems I'm not the only one here tonight with a death wish," she retorted.

Another step brought Fernando close enough to make out the girl's heart-shaped face. Her eyes were a mix of curious and wild, and her red lips were parted, struggling not to quiver in the cold. Her gaze widened in surprise as he stepped into enough light to be seen in return.

After a moment, he offered his hand.

She stared at it as though it were a ghost's and made no move to reach for it.

"There's no need for…" Fernando tried, but any comfort he could offer was beyond him. "Here, let me help you back down."

The girl frowned. "What?" Then she shook her head. "Oh. *Death wish.* It was only a figure of speech. I didn't come up to the top of this great big thing just to throw myself off the side of it."

Fernando's jaw hardened. "All right. Then guess what? You're coming with me." He couldn't begin to imagine the trouble if someone were to find them.

The girl didn't budge. Her eyes shone more brightly. The

delight at being high above Chicago had a hold on her. His eyes fell back to her lips quirking into a smile.

He swallowed. "Come on," he pleaded. Had the peristyle always been this high up? "I won't ask again."

It was inevitable the girl would agree and descend—only a fool would parade the sky above Chicago like the world beneath them were theirs to take. But when mischief lit the girl's glittery eyes, Fernando could see there was only one thing on her mind now that she knew Fernando posed no threat.

The thrill of the chase.

"Please," Fernando tried once more. The ambition that had brought him to Chicago did not extend to literal heights. "Before someone gets hurt."

To his horror, the girl's face changed into one of zeal. "Where's the fun in that?"

Then she spun around and ran off.

Fernando swore under his breath. She was racing toward the edge of the top tier, the exact opposite side of the spot where only moments ago a ladder had stood.

"Oh, you've got to be kidding me," he muttered before following as she crept along the ledge.

The girl looked over the ledge to the promenade, and when she stretched out her arms, Fernando wondered if this were the moment a death wish would come to fruition. Any prayers of desperation from years of living under the roof of Imogen Carolan returned—St. Jude, St. Michael, whomever he could pry from Heaven's Gates to ensure a safety net at the bottom. The icy currents of an April night fluttered the hems of the girl's night-black dressing gown, and Fernando forced his steps to be soft.

"Please. Get back from there," he heard himself order, but his voice betrayed his fear, and the girl grinned over her shoulder then grabbed the edge.

Fernando drew in a sharp breath as she let herself fall until she was dangling a good six feet above the second tier.

"Wait! No!" he bellowed, but the girl had already dropped, landing softly but wincing at the impact of stone.

Fernando searched for the easiest way to follow. On construction sites in Brooklyn, a structure like this would have been cobwebbed with nets and scaffolding, ropes and platforms. But Chicago's peristyle was essentially ready for the fair—enough to have already cleared away any safety equipment. In the light of the moon, Fernando saw the girl grin, retrieve her footing, and run to the next tier. Despite any rational thought, Fernando dropped down, too.

"You're going to get us both killed!" he shouted after her.

"No one asked you to follow!" she shouted back.

"God damn it," he said. "This is *not* a game!"

"It could be!" This girl was full of energy, like the moon above them were riling up every ounce of strength inside her. She ran to the edge of the last tier, which hung straight over the promenade. But once she reached its limits, she froze.

Fernando knew exactly why and shuddered a breath of relief. This final tier was not as simple as the rest. This one was perhaps a good twenty feet above the cement.

And even a girl like this must have realized if she tried to leap from such a height, she could kill herself—at the very least, shatter every bone.

Fernando took another step, but the sound of it betrayed him, and the girl spun around. Her eyes found his, and she squeezed them shut, like surrender pained her. The immortality she'd possessed only seconds before faded into the sky, and her shoulders slouched.

"Well, then. Get on with it," she said. "Who are you going to turn me over to—the Exposition guards? The police?" Her weight shifted awkwardly. "Are you going to have them summon my father?"

Fernando crept toward her with caution. "Just…please. Stay away from the ledge. There's nowhere else to run. But there is a way down on the eastern side," he added. "And I'm not sure if you've noticed just how molded the edge is. In those shoes, you could easily fall straight off this thing."

The girl's eyes dropped to her feet and then the tier. It was mostly décor—swirls and swoops of carved stone. A platform like that could easily let anyone tumble clear off if they weren't careful.

"If you would just give me your hand." Fernando's anger faded. Now he sounded unquestionably afraid while putting on the face of someone who wished for bravery. "Please," he added.

The girl glanced at Fernando's outstretched hand, shaking like spring leaves. He watched her for as long as he could before she glanced back. Gray eyes, like sky after rain. They stared at each other, and then the girl swallowed and glanced away. Fernando realized they were standing quite close—perhaps too close—and so he took a step of faith back, assuring himself she was not about to jump.

He nodded toward his hand. "I'm Fernando."

The girl relaxed, even as the wind grew stronger, fluttering her black dressing gown and white nightdress around her ankles. "Clara."

He nodded again. "Clara," he whispered, testing her name on his lips. "Let's get down now."

The girl frowned. "Wait. Why were you already up here?"

Fernando's eyes cut away from hers. "Just please take my hand?"

He wasn't expecting what would come next. How the wind would swirl mercilessly around them in a way that pushed Clara closer as she inhaled sharply. How his arm would suddenly have a mind of its own and wrap around her shoulders in a protective way that also carried the faintness of fear. To do this felt like the most natural thing in the world to Fernando. Then the wind passed, and Fernando dropped his arm from Clara's shoulders. But Clara did not move away.

"All right," she whispered, offering her hand.

Her skin was cold but soft. Together they stared at their fingers folding into each other. "All right," he said back.

He led Clara away and focused on the height of the peristyle, on the concrete, smooth and solid underneath. It felt good to walk upon these walls, like his very own castle lay beneath them. The power that lit his bones called it a feast for his soul. His heart pounded, but he liked that, too, and a strange feeling of hunger bit at his insides until—

"That part looks loose," Clara said as Fernando risked another step. "Watch out—"

Fernando's focus came crashing back, and his eyes snapped to his feet, but the sudden jolt of loosening stone came first. A slip followed. His heart panicked.

Clara screamed.

The fall came next, and Fernando grabbed frantically for the side of the tier, elbows pressing against the stones that were just as loose as the ones that had already collapsed. The muscles in his shoulders strained as he held on to his weight, so intensely he didn't realize Clara had dropped to the tier and yanked at his arms.

"Grab hold of me," she ordered. He stared at her, storm-gray eyes now full of terror. "Grab my shoulders!"

Fernando's entire world narrowed onto the bit of stone under his hands. The absence of matter under his swinging feet was all he could dwell on. He shook his head furiously as he tried to shift his weight toward her. It wouldn't work. He would fall. "Can't."

Clara seized his hands and pulled, but Fernando felt her slipping away from him.

Oh God, he thought. *This is it. This is how I die.*

"Use the peristyle for leverage!" Clara tugged more fiercely at Fernando. "Your arm!"

His arm swung around hers despite any worry she'd come tumbling off the peristyle with him. They locked elbows so Clara's weight countered his. She pulled back, her face tense from the strength they both knew she'd need. Fernando shook, and then with a long wince, his legs found themselves on the right side of the tier, and he kicked away from the ledge and its crumbling bits until their backs were flush against the tier above.

He heard Clara release a long breath of relief, and she unraveled her arm from Fernando's. She set her hand to her chest, calming a thundering heart. But then that hand turned into a fist.

"I told you to watch your step," she said, her voice lush with the sort of fury that comes about whenever someone is afraid. "You weren't being careful."

There was *no way* she was being serious. The very same girl who'd been scampering across the peristyle like it'd all been a game. Fernando scoffed loudly. Clara forced her eyes ahead, straight at the place where they both might have fallen to their deaths in another life.

"*I* wasn't being careful?" Fernando said, though he knew deep down this girl was right. "Why did you climb up here in the first place? God—what were you *thinking?*"

She glared. "I wasn't the one who nearly toppled off this thing! I knew exactly what I was doing—"

"Really?" he said, cocking his head to the side. "You knocked over the ladder from the promenade beneath us, and you knew *exactly* what you were doing? How were you planning on getting back down, huh?"

He felt the delight of victory when Clara shut her mouth in a tight line.

"Well, you said yourself there's another way down," she muttered under her breath. Then she looked pointedly at him. "Besides, you never answered me earlier. Why were you up here, anyway? There's no work to be done in the middle of the night other than patrol. And you are no Exposition guard."

Any victory diminished as Fernando felt his face warm. There was no reason to explain himself to this wild girl, but he did. "I come up here sometimes."

"So you work here."

"Yes. And if anything had happened, I'd have been the one to blame. Think I want to deal with that?" Fernando crossed his arms.

A sound drew Clara's attention to the Court of Honor, and she looked out at the Grand Basin. Fernando followed her line of vision to a group of three more girls by the water.

One of them called up, *"Clara! What's taking so long?"*

Fernando scoffed again. "And you have friends waiting. Great. Just perfect. So what was this, then? A joke? A prank? A dare?"

Clara's eyes flocked away from his, like the truth were beyond something he could ever imagine. "If I tell you why, I'm going to expect the same of you."

It'd be the first bit of true and honest talk Fernando had had with himself since leaving Brooklyn. He didn't know how much he should tell a stranger, but at the same time, he had long since learned strangers were the best people to hear the deepest secrets of the heart, and so before Clara could answer, he spoke first.

"This is the best view of Lake Michigan. I can't come here during the day because I work on the Midway, and I'd just be in everyone's way, perched up here like some lonely sparrow." He laughed once. "Someone would be liable to *fall*." He glanced at her in ironic amusement, and Clara reluctantly smiled. The mood grew lighter. "It's easier at night. Quieter. I can get away from life." Away from the noise, the fast pace, the need to always be moving for fear of one day standing still.

Clara hesitated before she pressed a little bit further. "Your accent—"

"New York. I've been here a few weeks."

"Came for the fair?" The question felt like small talk. Trivial chatter. But there was something beneath it that carried a genuine bit of curiosity.

"No," he said, the truth of being just a fair worker instead of something more a bitter taste on his lips. "I mean, yes, but that's not all of it." He would leave it at that. Let her make of it what she would.

Silence fell upon them. Clara looked out at the Court of Honor again. Some of the girls had started walking toward the east end of the peristyle.

"Why look out at the lake, then?" she asked. "What's so magical about that big old bog?"

Fernando glanced at his boots and how they shuffled back and forth at the ledge. "Promise not to laugh?"

"I guarantee you, it couldn't be any more ridiculous than my reason for being up here tonight."

Fernando looked over his shoulder at the lake. If he listened hard enough, he could hear the tug and release of the waves hitting the shore. "I know it's impossible to see New York from Chicago, but my home lies somewhere past Lake Michigan and then some. I just like knowing it's out there, I guess." When Clara didn't laugh, he nudged her with his elbow. "Your turn."

She answered quickly, like she had the response already planned. "A dare. It was a dare. Those girls out there at the Grand Basin didn't think I had the nerve to climb up and set off a firework at the top. I showed them."

Fernando didn't quite believe that was it, but figured they were all entitled to their secrets. "You could have killed yourself."

She leaned closer in a teasing way. "But I didn't."

"Well, if there's a next time, think carefully. Because it'd likely be my job to clean up your bones, cracked all over the pavement."

"Deal." Clara smiled and pulled her dressing gown more tightly around her body. Fernando caught sight of the emblem embroidered on the breast pocket. *St. Joan's Academy for Girls.*

He pointed at it. "The school of folklore."

Clara's gray eyes widened like she'd seen a ghost. "What?"

Fernando shrugged. "Earlier tonight, one of the lads on the Midway was trying to pull the wool over my eyes, and two girls from your school were there listening to him prattle on about some eerie fairy tale." Though the exact details of the folklore Antoine had alluded to between whiskeys—had those girls even told him?

Clara cocked her head in curiosity. "You…know about that?"

Fernando decided not to elaborate on the party on the Midway. "All I know is that some of the boys on the Ferris Wheel have it out for the men running this whole show, and with that, it's as easy as a skip to create monsters."

Clara settled back against the stone. "Oh." She had a strange look about her. "If I were you," she added, "I wouldn't bother with looking out to the lake."

It took a moment for Fernando to realize she'd changed the subject. Then he smirked and indulged her. "Oh no? Why not?"

"Well, the lake's always changing, the tide moving in and out, and it's only something we can see here in Illinois. New Yorkers don't get such a gorgeous view, I'm sure."

Fernando shook his head. "Definitely not." She was kidding, of course. Lake Michigan couldn't hold a damn candle to the sheer magnitude of the Atlantic.

Clara smiled. "But what they do get are the same stars we're looking at tonight." She glanced skyward at those very constellations.

A romantic, poetic thing to say, but Fernando had already spent hours up at the top of the peristyle searching for the comfort he'd lost in moving there and never finding it. She was right, though. He'd seen that night sky while traveling across the entire Midwest to Chicago. No matter where he was in the country—or even where he would eventually go—those stars would remain pinned to the sky. They'd been there long before he was born, and they would continue to shine long after Fernando had died.

There was a strange sort of peace in that.

He and Clara sat in silence for a long time. Until—

"CLARA, WHERE IN GOD'S NAME ARE YOU?"

Clara startled and sat straighter. Excitement blossomed across her face, like something amazing awaited her. "I have to go," she said breathlessly.

They stood, and Fernando fumbled his hands into his pockets. An awkward stance he took whenever he didn't know what to do other than step from foot to foot. Clara watched his feet in their clumsy dance, and then another bout of horror hit Fernando.

"I swore at you, didn't I?"

Clara hid a smile. "Not *at* me. But yes. You did swear."

He cringed. "I said the bad one. The one they tell you not to say to strangers or pretty girls scaling deadly peristyles."

Clara's smile turned into a full grin at his embarrassment. "That's right, you did."

Fernando squeezed his eyes shut and then opened them slowly. "Sorry."

"Oh, I've heard much worse," Clara remarked. "The pastor at St. Bernadette's has some fairly colorful vernacular. My father had me help out with the church's gardening during the summer I was twelve. Reverend Walsh wasn't a fan of tending to the tomatoes."

Fernando laughed, a big wide smile accompanying it. He didn't miss how Clara's eyes lit up.

"Who is?" He pointed to the other side of the tier. "Come on. I'll show you the way down."

He led her toward the peristyle's last tier, where there stood a ladder Fernando had used to climb to the top. When they landed on solid ground, they walked the promenade amongst statues of winged creatures and saints alike, and then at the end of it all, they found themselves facing a stairwell roped off, perhaps to prevent troublemakers from sneaking to the highest point of the fair.

"Off-limits," she remarked. "As I was promised."

"I won't tell the Exposition guards if you don't."

"Clara!" a girl shrieked, and then she and the shadowy figures of two more girls began running toward them.

"And now it's time for me to leave," Fernando said.

Clara faced him. "You're not going back up there to look out at the lake, I hope," she said. "This time I won't be there to catch you if you slip again."

Fernando smirked. "No. Tonight, I'm heading home with the stars looking down on me."

Clara offered her hand. "Well then. It was nice to meet you, Fernando."

Fernando grasped her hand and shook it once then tapped at his newsboy cap. "Clara."

He knew anyone wearing a crested dressing gown came from a place of money, and with that, Fernando made the safe assumption this girl would likely attend the fair. He might see her again, strolling the promenade or the exhibits or somewhere else in Chicago. Or he might not.

Christ, Fernando thought. *What if I'd fallen and she hadn't been there?*

He didn't let himself think of it beyond that.

Clara's eyelashes fluttered as her breaths quickened. She flexed her hands at her sides, like she was unsure of what to do with them. Fernando hid a smile as he felt her stare.

Until the girls were too close. Until it was time to go.

He drew away with another quick tip of his hat. "Good night."

And then he turned from her and walked the other way.

CHAPTER 9

CHÂTEAU PERLE

"WHO WAS THAT?"

Clara spun around to Sally and the rest. Marta and Lily rose to their tiptoes to catch a better sight of the tall boy strolling away, but Fernando had already gone too far.

"No one," Clara answered quickly.

She felt strangely protective of Fernando. He was a secret she didn't want to share, this boy who wore darkness on his clothes and in his eyes like he'd been born at night and had never forgotten it. She found herself unable to breathe, and she worried she'd lose herself entirely if she took a good and proper breath.

"A worker," she finally managed. "He helped me get back down because the ladder had toppled over." The explanation spilled out, one word after the next, jumbled but coherent. And then, as though the Alouettes couldn't see for themselves, she gestured to the shards of dark wood scattered over the promenade, like a tornado had swept through to wreak havoc upon the Court of Honor.

Lily frowned at the explanation but then shrugged. "I can't

believe you actually did it, Clara! We were ten seconds from starting a bet as to whether you'd tumble clear off that thing."

Clara scowled in a way that told Lily she wasn't entirely offended. The sweetness in Lily's voice kept her free from being the target of anyone's wrath.

"I believe you owe me something now, Sally," Clara said. Then she eyed the other Alouettes. "Girls."

Sally grinned at Clara. "You've more than earned it." She grabbed Clara's arm and hooked their elbows as they led the Alouettes toward the Midway Plaisance. "Definitely thought you'd chicken out," Sally added the farther the group strolled from the peristyle.

"Or sob at the very least," Marta added. "There was no sobbing at the top, was there? You'd tell us if there had been. Of course you would."

Clara fought the urge to turn back toward the peristyle in search of Fernando—the dark trousers and matching suspenders, his skin tan from sunlight and heritage, and eyes shining with midnight black irises. She imagined his enviable long lashes and thick brows arched in a way that transformed him into the personification of the best kind of trouble. His black hair with its touch of a curl from underneath a newsboy cap, and the expression on his face at seeing Clara at the top of the peristyle.

Had he returned despite his promise? Like he was a glutton for punishment and only felt at peace when there was none to be had?

Soon enough, the urge to see Fernando passed, and Clara listened to the Alouettes gossip about the teachers at St. Joan's and the workers on the Midway, some of whom had found themselves escaping scandals such as union arrests and rumors perpetuated with sharp words from even sharper tongues. And then the conversation drifted to the boys at St. Francis Xavier Cabrini's, many of whom Lily had courted, and nearly all of whose hearts she'd broken over two whole years.

"Well, what do they expect?" Lily protested loudly, her nose high in the air as she refused any shame. "I won't waste my time with someone who's more of a nuisance than anything. It's their fault if they fall to pieces when I walk away."

"You don't walk, Lil," Marta interrupted. "You run."

The girls laughed as they marched through the Midway Plaisance with its deep rich colors and tents surrounding the castles and villages from Europe, Asia, and Africa housing soirées they might have bothered with another night.

"No parties for us now, though," Sally said to Clara. "Because tonight, you become one of us. Tonight is your first night as an Alouette."

Lily cupped her hands around her lips and sent a loud song into the air.

"Alouette, gentille alouette.
Alouette, je te plumerai."

Clara had assumed they'd simply go back to St. Joan's. Perhaps to Sally's dormitory room, or Marta's—second floor, east end—or even to her and Lily's room. Though granted, Diana and Gabrielle were asleep in the room she and Lily shared, and common sense told Clara that wouldn't be it.

Instead of some magical grotto or a dusty forgotten basement, the Alouettes led Clara to a place on Bynum Island where in the thicket of the forest stood what at first looked like a small cottage tucked amongst evergreens and oaks beginning to succumb to spring. It was a one-story bungalow—very unfashionable compared to the current architectural brownstone trends of Chicago—with a dark trim on the roof's shingles and shuttered windows painted snow-white. The oaks planted around the cottage seemed to curl their branches inward to encompass it, like they hoped to conceal such a place from the rest of the world, and Clara noted they had been doing a very good job at that.

With Sally's arm looped through hers, Clara and the Alouettes approached the front door, which was made of wood Clara was surprised had been pristinely-maintained and with little rot. As she stepped nearer, she saw just how far back the cottage stretched across the land, like a spell had come over it, only revealing its true size to those worthy enough to find it.

"Whose place is this?" Clara asked.

Sally winked a clever eye and withdrew a long skeleton key from the pocket of her dress. The key was iron—so dark it could have doubled for coal. "Ours. And soon, yours. This is the home of the Alouettes. Welcome to Château Perle."

Pearl, Clara thought. *Like their rings.*

Sally slipped the key in and turned a full rotation. There was a click as the door unlocked. Sally stepped inside, glancing back at Clara under the veil of shadows.

"Don't be afraid. I promise it looks much scarier than it actually is."

"What sort of promise is that?" Lily asked, pushing past Clara to meet Sally at the threshold. "Girls *disappear* from this place, Sally. Something strange haunts this island."

Lily's words made Clara swallow with nervousness. Too close to the note in her mother's folktale for comfort. But one thing at a time.

"Quiet, Lil. Not now," Sally said.

The girls tumbled inside the cottage, Clara the last to risk the darkness of a place that might have been a witch's cottage if all this were a fairy tale. But when she breathed in the smell of the foyer, there wasn't any dusty scent of a home that had been dry of visitors for a long while. Instead, it nearly smelled like—

"Fire," Clara whispered. "Or...ash, at least." She squinted and searched amongst the shrieks of girls familiar with the nooks and crannies of the place, and all the while Clara still couldn't wrap her mind around the truth that a group of girls at St. Joan's Academy owned their very own *cottage*.

Next came the snap of a match and a burst of flame, illuminating Sally's face as she raised the dancing fire to a row of candles atop a stone mantle that took up a good portion of the wall. When the wicks bloomed to life, a grand living room brightened. Fine leather furniture studded with iron, and oil paintings that looked as old as history. Pastures and portraits seemed to follow Clara wherever she stepped, and the wooden floor she walked upon was covered with an enormous red area rug that muffled her footsteps and those of the Alouettes.

As Sally carried the fire to several gas lamps strewn throughout the room, Clara spied rounded doorways with fancy Grecian-style molding, each leading to a hallway that boasted a boudoir, a bookshelf, or a sitting room shrouded with the heaviness of long curtains. Trinkets lay atop table stands, and chairs stood in corners as though inviting wayward ghosts to sit amongst the living. The Alouettes raced throughout the tiny cottage, some lounging on archaic gray furniture with too few pillows for Clara's liking, others gallivanting elsewhere.

The fireplace was the last to be set ablaze, and once its enormous flames rose up and bit at the air, a chill came over Clara. The shadows had gone from too big to too small, and Clara now found herself in the middle of these dark woods on Bynum Island, away from home and her father and everything else she'd come to know these seventeen years of life.

"She passed the test, then?" came a voice, and Clara turned to Stevie, sauntering in with a little more coherence and less inebriation than before. Time was certainly a godsend when it came to sobering up. Stevie eyed Clara in a way that made her feel like a science project. "I had an inkling you might. Not too many girls are brave enough to wade through these haunted woods alone, after all. Where's the fear in climbing a lousy peristyle compared to that?"

Stevie's smile was cheeky, but it was there. And though something tightened in Clara's bones, she felt obliged to return the smile.

"This place is a circus, Stevie," Sally remarked as she waved the match free of its flame. "Did you bellow up to the dormitories to get everyone here so quickly? Goodness."

As if on cue, Château Perle rang again with delighted voices.

"So *quickly*? It took you hours! Headmistress nearly caught me twice in that time!"

Sally grinned. "Well, then. I can't believe we didn't hear you from the fairgrounds."

Clara remembered then why they'd come to the Alouettes' clubhouse. Why all of them had forgone the rest of the night's sleep. She might have passed the Alouettes' test, but she didn't know if nearly falling from the height of a peristyle had been more or less dangerous than what was to come next.

Before she could ask, Sally skipped over and grabbed Clara's hand. "Right, then. Come with me, Clara. A hostess should always give a tour of her home. And now Château Perle is set to become your home, too. Let's begin with the foyer."

Marta, Lily, and Stevie followed as Sally led Clara to the fireplace and the mantle. A strange spot to start with, but Clara indulged Sally and studied the lay of bricks on the mantle, their imperfections as natural as life, and the stone that hung overtop the fire, burnt slightly from use. Beside the mantle was a desk and a chair reminiscent of Clara's father's office. An inkwell pen sat in the corner with a long black-and-white plume curling into the air like the neck of a swan. Atop the mantle hung an arrangement of old paintings, small compared to the grandiose portraits hanging elsewhere. After studying in history class as photographs of the graduating classes watched her, Clara found this touch to be slightly antiquated.

"Blood to bone," Sally said in a commanding voice.

"And bone to ash," the girls replied in unison.

A kind of power came over Clara, like the words were as ancient as womanhood.

"These are our mothers," Sally said, pointing to each picture, one newer than the next. "Our grandmothers. The Alouettes' membership comes about through bloodlines. Blood, Clara." Sally's voice lured Clara's attention, and she could see how Sally meant for her to listen seriously now. "Blood rules over women in some ways. In other ways, we rein it for ourselves." It was a monologue that carried the air of generations.

Clara recalled reading about the men at Harvard and Yale who sliced their palms and branded their forearms. A lifelong commitment to a brotherhood. She wondered if this would be asked of her tonight.

"You do not have a mother or a grandmother in the Alouettes, Clara Banks."

"No," Clara said. No reason now to pretend she'd always been someone whose family could afford to send her to St. Joan's.

"So our invitation tonight makes you the first woman of your lineage to be a part of our sisterhood. We won't ask you for blood, though. What is blood to a woman? Our bond must go deeper." Sally's eyes darkened as though several of the candles in the clubhouse had suddenly extinguished. "As deep as marrow."

Clara went cold.

Sally's face softened. "Come along."

CHAPTER 10

EN GARDE

Sally led Clara toward the first arched doorway. The sounds of clanging rang close, with occasional orders and grunts and the light footsteps of battle. A pair of twin doors with carvings of ornate birds opened to a smooth-floored gymnasium. Clara and Sally walked inside as Marta and Lily trailed behind, and Clara's eyes immediately fell upon a silver bowl to the side filled with identical rings. The very same ones she'd seen the girls wear at St. Joan's. Clusters of pearls embedded on bands. Clara waited for Sally, Marta, and Lily to take theirs off—and she wondered when she would be given her own pearl ring if this were indeed a symbol of the Alouettes—but they didn't.

Instead, they watched a pair of girls spar in the middle of the gymnasium with a half dozen Alouettes observing from the sidelines.

Clara's eyes widened. "They're fencing," she said.

"Yes," Sally answered proudly. "Yes, they are."

Two girls wore the traditional white jackets and masks Clara had seen in newspapers of the fencing matches that had sprung up in Europe overnight. She hadn't even known there were people who practiced it in Chicago—never mind at St. Joan's.

The girls sparred, their foils singing as they moved like mosquitoes through the air. At the inevitable *en garde* and then *touché,* the match ended, and each girl removed her mask to shake her opponent's hand.

"Known as quite the avant-garde sport, you know." Sally led Clara through the sidelines of the gym. "But the Alouettes have been practicing it for decades."

"Ever since the first girl disappeared," Lily interrupted. "Precautions, naturally."

"Precautions like fencing were pointless at first. But maybe one day they won't be," Sally continued. "If you choose to learn, lessons are available. As much as Lily is a nitwit when it comes to keeping her mouth shut, she's quite the expert."

Lily straightened at the compliment and ignored the jab. "I've beaten every single Alouette since my first year at St. Joan's. My mother sent me to daily fencing lessons while I was at school in Rome and she was having her affair with my Italian professor. She and Father were quick to move to Geneva to live with the Swiss members of the Garner family after that, naturally."

A brightness spilled on to Clara's face. "Fencing," she repeated, ignoring the scandalous story she knew Lily was just dying to tell. "You could teach me how to fence."

Lily's keen eyes held the knowledge of an entire world Clara had never explored before. She slipped her arm through Clara's and led her onto the polished floor. The girls from the previous match had moved to the sidelines, and Lily marched straight to the side of the gymnasium where there stood an array of fencing gear. Bone-white jackets and masks and foils and gloves—they all hung inside a wooden armoire just waiting for any girls itching to fight.

One of the girls cupped a hand around her mouth and called out, "I haven't forgotten I'm owed a rematch, Lil!"

Lily spun on her heel toward her. "Perfect your form first, Chantel. There's no honor in defeating an amateur."

Chantel's face scrunched at the insult, and the girls with her laughed.

"Just say the word, Clara, and we'll put these away and continue with your tour of Château Perle," Lily singsonged as she strapped on a starchy jacket and slipped an oval mask onto her head, letting the mesh rest atop her forehead. "Are you frightened of a quick little skirmish?" Lily's right eyebrow slid up in challenge.

Clara had already scaled the peristyle at the fairgrounds of Chicago. She hadn't shied away from the first dare the Alouettes had assigned her—nor would she shy away from this one. She reached for her own fencing mask.

"I think you'll find I'm a quick learner."

Lily wasn't intimidated. "Excellent." She batted her eyes and reached for a fencing sword from the wall of about two dozen. Just like the real swords by the front door to Château Perle, these were rows of well-crafted blades, as thin as they were long with variants in threes.

"We'll start with the foil," Lily announced. Sally nudged Clara closer to Lily, who carefully chose a long sword with a rounded guard protecting the handle. "No use giving you any blades that would let you stab me in the eye, after all."

Clara fought the urge to roll her eyes. "Do you really think I'd do that?" She reached—albeit reluctantly—for her own foil. When she lifted it, she marveled at how light it was and how unnatural it felt in her grasp. Until suddenly, it warmed to her hand.

"Careful," Lily warned, backing away with ease toward the

middle of the gymnasium floor. "If that's the first time you've ever held a foil, I'll thank you to watch where you point it."

Clara lowered the weapon. "Sorry."

From the sidelines, Sally and Marta watched, whispering as they pointed with their free hands, the ones that weren't entwined together. Marta lifted her chin. "She's got a tell, Clara! Watch that left step! She only makes a leap when she's about to jab you in the side!"

Stevie settled herself on the floor, legs outstretched and ankles crossed. She batted at Marta's dressing gown. "Where's the fun in giving away all Lily's secrets?"

"Oh, quiet, Stevie. You're just miffed because you've never beaten Lily yourself."

Stevie glowered. "No one has."

Clara stood opposite Lily, her mask shaking as she set it over her dark curls. The white jacket over her night robe was too warm, and parts of it itched her skin. She tried not to look at the many chalked marks on either side of the stomach and arms, but the temptation to do so was too great, and she wondered whether it would hurt were she to lose.

Lily dropped the mask over her head. Clara did the same. The black mesh was thick enough that her sight was inhibited, but after a few blinks, her gaze resettled, and she eyed Lily carefully.

Lily snapped her foil up to her mask in one quick salute. "En garde."

Clara shook as she mimicked the move, a little bit slower than Lily, but accurately. *At least I didn't knock myself in the face.*

"I'm assuming you know what to do?" Lily said, as her foil drew down with a sharp whistle.

Clara nodded and did the same. "Strike or be struck. Isn't that right?"

Lily sidestepped to the right, her foil low. Clara likewise

circled, keeping as far away from Lily as she could. Behind her, Marta whooped and hollered as though intending to stir up drama. But this was all just a bit of training. Nothing more. Surely.

"That's right." Lily whipped her foil in a quick circle, faking an attack, and Clara leapt away. She heard the ringing of Lily's girlish laugh echo in the stadium, which had now gone silent—or was that just her own focus narrowing in on Lily? "But not above the neck. Not below the waist. No limbs. No arms. You must hit my torso."

"And say *touché*, I suppose," Clara added.

"We'll get to that if we need to."

The stadium fell silent. Not even their footsteps were audible as Lily made elegant jabs into the space around Clara, forcing her to step away at the last second. After missing twice, Lily retreated, her wrist whipping around the foil.

"Your instincts are good," she remarked. "You move quickly."

Clara's skin was damp with sweat, and her heart pounded against her fencing jacket like unruly thunder. She wanted to make a smart reply, but her eyes kept drifting toward Lily's feet. Carefully, they crossed each other in a slow dance as Lily readied for another attack. Clara would not concede any advantage—if that was Lily's game.

Then Lily made an awkward move. A left step instead of a right one. *A left step.* It was unconscious, and it was bulky. And then Clara remembered what Marta had said about Lily's tell.

Lily jabbed forward, aiming at Clara's ribcage. Clara folded away and lifted her foil. Lily stood defenseless. Clara turned and carried her blade with her, sending the blunt tip of the foil toward Lily's body.

A strong hand suddenly caught her right hand—Lily's. Clara couldn't move. With her surprise, she dropped the foil, which clattered sharply against the gymnasium floor, and Lily's foil tapped Clara's ribcage.

"Touché." Lily dropped Clara's hand and pulled off her mask, revealing her grin of victory.

"No!" Marta moaned from the sidelines. "Damn it all! I was hoping for beginner's luck!"

"Hoping against hope," Sally replied with a shake of the head. "Lily is unbeatable."

Clara removed her own mask, dark curls sticking to her sweaty cheeks. "That was incredible. What about your tell?"

Lily crossed her arms and scoffed. "Oh, come on, Clara. Did you really think I wasn't three steps ahead of you the entire time?" She tossed the mask across the floor toward the rest of the fencing gear. "You're definitely a quick learner. But no one beats me. Next time, wager your life on it."

Chapter 11

Newspapers

"Come on, now," Marta said, gesturing toward a second doorway in the gymnasium. "Let's show you the room I imagine you'll love the most."

As Marta pulled her toward the door, Clara looked over her shoulder at the next pair of girls preparing to fence—the one who'd heckled Lily earlier amongst them. Then Clara's eyes fell again upon the silver bowl with the rings. She'd forgotten about it as Lily's foil had flown through the air to meet hers, but now her curiosity was getting the best of her, especially knowing the Alouettes' clubhouse had been christened *The Pearl Castle.* "Why—"

"More on that later," Marta said.

"When is the initiation?" Stevie whined. "I spent all this time collecting the girls, and we haven't even *initiated* her yet."

Sally glanced over her shoulder at Stevie. "A proper hostess gives a tour," she said, her sentiments from earlier.

"For goodness sake, Sally, she's not a guest. Isn't that the whole point to this thing?"

Clara chuckled softly. "If I didn't know any better, I'd think you were looking forward to a simple initiation, Stevie."

She didn't have to turn to know Stevie grinned ominously. "More than you realize, Miss Banks."

Sally rolled her eyes. "Quiet, Stevie. This is Marta's bit."

The second room wasn't a gymnasium, but a library. Clara gasped as she took in the old wood lining the walls like bark on a row of snow-white birch. The shelves were gargantuan—rising to perhaps twelve feet—and the height of the library itself seemed all the greater. Clara had a distinct feeling she was no longer in the same cottage she'd stepped inside only moments ago but another world where the Alouettes ruled the land, and the concept of night was strictly ignored by all who'd rather lose themselves in the adventures that sang from count-less pages. Brontë, Austen, Alcott—there were first editions of all the classics Clara's parents had collected, and multiple copies of each.

And then, something more.

Newspapers.

"This collection is even bigger than the one at our school," Clara said, awe trembling through her voice. "I don't know where to look first."

"Thanks to *The Chicago Tribune.* Pays to have connections, Clara." Marta strolled to the closest shelf and ran an index finger along the careful creases of a stack of them, a fading gradient of browning sheets. Some crisp, others less so. As Marta selected one and shook out the dust with a loud rustle, Clara caught sight of the date.

"My God," she said, at Marta's side in an instant. She pointed at the front page. "This is the inaugural edition. 1847."

Marta handed Clara the newspaper, but before Clara could touch even one crisp page, Marta snatched it back. "Rip even one corner off, and your initiation into the Alouettes will include mounting your head onto the wall."

Clara was careful as she glanced over the tightly-arranged

words, the language so familiar and yet the world of Chicago so different.

"More on this another day, Clara," Sally announced. "Come on. The Alouettes await."

Clara folded the newspaper and set it back on the stack. Stevie was clapping gleefully beside her. "Hurry up, then! This is the dull room anyway."

Marta narrowed her eyes. "Only to the *very* dull, Stevie."

As Marta walked through the rows, Clara could see they'd eventually come to a great big space where in the middle stood a long table covered in pages and books and scribbled notes and blots of ink. A handful of girls sat amongst the chaos, fiddling with spectacles and looking down upon ciphers and codes of all different sorts. These Alouettes ignored Clara as she strolled by, her watchful eyes keen on every scribbled word in case there could be something of importance found among these notes—mentions of Aunt Miranda, perhaps, or the notion Bynum Island might be dangerous—and Marta held her finger to her lips in a request for silence until they passed to the next row.

And once they did, Clara asked, "It's still the middle of the night. What are they doing?"

Marta took a breath. "I suppose it's time. Surely, you know that girls go missing from St. Joan's and have been for decades. Common knowledge. What isn't so common is that the disappearings aren't accidents, Clara," she whispered. "And what we don't know is why each girl was chosen to vanish, and what connection they had to each other. If we can find out what they had in common, we can find the culprit of these crimes. Who took them—or what. If it's a creature or a bit of magic, perhaps."

A war between skepticism and possibility rang loudly inside Clara's head, but it was the familiar skepticism that found its way onto her face, and Clara could do nothing to stop it.

"Don't cast it off as foolishness," Marta said. "You know nothing about St. Joan's or the Alouettes. All you've known is what you've been told in the last few hours. We're here to tell you there's much more to Bynum Island than meets the eye. Sally told you not all wars are fought with rifles. We're readying for whatever lies out there. We're mastering fencing and studying cryptography so we won't be fooled by something that thinks it's smarter than we are." She paused. "You said you're the niece of Miranda Carveth, right? I suppose you had no idea before tonight she was a teacher here."

Clara's cheeks warmed. "No, I didn't," she admitted, and the desire to speak loud and true about the folktale on her nightstand pulled at her. These girls might already know more than Clara did. About the folktale, about the danger on the island—even about a peculiar note with an ominous warning that might be truer than Clara had originally thought. But Clara also didn't know these girls well enough yet to divulge family secrets. "Tell me about her?"

Marta reached for an old yearbook—its date, Clara couldn't exactly see—and opened it to the faculty page. "Here." She pointed at the humanities department, where a carefully calligraphed hand listed each of the teachers' names. "Miss Miranda Carveth of Chicago, Illinois."

Clara's finger brushed over the name like it could connect her to the past. "My mother said nothing about this. Just that Miranda had been her favorite aunt, and she, Miranda's favorite niece. They shared ghost stories." Clara wondered if it'd make any difference at all to tell the Alouettes about her mother's copy of *The Traveling Demon and the Peasant Girl*. Then another name caught Clara's eye. "Is that…Headmistress?"

Marta spun the book toward her and raised an eyebrow. "Look at this, Sal. Miss Florence McGill of Montréal, Québec is listed as a former student, now the poetry teacher."

Clara couldn't explain how that tidbit managed to tie her heart into a sailor's knot, but she now wondered if there was any possibility Headmistress had known Aunt Miranda.

"Clara?" Sally said delicately. "Are you still with us?"

Clara shook her head in wonder. "This morning, all I'd known about my own great-aunt was that she'd vanished without a trace. It'd never crossed my mind she'd been an actual teacher here."

"We haven't even begun to scratch the surface," Marta said. "You can still walk away from all of this, Clara." She dropped Sally's hand and crossed her arms, bracing her stance so she towered over the rest. "Or you can put your good mind to use and contribute to a noble cause."

"Patience, Marta," Sally ordered, always the leader. "It's a lot to take in all at once. But Marta also makes a good point. If there's any hesitation, Clara, best to walk away now. Go back to the dorms. Go back to sleep, and when you wake up tomorrow, none of this will be real. It'll all be a part of your imagination, a dream perhaps. The Alouettes will cease to exist in your solipsist world. The girls will simply invite you to join them and their mothers for tea downtown, and none of this will ever be spoken of again." Sally pressed a bit closer to Clara. "What'll it be?"

Clara could focus on nothing else. "I have to know, Sally. I have to know everything."

Sally cocked her head and declared, "Our girl is ready."

CHAPTER 12

BLOOD TO BONE

"SIT."

The Alouettes surrounded Clara, who sat in a chair in front of the desk. Beside her, the fire burned brightly, a testament to the good strong oak of Illinois and how well it held the flames. Clara tucked her dressing gown under her body and crossed her legs at the ankles. She wasn't sure what to do with her hands, whether to keep them in her lap or set them on the desk. Shadows bounced off all parts of the cottage walls in a way that was mesmerizing, and for the first time since the peristyle, Clara remembered it was still the middle of the night. Perhaps by now, almost dawn.

Sally stood behind the desk and ignored Clara for the rest of the Alouettes.

"The Alouettes have been a sisterhood at St. Joan's Academy for Girls since when?"

"1790," came the chorus of girls in unison.

"Our first leader," Sally continued, "was a girl by the name of?"

"Winifred Sinclair," the Alouettes replied as Clara watched.

"Winnie was affiliated with the New York Sinclairs, and in fact, it was she who brought them to power."

Clara was fascinated. This was a part of history she didn't know. "How?"

Sally opened a drawer in the desk and pulled out a black velvet pouch, which she unraveled and set in front of herself. Clara couldn't see what lay inside, but she did spot a shine of metal. "Winnie married into a Harvard family, which provided the necessary reputation, but her money and power through the rise of the Alouettes made it so her husband took her name rather than the other way around."

"That would have been quite the scandal," Clara remarked, unconvinced.

"It would have been," Sally agreed, "had the scandal ever been exposed. But whoever writes the news, writes history. Winnie knew that."

Clara knew the same. Scandals came from word-of-mouth, but they also came from the power of the press. Have control over the latter, and it seemed logical you would have immense control over the former, too.

Sally continued. "For generations, the Alouettes have secretly thrived. Our daughters will be invited to continue this lineage, and their daughters after them. Tonight, we ask you, dear Clara Banks, to become one of us. To be the first of the Chicago Bankses to join the Alouettes. Are you willing to give us that which makes you who you are?"

Sally lifted the shining tool in her arsenal, and Clara saw it was a knife. So it would be a blood ceremony, then. A finger prick and a drop of blood in a wooden bowl, a bit of hocus pocus here and there, and then the whole of it would be done. But then Clara remembered what Sally had told her.

What is blood to a woman?

Clara lifted her chin. "Yes, I am willing."

Lily nudged a tiny frame in front of Clara. Reflecting behind its glass was a yellowing bit of paper carrying flowery, black-inked script. "Read," she instructed.

Clara cleared her throat. "I hereby pledge my loyalty to the Alouettes of St. Joan's Academy for Girls. I understand that by taking this oath I become a sister to all the women around me, before me, and after me, and I do solemnly swear that everything I learn inside Château Perle will go with me to my grave, or may a flock of hungry vultures use their beaks to rip out my—" Clara paused as she read the rest. "Oh. Well, that's ridiculous. Is it really necessary to promise something so gruesome?"

Stevie's eyes widened in command. "*Read.*"

Clara scowled. "Use their beaks to rip out my throat and use it as a bowtie. Blood to bone, and bone to ash. There. I suppose Winnie Sinclair was a poet, too?"

Sally smirked. "More of an aficionado of the macabre. Give me your left hand." She removed her ring and set it on the desk. "And hold still. This will hurt, Clara. A lot."

Clara frowned. She did as she was told, but once Sally's own left hand found hers, Clara gasped. On Sally's naked hand, there was a careful yet deep indentation in the back of her index finger.

Almost as though someone had carved out a bit of bone.

Clara swallowed a surge of panic. "What are you going to do?"

Sally drew away as though having already anticipated Clara's reaction. "Let men ask for blood. Our bond goes deeper, Clara. It's like I said. We want a bond as deep as marrow."

The Alouettes removed their own rings, revealing their index fingers indented just as Sally's was. Stevie was last. There was not a girl amongst them without the mark.

"Oh, don't worry. I won't take off a finger or anything," Sally said. "It'll be a blunt stamp into your bone with this knife, and then a quick pull out again." She flipped the knife over in her hand. It wasn't sharp like a usual knife but had two dull edges. On the inside was a line of steel teeth. Teeth that would easily draw out shards of bone. "It'll be throbbing with a dull ache for a few days, but it'll heal properly if you take care of it. Feed the flames in the fireplace with your marrow, and you'll be one of us." Sally glanced behind Clara. "Or, the door is right there."

Clara stiffened at Sally's remark. The idea seemed barbaric—but also enlightening. The knife lay in Sally's hand, the same knife since 1790. Girl after girl after girl, all bearing the same mark, all promising the same promise. There was a love of history running through Clara's bones, and in mere minutes, history could make its permanent mark on those, too.

Clara stretched out her left hand. "Do it," she ordered. This was one step closer to finding out the truth of what had happened to Aunt Miranda.

Sally waited a beat, possibly in case Clara would change her mind. When that rescission never came, she opened the gate to the stove, now blazing hot with fire, and stuck the knife in, turning it once and then twice until it was hot and clean. She wiped the blade onto her skirt to remove the soot that had gathered on the steel, and then she stepped toward Clara and set her hand on the desk.

"Towels, Marta," Sally ordered, and Marta skipped away, returning with a set of pristine white cloths that would soon mop up the splatters of Clara's blood.

Clara gulped.

Lily offered her a silver flask that had been sitting on the mantle amongst the paintings of Alouettes past. "You'll probably need this."

Clara didn't argue. With her hand outstretched on the table and two Alouettes securing it in place, Clara took a long burning gulp from the flask. It was whiskey. And though it hurt to swallow, it cleared Clara's mind after a heavy drink of it.

Sally held Clara's gaze. "You might want to look away." She already had a brand new pearl-clustered ring sitting beside her own.

Clara knew that ring was meant to be hers in mere minutes and shook her head. "I've come this far."

Sally set the knife's dual bite to Clara's left index finger, right above the knuckle. Once it was in place, she lifted her fist and held it in the air. "On the count of three."

Clara nodded, desperate for the next few seconds to be over with.

"One."

Clara gritted her teeth and focused on the rush of blood from fear and spirits.

"Two."

The Alouettes tightened in on her, and Clara swore she could hear them assure her it would be all right, that Sally had done this a thousand times before, that it wouldn't be nearly as bad as breaking a limb, and that it'd be over faster than one could light a match.

"Three."

Sally slammed her fist down onto Clara's finger.

There was an audible crunch.

And Clara screamed.

ACT II

CHAPTER 13

BLADES AND ARMOR

HEADMISTRESS FLORENCE MCGILL WAS AN EFFICIENT administrator when it came to running an all-girls school, and her choice also to teach upper-level history courses would not diminish that efficiency. Likewise, she was a staunch advocate for learning through action rather than forcing a girl to scrutinize an entire textbook. These principles ensured Headmistress's girls received the chance to experience the biggest societal event in modern Chicago. And a week earlier than any civilian, at that.

Though Clara knew such success couldn't have come without a bit of help from someone with an 'in' to the fair.

"Naturally, if there's anything I could do to help with these girls' education, I'm happy to do so," she imagined Jonathan Banks saying to Headmistress, all too eager to prove to St. Joan's they hadn't been wrong in accepting Clara despite the Bankses' new money status.

Wherever the success had come from, the Alouettes set out on a field trip that day, the perfect opportunity to catch up Clara on all the research they'd done thus far on the school's missing girls. Research they were more comfortable speaking of now that they were off the ghostly Bynum Island.

Perhaps the note Clara had found in her mother's book could help somehow, but still Clara felt protective of it. A secret connected to an heirloom.

Not yet for the others.

Sally and Lily locked their arms through Clara's as the class marched the short distance to the Midway Plaisance. Clara shuffled the school's Kodak higher onto her back, its case having been blessed with two good and sturdy leather straps for just the occasion of carrying it across the fairgrounds. As they strolled past the Ferris Wheel, Clara studied each steel beam and the workers tightrope-walking them, their arms stretched for balance and their laughs punctuating shouts from the ground to *pull the ropes higher, watch the car over there, get that motherfucker back in line or this whole goddamn thing will fall over.*

"What on earth are you doing, Lily?" Sally asked, exasperated.

Lily was leaning across Clara, studying the Ferris Wheel just the same. "I'm looking for someone."

Clara's cheeks warmed as she remembered the dozens of times she'd spied Lily sneaking into their dormitory window. The boy Clara had met on the peristyle—Fernando, with his black eyes and unjustly-long lashes—could just as easily be one of them.

"Who?" Clara asked, her voice calm, though she wasn't sure why she needed it to be.

Lily's heavy lashes swept atop her cheekbones as she glanced at her black kitten-heeled shoes. She tried to hide a smile. "Never you mind."

"Antoine, I bet," Marta breathed dramatically as she trailed behind them, a sketchbook in hand. "Lily wants him to whisper scandalous French words into her ear tonight."

Clara's shoulders settled in a kind of relief she didn't understand.

Lily whipped around, aghast. "I said au revoir to Antoine a month ago, Marta. Why in tarnation would I be looking for him now?"

Marta grinned. "Wouldn't be the first time you've changed your mind."

"Quicker steps, girls," Headmistress called from up ahead. "Pick up the pace. And Miss Banks, I'll thank you for not letting that very expensive piece of equipment slide down your back."

Clara jostled the Kodak's straps higher onto her shoulders. "Yes, ma'am."

"Antoine knows what's good for his heart, I'm sure. He's staying away from you, Lil," Sally announced. Marta laughed from behind her sketchbook.

"Now, now," Lily protested. "Whoever said those boys knew much about anything when it came to courting me?"

"No. It's not Antoine," Marta decided. She cradled her chin in a dramatically investigative way. "No, maybe someone else you've seen around the Ferris Wheel before but forgot is actually stationed on the fairgrounds proper."

Lily's eyes widened, two full moons of surprise. She scoured the horizon ahead of them, where the Court of Honor awaited the girls of St. Joan's. "Oh, that's right. Dodger doesn't even work on the Midway."

"Aha!" Sally exclaimed. "He has a name!"

Lily could no longer deny a thing.

Once they passed the Ferris Wheel, the girls sorted themselves through Midway attractions Clara knew her father wouldn't know a lick about—dancers and wild animals and a market reminiscent of Cairo or Ireland with golden trinkets that caught the sunshine in a way that made them look new and ancient all at once. It was a fantastic spectacle, but as they walked, Clara couldn't help but feel as though there were a weight to the Midway, a bit of a fog, even though it was an overcast day free of humidity. A sense of shadows or eyes.

The Kodak slid further down on Clara's back, and she halted the Alouettes to shuffle it back into place, a difficult feat when her finger was still healing from the initiation. "Blasted camera," Clara muttered. "Where's Stevie today, anyway? How come I was tasked with carrying this wretched thing around? I thought no one else was allowed to touch it."

Sally shrugged. "Sick, from what I heard. I don't think the poor girl can manage a slight change of the weather without coming down with a fever."

"I hope I don't catch whatever she has," Lily said.

"Definitely," Marta added.

Clara turned to Marta. "Then why me?"

Marta barely glanced up from her sketchbook and then reset a bit of charcoal to the pages. "I'm busy."

"Marta has already taken pictures of the Navy Pier," Sally added. "It just wouldn't be fair for her to hog the Kodak. Mr. Asaka works for *The Tribune*, after all, so she can get access to cameras whenever she pleases. Seems you're the lucky one today, Clara."

The Alouettes marched along, staring up at the tents and buildings of the fairgrounds toward a checkpoint where they'd meet an Exposition guard who'd take them through the Court of Honor toward the Architecture Building.

Lily rose to the toes of her shoes. "Come on, let's catch up. Headmistress is going to be furious if we fall too far behind." She unraveled her arm from Clara's and marched with Marta toward the rest. They strolled amongst the new buildings, trees, and fountains of the fairgrounds. A tour of the Manufacturing and Liberal Arts Buildings awaited the girls before they would have ice-cold lemonade.

Clara noticed how quiet Sally had grown. "Sally?" she began. "What is it?"

Sally's eyes locked on the world around them. "Marta and Lily don't understand the way you might. May I tell you something now that they've run ahead?"

Clara nodded. "Of course.

"Sometimes I think about the girls who vanished," Sally said. "Not in the way we usually do. Not as victims, but as people. I wonder what their lives would be like today had they never disappeared into thin air."

Clara watched their feet tread along the path as she listened.

"Some of them might have come to these very fairgrounds in a few days. Imagine that?"

Most of the buildings were completed, architecture meant to dazzle people from all over the world and be recorded in history books to come.

And naturally, Clara's thoughts strayed to Aunt Miranda. "I have to know, Sally," she said, the same words she'd uttered before her initiation into the Alouettes. "I need to find the truth." Her mother's voice as it read a folktale of Chicago rang as a melodic song in Clara's mind. One tainted with sadness only known if one were to consider the care Bethany Banks had taken with each word she'd read.

Sally glanced at Clara as though she understood the frustration brewing a storm inside her. "Then we'll simply have to find it together."

Clara nodded. And then, in mild frustration, she glanced at the leather glove she'd put on before venturing out into the chilly spring air. Her forefinger was still swollen and sore from the blade Sally had slammed into it but was well on its way to healing, and soon Clara would comfortably wear her new pearl ring to conceal the scar. For now, a sharp pain would accompany her achy muscles from nightly fencing lessons with Lily.

Sally watched Clara stretch her left hand. "I promise, the swelling will go down in another day at the very most. The worst is really over."

"You said that yesterday," Clara retorted. But with her frustration and Sally's vulnerable words ringing in Clara's mind, she found her lips readying to speak about the note she'd found in her mother's book. "Sally, I—"

Another black-gloved hand reached for Clara's as both girls came to a stop.

"Something the matter, Clara?" Headmistress asked as she gently examined Clara's left hand.

Clara hid a twitch of pain as Headmistress's fingers turned her hand palm-side up, and with Sally's wide eyes promising retribution if Clara ever took off her glove to reveal the new indent, Clara shook her head furiously, dark curls bobbing around her chin.

"No, ma'am," she assured Headmistress. "Nothing to worry about—a paper cut only that's been irritating me all day." She smiled as though no girl could ever lie through the simplicity of one. "The glove makes it worse. But it's too cold to go without."

Headmistress's bright eyes narrowed only slightly, but if she sensed the lie, she said nothing and let go of Clara's hand with a nod. "Quite the nuisance," she agreed as she curled her own left hand into a fist. "It truly is remarkable," she then said, more to herself than to Clara or Sally. "The family resemblance, that is."

Clara stalled. Headmistress's kind eyes found hers in a way that was searching for something once lost but not forgotten.

"Yes, ma'am," Clara replied politely. "I've been told I look somewhat like my mother."

Headmistress's smile flourished. "No, not her."

It was on the tip of Clara's tongue to ask if Headmistress had known Aunt Miranda during the time they'd been teachers together. But Clara's courage faded.

Headmistress cleared her throat and strolled onward. "Don't dawdle now, girls."

"Those gloves stay *on*, Clara," Sally warned. "I don't care if it's the middle of Mrs. Dwyer's biology class and you have to dissect a frog using the spotty glass of her spectacles. That leather doesn't leave your skin until your finger has healed." She caught sight of their class and sighed with exasperation. "Oh great. Time for the tour. Should we try to catch up, or see if Headmistress miraculously carries on without us?"

The rustling sound of footsteps racing on the road suddenly drew close, and Clara slowed her step and tilted her lips into a subtle smile. A very familiar boy in a newsboy cap turned the corner—far enough away that he wouldn't notice that he'd stepped in front of her and Sally, but not too far off that Clara might have mistaken Fernando for someone else. Her eyes fell upon the dark vest over his white shirt, sleeves pushed up to the elbows revealing his deep tan. Set against his left shoulder was a set of steel beams, at least a dozen. And the dark curl of his hair peeked out from under his hat, resting against his neck.

Clara did not want to be a part of the Exposition guards' tour. Especially now.

Instead, something else beckoned her interest.

"The school of folklore."

On the peristyle, Clara hadn't asked Fernando exactly what he knew about the missing girls of Bynum Island or even if he'd ever heard of *The Traveling Demon and the Peasant Girl*, but perhaps she should have. Whatever stories an outsider like Fernando knew of Chicago might shine some light on to the Alouettes' mission. And Aunt Miranda's disappearance.

"What's wrong?" Sally asked.

Clara grabbed the heel of her shoe and twisted her face into a mild scowl. "Pebble. You go ahead without me. This shoe is impossible to take off without sitting down first." It was in fact a lace-up flat that did take time to untie and re-tie, so Clara's words were not completely dishonest for the second time in just as few minutes. But as for the pebble, it was more that there was some unfinished business she wanted to attend to first. And for some reason, Clara still wanted to keep Fernando a secret, even from Sally and the rest of the Alouettes.

Sally glanced ahead at their class, well out of earshot, and then back at Clara. For a moment, Clara wondered if Sally would buy a white lie as Headmistress had.

Sally lifted one shoulder in a quick shrug. "Suit yourself."

She stuck her hands into her pockets and followed Lily and Marta and the rest, many of whom were now calling back to her amid their shrieks and laughter.

Clara fiddled with her heel until she was able to convince herself there might have been a pebble after all. Then she straightened, righted the Kodak on her back, and tucked away a strand of dark hair as she followed Fernando off the path. Nearby was the Bavarian-styled architecture of the German Village, outside of which wove a moat that led to the drawbridge of a European castle.

Fernando picked up the pace toward the German Village and slipped past the entrance, under the careful watch of a great bird etched onto an arch overtop. Clara sneaked after him. A breath of confidence brought her to the tips of her toes so she could run a little faster, and as she did, she came alive. This wasn't something she would normally do, but she justified her actions by reminding herself she already knew quite a bit about the World's Columbian Exposition—as much as her father had told her, anyway. And as much as she'd seen through her trips to the various locations of The Cat's Whisker.

Besides, she'd been granted the opportunity to take photographs of the pavilions at the World's Fair for St. Joan's.

And even though the Midway Plaisance wasn't technically what Headmistress had in mind, it was far more interesting than the crisp white stone circumventing the Court of Honor, in Clara's humble opinion.

She reached the threshold of the German Village and stood under it, as Fernando had. The moat lay ahead of her, dark wood stretching across the gentle coursing of water in a fabricated body. Spindly branches crept over the edges, working their way toward the sky like they were escaping a marsh. Clara was entranced. But the darkness of the open door put her under a new sort of spell. One that begged to be remembered for all eternity. Her hands released the Kodak from the case across her back so she could set up the tripod, wind up the portable power supply, and duck under the camera's velvet curtain. She wouldn't use the flash today because the crisp overcast sky was enough to illuminate the magic surrounding her. A long click sounded as Clara activated the shutter, and she drew in her breath as she waited the handful of seconds it would need for the aperture to seize the image. Then she ducked out from under the curtain, the hem of it catching on her hair. A flat palm smoothed it down, and she blinked as the sky grew brighter.

She didn't know what lay inside the German Castle—nevertheless, she gathered the Kodak and stepped across the bridge, dipping into the shadows and past the castle's door. Her footsteps were too loud in the silence, and the dimness that greeted her, too dark. She could only see the shine and gleam of stolen sunlight against metal—*armor*. Suits of it lined the heavily sculpted walls. *Astounding.* And certainly nothing ever spoken of amongst the men and giants of Chicago in an ever-moving pub for the elite. Clara considered calling for Fernando but instantly cast away such a notion. That could wait. Soldiers from another era, another world, another time, all stood guard around her like they'd proudly do so for eternity. Holding her breath so as not to make the slightest sound, Clara set down the Kodak and aimed the lens at a row of them. It would be too dark inside to capture a hint of all that lay in front of her, but she'd be damned if she didn't at least try. Her finger fiddled with the shutter from underneath the curtain, but Clara did not duck her head this time. To look away might give these suits of armor the chance to come alive. She forced herself not to blink. The shutter clicked. The image, hers. She let out a long breath and crossed her arms as though that would protect her from whatever ghosts might be waiting.

And then, when Clara turned another corner, foregoing the annoyance of taking the Kodak with her, she found herself facing something of a personal sort of interest.

Swords. Any size, shape, and style she could imagine—they all stood, displayed like trophies. This was something Clara hadn't anticipated. In all her studies of contemporary history, she didn't know a scrap about swords or other medieval weapons. Only the fencing techniques Lily had been teaching her at Château Perle.

She ran her fingers across the metal. Upon contact, she gasped. "Like ice that never melts." Many of these were likely worth more than she could ever imagine, and Clara knew it would be improper to touch them.

But then there was a sword, a broad sword, one on the smaller side—just big enough for a seventeen-year-old girl to wield. One nearly the size of her fencing foil back on Bynum Island.

And Clara simply couldn't help herself.

Her fingers closed around the hilt and lifted. The steel scraped against the iron nails holding it pointed toward the stars, and Clara's breath caught. Heavier than she'd expected, but more than that, it was colder than her first touch had accounted for.

She backed away, her shoes sliding against the floor into the open space of the castle, and suddenly her surroundings vanished for Château Perle, the black ash of the fire flitting into the air. Real enough that she could smell the smoke that had abandoned it. She imagined Lily or any other Alouette standing in front of her—*en garde*. Her left hand extended behind her, and her right hand held the sword, readying to parry. She angled her toes to face her invisible opponent, and those two French words slipped past her lips.

As Clara's movements imitated her memory of Lily's form, Clara's thoughts found themselves in a place of wonder. Her imagination dove into the hundreds of thousands of possibilities that would explain the strange note in the pages of her mother's folktale and Miranda Carveth's disappearance—everything from sandpits in secret parts of the woods on Bynum Island, which grabbed unlucky girls from their midnight walks and sucked them into the ground, to an old pier no one had found but would lure girls onto its rowboats, like a siren's call, so they could sail away onto the waves of Lake Michigan, where there was surely a point that branched into a forgotten sea.

Clara's left hand throbbed as the bone in her finger struggled to heal, and her fist closed around the leather glove that tugged on the wound. She didn't need this hand to fence, but as she lifted it, she gave up on trying to stop the pain from taking her. She'd made that choice, and she'd known what would come of it. She wouldn't stop just because a sharpness in her finger was ordering her to. There were worst pains. But how much would she be willing to suffer before trusting the Alouettes with the whole truth of her mother's folktale?

How much longer would the sepia-toned note in the book's pages haunt her?

Another hand caught her right one then, the one clutching the sword's hilt. Clara gasped and pulled her fingers free. The sword tumbled, and two bodies stepped away from its clattering fall.

Fernando stood there, the steel beams from his shoulder now gone. His dark eyes were wild with surprise. "Hello," he said, like that were the only possible thing to say at such a moment.

Clara's cheeks turned hot. She was close enough that she could smell the sweetness of his soap, and she stepped away to regain her composure. "I didn't see you there."

"Are you sure? Because I think someone was following me when all I had to do was drop off some spare beams in storage." His words were gentle like he might not be suspicious. Just amused. "And other than you, I think I'm alone."

Clara's eyes squeezed shut in mild humiliation. "Perhaps I wasn't meant for the life of a spy."

"Oh, a *spy*." Fernando indulged her. "And here I was all this time thinking you were just a daredevil. Now it makes sense, finding you at the top of the peristyle. You're actually a spy, getting a sense of places at the fair where you're not supposed to be."

Clara grimaced. "No longer a spy as of ten seconds ago, I'm afraid."

Fernando shifted toward the door in a way that made Clara want to follow. "Maybe that's a good thing. I don't scowl as much as the German fellows here. Especially when they've found someone running their paws all over their swords."

"I'm sure there was a more appropriate way for you to say that."

Fernando blinked into the distance, his lips quirking in a smile she liked. "Probably."

When they left the castle—the Kodak in tow—and found themselves on the bridge, she saw a sense of exhaustion around his eyes. Exhaustion that deepened by the second, like perhaps he might not have been sleeping well.

"What are you doing here, anyway? You're too early for opening day." He leaned against the wooden railing of the bridge. Clara didn't know if he meant to elongate his frame in a smooth line, but she wouldn't complain. "Or if you're planning on setting off another firework at the top of the Agriculture Building tonight, well, you're early for that, too."

Clara set her hand over her heart. "I promise. I come to the fair today with wholesome intentions, the main one being my class is here on a field trip to learn about how life in Chicago will change from all these great and glorious miracles of progress."

"I don't know," he teased. "It's hard to believe a spy. Even one who's only recently resigned."

She narrowed her eyes playfully.

"Suppose that's better than sitting in a classroom," he added. "At least this way, you have a valid excuse and I don't have to report you to any suits."

Clara figured he meant the investors aplenty throughout the fairgrounds—men whose money made the world go 'round—and she shrugged, choosing not to reveal the tiny detail of her father being one of them. "Most of the trivia they'll spout as they drag us around the fairgrounds is trivia I already know. Did you know New York was a contender for the fair? You must—you come from there."

She watched Fernando's eyes crinkle with delight. "Everyone knows that. Is that all you've got?"

Clara lifted an eyebrow in challenge. "I know the plans for the World's Columbian Exposition include a hot air balloon that'll be tethered to the ground, and it'll be a fortune for anyone brave enough to try it. I know the wheel you're working on is terribly behind schedule, enough that I don't think anyone will get to ride it opening day. And I also know that anyone who claims to have come from New York without any animosity toward Chicago for winning the bid is a liar." She said the last word with a flair of drama so he'd know she hadn't been entirely serious.

Fernando set his eyes on the Midway and just as quickly blinked away from it. "Well, you've caught me. I'm here to ruin the fair in the good name of Brooklyn, New York." But though he'd joined her in a silly joke, Clara heard a slant of sadness in how he said the name of his old home. Even as he smiled. "Looks like we're both guilty of something today."

She thought of her first days at St. Joan's, days she'd been away from home for more than a night and how she'd left her father alone in a house that had once had music and life in it. "I was only teasing."

Fernando nodded. "I know."

Clara begged for another tidbit about the World's Columbian Exposition to find her, something that would lead to a natural flow of conversation, but chitchat had never been her strong suit. There was no other way to ask. "What monster stories did you mean?"

Fernando glanced up but wasn't surprised. "Ones told to me by my foreman about the World's Fair in Paris. Monsters or rich men. Fairy tales."

"Paris? Not Chicago?"

Fernando shrugged. "Well, that remains to be seen, I suppose. But I'll keep an eye on the fairgrounds, just in case." He smiled a smile of someone who didn't exactly believe what he was saying.

Or someone who didn't want to say any more than that.

Clara gestured toward the Terminal, where Headmistress was already ushering the girls together. "I should hurry up, then."

Fernando caught sight of the troop just as she did. "Oh, right." Then he blinked at her. "Clara." A point to show he hadn't forgotten her name. She liked how his voice wrapped around the letters of it.

"Fernando," she answered back. And then she smiled politely and turned on her heel and marched across the moat. But she'd only gone a handful of steps when Fernando called again.

"Clara?" A request.

She turned back.

His eyes searched hers. "I didn't exactly tell the truth that night. The night on the peristyle."

She blinked. "Oh?"

He glanced at the ground as his foot kicked at the dirt. "Suppose it doesn't exactly matter, but for what it's worth, I'm here for the fair and a new life. But if nothing pans out in Chicago, that new life is going to be in San Francisco." He glanced at her, his dark eyes as warm as she'd ever seen them, like he was admitting a secret out loud, one nobody had ever heard before. "After the fair."

Clara nodded. She told herself not to let her face give away her thoughts. Because if they did, she knew Fernando would see just how strangely disappointed she was to learn he'd leave soon. Someone she'd met only once before now. Someone whose last name she didn't even know.

"I mean," Fernando continued. "That's all of it. The rest was true. Even that insanity about how I was up there because I was looking for home. Thank you for not laughing, by the way."

Clara dropped her eyes to the dirt road of the Midway. She watched his feet shift back and forth, like he was nervous. "I'd never do that."

"All the same."

Clara smiled. "I hope to see you before you go, Fernando." It was the truth, but she forced her face to remain stoic.

And then, not able to bear the intensity of his gaze any longer, she turned without waiting for a reply and walked toward the Terminal. Being drawn to Fernando, even in only a few moments of innocent words, wasn't something Clara understood, a sentiment that frustrated her beyond belief. There was something illogical about how she thought of the boy in the newsboy cap. He was a mystery she wanted to unravel, but he was also a person who deserved his own privacy.

"Pebble in your shoe indeed, Clara Banks," a voice suddenly said.

CHAPTER 14

WHAT SALLY KNOWS

CLARA SPUN AROUND. HER EYES FELL UPON THE GRAY BRICK OF the Blarney Castle, where in the shadows stood Sally, who had pointedly *not* left her behind and now grinned. "Oh, I don't care about the boy. You were about to tell me something before Headmistress interrupted. Don't you dare think I forgot."

"Gracious, Sally. Give my heart a minute to restart."

Sally laughed as she looped her arm through Clara's. "Hard to restart a heart when you've given it to someone else."

Clara peeked over her shoulder, but Fernando was already walking back toward the Ferris Wheel. "That's ridiculous." And though she'd crossed paths with Fernando twice in the span of a week, she couldn't imagine Chicago were small enough ever to see him again.

Besides, Fernando had just admitted it wouldn't be long before he'd move on to San Francisco. Why fall into a daydream that could never be?

"Well, then. What was it?"

Clara took a breath. *How to begin?* "What if there are others—

were others on Bynum Island who knew about the missing girls? What if, Sally, we aren't the only ones?"

Monsters hide on Bynum Island.

I fear they'll take me next.

Sally shifted from one foot to the other, and she blinked rapidly as she considered Clara's question. "Like the other students? Girls who aren't Alouettes? Clara—no one remembers the missing girls outside those at St. Joan's. It's like everyone in Chicago has fallen under a spell."

"No, not everyone else. Not exactly." How much was Clara willing to say? How big of a risk would a suggestion of this magnitude pose? "But maybe someone who knew the best way to solve such a mystery was to pass it along to the girls who'd come after in a way that wouldn't arouse any suspicion. A secret. A legend. A folktale, disguised as a warning." Her eyes fell on Sally's, drawing in the spinning cogs behind her friend's eyes as she let slip that final word. The one that'd surely clue Sally in to what Clara was thinking.

"The only folktale I can think of is *The Traveling Demon and the Peasant Girl*. But, Clara, it's just a story."

Only a few months in at St. Joan's, and Clara had resorted to figurative language against her better judgment. But then a song of victory from girls past sang loudly inside her as she posited such a thought, and she reached into her pocket for the note she would keep secret from the girls no more.

"I found this in my mother's copy of the folktale."

Sally opened it and read the words. Then she stepped away with a light scoff. "The—" But she, too, must have realized it'd be foolish to disregard anything now. "You're serious, Clara?"

Epiphany struck Clara as she spoke. "What if it's a clue, Sal? What if the story is everything we need to solve this mystery? What if it had been passed onto us under the noses of whatever stalks Bynum Island as a means to warn us?"

Sally nodded slowly. "We'd been looking elsewhere all along. Newspapers. Census records. Journals. We never considered there'd be a folktale taught to every Alouette all these years that could tell us everything we'd ever need to know. It's as good of a theory as anything we've tried so far. What if?" Awe faded for pride then, and Sally nudged Clara. "Well done, new money."

Clara smiled. "So what now?"

Sally's voice quietened in an unusual way for her. "Well, I suppose it's time. You know the *what* of the Alouettes' quest, but you don't exactly know the *why*." She swallowed. "My *why*."

"What is it, Sal?"

"You might be Miranda Carveth's niece, but the girl standing in front of you is also part of the legacy of missing girls."

Clara's eyes widened in surprise. "How are you—"

"My grandmother was the first Black woman to attend St. Joan's, but you wouldn't know that—no one does. She was an Alouette. And so was her younger sister. My great-aunt, Theodora. Grandmother still speaks of Dora—every Christmas the stories come out. How they shared a room together at St. Joan's. How Dora's uniform skirts were too big until she was fifteen, when she finally grew into them. How they both hated math just as much as they loved science."

Clara felt a hollowness inside her as Sally spoke. "What happened to Dora, Sally?" she whispered.

Sally stared plainly at Clara as though it would be easier to speak that way. "Dora wasn't the first girl to have disappeared, but she was the first Alouette to." Then she shook her head furiously. "No, wait. Let me say that again. She was about to become an Alouette when she went missing. In the middle of the night, Grandmother woke up. The window was open, the wax of a nearby candle was spilling over the nightstand, and a strange scarlet hair ribbon was lying on the floor, like it'd fallen from a girl's night braid. Dora was gone from her bed. Never to be seen again, and now you're the only Alouette to know that." Sally's eyes welled, but she lifted her chin and brushed at her cheeks. "Dora was one day away from her initiation, Clara. One day." From inside her blouse, she pulled out a gold necklace adorned with a small pearl ring Clara knew had never been worn.

Clara clutched Sally's hand. "I'm so sorry."

The despair in Sally's eyes fell away for resolve. "I took over the leadership of the Alouettes because I knew it'd give me access to the research they've done on the girls who've disappeared. The only missing thing was the connection—why do some girls vanish, Clara, and not others?" Sally faced Clara. "And then you waltzed into our lives and told us you were the great-niece of Miss Carveth, the only teacher to have disappeared. Girls who come to St. Joan's might be cursed, Clara, but it doesn't make them stupid. *This* is why I chose you to become an Alouette. Because I think together, especially if there's any promise in studying the folktale, you and I can save the next girl from disappearing."

A hundred thousand thoughts sailed like ships inside Clara's mind. "How?" The folktale's story of a traveling demon seizing lives from here and there, not to mention the wily sprite who fooled them all—it was all coming to life in front of her, a performance in the theater of her mind. And it called upon Clara to play a starring role.

Sally took a breath. "Great-Aunt Dora, Clara. And Miranda Carveth. There's a family connection. I have a strong suspicion the next girl to disappear might be one of us."

Nighttime dusted Château Perle with a familiar aesthetic, like Clara might be lost in the woods of a story but had just found solace in a place she wasn't sure she could trust. She and Sally had sneaked out of the dormitories to go through the mountains of research that had only been made privy to an elite group of Alouettes, just in case word of the true danger at St. Joan's ever got out.

Danger that had long ago spidered its way inside Clara's family and now left her wondering how anything about her mother's Aunt Miranda could be tied to the missing girls of St. Joan's.

There just had to be clues somewhere. Clues about other families and other girls. Family legacies cut short by something unknown, unspoken, or perhaps both.

"Not to worry," Sally told Clara. "About anyone else on Bynum Island knowing you're Miranda Carveth's niece, that is. The top Alouettes are as tightly-locked as a safe when it comes to confidentiality. Promise." She turned the skeleton key in the door's lock and they stepped inside. The mantle was more an altar now than a fireplace, and Clara watched as Sally lit a fire, sending smoke skyward through the chimney.

"Blood to bone," Sally said as the embers burned. She waved the match of its flame. "And bone to ash."

"And bone to ash," Clara repeated.

Her finger throbbed at the memory of the jagged knife's edge cracking through bone, but Sally was already on her way inside, and Clara raced to keep up. They breezed past the empty gymnasium—no girls fencing at the clubhouse tonight—and into the library. A familiar dog-eared novel, as thin as a tea biscuit, sat on the edge of the giant table in the middle.

"I wish I could say *speak of the devil*," Clara announced as she picked up Sally's copy of *The Traveling Demon and the Peasant Girl*, "but it all seems so gauche now." She tried to lighten her voice, and yet it felt like she were staring at a beacon that announced Bynum Island, St. Joan's, and all of Chicago as damned. A warning of danger a monster would quietly seek and perhaps had already found.

Sally shrugged. "Who would have thought a potentially monstrous warning in disguise would turn out not to be drivel? I actually enjoyed parts of it."

Clara calmed her nerves, opened the paperback, and read the first bit of prose she found. "*Then they'd forget her face, and that was the sprite's final game. For how could anyone find danger without knowing its name?*" She shut the book more forcefully than she normally would and tossed it back onto the table. "It had to be dog-eared at the spooky part."

"Oh, calm down. We're safe here."

Clara ordered herself to believe the same, all things considered, but Bynum Island in the middle of the night wasn't exactly the best place for rational thought. "I thought the others would be here."

Sally leafed through a stack of crisp papers. "Kimiko Ando told me Stevie is still indisposed. And silly Marta is days behind on her history homework." She smiled the smile of a girl in love. "She promised she'd come once she's finished. Lily, on the other hand, is meeting us here after she gets back from her rendezvous with that fellow we were teasing her about earlier."

Clara had a feeling Dodger wasn't one of the upper-class St. Francis Xavier boys at the school across the way.

"All right," Sally announced, her natural leadership as prominent as ever. "Before we dive into the story, let me show you what we've done. I've been through the yearbooks."

Clara blinked at the seven shelves beside Sally, each containing a thick leather-bound volume more suited as a Bible than a school history. "All of them?" She looked for the one that contained her aunt's name beside that of Headmistress McGill—it lay to the side, and Clara ran her hand over it.

"I've been busy," Sally replied, sitting at the desk in the

middle of the room. "Three decades' worth of books only took a year, but no, not all," she added with a shrug. She opened a thick journal with ink-blotted notes written in her own hand. "There's nothing, actually *nothing*, in the yearbooks about the missing girls. No memorials, no mentions, nothing."

"Goodness." Clara shuffled in her seat with unease and took in the dim candle light of the room with its layers of dust on the shelves. "This place is already eerie enough without any added ghost stories."

"Seems worse when there's none at all." Sally licked a finger and flipped another page. "I had to cross reference everything with prior editions. Year Ones become Year Twos—which Year Twos disappeared from the rosters? Did they say why? Is the family still in town according to census records or *The Chicago Tribune*? Did they leave? Why? Track them down, figure out if the girls are still alive and well. Try again. Year Twos become Year Threes."

Sally counted each step on her fingers, and Clara listened, bewildered. "That's quite the devotion."

Sally's face fell slightly before she pulled her chin up again. "If it means my grandmother finds out what happened to Dora, it'll be worth it. I'd have asked Marta for help, since her father works for *The Chicago Tribune*, but she's not nearly as thorough as you are with the details, not to mention how bored she grows with homework—faster than you can say jack o'lantern." She reached for another yearbook and handed it to Clara with an air of sheepishness Clara had never seen in her before. "She should be in this volume." Clara knew Sally didn't mean Marta now. "I haven't looked in it. I was hoping you would. See if any similarities to that folktale of yours spring to life."

Clara ran her fingers over the soft brown leather. The year embossed on the front was in gold lettering: 1835.

"Of course," Clara replied, the memories of a hundred girls

under her fingertips, one of them never to be heard from again. "What do we do once we find out, Sally?" she asked. "What are you hoping to find? How do you propose we stop whatever has been responsible for all this?"

The real question was what had happened to those girls. To Miranda Carveth. To Sally's Great-Aunt Dora. *Are any of them somehow still alive?*

She could tell it wasn't the first time Sally had considered that question herself. Sally's confidence deflated, but she nonetheless nudged the journal across the desk and pointed to a chart. "Mark down any girls I noted in the prior year and see if they appear in the following one, too. If they don't, we'll investigate."

"All right," Clara whispered. But on the following page, a figure of some sort had already been inked. A shape bleeding into the paper. A chart that wasn't exactly that, but something curved, formed like a seashell she'd found at the beach the summer prior. One her father had called a remarkable entity to wash up on the shores of Illinois. "Sally," she said, teasing at the page with her fingertips. "May I?"

Sally nodded. "You can look."

Clara flipped the page, and a swirl of numbers and dates arranged themselves into a spiral. She recognized it as the golden ratio, a number she'd learned about not there at St. Joan's but from a textbook she'd managed to get a hold of at Curtis School. "I know this figure. What's it for?"

"This is what we're looking at next. The girls are mostly plotted, their disappearances, graphed. The first girl was forty years after the incarnation of the Alouettes: your great-aunt, Miranda Carveth. And then the rest, the increments decrease at a consistent ratio the closer you arrive to the present. See?" Sally traced the shape. "Whatever's causing these girls to vanish is moving faster. Like it's hungrier."

Clara glanced at the center. "What's in the middle, Sally?"

"That, Clara Banks, is what you and I know, and no other Alouette. That is Monday." She drew a bright red X. "And according to this chart, the next girl will vanish sometime that day. The first day of the World's Fair."

Clara's eyes welled with hot, frightened tears. "You mean one of us. You or me. One of us will simply…vanish."

Sally swallowed. "Or another girl entirely. Someone else who might have an aunt or a mother or any other family in her life who disappeared from this godforsaken place. Or maybe even some poor unlucky sap who has nothing to do with any of this at all."

Clara's fingers drifted across Sally's copy of *The Traveling Demon and the Peasant Girl*. Her mind raced with memories of sitting on her mother's lap in the dining room in the house they'd lived in before Jonathan Banks had reached the loftiest perch of high society. In the parlor, there had been a window seat with a thick woolen blanket, and Bethany and Clara had sat there time and time again, hot tea steeping on the small table beside them as they read together. Clara's mother's fingers were long and thin, drifting over each word carefully, and Clara had well known she could make out the meaning of each string of symbols before her mother. It hadn't mattered. Snow had been falling outside like thick fat feathers, and the chill from winter had permeated the entire house, begging Clara to pull the blanket closer. Her mother's voice had been but a whisper, loud on such a silent winter day, but one that had brought to life the apex of the folktale they both cherished so much it seemed to dance before Clara's eyes.

"Girls would lose hope," Clara whispered. *"They'd forget each one's face. And then simply vanish—"*

"Without even a trace," Sally finished.

Were she and Sally a part of the folktale now?

A scream sounded, and Clara and Sally startled out of their seats. But Sally was the one to race out of the library first.

"Marta," she breathed.

Before Clara could speak, Sally was out the door, and Clara clambered after her. "Wait! Sally! Be careful!"

A gust of wind burst through the clubhouse as Sally yanked open the heavy door, nighttime spilling inside with the smell of cool cedar and fresh earth. She searched the woods.

"Marta!" Sally cupped her hands around her mouth as panic forced her voice louder. "Marta!"

Clara's eyes fell upon the school's Kodak, lying in the tall grasses. Together they ran toward it. "Sally, what—"

"Marta," Sally said, and nothing else.

Clara hiked the Kodak onto one shoulder, the other struggling with the awkward flash, and together they ran onward.

The screams heightened, a thousand pitches of fright. A violent harmony in a timbre Clara recognized. Sally searched the trees and branches, the whispers of balsam needles and those of pine. Her and Clara's breaths fogged in quick puffs in front of their faces.

"Marta!" Sally called again as she trembled. "Where is she?" A quiet voice. "Oh God. Where is she?"

With one hand shuffling the Kodak onto her back, Clara reached for Sally's arm and held it. The screams grew louder now, a horrific crescendo that rang from everywhere at once, like Bynum Island weren't just an island location for a girls' school in Chicago but a realm in its own right: cut off from the rest of world, locked in place, and forbidden to escape.

Like we're bound to these woods, Clara thought.

"Clara! Sally!" came the brave call of another girl.

Running through the field toward them was Lily in a flurry. Her light hair was a waterfall of cascading unkempt locks. Upset —no, *furious*. She tread through the tall grass cresting the hill, grabbing at its strands like it could keep her alive.

Alarm flooded Clara. "Lily? What—"

"He took her!" Lily screamed in a fit Clara had never before seen in Lily. "*It* did. It took her!"

The Kodak weighed on Clara's back as Lily's fingers pressed into her arms. She shuffled the camera free, lowering it carefully to the dew-covered grass at their feet, and grabbed Lily's hands in an attempt to calm her. "Who did? Do you mean Marta? Where is she?"

Sally was at their side in a second. "Were you with her, Lil?"

Lily was panting as she fought to catch her breath. "I came from the other side of the island after I left Dodger." She pointed past Sally to where the woods swallowed any light. "I saw Marta coming up the hill toward Château Perle. But then someone— some*thing*—snatched her and dragged her away, and—"

That was enough for Sally, who tore away from Clara and Lily and raced into the thick of the trees like her life depended on it.

"Sally!" Lily screamed, but Sally wouldn't stop running.

Clara hoisted the Kodak higher onto her back. Her other hand grabbed Lily's. "Come on." They raced after Sally through cobwebs and hand-like branches onward. The loud crunching of dried leaves on the ground sounded each of Sally's steps with her persistent, "Marta! Marta!"

Clara's veins scorched with fear. Danger hummed around her, daring her to conjure up any courage. Her lungs tightened with exhaustion—it'd been forever since she'd taken a good long breath—but something otherworldly pushed her forward.

She slammed into Sally, who barely moved at the impact. They were at the edge of a field Clara had never seen before, the dusting of silver moonlight shimmering over each blade of grass and shard of forgotten bark. The buds of spring flowers hadn't yet forged their wild blooms, but that wasn't what had stunned Sally into stillness.

"Marta," Clara whispered.

In the middle of the field stood a man, tall and thin like a shadow stretched at sundown. The moonlight illuminated his fine features, the angles of his jaw, the careful yet unnatural way he stepped around a girl curled up on the ground, her straight black hair a curtain shielding her face and muffling her cries.

"That's him," Lily whispered with fury. "That's *what* I saw before it seized Marta straight from the path. That man is *not* human!"

Clara frowned. The man and Marta hadn't yet seen them, and for the life of her, Clara couldn't understand why they weren't charging forward to help their sister, if not by blood then by bone. "Why do you keep saying that, Lil? Sally, what in God's name are we waiting for? Marta is right there—"

"Clara," Sally interrupted, a worried ripple on her voice. "What is he doing?"

The rumble of danger on Bynum Island grew louder, and Clara tilted her head back toward Marta and the man circling her. The steps he took were awkward, like his bones were rebelling against him, but Clara knew the long black tails and white bowtie would ensure he fit in well at the galas in Chicago's high society.

Or maybe not so much.

Clara sucked in a sharp breath as the moonlight shifted in favor of the clouds passing over it before the darkness found him again. She clutched the Kodak's flash and bit her lip. In the right setting, its brightness could come across as lightning from a wayward storm and might scare him away. Clara narrowed her eyes on the man and switched on the power source of the flash. It hummed alive.

"Clara," Sally warned.

Too late. Clara lifted the flash and ignited it. Yellow light exploded into the black sky, and as it did, the white skin on the man's face paled, deepening his cheekbones and jaw until there was none of it left—only a darkness on his face that desperately crawled over his bones.

Marta screamed again.

"Oh God," Clara breathed. It was an illusion. A trick of the woods. The man and Marta startled at the split-second aura of brightness, and Sally yanked on Lily and Clara's arms, drawing them to the ground until all three of their backs pressed against the roughness of a nearby elm.

"See?" Lily hissed. "*Not* human!"

Sally clenched her hands into determined fists. "Whatever it is, it's not taking my Marta."

Lily took a deep breath. "Stay here. Don't do a blasted thing. I'll be right back."

She stood and spun on her heel, as silent as a thought, and stormed off.

"Where are you going?" Clara whispered frantically.

Lily cocked her head like the answer should be obvious. "To get a sword."

And then she ran into the woods toward Château Perle.

Another cry from Marta pulled Clara and Sally back to the center of the field, the phenomenon of light now forgotten. Sally gripped Clara's hand. "I can't lose her."

Clara's dark curls tumbled around her cheeks as she shook her head. "You won't. But let's be wise about this." And though there was something terrifying occurring not fifty yards away, Clara knew this was absolutely not the time to act rashly.

The man grabbed Marta by the shoulder and lifted her clear off the cold ground. Clara gasped at his sheer strength. Marta hung in midair, short breaths punctuating her fear. The man pulled her closer, his eyes once again those of a human as the clouds drifted away, letting moonlight blanket the whole of Chicago.

"It's not my fault, you know. It's the anchor. She grows *weak,* close to her end. Stupid human. You can't begin to understand how much this irks both my impatience and my hunger." His lips turned upward in a ghoulish smile. "I assure you, dear girl, a snap of the neck hurts less than you think."

Clara couldn't help but search her mind for the word *anchor* for a clue. As though Aunt Miranda's folktale might have mentioned such a hint that could give Clara and Sally an edge over this thing that cowered over Marta. Then suddenly, a bout of familiar unkempt hair stormed past.

"Lily?" Sally said.

The long broad sword from the foyer of Château Perle hung sturdy and safe in Lily's grasp. She held her chin high and lifted the blade. And then she marched into the field, as plain as day despite the moonlight, and beckoned the man she knew to be a monster.

"Put her down!" Lily cried into the silent night.

The man in the suit froze, wiry limbs reverberating against his shadows as he cocked his face toward Lily. Clara's heart thudded against her ribcage, a moment in time she could only describe as that of a children's story, but with Sally strong beside her, she drew strength from the Alouettes and watched as Lily took a careful stance only yards away.

"Sally," Marta breathed, a frightened whimper Clara had never heard before in her voice. "Sally!"

"I'm here!" Sally called back.

In the corner of her eye, Clara watched Sally suck in a breath of agony as the girl she loved balanced between danger and solace. "It's all right, Sal," Clara whispered. "She's going to be all right."

Sally's face hardened. "I'll kill him. I'll kill *it*."

"Girls?" the man questioned. He straightened, lowering Marta to the ground with a simple pat on the head as though he were nothing more than a concerned gentleman searching for the family of a lost child. "It's after midnight. Have you gotten lost?" He tsked in a way that showed disapproval. "What would your parents think?" If it hadn't come out as a nasty sneer, Clara would have thought it the most condescending way to speak. "And with one of you carrying such a barbaric weapon as though it were a toy."

Lily didn't move. She stared at the man's bony grip on Marta's dress collar and the shining tears on Marta's cheeks. "Free her. I won't ask again."

The man took a moment for Lily's words to sink in, as though there were a way to ingest orders like one did food or wine. Then he dropped Marta's collar with a ferocity that cast her away with a scream. Sally rushed to Marta, all fright abandoned. She fell in the grass and clung to Marta like her heart could beat once more as long as they could embrace. The man didn't care. He eyed Lily, and Clara caught up to Lily's side so they might somehow fight together while the other two got away.

Lily didn't as much as glance at Clara, her eyes on every awkward movement the man made toward them.

He took another step—crunches on the cold ground as his heel found forgotten bits of winter—and rubbed his hands together in a way one might before a roast dinner. "I had set my sights on one. But two is better." Then his cold black eyes found Clara. "And three—no *four?* A gift."

With a snarl, he charged toward Lily—no weapon in hand, but brute strength in stance. Lily gauged her time, her weight light on her heels, and then she swung her sword. The man lifted a long arm, too thin to be real. The blade struck, and there came a loud bang of a sound. Clara froze.

Lily's lips parted in horror as her blade cut into his arm. The sword's edge had failed to hurt or maim or even spill the tiniest drop of blood—instead it stuck there, wedged inside bone.

"What are you?" Lily breathed.

The man's eyes darkened into those of a hungry wolf. "Silly girl. I am much stronger than the new ones in this young city of ours."

Clara's heart skipped a beat. Lily's eyes widened. Desperation intact, Clara's hands tightened on the metal shield of the flash. Her steps were quick, and she couldn't retreat now. If there were no other way to ensure the Alouettes survived this, she would be damned if she were to go down without a fight.

She swung the heavy flash at him. It struck the small of his back, shattering the already-dead bulb and cutting through the silk blazer he wore—as ash-black as the night and the shards of bones the Alouettes sent up a hearth, little by little. A gasp sounded from his skeletal lips, and a howl followed, piercing the quiet of Bynum Island. Clara forced the rounded edge of the flash through as much as she could, her eyes squeezed shut as she struck again.

It's for Lily, she told herself. *This is so all of you can stay alive.*

She wanted to be sick at the thought that the metal she was holding was chipping away bone. But as though kismet or the stars themselves had different plans all together, the sensation of skeleton and body vanished from under the flash of the Kodak, giving way to nothingness. Clara opened her eyes in time to see the man's skin and suit shift into shimmering sand. His cries were mere echoes now, memories of a nightmare to four girls in a field. He trickled away from his form until he fell completely into the grass.

And then he vanished entirely.

Clara didn't dare breathe. She stared at the spot where the man had once stood, but now there was only Lily. Her sword fell. She covered her face with both hands. Clara exhaled, thinking she might be sick—lemonade and Cracker Jack from the fairgrounds destined to make a reappearance—and glanced at

Marta and Sally holding each other, their eyes saucepans as they gaped.

"He asked me for the time," Marta whispered with a shake of her head. "That's all. He was completely normal. I didn't understand why he was on Bynum Island and said as much, but all he did was ask me for the time."

Sally clutched Marta closer, pressing kiss after kiss to Marta's temple and cheeks. "You did nothing wrong." She set her forehead to Marta's and held her tightly.

Lily stood tall and nodded. "Right. Fencing practice has to become mandatory now, Sal."

"Lily," Sally said, exhaustion in her eyes. "Please, let's just take a moment—"

"No!" Lily cried. "I don't know what we came across tonight, but I've been saying this ever since Mary-Anne got married and left the Alouettes and St. Joan's all together. Girls vanish from this island. And if there's a chance something like this could happen again—" She kicked the grass where any remnants of the *thing* might still be lingering "—then *everyone* has to be prepared. *New ones*, that monster said. So there are more to come. Tell the Alouettes, Sal. We have to be ready. With proper swords, too. Not just fencing foils."

Sally stood and helped Marta to her feet, and then she nodded. "All right."

Clara's eyes fell to the ground. She imagined what sort of flowers might blossom in the coming weeks in this field—or if none at all would. There was nothing in Miranda Carveth's story about a scrap of metal from a school's camera destroying a monster—*nothing*, and Clara knew that for a fact. Perhaps she'd been wrong about all of it. Perhaps the story she knew and loved so well wouldn't make a lick of difference after all. Any hope left inside Clara's heart vanished.

How could the Alouettes defeat something they couldn't even understand?

CHAPTER 15

CRACKER JACK

PAY DAY MEANT LONG LINES.

Even lifted up onto the steel toes of his boots, Fernando couldn't see the front of the queue, where the foremen superior to Antoine distributed wages for the week. Beyond frustrating.

Frustrating since the terms of Fernando's deal with Rex Winston had given him three weeks to pay the remainder of the debt his parents' savings hadn't covered. Three weeks ended in three days—rather poetic or entirely cruel, depending on Fernando's mood.

Today, he was anxious.

"No use jumping around like that," Dodger said behind him. His arms were crossed—not out of annoyance, but boredom. "This line won't get any shorter just because you're dying to get to the front of it."

Fernando fell flat-foot and scowled. He hoped Dodger took it as impatience instead of what it really was: stark-raving worry that however much he was set to make that week was never going to be enough. That he was no closer to his goal of making it in Chicago than when he'd arrived.

"Calm down," Dodger said. "Once everything starts moving, it'll be quick."

"Yeah, but the trick is knowing *when* everything'll start moving," Fernando grumbled back.

"Okay, I see standing behind you like this is going to send me straight into that god-awful lake before I get my wages, so how about we play a game?" Dodger cradled his chin and then snapped his fingers. "The first thing you'll buy once you're paid. What'll it be?"

Fernando frowned. "Not a game, Dodge. That's a question."

"I'm not done. Tell me what you're going to buy first, and I'll tell you what I'm going to buy first, and whoever is spending the least amount of money wins."

Fernando scoffed. The line still wasn't moving, and all of the men standing in the vicinity of the half-finished Ferris Wheel looking over the Midway were just as impatient as he was.

"C'mon. It'll pass the time."

Fernando pulled away from the apprehension eating at his bones and let his thoughts scatter. It'd been a long time since Fernando had considered purchasing something simply because he wanted it. So, being careful not to say a word about his debt to Mr. Winston, he blurted out the first thing that came to mind.

"I don't know. It'll be at the fair, probably. Yeah. That popcorn and caramel shit that's been turning the air up and down the Midway into a candy factory. Cracker something."

"Cracker Jack."

"That." Fernando let the cruelty of the world vanish for a handful of precious seconds. He was hungry, and time wasn't helping. "A whole big bag of it. All to myself. I'll find a bench right beside the Grand Basin and sit in the sun and let sugar melt onto my hands until I'm sick from it."

"Lily likes flowers." Dodger wasn't speaking to Fernando as much as he was speaking out loud. "I've teased her a thousand times about having a flower name herself, like she had no choice in the matter." A gentle laugh followed, as though Dodger wanted to make sure Fernando knew it was entirely innocent and no hearts were invested. But then, "Roses. A whole dozen of them."

To fall in love is one of the greatest pains the heart will ever know, Fernando's father had once told him. "Dodge."

Dodger shifted from one foot to the other, like admitting this had been the hardest thing he'd ever done. "Almost got enough saved up for a bouquet. Maybe by next week. After the fair opens, but it'll have to do."

Fernando decided to let it go. "Guess that means I won."

Dodger lifted a shoulder. "Guess it does."

The line began to move, and Fernando stiffened as the onslaught of men pushed him forward.

"God damn," Dodger said behind him. "Like there's an expiration date written on each of those dollar bills."

Fernando's wages had afforded him food and a partial bit of board, but not entirely. Chicago was expensive, and the prices of small everyday things—bread or milk—crept up by the hour now that the Columbian Exposition was less than a week away. Mr. Winston's contribution had been a life-saver, and his promise not to charge interest for a personal loan, generous, but something in the deepest corners of Fernando's heart made him think twice about that.

A strange voice suddenly echoed inside his mind, one that had told him stories before. Today it was a tale about one Sunday in particular when Fernando was eight. After the celebration of the Eucharist at Holy Mass, Juan García Díaz had taken Fernando to the corner store to get a newspaper.

"I don't know if they'll print my letter about the way construction workers are paid in this greedy city," Fernando's father had said as the bell chimed when they walked inside.

Fernando hadn't cared two licks about the newspaper. There'd been penny taffy in the window display, and on the way to St. Ambrose, Fernando had spotted baskets of it, just waiting to be eaten. At Mass, as the priest lifted the Chalice and deemed it the Blood of Christ, Fernando couldn't stop thinking about the taffy. As the choir sang Agnus Dei, Fernando had fantasized about tasting it. How rare something such as taffy was in his home when his mother considered it a vile knob of sugar that would rot his teeth and spoil his dinner. How his friends had always had spare candy in their homes even when it wasn't Easter or the birthday of someone very lucky.

As his father purchased the Sunday paper, greeting the clerk Viggo at the front of the store, Fernando had stood in front of the taffy display.

"Papá?" he'd called. "Papá? May I have one? Just one?"

Juan García Díaz had clicked his tongue. "No, mijo. Mamá está haciendo la comida."

Fernando hadn't forgotten his mother had promised to have lunch ready by the time they returned from Mass.

But Fernando had wanted the candy—

"Hey," Dodger said with a nudge of his elbow against Fernando's back, jostling him from the memory. "It's moving."

The line pressed onward, and Fernando caught up with it. Soon enough, the workers ahead of him walked away paid, and Fernando and Dodger stood next as a white man in a suit and a black bowler hat thumbed out a small envelope and handed it to the foreman beside him.

The foreman's eyes settled on Dodger, and he gave a quick nod of the head, a toothpick dancing in his mouth as his teeth bit down on it. "Been a while, Dodge," he said.

Dodger opened his envelope. His expression turned dismal as his fingers peeled the bills apart. "Some of it is missing."

"Not me, Dodge. The city took it. Or have you forgotten the riots?"

Fernando frowned at Dodger, whose cheeks warmed as he glared back at the foreman.

"No," Dodger replied in a small voice. "I haven't." And though he made a point to keep his voice low, Fernando could also detect notes of ferocity and none of regret as Dodger spoke.

Fernando's internal map of the city showed him street corners burnt with lingering ash and blackened with the memory of fire. Neighborhoods in the west side whose dilapidated buildings stood empty and quiet, and through each of their open windows, the whispers of what had happened on a cold winter evening in Chicago only a handful of years before.

"Pretty fair amount if you ask me," the foreman continued as he spit out the toothpick and stuck his two thumbs in his pants pockets. He inched closer to Dodger. "Considering all the trouble you left behind. Still strange, though. Your sass for working conditions in Chicago might be the height of annoyance, but you've also got some of the most powerful suits in the palm of your hand now, don't you?" A tilt of the head, and the men surrounding Dodger turned to see how he would react.

Fernando shuffled beside him. "What's he talking about, Dodge?"

Dodger's eyes flitted to their corners as he glanced at Fernando. For a minute, he was silent, as though considering whether to respond or leave it be. "The Cat's Whisker," he finally admitted. "I relocate it every week. All the work that goes into moving around that damn pub. It's all me."

"Not only that—from what I hear, you've got a big ol' plan for opening day," the foreman continued, a conniving grin accompanying his words. He lifted a hand and waved it in front of his eyes, as though indicating script on a theater's marquee. "Electric lights, courtesy of George Westinghouse. Replacing the firelight of Chicago once and for all. Isn't that right, boy? They should have taken more of your wages, you patsy to the rich. Or is this what keeps them from taking every single penny?"

Dodger went silent. He stuffed his envelope into his inner vest pocket and turned away from the crowd, pushing aside Fernando as he did so.

"Dodge!" Fernando called, but Dodger would not turn back.

"Let him be," the foreman said. "García Carolan, right?"

Reluctantly, Fernando nodded.

"He never sticks around too long after pay day anyway. Has to get money to the *families*." The tone was mocking, cruel. Like Dodger might be foolish for how he chose to spend his wages.

Fernando blinked. "Families?"

Another worker beside Fernando pushed closer, old enough to be Fernando's grandfather, but with a cynicism in his scowl fit for a jaded clergyman. "Union friends. Scalawags who got caught during the riots and left behind wives and children. Bah!" The man's frostiness vanished with a hesitant shrug. "It's good they've got Dodger's dime, though. He was the one responsible, after all."

There'd been a hundred moments Fernando had spent with Dodger, and not once had he hinted at the ties he still kept with his neighbors. Those who were family not by blood but by circumstance or necessity. A deep admiration grew inside Fernando, one he wasn't sure he should ever speak of, and he wondered if the kindest thing to do were to say nothing at all.

But then his hands tensed at his side. The frustration amongst the men around him—their shouts, their complaints, their angry frowns that spat out ugly words—they all swirled in his head like wine, a loud clang of a bell that silenced his thoughts and quickened his heart. Hunger grew, and Fernando's gaze fell to his right hand, a clenched fist at his side.

Bone.

The foreman slapped the envelope into Fernando's chest. "Move aside."

Fernando jumped and stepped away from the workers. He checked his fists, studying the usual flesh he saw every day and every night. A relieved breath loosened from his chest. He opened the envelope and flipped through the bills, counting the amount. He told himself to forget what had happened. Exhaustion had a strange way of making eyes see what they wanted to see.

Fernando told himself it was nothing more than that.

"Oy!" called someone from the back of the line. "Let me pass!"

The suits ahead of Fernando glanced past him and scowled in irritation. Fernando turned as Antoine pushed through a handful of men to the front of the line.

"You're stiffing the boys on the Ferris Wheel," Antoine said, matter-of-factly. He pointed a finger at the suit who'd doled out Fernando's wages and pressed it into the crisp linen of the man's vest. "Work doesn't stop just because suits feel like playing hot potato with the contracts. You owe seven of my men an extra week of wages."

An additional crew of Ferris Wheel workers stood a good distance behind Antoine, each of their faces familiar to Fernando from the days he'd seen them on the wheel, but never in the shade of hot anger they boasted now.

"These ones shouldn't have been working last week," the suit calmly replied, like speaking to a child. "Their foreman shouldn't have hired them when there'd been negotiations that didn't concern him." He eyed Antoine with a grin that seemed nearly happy saying such a thing.

Antoine stood his ground. He pressed harder into the man's chest. "You owe my men wages." Each word was spoken with flames.

The suit cocked his head and leaned closer to Antoine. He whispered his response, but Fernando could still hear it. "I owe scum like you nothing."

It was loud enough that the men behind Antoine could also hear it. One wrestled past Antoine into the suit, shoving with ferocity and throwing a lone punch. "We work nonstop for your fucking wheel!" he growled.

Chaos brewed quickly in the line, and just as quickly, suits and workmen fought to extinguish the fire that was spreading. Antoine held back the worker and eyed Fernando to do the same. They each took an arm. For a man nearly a head taller than him, Fernando was surprised at how much he was shaking with fright.

"Easy, Will," Antoine whispered. "It's not how we do things."

The suit who'd been struck handled his chin with a sour grimace. "Get off the fairgrounds," he told Will. "There's no work here for you. Get off the fairgrounds or into a jail cell. It makes no difference to me, vile and ungrateful rodent."

Will shook harder now, and Fernando didn't know what to do.

Antoine stepped between them. "Give them wages and give them their work. Or you'll lose me."

The suit glanced over his spectacles at Antoine. "So be it."

Fernando's immediate thought was how Antoine would make it through the month, the week, the day—who could afford to lose a job in a city with so few options?

Antoine turned from the suit and brushed against Fernando. There, he paused. "For so long, I thought I was looking for monsters in the fairs of the world," he told Fernando. "I never thought they'd be in the shape of actual men this time."

With his workers following, Antoine slipped back into the line and off the fairgrounds, a quiet lull left behind in his wake.

"Problems with your own wages, Mr. García Carolan?"

Fernando's heart skipped a beat until he remembered he'd

had nothing to do with the scuffle. And in his hands were wages he'd been promised. With that, the sum of his salary was correct —Fernando had always been very good at math—but with the necessary expenses until the next pay check, it was not enough to pay back Mr. Winston. Not yet.

He'd been praying for a miracle his saints had chosen to ignore.

This meant that much longer before Fernando would be independent of not just his parents, but the old family friend holding debt over his head, even if ever so kindly. He was a thousand miles away from stepping inside that room behind the door on Mr. Winston's verandah, the one with drink and music for those who'd earned their invitations, through birthright or opportunity, and especially both.

Fernando didn't know how Mr. Winston would feel about a late payment, but if there was one thing he'd learned from Juan García Díaz, it was that a man didn't hide from his problems. A man confronted them head-on.

And yet I still ran from Brooklyn, Fernando thought.

"No, sir," Fernando told the suit, echoes of what'd happened with Antoine still haunting him as hunger gnawed quietly at his bones. "No problem at all."

Now determined to step away from the past, Fernando stuffed his envelope into his trouser pocket and jogged away from the fairgrounds.

He was going to pay Mr. Winston a visit.

CHAPTER 16

A NEW DEAL

AT SEVEN O'CLOCK, THE SHADOW OF THE FAIRGROUNDS CHAOS darkening his mind, Fernando knocked on the door to the Winston estate. Timing was important: Seven was too early for a nightcap and too late for tea. In the most ideal situation possible, Fernando would speak with Mr. Winston, inform him of his late payment, bid good-bye until next time, and leave. His goal was five minutes and not a second longer. He hoped Mr. Winston was not the slightest bit interested in speaking with anyone at great length that night. Perhaps there was another soirée to host, and he would be inebriated enough to have a merciful heart. One that would wave a hand at the idea of someone needing more time to pay off a debt. Fernando imagined the swollen eyes, the crystal decanter of spirits. The sense of joy that begged Fernando to stay and mingle with the richest of the rich but forgave him for leaving early.

"Of course, dear lad. Take all the time you need. By the way—your father has attempted to get into contact with you, so I've passed on your current address to him and your mother. A family reunion could be in the works. I hope that's all right."

The imaginary Mr. Winston was about to offer Fernando a house of his very own—a summer cottage on the east coast of New York—as well as organize a meeting between Fernando and Mayor Harrison when the door opened. The housekeeper Mrs. Grant eyed Fernando up and down. He'd done well to wear his cleanest outfit that day, which just so happened to be his nicest: a black jacket overtop a white button-down and black trousers to match, not to mention freshly-shined black shoes.

Fernando removed his newsboy cap and smoothed his hair. Antoine might no longer be on the Ferris Wheel, but Fernando had found himself in a different sort of circumstances, and he'd be a fool not to take advantage of them. There was no going back.

"Mrs. Grant," he said. "I'm not sure if you remember. I'm—"

"Fernando García Carolan," she said indignantly. "Come inside at once before a draft chills this place to its very core." She turned on her heel and led Fernando to the verandah. "I assume you're here to deliver your wages to Mr. Winston."

Fernando cringed inwardly at the white lie he'd have to tell. "Yes, ma'am." But he consoled himself by remembering it wasn't her business.

"Very well. You came at an opportune time."

The verandah was chalky as the day lost grip of light. Sunset had already passed, and the candles on desks and mantles stood ready with illumination of their very own. Fernando stared at them and remembered the night with the electric street lamps and the boy who'd ignited them. A shiver ran down his spine when the memory of that ghoulish face returned—surely, though, it'd been because of exhaustion or shadows.

Something harmless. Certainly.

Mr. Winston sat in front of the white linen tablecloth empty of any platters or plates or soirées in the neighboring room. The only thing to occupy his attention was a set of documents, a long feather quill, and an ink pot. Spectacles, rounded and wiry, sat on his nose, and his skull-encrusted ring wound around the index finger of one hand.

"Fernando García Carolan, sir," Mrs. Grant announced as Fernando stepped beside her.

Rex Winston glanced up, the translucence of his eyes startling as he peered over his spectacles. "Fernando," he said, his voice not wavering in either direction of annoyance or pleasure but resting in a comfortable indifference.

Fernando shuffled his newsboy cap from one hand to the other. "Mr. Winston. A pleasure to see you again, sir."

Mr. Winston made no effort to stand in greeting. Instead, he beckoned Fernando to sit beside him. "Please."

Mrs. Grant gestured the same of Fernando and then strolled away, calling, "I'll bring tea," over her shoulder.

Fernando cringed inwardly at the implication he would be there long enough *for* tea, and he didn't miss how Mr. Winston's face seemed to tense in a similar way. But civil matters required refreshments, and so tea would come.

Fernando prayed there'd be no cakes this time.

Mr. Winston scanned the documents in front of him. "To what do I owe the pleasure of this unexpected visit?" The words felt scripted.

Fernando realized he was still holding his cap. He didn't know what to do with it. Whether he should set it on his lap or the table. The table would be a bad idea, though, considering how clean the linens were. He stuffed it in his jacket pocket, hoping Mr. Winston wouldn't notice.

"I owe you wages, sir." From his other pocket he withdrew his envelope and handed it to Mr. Winston.

Mr. Winston received the envelope. Sitting back in his wooden chair, he opened it and pulled out the small stack of bills.

He counted. "This is not what we agreed upon. You're short by ten dollars."

A fortune. "I know, sir. It seems the workers at the Midway don't make as much as I'd anticipated, so for now, I have some of my payment—"

"I didn't give you *some* of what your parents requested. I gave you *all* of it. I'm surprised you wouldn't offer me the same courtesy. This means we now have to discuss interest payments."

Fernando took a breath. He gauged his surroundings, at the décor he was certain cost more than his parents' apartment in Brooklyn. At the sprawling flowers that served no purpose other than as ornaments in a sterile white home. He wanted a life like this. But none of that mattered now. Interest could mean the rest of his life would be tied to Rex Winston.

"I'm a man of my word, sir. I will pay you back everything you gave me. That's why I'm here tonight. I came to ask you for more time to honor my debt. Without interest, if I could be so bold as to ask."

Mr. Winston eyed Fernando carefully, but he didn't speak. This was unusual. In the years Fernando had known him, Rex Winston had never hesitated in voicing opinions whenever a fight called to him. There'd been many nights in Brooklyn when Fernando's father had suggested something like an eight-hour work day at the construction site instead of the exploitive fourteen that had become common practice, and Rex Winston had protested immediately with fiery rhetoric. Either Mr. Winston was much slower now than he had been in the past, or there was going to be an agreement.

Mr. Winston cleared his throat and sat straighter as Mrs. Grant returned with a piping hot pot of steaming tea smelling sweet like lavender and a plate of fresh cakes with sliced bananas and cream around the edges. Despite the hunger he'd felt earlier on the Midway, Fernando nearly went sick at the sight of them.

So it would be a long visit. At least there were some sugary treats to dull his worry.

"More for you than him," Mrs. Grant said, a quick nod to Mr. Winston, who ignored her for the tea. "He won't eat any of them. Not a single bite."

"When you're as old as I am, not even desserts with sugared fruit are worth the effort," Mr. Winston replied.

"Such dramatics." Mrs. Grant set the cream for the tea beside Mr. Winston—who ignored that, too—and then she left.

"All right, Fernando," Mr. Winston said. "I'll agree to your request."

Fernando exhaled in a way that made him wonder if he looked pathetic. "Thank you, sir."

Mr. Winston nodded slowly. "On one condition."

Hope deflated inside Fernando. "Sir?"

Rex Winston pointed to his stacks of papers on the table. "Do you know what these are?"

Fernando squinted at the papers and made out words associated with legislation and ownership. He understood them, but he didn't know specifically what they referred to. "The language is formal. Business documents?"

Mr. Winston laughed abruptly. A good, hearty laugh that seemed to twist his face. "Yes, that's the pinnacle of what they are. These are from a one Mr. Jonathan Banks, George Westinghouse's liaison to the fair. Have you met Mr. Banks?" He set a pair of wireless spectacles to his nose and stared down at the papers.

"I don't believe so, sir."

Mr. Winston stood and strode toward a bar cart on the verandah with images of orchids cut into the wood. Atop it sat a photograph in a black frame. A real and true photograph from an actual camera.

Fernando had never seen a photograph before, and he

couldn't help but stand and follow Mr. Winston. The faces in the impossible image were just like real life, as though a photographer were nothing more than a thief of souls, able to pluck them from human hearts and glue them to paper.

"That's Banks," Mr. Winston said.

The photograph showed a row of men in cravats and ties in the sunniness of daytime. One of them was Rex Winston, no older than he stood right there. The man next to him was someone Fernando had seen sketches of in daily newspapers, but it was the scowl beneath a thick moustache that triggered Fernando's memory.

"Mr. Westinghouse," Fernando said. The papers had been wild with the news of how George Westinghouse had claimed the contract to the World's Fair, just narrowly beating Thomas Edison's General Electric.

"Beside him," Mr. Winston said.

The man beside Westinghouse was younger, perhaps in his late thirties. He had longer hair he kept tidy and tucked behind his ears, but he carried himself with the look of someone who didn't outright belong amongst financial giants. There was something about his sensibility Fernando recognized. This was a man who'd lived a hard life. A man who'd once owned second- or third-hand shoes.

"Jonathan Banks was not born into wealth," Mr. Winston said as though he could read minds. "Instead, he made a name for himself as a superb business consultant in the great city of Chicago. Sadly, it came with consequence." Mr. Winston handed Fernando the frame so he could get a better look, and Fernando clutched it with great care. "His wife was taken by consumption before his career led him to greater things, and all that left him to raise a daughter alone. Afterward, he threw himself into his work, which brought him higher up the ladder and let him meet industrial titans of our times. No wife anymore, but now he can dine with the likes of John Morgan and Henry Ford."

Fernando blinked in amazement that such a change in status could ever happen. "What does this have to do with me, sir?"

Mr. Winston reached into his pocket and withdrew a handkerchief, tucking it around his fingers like he might be preparing to squash a beetle. Then he opened the drawer of the desk that the frame had been sitting on and pulled out what appeared to be a cloudy glass orb with soft pliable metal on the bottom. The cloth of the handkerchief cushioned it in Mr. Winston's hand, like a treasure.

Only it wasn't.

Mr. Winston held it high—a glass raindrop in reverse. "This is one of the first lightbulbs General Electric ever produced. Edison gave me this as a Christmas gift last year, before they started putting direct current into practice and sprucing up the cities of this country with electric street lamps."

The bulb hung between his index finger and thumb as though Mr. Winston wanted a trinket of this kind as far away as he could get it, despite the handkerchief. Then he scoffed and shoved it back into the desk drawer before Fernando could get a better look. Mr. Winston shook his fingers free of any invisible dust that had somehow managed to find his skin, and it reminded Fernando of how his mother would do the same whenever she touched a hot stove by accident. Curious.

"As if I'd ever have a need for such a troublesome thing when candles and controlled firelight certainly suffice. It's the great secret of the World's Fair, that on the first night, and every night thereafter, the city will light up without any fire at all, bathing us in luminescence, Fernando, and changing the way we live, as you once so eloquently put it."

Fernando's eyes widened with wonder. "That's remarkable,

sir." So this was what the foreman had alluded to about Dodger earlier that day: The World's Fair was truly meant to be the beginning of the future of the world.

"Remarkable? A damn waste of money." Mr. Winston snatched the handful of papers on the table. "Westinghouse went through months of irritating legislation to ensure he'd get the contract. He had to deal with Edison, and now he has to deal with Tesla to get around the patent of G.E.'s original bulb, and after all of this nonsense, he refuses to give in to common sense and abandon the idea all together."

Fernando frowned. "But why would he, sir? There are lights just like those on the west end of the city." The memory of the skull-like face through the window found him again—but it had been the shadows, the late hour. "They're incredible," he said, more to himself than Mr. Winston. "This sounds exactly like what the rest of the world needs to see. It's human progress."

"It's elaborate and costly, and it'll run the fair straight into the ground. We can't afford such a thing, Fernando." Mr. Winston eyed him carefully. "I've known you since you were a child. Longer. I remember when your mother carried you. How she and your father were so excited for you to arrive. Your mother decorated a simple crib in that one-bedroom apartment in Brooklyn with pictures of the Virgin Mary and draped it with Kenmare lace. Did you know that?"

Fernando felt a lump in his throat. He shook his head. "No, sir." He wouldn't cry, but his eyes betrayed him.

"Don't weep, boy. You've left home, and you're a man now for it. I don't care what sort of wedge came between you and your parents after those men died on the construction site."

Fernando's eyes hardened. "Mr. Winston, respectfully. That is not your business," he remarked carefully.

"It is when it's my money helping you out of that mess." Mr.

Winston waved a hand. "Irrelevant. We have history, Fernando. You know I care deeply about your family."

Fernando's gaze flocked to the envelope of bills on the table, ones that seemed to sing about how he might soon enter a renegotiation with Mr. Winston.

"I will help you tonight, Fernando. In exchange, I ask for something else."

"And what is that, sir?" Fernando asked.

"The bulbs. They're ready now for the opening night of the fair, yes?"

"I'm sure they would have been for some time."

"There's a switch board that activates the alternating current the fair will use—it's in Machinery Hall in the Court of Honor. Banks has told me in passing the lights will be controlled there. You should have access as a worker, and in going there, you should be able to permanently dismantle the lights. This charade of technological progression has gone on too long, and those ghastly things need to be stopped if our fair is to be saved."

Fernando stared. "You want me to destroy fair property, Mr. Winston?"

Rex Winston took a step closer. "I want you to be a hero, Fernando. I want you to give the city of Chicago profit, not debt. I want you to stand against the foolish gods of our time who play with money that isn't theirs and prevent them from seeking more of it for something our city simply cannot afford. It's an absurd idea that we would ever need electric light. It's hellish enough we already have it here." He pulled at the knot of his tie in an unconscious way. "I can't begin to tell you what sort of headaches they give me. The horrible shine of them. It's impossible to enjoy the city past sundown. We shouldn't stand for this sort of waste when there are more productive means of time at hand."

Fernando considered what Mr. Winston was asking of him.

"If I do this. If I get rid of the bulbs at the fairgrounds, you'll forgive the extra time I need?"

Mr. Winston set his hands on Fernando's shoulders. "Better. If you disconnect the lights' electricity before they brighten on opening day, I'll forgive your debt entirely. I'll introduce you to the men in this city who could make your life so much better than you could ever imagine. The time of your initiation into high society nears. Isn't that what you're truly here for?" He picked up the envelope filled with bills and set it inside Fernando's jacket pocket. "Now come, boy. The tea's getting cold, and Mrs. Grant brought you cake. You must be hungry. Eat."

The envelope inside Fernando's pocket was heavier than it had been when he first arrived. He didn't want to touch it.

He wanted to run out of Mr. Winston's estate and into a place of solace, wherever that was.

But he also wanted more.

He wanted the keys to a life he deserved. One that had been impossible in New York.

"Mr. Winston," Fernando said, his eyes unfocused on a spot in the room. "You have one of those lightbulbs yourself. What's wrong with them? Is it truly just that this idea is unaffordable?" He thought of the Ferris Wheel and how much more money that certainly cost.

Mr. Winston glanced over his shoulder at Fernando. He sipped his tea carefully, the steam rising into the air like ribbons.

"Some things should be left untouched, Fernando. And sometimes, the world does better without progress."

Fernando left after tea and cakes—those on Mr. Winston's plate left untouched, as promised—and when he did, the electric lights on the streets were already illuminated.

He caught a quick glance of his hand before descending the front steps to the street and saw once again the bones in his fingers, with no flesh at all, before the illusion disappeared as though it had never happened to begin with.

CHAPTER 17

LIGHT

As the city darkened, Fernando drew his newsboy cap low over his eyes and slipped into the streets. The lamps were bright with the same electric light he was now on a mission to stop, but he focused on the road ahead and nothing else. His shadow stretched more and more with every step toward a wagon en route to the fairgrounds. One that would transport construction materials to reinforce the whimsical white buildings forged to stand for as long as the fair would last, and even though the hour was late and there was certainly not a single foreman on the fairgrounds, work would continue into the night.

That wagon soon pulled up to Terminal Station, just west of the Court of Honor. Exposition guards were patrolling, though if Fernando were being honest, they were mostly interested in chatting as they skipped stones off the silver water of the Grand Basin. Sitting to the right of the pool was Machinery Hall, a white-stoned wonder with neoclassical columns holding up a triangular roof like they'd been charged with carrying an emperor. The building extended nearly as far as the peristyle, and Fernando smiled at the memory of being in the company of a girl who'd saved him from falling. He hopped off the wagon and dashed between the columns.

But when he tugged on the handles of the doors to Machinery Hall, his shoulders slumped. Locked.

"Not making this easy." He squinted in the darkness. The handles gave slightly with another pull, but nothing more than that.

But Fernando had expected that. From inside his jacket pocket he pulled out a crowbar no longer than his forearm. He nudged the slant of it between the doors until it caught on to the latch, and then with a quick tug, the lock popped. Fernando opened the door and stepped inside Machinery Hall.

Pitch-blackness greeted him with silence in its wake. Fernando had expected that, too. But he also had on good authority most of the buildings had extra sets of gas lamps ready.

In case the light show promised by Westinghouse failed, perhaps.

There was a shine to the curved glass ceiling speckled with steel beams, and through it, moonlight let Fernando catch sight of the structures in the pavilion—shadows made of steel and copper and wheels and pipes on either side of a path, everything a bona fide guarantee the world was charging head first into the future.

Fernando crept toward a desk with the usual tools one would find at a work station. At the Ferris Wheel, Antoine's crumbling workspace had become a shrine to specifications that had sat out in the sunshine long enough to turn tea-brown. Fernando ran his hand across the edge of the wood, finding ink wells and legislative documents—all so painfully similar to those he'd find on his father's construction sites back in Brooklyn—but nothing particularly useful beyond that.

Until his hand reached into a drawer and brushed past something solid and steel and shaped in a fashion he wished he couldn't recognize.

He yanked his hand free of a cool silver Remington revolver. The barrel rattled as Fernando jerked away from the gun, clicking like the hands of a clock until it settled against the tools.

Fernando squeezed his eyes shut, and not for the first time that night did he wish he could be anywhere else. "Jesus," he swore softly. He knew his mother would scold him for such a crime and then point out how Heaven was damning him for it.

A duet of voices sounded from the other end. "*...Edison wouldn't give up the patent. That's why Westinghouse had that Tesla fellow create the double stopper.*"

"*An ugly thing it is, too. And they'll have to be changed constantly. Such a damn shame General Electric lost the contract.*"

Fernando dropped to the floor, backpedaling against the desk until he nearly split the wood. He held his breath. Shut his eyes. As the voices faded, Fernando scoured his mind for any sensible reason he'd ever do something so stupid.

Because it'll all be forgiven. That's not stupid.

Nor is it a sin.

That's an ace in your hand you'd be foolish not to play.

A new life awaited him. One he could easily adapt to. One with opportunities and relief, without needing to worry about where the next bit of money would come from because worries like those would be long in the past. Fernando wondered what his father would have said at this proposition, if his mother would have exiled him twice over from their Catholic home for something she'd call making a deal with a devil or a monster.

Monster—like Antoine had said.

But Mr. Winston wasn't a monster—he was a friend. Even more than that to Fernando's parents. *Family.*

Machinery Hall went quiet. In the daylight it was destined to be a headache of moving, churning parts. But the ghosts of such things had gone to sleep, and it was time for Fernando to work. He offered shameless pleas to whichever patron saint had any experience in illegal acts, hoping for a bit of sympathy from Heaven, and then he searched the desks for a source of light.

Until finally, his foot hit something, and Fernando glanced down.

"Aha."

He crouched and picked up a rusty gas lamp, fumbled in his pockets for a matchbox, and then struck a flame into life, illuminating the cloudy glass dome that shone into the entire hall. The great machines came into view with that light, engines that would soon rest inside motor vehicles, propellers for commercial planes and ships, the canopying marquee with block letters: **WEST-INGHOUSE ELECTRIC & MANUFACTURING**.

Fernando stared in awe at the formidable giants they were and then moved on.

The switch board at Machinery Hall was a wall of levers and numbers. Accessing it required a rolling ladder on a platform about ten feet high, but still the entire thing was being touted by Dodger as something only one man needed to operate—surely a way to save the fair some money—and it now stood ready for Fernando to find the appropriate switch to kill the lights. It wouldn't be as simple as yanking the appropriate lever and pulling down. There would have to be some sort of sabotage involved to ensure the lights stayed off. At least long enough for Fernando to figure out what to do next.

He lifted the lamp higher and stepped toward the switch board, but his foot hit a box, and a jingle followed. Fernando's eyes snapped down. At his feet was a row of wooden crates with glass inside. Fernando knelt and read **WESTINGHOUSE** on the lid. He slid it off and peered inside, the lamp illuminating the darkness. Bulbs.

"Replacements," he whispered. Because Westinghouse's bulbs

were not as long-lasting as Edison's. These months of litigation had been the topic of many conversations on the Midway.

"Nothing quite like seeing a bunch of suits lose their shit over stacks of paper."

"Imagine they had to box to settle a fight like that—just imagine it! Do you supposed they'd keep their neckties on?"

These bulbs were lined up in rows, like toy soldiers. They were separated by a checkerboard of wood, but nonetheless, the delicate things clinked against the sides at the slightest movement. Fernando gathered his courage and picked one up, examining it under the firelight. It was strikingly similar to the bulb in Mr. Winston's desk drawer, but Fernando couldn't see how such a trinket could be so terrifying.

Suddenly, a tremendous flash of light forced Fernando's eyes shut. He gasped and dropped the bulb. It shattered against the concrete.

"Who the hell are you?" a gruff voice growled.

Fernando froze, one hand shielding his eyes from the harshness of the light. "I…"

Then, another sound: a click. *The Remington.* Fernando sucked in a terrified breath.

"Move, and I pull this trigger," that voice warned. "You're not allowed in here. What have you stolen?" A strong hand grabbed Fernando's arm and yanked him to his feet.

Fernando swallowed. "I work on the Midway. My foreman is Antoine. The French guy at the Ferris Wheel?" As soon as he said it, he remembered such words were no longer true. Fernando shut up, despite the cold barrel facing him. His palms filled with cold sweat, and any possibility of breathing quickly vanished.

The man stepped forward and lifted the lantern higher, revealing his face. It was older, but not by too many years, and oddly familiar to Fernando. He couldn't quite place the man until he recognized the sheer drive in his eyes. This was the same man from Mr. Winston's photo.

Jonathan Banks.

"Thief!" Banks shouted. Remington in hand, he grabbed Fernando by the jacket and hauled him with enormous strength away from the switch board. Fernando didn't fight it—he wasn't even sure he could. Banks was a good half-foot taller than Fernando and an ox of a man in a formal suit. Fernando landed in front of Westinghouse's engine. The lamp went scattering across the floor, and its light extinguished in a heartbeat. There was no need for it now, though—not when an arc light faced Fernando that seemed too big for most men to lift. Panic raced through Fernando's blood and spliced his bones, but he stayed where he was, not about to budge when a weapon bound him still.

"I swear, I'm not a thief," Fernando said. "You've got it all wrong." And though he wasn't lying, the truth he hadn't confessed to would be no better.

Banks lowered the gun as the moment passed but pointed an angry finger. "I'm calling the guards. There's no reason for you to be in this building at this time of night. Your foreman would have told you that."

Fernando panicked and clambered to his feet. "No, sir. You don't understand—"

But then, "Father?" came from the doorway.

Fernando recognized the voice like he would recognize the quench of thirst once water touched his lips, and even though it usually took him quite some time to place peoples' faces, names, and voices, this one stood out like a splash of color in an otherwise black-and-white world.

Clara stood by the doorway to Machinery Hall, her long shadow cast by way of moonlight. Her face was not well-lit in the dimness, even with Banks's arc light, but Fernando could still see the soft curls of dark hair bobbing around her chin, the simple yet clean line of a dress whose length stopped at her calf. She was carrying a small clutch in one hand and a wool coat in the other. Fernando wondered why she'd ever be here.

And then he registered how she'd addressed Jonathan Banks.

Father?

Oh for the love of every single god damn there ever was.

Clara's shoes clacked on the floor. "What is all this? I heard a commotion." And then, when she was only about six feet from Fernando, she halted, her posture straightening with surprise. "Oh. Hello."

Fernando watched her eyelashes flutter and a smile broaden her face. "Hello," he whispered back. *Help,* he silently screamed.

"Clara, wait outside," Jonathan Banks said. "This is a trespassing matter, and I won't have you involved—"

Clara swung her face toward her father's, her curls bouncing. "Trespassing?" She hesitated, and then, "Father, you misunderstand." She shot Fernando a wide-eyed look, and he knew it to mean *play along.* "This is Fernando," she said with a nervous laugh. "He was supposed to meet me here at seven-thirty, but I was running late. It seems he got here first."

Banks stiffened at the sound of Fernando's name. As though there were something unsettling for a man whose daughter knew the name of a boy he believed to have more original sin than most. "Why was this boy supposed to meet you here? It's Thursday. We have dinner."

"Yes, of course, but Fernando wanted to ask you permission to be my escort to the fair when it opens. He wasn't going to join us, naturally. But clearly what was supposed to have been a friendly meeting has gone disastrously wrong." Without waiting for Banks's response, Clara turned to Fernando. "I imagine it would have been better to have scheduled this for the daytime, as you'd suggested. Oh dear, this is all my fault. I really thought it'd be easier this way."

Banks blinked several times in the darkness as though unpacking everything his daughter had just blurted out. "Escort. But St. Joan's—"

"Yes, St. Joan's is sending its students together on Monday, but you can't honestly believe all of us will stay as one flock of geese throughout the entire day. Goodness, so many of the girls don't even get along."

Banks gripped the bridge of his nose. "And how did you meet this boy?"

Clara shifted from one foot to the other, but she didn't miss a beat. "Several of the girls at St. Joan's have made friends with the boys—pardon me, with the *gentlemen*—who work at the fair-grounds. Naturally, through them." She cocked her head as though such a roundabout explanation were obvious, and Fernando nearly laughed at the absurdity of it. Nearly.

Banks leaned on the counter. "The doors were locked."

"They probably weren't," Clara assured him. "Whoever is in charge of locking these doors at night, Father, I can tell you they've left them unlocked many times. I told Fernando to meet me inside. He was just looking for me. But it's hard to find someone when there's no proper candlelight inside this dismal place."

"This dismal place is not to be visited when there *is* no light," Banks said carefully.

Fernando forced himself to breathe through his panic. "I'm sorry, sir. Very sorry. It won't happen again."

Banks swallowed a sigh, resigned. He rolled a shoulder, and his hand went to his chest in an unconscious way, as though moments of stress had a tendency to cause pain. "Is it true, then? You want to escort my daughter to the fair?"

"Yes, sir." Fernando felt shy in admitting it, even though for all Clara knew, it was merely a way to get out of trouble.

Banks eyed Fernando. The silence was thick. And then, "Where did you say you worked again?"

"The Midway Plaisance. The Ferris Wheel," Fernando quickly clarified. He wondered why Banks would ask such a question before settling on the most likely answer: Perhaps someone like Fernando García Carolan might not be good enough for the daughter of Jonathan Banks, liaison to George Westinghouse.

And Clara caught that immediately. "What would it matter? Don't you remember the days when Mother was still with us? She called you a stooge for worshipping the wealthy while we still wore second-hand winter jackets. A person is not the money they make or the work they do. What would Mother say now?"

Banks's gaze snapped to his daughter's. "Careful. That is not a card for you to play whenever you wish."

But Clara was not resigned to humility. "It's all right with you then? Fernando is a gentleman, and I enjoy his company very much."

Fernando thanked his Patron Saint of Trespassing With Intent To Sabotage—whoever was clearly watching over him. And now his cheeks burned at Clara's comments. Even if she was pretending.

Banks eventually nodded. His right hand clutched his chest a little more. "Fine. You have my permission. But don't test my patience again." Fernando had thought he meant Clara, but Banks glanced at him, too. "Either of you." A glean of sweat lined his forehead.

Fernando nodded furiously.

"Then it's settled," Clara announced. "Shall we say good night to Fernando and go to dinner now?"

"Confound it all." Banks leaned against a nearby desk. "I'm afraid not, Clara. All of this has upset me greatly."

Clara stepped closer, a tender hand pressing to his forehead. "Oh, poor Father. Then let's reschedule for tomorrow or Saturday. I can return to St. Joan's in another taxi. Why don't you take the one outside? Get home and take your medicine right away."

She took Banks by the arm and led him toward the doorway, a quick glance at Fernando so she could jerk her head with big eyes.

This way. Come on. NOW.

Fernando followed, keeping a safe distance for more reasons than one.

"It would be improper to leave you alone," Banks protested.

"Don't be silly. There are guards patrolling outside Machinery Hall. They'll be our chaperones until another carriage arrives."

Banks grumbled, "Very well," and Clara led him into the Court of Honor, where a carriage waited. Fernando gave them a sufficient amount of privacy and watched as Clara kissed her father's cheek before Banks climbed into the carriage and left. In the firelight of the fairgrounds, he glimpsed the details of Clara's clothing: how meticulously the garments were stitched, how they fell against the long lines of her body, which he'd already made an effort to remember in the moments before he fell asleep at night. He couldn't believe his luck that he had run into Clara once again—*Clara Banks*, he now knew.

Clara waved as Banks left, her smile that of a beaming actress. Fernando inched toward her, tipping up his newsboy cap in a way he hoped would appear polite.

"Thank you so much for that. Really, you have no idea—"

"What *on earth* are you doing here?" Clara erupted, more shocked than angry.

Fernando took a few surprised steps back. "What?" he said, the stupid response it was.

"I said, *what on earth* are you doing inside Machinery Hall at this time of night? I *know* it was locked—it *always* is. You just about terrified my father. The man has a heart condition, you know! Ever since my mother—" Her lip wobbled, but she brushed any sadness away. "At least I had the common sense to follow you through an *open* door in the German Village. Why did you break into Machinery Hall? Is this the new peristyle for you? Your own sort of *death wish?*"

Fernando shook his head. "You wouldn't understand."

"I understand it was divine intervention or kismet or just plain old dumb luck that had me here tonight at the right place and time. If I'd been even a few minutes late, the guards would be hauling you downtown to the police station right now, and that would have been quite the time, explaining why you were inside one of the fair's buildings for no apparent reason at all! I just had to lie to my own father to keep that from happening. So, Fernando, the least you owe me is the truth."

Fernando opened his mouth to respond, but no words came. He searched for anything that would seem rational.

"I was just…making sure," he finally said, a slouch in his shoulders as the vague explanation spilled free.

"Making sure of *what?*"

"Making sure that…" Fernando growled in irritation. It would be the end of him to confess, but there was another card to play if he could only bend the truth. "Making sure all of this is…safe. As safe as it can be."

Still too vague, and he knew it, but he hoped an idea would spring to mind as Clara asked more questions.

Oddly enough, though, Clara did not ask any more questions. Instead, Fernando watched her gray eyes go wide and a veil of mystery come over her, this girl who had climbed the peristyle only steps away and set off a firework in the middle of a dark Chicago night.

"Because it's supposed to happen," Clara pressed, her voice

woven with intrigue and stitched with certainty. "On opening day. Right? Something we've all been waiting for."

Fernando supposed it would be true to say that Mr. Westinghouse's electrical lights could indeed be worth waiting for. He couldn't begin to imagine what it'd be like to live in a world that had erased the elements of night. But Fernando was also not exactly sure he and Clara were talking about the same thing.

Clara set her fists to her hips. "It's not happening, though. Not on my watch."

Fernando stammered. "I…I don't understand—"

"Not again, and surely not even here," Clara added, running back toward Machinery Hall.

Fernando's heart pounded a mile a minute as Clara raced back inside. It would be madness to follow, he knew. But this was also a second attempt to be square with Rex Winston.

Fernando raced after her—*"Wait! Clara!"*—cursing his own stupidity every step of the way.

CHAPTER 18

STAY

EXCITEMENT ROSE LIKE A SOUFFLÉ INSIDE CLARA AS SHE RACED toward Machinery Hall. Her heart pounded so loudly she was certain Fernando could hear it and had probably already guessed she'd been more than simply surprised at finding him tonight.

With one quick move, Clara yanked open the doors to Machinery Hall and ran inside. "Come on!" she shouted over her shoulder, guards in the vicinity be damned—she was Jonathan Banks's daughter, and with this came a newfound privilege. She would do as she pleased.

"Clara, wait!" Fernando called. His dark hair sprouted wildly from underneath his cap, and his brown eyes carried the same intensity one could only get from standing on top of the world. She watched him stare across the inside of Machinery Hall at all the mechanical madness around them, and though Clara had been there to visit her father many times before, she understood its overwhelming grandeur. But that wasn't it—Fernando stared in such a way that whatever reason he'd had for breaking in, it surely hadn't been for anything wicked.

Clara paused at an intersection of paths. She could see the

massive machinery her father had ordered into place a few months earlier, but everything was backward in the dark, and the switch board was not where she expected it to be.

"You said the lights," Clara remarked, Fernando beside her. "I don't know where they keep those."

"Clara, we shouldn't be in here."

"Don't be silly. Only a few moments. Promise. Now, where would I keep the fair's bulbs if I were my father?" Clara let the wheels spin in her mind as she put herself into Jonathan Banks's shoes. Then she rolled her eyes. "Likely at the bottom of Lake Michigan. Those things have been nothing but an annoyance ever since Edison protested Westinghouse's use of his patent." As a way to alleviate any nervousness—but mostly to flirt—she touched Fernando's sleeve. "Don't worry—I won't make you dive into the cold waves to get them."

"That's good because I didn't bring my swimming trunks," Fernando quipped back. His voice was light.

Clara laughed politely, but then an image of this boy in swimming trunks ambushed her mind, eliminating any possibility of focus, and she went silent.

Fernando touched her arm back, the only thing she could feel in the darkness. "There were a few crates over here. Come on— this way."

Clara walked with him between several attractions.

"Hold on," Fernando said, pausing again. She could tell he was looking behind them. "No. Maybe it's somewhere else. I've turned us around. Where'd that lamp your father—"

There was a loud crack, followed by an eruption of hissing.

The round shape of a bulb burst to life in the hands of four or five figures only feet away, none of whom Clara could make out clearly.

"Oh!" she exclaimed.

They snapped their faces toward her. One was lifting a crystalized teardrop high into the air, studying the shape of a light-bulb shining with bright rays. But the strange and long figure had lifted the bulb for only a second before the sheer touch of it generated the strangest effect.

Every piece of him seemed to come apart. Like a sand-castle knocked over by children or wind, all the way from the fingernail down the arm, he unraveled like he'd never been whole to begin with. Exactly like that...*thing* that had dissolved into shimmering pieces on Bynum Island when Clara had stricken the Kodak's metal casing against its back. That *thing* that'd had the sheer gull to select an Alouette from St. Joan's and threaten her with harm. That *thing* Clara now knew hadn't been a man at all, but something extraordinary and inex-plicable.

A wolf-like growl penetrated every bit of Machinery Hall, only silenced when there was nothing left to scream.

The faces watched.

But they weren't true human faces Clara saw for the split second before Fernando yanked on her arm and pulled her in the other direction.

They were much too pale.

Distorted as though part of a painting whose oil colors had run, or a candle left out in the hot sun.

Not human at all, Clara realized.

They *were* just like that man back on Bynum Island—bones clothed in garments, and hats atop skulls as their empty eyes glared with shock and greed.

No, not human at all.

The sound of Clara's own scream was much louder than Fernando's shouts of, *"Shit. Go. Run!"*

He pulled her toward the doors to Machinery Hall. As she glanced over her shoulder, the last thing she saw before racing into the night was chaos: the smashing of crates, the extinguishing of lights. A sharp ringing filled the air. The room went pitch-black.

Clara's terror increased a thousand fold. She trembled as she ran.

Despite Sally's assertions the World's Fair was certainly the day when the next girl would go missing, Clara wondered if there'd be anything to stop these things from taking someone tonight, days ahead of the exposition's opening. One had made a sore attempt only a few nights past—why not try again when another St. Joan's girl coincidentally appeared on the fairgrounds?

"GO!" Fernando shouted.

Clara's feet ached as she kept speed with him. They raced across the Court of Honor toward the Terminal. Her muscles strained to move faster, but she had no idea what the plan was now. Would they stop at the Midway Plaisance? The Ferris Wheel?

They wove around the Terminal's railway tracks until they were racing past tents and attractions, shut for the night with echoes of laughter and hints of shadows from whoever might still be there.

Clara gasped for breath, but something new had risen from inside her: a fear she'd refused to give in to when she'd helped Lily slay the thing that'd tried to take Marta. She wasn't about to quit. Not when those skeletons might be on her kitten heels, ready to seize her and Fernando with their bony hands. But there were at least six of them—a good chunk more than the solitary fool she'd bludgeoned with the Kodak's flash.

"What on earth do we do now?" she screamed.

Fernando didn't answer.

Clara didn't know the Midway Plaisance. The weekly carriage she took to meet her father usually brought her straight to wherever The Cat's Whisker happened to be that night, which was never Machinery Hall. It was sheer luck, as she'd previous declared, and a late arrival—due to that damn literature essay on Tolstoy—that'd had her arrange to meet her father at Machinery Hall that week. Everything was catching up with her now, and she couldn't remember how to get out of the fairgrounds.

As though that would make a lick of difference.

They reached a fence surrounding the Midway Plaisance, and Fernando cupped his hands and gestured for her to step into them. "Come on!"

Clara stepped into his palms and grabbed his shoulders, and Fernando lifted her so she could pull herself up on top of the wooden fence.

"How will you get up?" she called as she threw her legs over to the other side.

Fernando took a few steps back and made a run for the fence, shuffling his feet up a few steps before he reached the top and threw himself over. "Drop!" he ordered.

Clara let out a scream as she fell, but the soft ground near the edge of the woods was a cushion to land upon. She scrambled to her feet, and they ran onward through a thicket of cedars and oaks.

A familiar set of street lamps stood in the distance, and Clara pointed. "There! Bynum Island is just past those lamp posts!"

St. Joan's was within reach. Clara had no idea where Fernando would go now, but he followed like he was as afraid of solitude as she was.

They ran until they could disappear across the foot bridge leading to Bynum Island and into the woods near St. Joan's. Clara risked a second glance to see if the monsters had followed. But she and Fernando were alone.

Clara stopped, panting breathlessly. "I think we're safe." That meant nothing, though, on an island alive with danger and magic.

Fernando set his fists to his sides as he bent over to catch his breath. "What happened back there?"

Clara glanced at him in question. "Didn't you see?" Her memory went wild with everything that'd happened tonight and only a few nights before.

Fernando met her eyes. Drops of sweat rolled down his neck. "They were testing the bulbs. Damn it. We shouldn't have gone back inside."

Clara blinked. "No. Didn't you *see?*"

"See what?"

Clara gestured dramatically toward the fairgrounds. The shimmers of gas lamps were blinking along the roads they'd just raced down, and only then did Clara realize just how far they'd run. "Who they were. What *happened* once one of them touched a bulb."

Fernando rested against a willow and pressed his palms to his eyes. "I only saw a flash of light. You screamed. They dropped the bulbs."

Clara stormed for him. He straightened once she was inches away. She pressed her index finger into his chest. "You were *there* with me. You must have seen it."

Fernando cocked his head at her. "If you would just *tell* me, Clara, what it is you're talking about, I could tell *you.*"

She pressed her finger harder the longer time passed until the memory of the skulls faded from her mind. Fernando caught her hand and held it.

"Tell me. Please?"

Clara blinked, her heart speeding up until she was certain it would catch flight like a wayward bird. "It's crazy." All of it. Ever since she'd joined the Alouettes. She could no longer deny how a folktale was coming to life in front of her. The warning in the note, written now for her.

Monsters hide on Bynum Island.

I fear they'll take me next.

"You don't know crazy like I do," Fernando replied. "Trust me." He held her hand tighter, and his grip began to shake.

A few shrieks caught them off-guard, and Clara jumped. She glanced in the direction of the sound. St. Joan's was closer than she'd realized, and there were girls nearby. Nightfall had already gotten a head start, and if Clara wasn't out for dinner with her father, she was supposed to be inside by eight-thirty. Curfew was essential for young girls. Reputation, crucial.

And there she was, standing in the woods, bathed in soft silver moonlight, her fingers caught in the hand of a boy she barely knew who stared at her and waited for an explanation. Clara stared back, a dangerous idea if she ever had one.

"Come on, Clara," Fernando whispered. "What happened?"

She didn't know how to answer, so instead, she inclined her head to study his face. Fernando was around her age, but there was something in his gaze that suggested he was ancient. Long ago Clara had realized anyone who'd experienced loss would gain a bit of sadness in their eyes, sadness that would remain with them forever and never budge, never leave, only become a shadow for all to see, even in moments of inexplicable bliss. Grief changed a person, only seen by those who knew it, too. Though when looking at Fernando, Clara couldn't tell what sort of grief had taken him. It was there, but it was different from the kind that had imprinted itself on her heart when her mother died.

She wanted to ask Fernando about it. She wanted to know why sadness had become a friend. Why he'd come to Chicago if he still missed New York so terribly.

Instead, she conceded that Fernando would probably not believe her if she were to say she'd seen a group of monstrous skeletons fiddling with Westinghouse's lightbulbs, let alone having slain one herself there on Bynum Island.

And there was something disappointing about that. She could

very well be the next girl to disappear in only a few days and fade from his memory, and still her word would never be trusted.

The thought chilled her, and her eyes began to well. "I was afraid. That's all."

Fernando frowned, like he didn't exactly believe her, but Clara stepped away before he could demand the truth.

"I wasn't expecting anyone inside the building, not when my father had just left. I didn't want to get into trouble. How stupid, right?" She kicked a pile of rocks that formed a path at her feet. A few scattered.

Fernando's silence told Clara he knew she had more to say, and that he was listening.

Clara took a breath. "I don't want to disappoint him, and getting in trouble does that. Maybe more—maybe it hurts. It devastates him that my mother is gone. So unfair of the universe to take someone so much younger, someone who'd been in good health until she truly wasn't, someone with a better spirit than he or I could ever have. It all happened so fast."

Whenever she shut her eyes, Clara saw visions of her mother: the dark hair that had been passed down to her, the sharp gray gaze that always seemed to know whenever a lie was afoot, the confidence in how she carried herself, like Bethany Banks had once come from a line of queens.

"So, so fast," Clara repeated softly.

She couldn't recall the lemon-cake bake-off at their church as her twelve-year-old self stood in the wings of the stage rather than the audience. But she did remember how Jonathan Banks had had to work that day for the seventh Sunday in a row and so missed his wife's vanilla frosting being declared the clear winner. And she'd never forget how her mother had laughed in celebration under a buttery-yellow sky all the same.

The following day, a gray cloud descended upon the family

home, and a mere three weeks after that, consumption made its permanent mark on the Bankses.

"It's so very strange," Clara whispered. "When I was a girl, I read books quickly. I ran a lot. I climbed trees—it's likely why I wasn't too afraid to climb the peristyle. I've always loved the idea of moving fast." She faced Fernando and was surprised to find him standing close—not slumped against the tree like she'd been expecting. Like he'd wanted to be near her, like he could sense that the thrill of the night had made her fearless in divulging secrets no one else had ever heard.

Fernando stared at Clara. "Moving fast doesn't let you feel anything."

She stared back. "Sometimes it does." Then she thought about his response. "What do you mean?"

He shrugged once and took a step away, like to explain would be too much. "I don't know. I guess because I know what it's like. I left home very quickly."

"Why?"

Fernando's eyes dropped to the ground. His boots pried the path of rocks away from the dirt. "That is a long story best saved for another day." He forced a laugh. "Ask me again when you're in the mood to hear about a good old-fashioned family business scandal."

Clara's eyebrows rose. She had a hunch he'd only added that because there was a part of him that wanted to tell her. So she pried a little further. "I won't tell, if that's what you're worried about. Or if it's judgment—short of murder or something just as evil, I suppose I wouldn't care too much."

Fernando cupped his hands behind his neck and let his elbows fall to his chest. He seemed tired, and not just because they'd been running. He blinked at Clara once in the sort of way that indicated he was considering it.

"Ask me again another day." His arms fell to his side.

Clara conceded and glanced toward the Midway. "Fernando? Something is meant to happen at the fair. Isn't it? You know it as well as I do." The woods hummed with girls' voices, and Clara imagined one of them as belonging to Aunt Miranda.

He swallowed purposefully. "Forget it. Spare yourself the trouble of getting involved in this mess."

"Forget it? How? My God, people are at stake. Girls I care about!" The Alouettes were readying for a war if it meant no St. Joan's girl would ever again disappear, and by the day, the likelihood it might be her or Sally came to Clara more and more in waves of bitter fear.

"Your friends from the peristyle, I assume. They have nothing to do with it."

"It's not true. I don't believe that for a second." Clara considered the bulbs in Machinery Hall, and how the Kodak's flash on Bynum Island had revealed the man who'd taken Marta as something other than human. "It must be connected to the lights somehow." *Monsters in the light and disappearing girls—two unbelievable events happening in the same place, at the same time?* she thought. *That's not how history works. Everything has a connection.* She blinked ferociously, but all she saw were eyes that had never been eyes to begin with. "There's something in the air, and everything's gone backwards, upside-down. Tell me you don't feel it like I do."

Boldness coming over her, she caught his hand and squeezed it, and Fernando stared at her lips. They were standing too close for anyone to think Fernando might not try to kiss her.

Suddenly, that was all Clara could think of. Electric lights and forthcoming wars against monsters in Chicago be damned.

But as Fernando's gaze lifted, he pried his hand from hers. "I don't know," his said, speaking slowly. "And whatever it is, it has nothing to do with me. I can't be involved."

"You already are! That's why you were at Machinery Hall

tonight. Tell me, Fernando!" She touched his arm again to keep him close, but he pulled away.

"Don't," he warned.

She dropped his sleeve. "Please," she whispered. "Tell me you saw what I saw tonight." But Clara wouldn't say any more in case oncoming madness were the reason behind everything.

Fernando's eyes turned dark. "I have to go, Clara."

Clara felt the same tears at her mother's death strangle her again. "No. Don't leave. Please? Not yet."

She knew it was a strange thing to ask of Fernando, that she had no business telling him what to do—someone who was still essentially a stranger. But the threshold that divided Clara and Fernando as strangers shattered, leaving behind a kinship. Clara knew this as deeply as anything, and she could damn well see it in Fernando's eyes, too.

With one look, she knew that no, he wouldn't leave, not yet.

"Please?" she asked again, ensuring she was right.

Fernando slipped his arms around her waist and pulled her close. As he did so, she breathed him in—wood and leather and soap that reminded her of a memory in another life.

"It's all right, Clara," he whispered, his lips brushing the edge of her ear.

But Clara knew that wasn't true.

She'd run tonight from something that had scared her, but now she was only filled with regret. She wanted to return to Machinery Hall and face that which had frightened her.

That's what her mother would have done.

She would have stood up to it, Clara thought. *She would have faced it until it couldn't scare her anymore. She would have stripped it of its power.*

Her face turned wet with the tears that come quickly when the presence of a loved one long past is near, and her arms circled Fernando's neck and held him in return. He didn't fight it but drew her even closer. She'd never embraced a boy like this before, but it was wonderful and confusing at the same time. Fernando's body was hard against her softness, but gentle. It wasn't just safety in the moment she felt with him—it was a sense of pure, intimate understanding. Which suddenly alarmed Clara.

Enough that she pulled free.

Fernando let her, and Clara looked into his eyes as the light of night tried its damnedest to let them see. She watched how his lips moved like there was a prayer escaping them or like he had the unconscious habit of trying out words before speaking. She fantasized about kissing Fernando. She imagined what it'd be like to taste him. Right then, with all the excitement surrounding them, it was all she wanted.

A flash of light struck them. At first, Clara thought it might be lightning, but Fernando's sudden reaction of dropping her waist and stepping away told her there were no guilty thunderstorms in the vicinity.

"Was that an arc light?" Fernando asked, amazed. "No, they couldn't have followed us."

Clara searched the grounds of St. Joan's, but it was too dark.

Until, "Clara? What in blazes are you—" And then, "*Oh.*"

Clara's eyes adjusted back to the night, and then she blinked at Marta holding the Kodak with its flash pointed toward the willow tree. Clara took another step away from Fernando until she was certain the distance between them was appropriate. "Marta? What are you doing out here?"

"I flunked my last assignment, so Headmistress told me to submit ten photographs of the fairgrounds for extra credit by tomorrow. I only had eight good ones from the Navy Pier. This kind of looks like those bushes by the Architectural Building, right?" Marta narrowed her eyes on Fernando. "Fair boy. Fancy meeting you here."

Fernando stuffed his hands into his pockets and inclined his chin. "Marta, wasn't it?"

"Had to see Bynum Island for yourself?" Marta's tone turned cheeky. "Or are you here for extra credit as well?"

Clara clicked her tongue disapprovingly. "Marta," she scolded.

Marta grinned, and though Clara felt her cheeks warm at being caught with Fernando, she was also amazed. *I wish I had her resilience*, she thought. *If I'd been captured by that thing, I'm not sure I would have ever returned to St. Joan's.*

Clara glanced at the willow. "You really think the school grounds look like the fair? Headmistress is going to scold you terribly."

"Well, that's my fault, isn't it?"

Then, "All girls to their dormitories, please!" Headmistress called from the school.

Marta glanced at Fernando and then back at Clara. "Come on," she said, cocking her head once to the side. "Curfew."

Clara nodded. "I have to go," she told Fernando in a soft voice.

"Yeah," he whispered back.

Clara glanced at Marta again. "Go ahead. I'll catch up."

Marta shrugged. "Careful, Clara Banks. Headmistress isn't as understanding as I am." Then she hoisted the Kodak onto her back and raced back to the dormitories.

Clara dug up the remnants of courage she had inside her and faced Fernando. "President Cleveland's commencement ceremonies will take place at noon. Is that correct?" She forced her voice to sound normal and praised it silently when it did.

Fernando blinked. "What?"

"You're taking me to the fair, remember? Monday is opening day." And classes would be canceled in favor of this historic event.

Fernando blinked again as the memory hit him. "Oh. Yes. That's right. That's what you told your father."

"I'm assuming it's still all right. I mean, I have to arrive with the girls, but I should be able to sneak off in no time."

Fernando shoved his hands into his pockets. "I just thought it was for…show?"

Clara blinked. "You don't want to go to the fair with me?"

"No, it's not that," Fernando stammered. Then he smiled. "Yes, Clara. I'd very much like to go to the fair with you."

"Do you work that day?"

"No. The Ferris Wheel operators will be there but not construction. Not with so many people. I suppose we'll finish building the wheel on Sundays."

Whatever danger faced the girls at St. Joan's surely lay within Machinery Hall. Clara needed to know who those skeletons were. And Fernando, with his access to the fairgrounds she wouldn't have on her own, was her key to finding that out for herself.

"Then I'll meet you on the Midway at eleven," she told Fernando.

Clara spun on her heel and ran back through the soft grass of St. Joan's grounds, calling over her shoulder, "Eleven o'clock! Don't be a minute late!"

ACT III

CHAPTER 19

MARINE CAFÉ

"But Sally, we don't know how to recognize——" Clara curled her fingers around a small pile of papers on the table and released them. "I don't even know what they *were*! I thought they were ordinary men. But something was terribly wrong." She shook her head to emphasize the point.

Sally paced the library at Château Perle, and Marta and Lily slumped into their seats on either side of Clara. Dawn had long since broken on the morning of May 1st, the opening day of the World's Columbian Exposition. And if Clara were to listen carefully, she'd swear she could already hear the hundreds of thousands of people—from down the street and across the Atlantic alike—rushing for the Court of Honor, not willing to miss a thing if it'd mean they'd all forever be a part of history.

But here were the Alouettes, awake for hours now, scraping for mere minutes and irrefutable evidence—anything that could help them solve the mystery of the missing girls at St. Joan's before time would eventually run out and one of them would disappear.

Maybe Sally Carter.

187

Maybe Clara Banks.

Maybe another girl entirely.

It didn't matter—it wouldn't happen. It couldn't. But Clara's fists clenched nonetheless around the papers that were becoming more and more irrelevant by the second, not to mention the very truth that her mother's favorite folktale hadn't accounted for a once-solid man vanishing into iridescent sand. No one knew how to spot the danger lurking in Chicago. All the Alouettes knew for certain was the terrifying incident with Marta and Clara's recollection of what had happened at Machinery Hall.

Omitting a few details.

"I have to say, Clara," Sally added, fatigue weaving its way through her voice. "I'm rather impressed that you sneaked inside Machinery Hall all by yourself." She pulled out the chair beside Marta—an old and heavy one that made the loudest of creaking sounds—and collapsed into it. "I just have to think of that horrible night we all barely escaped, and I'm frozen with fear."

Marta leaned her head on Sally's shoulder. "I'm all right now, Sal." And then she cut her eyes to Clara's.

Clara understood instantly. Marta hadn't told a single girl about how she'd caught Clara with Fernando under the willow tree. That sort of a secret was a great kindness—especially since even Sally didn't know, and from what Clara understood about love, one of its best parts was sharing your entire soul with another and never holding back.

It's a debt you'll one day repay, Clara told herself. She would honor it. Somehow.

"Well," Clara replied to Sally. "In so many ways, I wish I hadn't."

"You're much braver than I could ever be, Clara," Lily announced. "I don't know what will happen today, but I do know if none of us had spent the entire weekend fencing, there'd be no way on God's green earth I'd be stepping onto those damn fairgrounds today." She licked a finger and flipped over another newspaper, glancing at the words for no more than a second before choosing another one.

Marta offered a bit of a scowl. "Oh, really? Then I guess it doesn't matter if a certain gentleman you've been secretly seeing works there, does it?"

Lily's sticky finger dropped the next edition, but while she didn't deny it, she didn't acknowledge it either.

Clara stretched her arms across the table. "There isn't much time left." She glanced out a window, each quadrant showcasing a different view of Bynum Island. The dark branches from the oak outside Château Perle, its buds insistent on their arrival. Overcast clouds and birds flying against them. The hills leading toward the academy itself. And then there was a path. One she and the Alouettes had hastily taken to save Marta only a week prior, and now it would lead to the very field where that... *monster* had collapsed into ashes. But it would also lead to the footbridge that would take the Alouettes into a maddening folktale that was more real than Clara had ever imagined. "And we're no better off now than we were before this whole mess began."

The hopelessness of her statement carried through the whole of Château Perle's library and washed over the other girls. Marta's dark eyes widened in surprise. Lily looked aghast. But Sally—Sally's reaction to Clara's assertion was the worst of all.

Hurt. And betrayed.

Clara shut her eyes and pressed the cool silver band around the delicate scar on her left index finger. As she flexed her hand, the echo of its pain ached all the way up her arm, but it was finally healed-over enough for her new pearl ring.

"I'm sorry. I didn't mean it the way it sounded. It's just that..." She searched for the words, but the only ones she found were just as desolate. Full of grief. Empty of hope. "The folktale hasn't helped, and I personally can't connect everything we know, everything we've learned. Can any of you?"

It was a question for the entire table, but all eyes turned to Sally.

"Please, Sal," Clara continued. "Tell me there's something we've missed. The key to everything. Tell us you believe we can save this city from losing another Alouette and forgetting her entirely."

Sally's gaze fell to the stacks of newspapers and research on the table. Each one had been scrutinized relentlessly. Analyzed down to the choice of paper for each handwritten note. The one from the folktale, no less. Scrawled in a hand that tried to remain calm but couldn't help the desperation it bore. No iambic pentameter in this one—perhaps no time to think of something more clever than what it claimed.

All done for Sally's great-aunt, Dora. So the Carter family could learn the truth of what had really happened.

Sally hesitated at Clara's words. "Don't give up, Clara." Her voice grew stronger. "No Alouette is disappearing today."

Frustration grew inside Clara like a stubborn weed, and the thought Sally might be the next girl to vanish was too horrible to bear. "We should at least tell Headmistress. Maybe it'd be better if none of the girls from school were at the fair today." To Clara, it would make sense to avoid the fairgrounds, given the enormous coincidence that the next disappearance was bound to happen that day.

"No," Sally replied thoughtfully. "I don't think that's how it works. Every missing girl we've made note of has disappeared from Bynum Island. Like the disappearances are somehow attached to this place. Linked, or bound, or...*something*. It makes more sense to leave."

But the more Sally spoke, the less convincing her words became.

Fairgrounds or not, Clara was determined to slip away from the Alouettes after morning tea with the girls' families—not a tradition as much as it was a way for St. Joan's to show off that year's crop of bright minds in a spectacular setting. Fernando had agreed to meet her at eleven, and come hell or high water or monsters mixed in with both, she was determined to sneak inside Machinery Hall to investigate anything to do with those *things* she'd seen amongst the lightbulbs. With any luck, the pieces Clara was so eager to find would fall into place.

"How will we know we've found the answer to all this, Sal?" Marta asked.

But Sally's focus was on something else. "Every missing girl…" She stared at the scraps of newsprint in front of them. "Perhaps it's been staring us straight in the face." And then she pushed her chair from the table and stood as though the key to solving an enigma had fallen over her. "All this time."

Clara frowned, but suddenly the library door burst open and all four girls startled away from the table. Kimiko Ando stood there, an Alouette a year younger than Clara.

"Headmistress says we're all to meet at the footbridge in ten minutes, Sally," Kimiko announced with not even a look at the mess on the table. Then she eyed Marta and Lily. "Except you two, Miss *I-Couldn't-Be-Bothered-To-Complete-A-Single-Assignment* and Miss *It-Must-Have-Slipped-My-Mind*. She said she wanted to see you personally in her office in five minutes." Kimiko gave a shrug. "And that was ten minutes ago."

Marta rolled her eyes, and Lily feigned a dramatic sigh, but the two girls stood and followed Kimiko out of Château Perle with a quick wave to Clara and Sally.

Clara stood herself. "Well, then, Sally. Let's go."

"No. There's something I need to look into first. Make my excuses. Please? I'll meet you after Marine Café."

Clara frowned. "What? You're missing tea? Sally—"

"Clara," Sally said, leaning close enough that Clara imagined she were actually speaking to Great-Aunt Dora instead of her dear friend. "You need to find out how the fair fits into all this. Where the danger is."

Clara's eyes widened. "We shouldn't be alone—"

"I already said no one is disappearing today. Trust me, Clara Banks." Sally held Clara's hand tightly. "Blood to bone."

Clara kissed Sally's cheek. "And bone to ash." She could feel Sally's determination running through her own veins, like strength was a gift a girl could give to another.

And then Clara raced out of Château Perle and into the woods of Bynum Island.

***

The students of St. Joan's Academy for Girls arrived at Wooden Island on the fairgrounds promptly at nine o'clock for morning tea. The bright white outlines of the Court of Honor were visible from Marine Café, though still far enough away that those who'd never sneaked onto the fairgrounds would still be surprised once President Cleveland officially declared it open.

Clara told herself to relax amidst the quiet of porcelain tea cups and mild chatter, but Sally still hadn't arrived, and that was unsettling. Crisp white linens, towers of miniature sandwiches, echoes of string music all playing in delightful harmonies surrounded her: an atmosphere fit for the wealthy and the elite.

Find out how the fair fits into all this, Sally had said.

"Clara." Jonathan Banks kissed her cheek and stepped around the table to sit across from her. Dark circles scored the skin under his eyes, and a puffiness highlighting them suggested yesterday's nightcap had been a bit stronger than usual. "You look lovely. And you'll be meeting your escort when?"

"Eleven o'clock sharp," Clara said with a frozen smile. *No one's disappearing today,* she reminded herself. *Especially not our Sally.* "We'll start in the Court of Honor for the opening ceremonies, and then we'll tour the pavilions," she said, an actress on an invisible stage as she managed to get through the entire sentence without the slightest wobble in her voice.

"Excellent. Well, I'm glad to see you before the chaos begins." Banks lumped three spoonfuls of sugar into the white teacup in front of him.

Each spoonful was an eternity.

Clara sipped her tea. Black, with a bit of lemon. "Chaos?" Anything to make small talk.

Banks waved away any concern. "Politics and paperwork and the like. Within the hour, the majority of the investors here will have left this place to drown their worries in bourbon."

"At The Cat's Whisker, you mean?" Clara asked. "How interesting. I wonder where it is right now." Her words were not subtle in the least, and she stole a bit of happy delight in that.

Banks cleared his throat. "Maybe it's best we talk about something else."

Clara's eyes darted toward the café door with its linen curtains gracefully ballooning inside from the wind. Still no Sally, and any grace in a proper setting suddenly seemed frivolous. "School is fine. My classes, also fine. I just turned in an English paper I'd rather not talk about, and so now we're caught up." A touch of venom coated her response, and her shoulders slumped once she realized it. Oh, how she wished she could be sparring with Lily at Château Perle, preparing for the Alouettes' war. "I'm sorry. I don't mean to snap."

Banks narrowed his eyes at Clara—confused, not angry. "Is everything all right, dear?"

Clara forced another smile and imagined a cigar-smoking director guiding her in the stage performance of a lifetime. "Perfect." *Gracious, Sally, where are you?*

She stirred her tea as the quiet yet joyful banter of those around her peppered the café: families of St. Joan's girls on this momentous day and men of power, their pipes lit and aromatic, smoke billowing while tea was drunk and cucumber sandwiches eaten.

Until a voice spilled through all of them. A brash voice that could cut silence like a blade. And though Clara did not turn to see, she could tell this was a *suit*, as Fernando would say.

A suit standing behind her.

"…only place I can get refuge from those god-awful electric lights. Can you believe they've already installed them in my own neighborhood? And that chap Westinghouse thinks I should be here the entire day just to have the headache of a lifetime. We'll see about that."

"Of course," Banks muttered. "Of course today of all days."

Clara glanced at her father, whose disposition had changed dramatically in a matter of seconds from calm to irritable. Banks stood, buttoning up his jacket as he forced a pleasant smile.

"Hello, sir. Congratulations on what's sure to be a marvelous day."

Clara set down her tea and looked up at a man much smaller than her father in stature but with an air of confidence so strong no one would ever notice. The black hat he wore was clearly expensive, and the scarf around his neck an odd choice for a spring day but would do well to keep his skin free of sunlight. He was probably much older than Clara could guess, but there was a sharpness in his light eyes that showed clarity, intelligence, and a want for control.

The man shook her father's hand. "Jonathan. Good to see George's own here today."

"Good to be here, sir. An honor."

Clara blanched at seeing this side of her father. He was nervous around this man. Uncomfortable.

Banks gestured to her. "My daughter, Clara. Just started at St. Joan's this past winter."

The man's eyes flicked toward Clara. He studied her as though attempting to figure out why on earth he should care about her presence. Clara responded by sitting straighter, but she did not stand. Etiquette wouldn't demand that of her in these circles.

"Quite a challenging school, St. Joan's. Florence McGill is your headmistress, correct?" His voice was as heavy as iron.

"Yes, sir," Clara responded with not a dip of confidence. "And it is challenging. That's why I like it."

"What sort of sights do you have after you graduate?"

The question took Clara by surprise. Marriage to a man of high society was the usual assumption for a St. Joan's girl. Clara stuttered her answer. "Ideally, sir, one of the schools on the east coast for their history classes. Radcliffe or Sarah Lawrence."

The man nodded, thinking carefully. "Jonathan, should I introduce myself to your daughter, or will you have the good graces to do it for me?"

Banks ran his leg into the side of the table as he ambled toward them. "Of course. Clara, Mr. Rex Winston, a friend of Mr. Westinghouse—"

Mr. Winston tensed. That sort of connection to Westinghouse was clearly not the kind he appreciated.

Banks corrected himself right away. "A colleague. They've worked together on the fair's lights. There were many contracts, naturally, and Mr. Winston is one of the finest attorneys the country has ever known."

Mr. Winston seemed to forgive Banks. He offered his hand to Clara, and despite herself, she shook it. His skin was cold, and he grasped her hand in a way that made his bones press unpleasantly into her palm.

"Very nice to meet you, and the best of luck to you at St.

Joan's. Florence McGill is not an educator to be overlooked. Now if you're a smart girl, you'll look me up after this to arrange a meeting about any recommendations I could give to the old dogs at Radcliffe." He tried to smile, but Clara noted how it didn't quite reach his eyes.

"Thank you, sir. I will. I assure you, my grades are impeccable."

"I'm not worried." Mr. Winston turned away from Clara, his conversation with her now finished. "In fact, since you do plan on coming to the pub this afternoon, Jonathan, there are some associates of mine I'd like you to meet. Many of them have connections to the schools on the east coast, Radcliffe amongst them, by chance."

Clara watched her father pale. She expected him to respond with one of his usual answers, *"Oh certainly,"* or *"I'd be delighted,"* but instead, Jonathan Banks surprised Clara in what he said next.

"Yes, sir. I think I will."

And nothing more. Clara frowned.

"Splendid." Mr. Winston fiddled with a small pocket hand-kerchief in his breast pocket until it was straight. The dark blue shine told Clara it was silk. "Navy of all shades," he said. "Perhaps I'll start a trend." Another smile of insincerity. He slid a business card into Jonathan Banks's shaking hand. As navy as the handkerchief sprouting like a tulip from his pocket.

Banks stared at the card, but he didn't read it. "Indeed."

Clara turned away from their conversation and stirred the lemon wedge in her tea until bits of pulp saturated the entire cup. Sally still hadn't shown up at Marine Café.

No matter, Clara thought. *Anyone strong enough to cut bone from the fingers of dozens of girls is nothing less than a force to be reckoned with.*

"Excuse me? Miss?" came a whisper.

Clara glanced to her left, where out of view from Mr.

Winston and Banks knelt a boy nearly a foot taller than Clara with kind eyes and floppy dark hair.

The boy gave Clara a crooked but well-meaning smile. "I know the girls here are from St. Joan's. Don't suppose you know where Lily is?" He held a bowler cap in his hands. "Oh. The name's Dodger." He offered her a handshake.

Clara shook it. *So this is Dodger.* He was handsome, the sort of handsome she knew Lily would seek out in a boy, and somehow wore the same puppy-love smile Lily had been boasting these last few weeks at St. Joan's.

"Clara. I'm afraid Lily was called to our Headmistress's office before the rest of us left for the fair." She searched Marine Café, but there was no sign of Lily or Marta. Or Sally.

Dodger shuffled back and forth and nodded. Disappointment dropped his gaze to the linen napkin on Clara's lap. "Thank you anyway, then. Sorry to disturb." Then he took a deep breath that puffed out his chest, like he might be gathering courage. "Could I ask you to pass on a message for me, if you do happen to see her?"

"Of course."

"Tell her Dodger would be honored to take her on the Ferris Wheel once it's finished, but it won't be today. Blasted thing is still half-done. Otherwise, I'll be at Machinery Hall if she wants to say hello. Would love to buy her some hotcakes and syrup." Another delightfully crooked smile as Dodger stared off into space as though already imagining Lily there.

But something else took hold of Clara's attention. "Machinery Hall? You—"

"Dodger," Mr. Winston commanded.

Dodger straightened instantly, nearly dropping his bowler cap in the process. He clutched it to his chest. "Yes, sir."

"One does not bother a lady at tea, and one especially does

not bother her by crouching in front of her like some sort of misbehaving child." Mr. Winston's eyes were cold.

Dodger nodded. "Of course, sir. My apologies, miss."

Clara opened her mouth to say no apology was necessary, but Mr. Winston had already drawn closer to Dodger, and suddenly the mood in the café grew tense.

"Is everything ready for tonight?"

Dodger nodded again. "Yes, sir. The lads and I worked late into the night. The last spot was a bit of a tricky one to relocate, but The Cat's Whisker's patrons will find an extraordinary experience awaiting them today."

Clara eyed her father, but Jonathan Banks was staring at the navy business card in his hand. Like it were hot iron instead of pressed paper.

"Excellent," Mr. Winston said. "Tell the patrons the new location at the appropriate time. Not now, mind you. This morning is for celebration and family—not business. See to it after the opening ceremonies."

"Yes, sir." And without another glance at Clara, Dodger left the café.

Machinery Hall, Clara thought. If nothing else, seeking out Dodger there might lead her to understanding who those men— those *monsters*—were that night she and Fernando sneaked inside. It wasn't much, but perhaps it was something.

"There's still some unfinished business I need to take care of, unfortunately. Just know that the record states I was opposed to such a wasteful display. Machinery Hall should have been enough," Mr. Winston was saying in the meantime.

Clara's spoon froze mid-stir in her teacup. She held her breath in case that would help her eavesdrop better.

"Sir, with respect," Banks said in response, "I think you'll find the light show quite incredible. I've already seen specifications of what to expect, and—"

"*I* expect a huge debt will settle upon Chicago, which would mean no return on any investments. What could happen in that case is a great and sudden halt to the wages of everyone on the blasted Ferris Wheel, the damned thing itself sold for scrap metal, and anyone working on it penniless in the streets."

Clara exhaled. *Fernando.*

Banks's voice took a low tone. "Begging your pardon, sir, but to take their jobs…the riots would rival those after the fire."

"Let them riot. My job is to ensure Chicago prospers. Enjoy the fair, Banks. I'll expect you by nightfall."

Mr. Winston took his leave, a handful of suits following him. Clara stared at the decorative designs of the linen napkins on the table as her father sat back down. He unbuttoned his jacket like a weight the size of the Blarney Stone had been dropped from his shoulders.

Banks reached for the sugar and added a fourth lump of it to his tea, which Clara imagined was probably now ice-cold. "Try the sandwiches, Clara."

Clara reached for a triangle cucumber sandwich and took a bite. She winced at the sogginess of the bread. Her eyes found the door, but Sally still hadn't arrived.

That merely meant Clara Banks would have to solve this mystery alone.

CHAPTER 20

UNORTHODOX ADMISSION

"Turn away from the clutches of sin and come back into the light, or be doomed for all eternity!"

The pastor stood at the edge of the Midway Plaisance as Fernando and Antoine—employed now at the French Pavilion and all the happier for it—strode past an entire brigade of church-goers and their respective ministers amongst patrons of the World's Columbian Exposition. Fernando's eyes widened in gentle mockery as they passed picket signs declaring the sacrilege of the belly-dancing displays that had begun after the arrival of the Egyptian performers.

Antoine leaned in close. "Dodger's pastor, a man named Bennett, says all this is two steps closer to the devil, but he's also miraculously decided to wear his spectacles for the first time in thirty-five years, according to the Chicago church ladies."

Fernando smirked, the idea of a morality brigade protesting the Midway Plaisance ridiculous enough to distract from the pangs of worry he worked to suppress.

Dismantle the lights, he told himself. *Dismantle them, and you've paved a path to becoming a successful man.*

"They'll calm down soon enough," Antoine remarked, and Fernando wondered if Antoine had given up on his search for monsters. "There's so much more to be worried about than the fair's calls to the devil." Poking fun, Antoine stuck an index finger on each side of his head and growled.

Fernando laughed, and Antoine led him inside a tent on the Midway, one Fernando had never visited before.

"Alors," Antoine muttered to himself as the French workers there chatted with each other and ate hotcakes with syrup. He sorted through a rack of traditional French chemises with polished lines and carefully-embroidered suspenders.

Fernando stood awkwardly and waited, catching a glance of his reflection in a tilted mirror in the corner, just past the tables of pressed powder and rouge for any performers frequenting the tent. A French girl with long hair caught his eye in the mirror and smiled, and Fernando knew why. Before arriving at the fairgrounds, Antoine, in one of his more brilliant moments, had smudged a bit of kohl under Fernando's eyes, just beneath the lashes, and then on his upper eyelids, too. The look was certainly dramatic, one that let Fernando appear as though he belonged on the fairgrounds as a performer, if nothing else. He looked like a shadow. Like danger. Like someone who'd walk through the night and not fear a minute of it.

"You're taller than me," Antoine continued, "but not by much. This one should do, but on payment of death, if you don't return it to me by the end of the day, it'll be my neck on the line, and whatever happens to me will be ten times worse for you. No —a *thousand*." Antoine had a unique ability to threaten someone in a way that didn't outright hurt as much as it tickled, but Fernando knew better than to test that.

Fernando looked away from the girl in the mirror and unbuttoned his own cheap shirt without any thought to modesty. Not when everyone on the Midway had long since boasted their liberal views of clothing and how much skin a person could show. Morality police these folks were not.

Fernando slipped off his shirt and fiddled with the French one. "Is it really that different from the one I'm already wearing? No one will notice if—"

"Hello," Antoine interrupted as he glanced past Fernando.

"Hello?" Fernando said, turning.

At the front of the tent stood Clara.

She'd managed to sneak away from the girls at St. Joan's, as promised, and now stood there in a black sheath of fabric that hit her knee. While so many girls and ladies arriving that day followed the trend of wearing a bustle, Clara didn't. The sleeves on her dress bunched just before her elbows, and the neckline went fairly low, enough that Fernando's second thought was how she fit in quite well on the Midway. There was a black ribbon wrapped around her neck, and from it dropped a careful arrangement of delicate pearls. Her dark hair in its unruly ringlets bounced around her chin, and Fernando swore she'd reddened her lips, but that might have been wishful thinking. When she spotted him, her eyebrows lifted, and a strange expression blossomed across her face.

"I might be a tad early," she finally said.

Fernando felt naked. He whipped on Antoine's shirt and fastened the buttons, wishing away the warmth on his neck and cheeks. "No, not at all," he stammered. "Well, yes, technically."

Having fastened the last button, he quickly set the suspenders to his trousers and then stilled, feeling like an attraction thousands had come to gawk at.

"We agreed to meet at eleven." It couldn't be any later than quarter to.

Clara's lips tipped upward in a shy smile. "We did. But with all the people here to see President Cleveland, I was worried I'd miss the show."

Fernando wondered if her wording was intentional.

The silence that lingered between them was thick, a kind that encouraged the eventual confession of secrets, just like the night in front of the school when Clara had spoken about her mother with abandon. Fernando's pulse sped as their silent staring passed the point when the reasons behind it were beyond obvious.

Antoine stepped forward, offering his hand to Clara, and the spell broke. "Antoine," he said. "Excuse Fernando here. His manners lack in moments of revelation."

His cheeks even warmer now, Fernando glared at Antoine. "Traidor." He was certain the insult transcended languages.

Antoine grinned. "Bâtard."

At that, Clara smiled as she shook Antoine's hand. "Clara."

"Welcome to the Midway, Clara."

Fernando moved to Clara's side and gestured to his clothing. "Am I all right now?" he asked Antoine.

He shouldn't have been surprised when Clara caught on immediately. "These aren't your usual clothes. You're sneaking in? Or are you getting in for free?" Delight blossomed in her eyes. "Reporters get in for free. Did you know that? So does the fair's official photographer." She glowed with excitement.

Antoine shrugged as he studied Fernando. "I suppose this'll do. Just mention you're courting this savvy girl beside you, and they'll waltz you right on to the fairgrounds."

Fernando froze. He couldn't see Clara's face turned away, only that she tensed at Antoine's assumption. "Actually, for me, it won't be a problem," she said. "My father is one of the liaisons to Westinghouse. Fernando is simply escorting me as a favor."

Is that the only reason why?

Antoine stared. "Oh. Well, then. Enjoy yourselves, you two." He eyed Fernando again. "Keep the shirt, but just for today. Don't forget—it's your head on a prickly wooden spit if I don't get it back by nightfall. I'm serious. I will cut down this tent with my own hands and sharpen the wood myself."

Fernando gestured to Clara to follow him. "I promise."

"Yuki said the hotcakes and maple syrup are the best foods here, by the way," Antoine called after them. "Have fun!"

But even with Clara at his side, fun was the last thing Fernando had on his mind.

With Machinery Hall in their sights, they exited into a herd of fair-goers, all storming the Midway toward the Court of Honor, and even more awaiting President Cleveland's official opening of the fair. As the starchy shirts and soft linens of strangers brushed up against him, Fernando felt his chest tighten with the pressure of so many watching, so many pushing bodies inching toward the row of camels on the Midway, pausing at the Japanese Theater, where Yuki and others were performing pantomime. *Céad míle fáilte* sat above the Blarney Castle, and close by, the applause from the Chinese Theater in the middle of a captivating tale.

Fernando reached for Clara's hand, her gray eyes on his as he wrapped their fingers together. She squeezed in return, a silent message she wasn't going to be separated from him in this crowd of thousands. Fernando's sole focus narrowed on the feel of Clara's skin, a persistent reminder he wasn't alone, and though it was something that couldn't last forever, for now, it was a comfort. His heartbeat slowed to a normal pace as they pushed through the crowd.

Until something ahead forced him to halt altogether.

"Fernando?" Clara called over the loud and rambunctious voices awaiting the opening ceremonies. "What is it?"

Fernando's skin chilled with nervous sweat. A plethora of suits, their eyes dark with intent and malice, scanned the crowds in the opposite direction of the Court of Honor. Like they were looking for something. Or someone.

Like they were hunting.

"No," he whispered, low enough he was certain Clara wouldn't hear.

"Fernando?" Clara asked again beside him.

The suits beelined for them, and Fernando felt time slipping away, costing him the precious seconds he'd need to sort out this mess. Clara wouldn't be complicit in whatever deal he'd made with Rex Winston.

"Change of plans," Fernando said, tightening his hand around hers. "We have to go." He risked a glance only to see confusion in her eyes.

Any explanation would have to wait. He tugged her along the Midway until they reached a slab of land where an impromptu magic show inside a tent had been set up. Fernando sucked in a surprised gasp and stopped. The low wooden stage ahead of them boasted a short man wearing a black suit with a white bowtie, and his gaze from under tilted eyebrows stared out.

A tall skinny chap in a bowler cap pointed at Fernando. "He must be your assistant, Houdini! Look at those eyes!"

Fuck, Fernando thought, shrinking into himself.

The man Houdini cocked an easy smile. "I'll be in the market for a volunteer in only minutes. My boy, if you wouldn't mind?" He offered a hand.

Hundreds of people gaped at them, and Fernando felt heat rise to his cheeks with the unwanted attention.

"Well, you *were* hoping to be mistaken for a performer, weren't you?" Clara muttered with an airy laugh. "Ha, ha?"

Fernando shook his head at the magician. "Not interested in vanishing today, pal." And then he and Clara slipped back outside.

They found themselves in a crowd with people pushing onward, a menagerie of women and men all heading toward the Grand Basin in the Court of Honor with its fountains bursting from within. Fernando ran, knowing Clara's very safety depended on finding a place to hide.

The suits were growing close.

"Stop them!" one shouted.

They were pushing through the crowd as Fernando suddenly spotted a point of sanctuary in the least likely of places—one he considered to be the epitome of irony, and if Clara knew the significance, she would, too. Applause was ringing all the way from the Court of Honor as President Cleveland's voice rang through the crowd. The World's Fair was coming to life.

The suits raced faster. There was no time.

Fernando held tightly to Clara's hand. "This way. Almost there."

"Fernando, what—"

"Trust me."

There was one place Fernando knew he and Clara could hide without any chance of being found.

The only place at the World's Fair that would not open today.

The only attraction that would not be finished for another month.

CHAPTER 21

THE FERRIS WHEEL

CLARA REALIZED TOO LATE WHERE FERNANDO INTENDED TO GO. Her eyes crept up the entirety of the Ferris Wheel—beam by beam, car by car. From the ground, it looked more like a torture device than an actual vehicle for special occasion pleasantries.

Straightaway, she dug her heels into the ground until both she and Fernando came to a stop.

"No," she declared as Fernando faced her. "You can't be serious. *Up there?*" She pointed at the many cars lining the wheel's circumference. She didn't know what sort of panic had come over Fernando. She needed to search Machinery Hall. And there was only so far she was willing to follow him.

"Just listen," Fernando pleaded, his words a long desperate hiss. "It's the only place we can hide."

"Hide from what? This thing is not even scheduled to open until the end of June!"

Fernando frowned. "How did you know that?"

"Remember? My father is the liaison to Westinghouse. I probably know as much about this place as you do!"

"We'll be safe. I promise."

Clara wretched her hand free and let out a good loud laugh. "Safe? If the wheel starts moving, anyone with half a brain will notice!"

"It's not going to—" Fernando's eyes flew past her to something in the distance and widened with horror. "No time, Clara. *Please.* We have to leave before they catch us. Trust me?"

She followed his line of vision and saw. There were two suits, and then there were seven. Moving in unison like they shared a heartbeat. Their faces were solemn, and they marched toward her and Fernando and no one else.

Clara had never before felt the danger that now rippled over her skin. Her throat tightened. In a moment, she could be captured for something she didn't understand.

"All right," she whispered. She could barely breathe the words. "Go."

"What?"

She faced Fernando. *"Run!"*

Right away she knew she'd said it too loudly. She stole a glance at the suits. The one in the front followed the music of her voice until he spotted them. He gestured to the rest, one wave of a hand with his fingers curling inward like the delicate choreography of a ballet.

Clara and Fernando ran to the Ferris Wheel. They wove around a group of children chasing balloons toward the promenade. The panic in Clara's bones cooled her blood until she was certain icicles were forming in her veins. The suits were gaining on them, but they ducked under the arms of an elderly couple holding hands, and from the other side, Clara saw the suits were lost. But then the one who could only be their leader stopped in the pathway and looked above the faces and heads of those around him, cold eyes straight on Clara's.

Her hand squeezed Fernando's in fright. "He saw me!"

Fernando stole a glance over his shoulder, a short curt word slipping from his lips as he yanked back the rope past the turnstile of the Ferris Wheel, urging Clara to slip under first. Clara's breath shortened as she moved as quickly as she could, not bothering to see who on the Midway might be watching or pointing or calling to a nearby guard. Her heart was pounding in time with the rhythm of the fair's chaos like she were a conductor and Chicago an orchestra performing a symphony of madness.

Up close, the Ferris Wheel seemed much more ominous than Clara had initially thought.

"It's all right," Fernando assured her once they were safely stowed away in the shadows of the ride. "We're only hiding here. I promise you, it won't move. And even if it did, it's as solid as iron. I worked on this thing myself."

Clara thought of the peristyle and how she'd met this very same boy at the top. And yet the Ferris Wheel was so much bigger. "Is that so?" Her voice teetered on annoyance. "How were your math grades in school, Fernando?"

"Perfect," he quipped back, no jostling smile now when panic surely rattled his bones. Suddenly, his hand gripped hers more tightly. "Clara," he said in worry.

The deep browns of Fernando's eyes were flush with fear and staring over her shoulder. Clara turned. The suit was storming toward them, no expression on his face—no anger, no determination, not even the mildest bit of irritation. Clara loosened a frightened gasp. This man was charging toward her and Fernando as though they were prey.

"Go!" Clara ordered, pulling Fernando into the first car of the Ferris Wheel, a great big space with benches that would let a few dozen fairgoers watch the clouds.

As soon as they'd dashed inside, Fernando grabbed her arm and pulled her against the wall of the car. A desperate attempt to hide, Clara knew. But useless.

"He's already seen us," she breathed. She didn't understand

the chaos that had found them, the target Fernando had been. Her foot inched backward until there was no more ground in the car at all—only air. She gasped at the empty space—a window to her left which hadn't yet been barred with a railing—and clutched Fernando's hand tightly.

Fernando tilted his head to look out the window, down to the Ferris Wheel's turnstile. Clara ducked her head beside his shoulder and likewise watched.

The suit sauntered closer to the turnstile, a well-manicured hand with a polished silver band on his pinky smoothing the lapels of his silk suit. That predatory glare vanished for amusement, pleasure, intrigue. He looked like a wolf that enjoyed the thrill of the chase.

"Come out, boy. Come out without a scuffle, and I'll make sure the girl goes free. You have my word. No scene. No calling the officers strolling the promenade." The words were honey-coated venom.

Fernando squeezed his eyes shut and rested his head against the wall, like he might be anticipating the worst but praying for deliverance from it. His lips moved in the shape of another curt word Clara knew very well from the pastor at St. Bernadette's.

The suit's eyes raked over the entire Ferris Wheel, like perhaps he truly didn't see where she and Fernando had hidden. Like they had the advantage, and not him. There were so many cars, and even though they were limited to how many were close to the ground, perhaps they could wait out the suit. Confidence buoyed Clara's strength, enough that she was a split-second away from squeezing Fernando's hand to reassure him the worst was nearly over.

Until the suit's face turned back into that of a hungry wolf's. Until his cold eyes seemed to find hers in an impossible way, like the entire time he knew exactly where they'd gone, and this was a wolf who liked to play with his food. His bone-white hand reached for a long lever by the turnstile and gripped it. Clara flinched as his fingers curled, one by one. The long, scratching churn of a clutch soon followed.

The wheel lurched.

Clara clasped her hand over her mouth and fought back a scream.

Fernando pressed against the wall of the car. "Jesus, Mary, and Joseph," he whispered brashly.

Clara righted herself properly and glanced again out the window.

The wheel moved.

The suit leapt toward the car as it lifted off the ground. His polished black shoes landed perfectly in front of them, and he narrowed his eyes on Fernando and then Clara. He stilled, unaffected by the swing of the ride.

The wheel swayed.

Then it swayed a little more.

Clara's frame bolted forward as the quiet rumble of an engine sounded, moving the car. She gasped and steadied herself.

"Now, now," the suit scolded gently. He took a step closer. Then another. Fernando dropped Clara's hand so he could stretch his arm in front of her. But the suit merely laughed. "Enough of that. I have no time for children's games."

His lip curled on the last word, and without any warning, he lurched forward, fingers like claws grasping for Fernando.

"Fernando!" Clara screamed. Futilely, she grabbed his arm and pulled, as though that could save him from the suit. But then her foot found that empty space of air again. Clara dug her nails into Fernando's arm. Her weight shifted. As the suit with his tobacco-scented threads seized Fernando and threw him against the opposite corner, Clara was forced to drop Fernando's arm. Horror clenched at her throat as she found herself falling from the moving Ferris Wheel. Her eyes widened, and her arms reached for anything that would save her.

She screamed.

"Clara!" Fernando shouted.

Clara's arms slammed on to the steel floor of the car, and she clung to it desperately. There were no rivets she could dig her nails into for leverage, but there were beams holding the structure of the car together, and her hands flailed to grab hold, moving so quickly, she was certain time had stopped.

Her grip was like vices around two beams, and the world rushed back. Her legs dangled from the Ferris Wheel's climb toward the sky. The cool May wind bit at Clara's skin, raising goosebumps over the back of her neck and arms. Her teeth chattered, but relief took her. She was alive—she hadn't fallen to her death.

Do not let go, she ordered herself. *You will not die this way.*

She glimpsed Fernando in the far corner. He scrambled to stand, but the suit divided them.

"Clara! Hold on!" Fernando shouted, and Clara realized he'd shouted it more than once by now. *Was this how he'd felt on the peristyle?*

The suit's fingers curled around the collar of Fernando's shirt and tightened. "You're dawdling, aren't you, boy?" he growled. "We don't like it when those with a job dawdle."

Clara's fingers numbed around the beams. *Help. Help.* She focused on Fernando—his eyes big and dark and just as terrified as she felt, like if Clara were to drop, he might consider diving after her.

"She's going to fall!" Fernando screamed as he fought against the suit. *"Get out of my way!"*

The suit tossed Fernando against the wall of the car, and he fell with a wince and a groan. In a flash, the suit's icy hands were around Clara's wrist, yanking her grip free of the beams and lifting her high. Not to safety, and not onto the floor of the car, but over the edge, with not even a beam to save her were he to let go.

Sweat drenched Clara's brow. She squeezed her eyes shut as she prayed for the wheel to stop moving. But it couldn't. A smart girl could very well figure a motorized ride would only stop once someone pushed down on that horrible clutch that had started this whole thing. In one rotation before sweet solid ground, a lot could happen. Perhaps the patrons on the Midway Plaisance would think this was yet another routine check before the Ferris Wheel would actually open. Perhaps they'd think this was a show for their delight and amazement.

Perhaps no help was on its way.

An icy breeze hit Clara's skin as the wind stirred up plans of its own.

Clara imagined she were home, knowing nothing of all this. Home with her mother, warm arms tight around her shoulders, the clean soap Bethany Banks used to wash her hair. Gentle sobs tugged at Clara's throat, and though she wanted to appear brave against this suit who held her life in his hands, Clara stopped caring and let the tears fall.

"She's afraid," the suit said in a low growl, and Clara opened her tear-swollen eyes to his. He spoke in a way that made her feel invisible. "And why wouldn't she be? She knows she's just one drop from the end of all this." He whispered the last part, leaning close as Clara clambered for something to stand on.

"Jesus," Fernando begged, exasperated. "Just let her go. This has nothing to do with her. Wrong place, wrong time. This is about me."

Clara forced herself to look upon Fernando. His eyes avoided hers purposefully, and his jaw clenched in the same way it had when she'd caught him in Machinery Hall, her father's angry glare on him because he'd found an intruder.

"You're right," the suit replied. "It's about what must happen if all is to be saved. It's about *you*. The deal you have yet to fulfill."

Clara watched Fernando swallow as her body shook in midair. She clasped her hand around the suit's arm—steel or bone. She saw in Fernando an admission of guilt. Proof of shame.

"It must be dismantled, boy," the suit continued. "None of it can happen come sundown."

Clara's eyes widened on Fernando's. The flicker of the light-bulbs in Machinery Hall brightened her memory as clearly as the sun. *He'd been there for the lights,* she told herself. He *had* been breaking in.

But why?

Fernando straightened. "What do I have to do for all of this to stop?" Each word was a heavy sword he fell on a thousand times. "Please."

Clara curled away from the suit as his eyes gleamed with victory. "There's a boy standing at the bottom of the wheel. Beside the turnstile. I believe he works on the fairgrounds."

Fernando took a breath. He peeked down without an ounce of fear like he'd climbed mountains his entire life and never feared the danger of heights. "He does."

"Good," the suit crooned. "Tell him to let us off after this circuit. I'll set this girl back inside, where she'll be safe. You'll go with me as we exit the Ferris Wheel. A gentleman's promise."

Clara gritted her teeth. *You're no gentleman,* she thought. *Monster.*

She thought of the skeletons in Machinery Hall, of the effervescent suit that had nearly captured Marta forever, and then she wondered just how true that declaration was. Because if to become a suit was to become a monster, what did that mean for her father?

She forced the thought away.

The loud bravado of President Cleveland echoed through the city from the Court of Honor, and to roaring cheers, he moved toward a small box on the stage and flipped on a switch. Fountains sprang to life, raining their dances in the Grand Basin to the delight of all. A subtle yellow glow churned from each part of the Court of Honor, as though the sleeping stars had fallen, catching in the white plaster of each building—Ancient Rome or Greece reborn on the same shores of Chicago that Clara had known her entire life. The air sang with magic.

Maybe I've already died. Maybe this is what Heaven looks like. The world coming alive in front of you.

The wheel lifted a bit higher, and with every foot, Clara watched as the black and white of the fairgrounds—all of Chicago—vanished for muted color, pastels peeking through the gray clouds like springtime were not quite as distant as the chill of the city promised. She told herself to focus on the peace of the world. She told herself not to show any fear.

But Clara Banks had never been very good at taking orders.

"Well, Fernando?" the suit continued, his tight grip loosening around Clara's wrist. It drew a pained gasp from her lips. "It takes no effort to let someone fall. They'd call it a tragic accident, not unlike that which you've seen before, I wager."

Fernando's eyes darkened with hatred.

The suit's smile crawled across his mealy cheeks like a painter pulling a brush across canvas. "The wheel is on its descent. Tell that scrappy boy at the bottom to stop it when this car reaches the ground. Get off the ride and follow me. Anything less than that will loosen my grip from this girl's hand."

The hot tears on Clara's cheeks turned to ice with the wind, and her body fluttered like a feather.

Fernando shut his eyes and leaned out the window. "Hey! Jason!"

"Fernando?" called back a boy no older than fifteen. "What are you doing up there? Who started the wheel?"

"Long story," Fernando called back down.

"*No* story," the suit corrected.

Clara could feel the skin around her wrist stretch as her weight pulled her toward the ground. A sharp pain traveled from her fingertips all the way to her shoulder, her tendons stretching with every passing second. Her breathing grew labored, and she knew Fernando saw that pain.

"Stop the wheel when this car hits the ground!" Fernando called.

"You got it!" the boy called back.

The suit lifted his chin. "Wise decision." Then, without warning, he tossed Clara back inside.

She landed on the unstable floor, and a shock of pain electrified her bones. The car wobbled unsteadily, but even with the risk of falling, Fernando slid on his knees toward her and took her into his arms. She sucked in breath after breath as her hands climbed his chest until she could clasp them around his neck.

You're all right, she told herself. *You're alive.*

Fernando pulled her into his lap, two shaking hands around her face as he stared into her eyes. Words hung in midair between them. A hundred thousand questions desperate to spring free, she knew, but none of them would. Giving in to defeat, Fernando settled on tightening his arms around her body and rocking her in sheer relief.

"Jesus," he finally whispered against her neck. "I'm so sorry."

"I'm all right," she whispered back. "I'm here."

A soft thud sounded as the wheel completed its circuit, and

the door rattled open. A wide-eyed boy stood there and brushed a hand over his dark hair. His eyes narrowed, and Clara imagined how all of this must look. A terrified girl in the arms of one of the workers. Both of them with equal looks of fright, though only one with tear-stained cheeks. And then a suit with cold eyes and a wolfish disposition straightening his tie.

"Fernando?" the boy asked.

Fernando pulled away from Clara. His gaze changed from worried to defeated in a matter of seconds, a devastating thing to see in such dark and beautiful eyes.

"Fernando, what happened—" she began.

He unraveled his arms from around her waist and helped her stand. She swallowed her question. She knew what was to come.

"This way," the suit said, beckoning them to follow him out of the Ferris Wheel car.

Clara's hand warmed in Fernando's, even as his fingers twitched nervously. Together they walked off the Ferris Wheel, past the suit and a bewildered Jason, to the shadowy sanctuary of the turnstile. There, Fernando stopped, out of earshot of both, though the suit's gaze lingered.

Clara had heard the deal made in the middle of the sky. The one that ensured she'd never fall from the Ferris Wheel to her death. But now, she refused it. "I won't let you go alone with him."

Fernando's eyes softened. "Clara—"

"No," she said. "I won't leave you." She felt the weight of those words, like in the sky with his arms around her, there'd been something to tie them together.

Fernando searched her. "Leave it alone," he told her. "Please." He glanced over her shoulder, and Clara turned to follow his line of vision. On the Midway, ribboning toward them between a thousand people, was Sally Carter.

Sally.

Clara's heart lifted in joy. She dropped Fernando's hand to wave. It caught Sally's attention, and Sally responded with a grin of delight. But then Clara's heart sank just as quickly. Her other hand was tied up in Fernando's, and Clara didn't want to let go.

"Come with us," she told him, a quick glance at the suit waiting in the shadows of the Ferris Wheel. Her lip quivered with worry, but she chased it away. "There are enough people on the Midway that we could easily lose the suit. At the very least, if we're caught, no harm will come. Not with the Exposition guards patrolling. Right?" A flat and unconvincing voice. Hundreds of suits patrolled the Midway, too, at any given moment. If she were to find one in the crowd, there'd just as soon be ten more behind him. But desperation was not always rational. "Fernando, please."

Fernando shut his eyes and opened them again. Their warmth had vanished, and in its place now shone hard resolve. "This has nothing to do with you, Clara. You think you know what happens when you work on the fairgrounds? You don't. You don't know what this life is like. Don't pretend like anything you could come up with now wouldn't put me into any more trouble than I'm already in."

Clara stepped away. She waited for any brute anger to strike from his words, but none came. Try as Fernando might, he could not summon up enough fury for Clara to think he'd turned cold against her.

But words could always be used in a million other ways.

"Go, Clara," he said again. "I don't want you here."

Fernando dropped her hand and turned, not even a glance over his shoulder as he walked toward the suit who set his arm around Fernando's shoulder like a father might.

Clara watched them go.

"Clara?" Sally tugged at her sleeve, and through the tears clouding her eyes, Clara faced her. Sally was there—she hadn't found any danger on Bynum Island, and in utter relief, Clara pulled her close so she could kiss Sally's cheek.

"I'm so very happy to see you," she whispered.

Sally pulled away. "Me too, Clara Banks. Especially since I've discovered where the monsters are hiding."

CHAPTER 22

A Disappearing Act

Fernando barely registered the heavy hand on his shoulder.

Not even the pinch of two bony fingers was enough to distract him from the hurt in Clara's gray eyes before he walked away with the suit in a manner he hoped would deter her from following.

It had worked.

The world and all that was in it—the Columbian Exposition that promised to dazzle and amaze—slowed as suits appeared out of nowhere, each walking alongside the one who'd chased him and Clara onto the Ferris Wheel. Escorts, not guardians. Watchdogs, not security. Monsters, surely, instead of men.

They were leading Fernando farther away from the Court of Honor on the fairgrounds proper—including Machinery Hall, which meant it was dire. If they weren't taking Fernando directly to the place where he was supposed to complete his job for Rex Winston, then where were they taking him?

"This way, boy," the suit crooned, the cruel and cold words he'd used on the Ferris Wheel locked in Fernando's memory

when glitz and adventure now surrounded them on the Midway.
"This way."

The suit's fingers curled deeper into Fernando's shoulder and
led him toward a tent whose waving front flaps beckoned like the
flick of a wrist. A tent Fernando recognized from the minutes of
chaos when suits had been following him and Clara. A tent
they'd inadvertently raced inside, calling more attention to themselves than they'd ever hoped to, with a man of magic named
Houdini standing on the humble beginnings of a stage in front of
them.

The heavy cloth curtains swayed across Fernando's shoulders
as the suit urged him inside. A hum of firelight flickered in the
shadows against the dark fabric. Fernando had to commend the
magician for the tense yet mystical atmosphere, especially since
the captivation on each audience member's face clearly indicated
his illusions were more than simply amazing.

Houdini stood on the stage, any words he shouted out to the
crowd lost in an indecipherable cloud of noise. The suit led
Fernando toward the back of the tent, where a long row of men
smoking woodsy pipes and cloudy cigars sat in their rich black
linens, an occasional hand pushing back pomaded hair. These
were the rich, escaping the prestige and showmanship of the
Court of Honor for a bit of Midway fun, chattering and
gesturing to the stage as the day's brandy shaped their words into
whatever deemed appropriate.

At the row's end sat a man Fernando recognized. Here in
Houdini's tent, Rex Winston stood out painfully. His white skin
didn't reflect the candlelight as much as it transformed it into a
shade of stone. Although he watched with intrigue as Houdini
vanished rabbits and cuffed his wrists together, it was a quiet sort
of interest—not the intoxicated, obnoxious demeanor the rest of
Chicago's rich boasted, enough to call attention to themselves in
the whole tent.

An empty chair waited beside Rex Winston.

The suit slipped behind Fernando, and when Fernando glanced back, the suit had already left.

Rex Winston kept a steady gaze on the stage, never acknowledging Fernando's presence—not even a gesture of the hand to sit.

"Fernando," he finally said.

Fernando swallowed carefully and stared at the empty chair beside Winston. Was it meant for him? Was it being kept empty for someone else? He asked himself question after question—frightened enough to analyze the grain of the stained wood it was if only that would mean respite from his fear—and ordered himself to dismiss the sharp tickle fluttering up his neck, raising the hairs there. But he knew it was a sign that dug into his intuition. There would be trouble. More specifically, trouble had already found him.

Fernando had always had very good intuition.

"I'd expected you this past weekend," Winston said. "At least to stop by for tea so you could catch me up on any last minute happenings."

Winston was wearing his Sunday best despite the warmth of the day now that the sunshine was peeking through the clouds. The lines to his dark blazer were pinstriped, and the dusty gray of his tie was soft, creamy, elegant. A sharp contrast to the navy square peeking out of his breast pocket. His skin gleamed against the black of a bowler cap, heavy over his eyes like he wished to remain in the shadows wherever he stepped. The crystal-light of his irises pierced right through Fernando.

"Instead, I had to seek you out myself." Winston's eyebrows rose in disappointment. "You made an old man give up a restful morning to come find you."

An announcer in a flashy costume took to the stage and rallied the audience's applause as Houdini slipped behind the curtain. "You have seen how the magnificent Harry Houdini is not of this world! Indeed, he has just cut a woman in half and put her back together again! Not only that—he has made an entire man vanish straight from this stage! Are you ready to be even more astonished?"

The crowd erupted in ferocious and gleeful roars. Fernando searched their faces and wondered if any of them had ever heard of St. Joan's and how Lily had said girls would disappear as easily as this magician's tricks. He wondered if illusions were nothing more than jabs at the horrors forgotten in Chicago.

"Sit," Winston now ordered in a low voice. "You are not on trial."

Fernando took the chair beside Winston, but no matter how he positioned himself, comfort seemed impossible. He prayed to his saints for more time. "It wasn't my intention to keep you waiting, sir."

Mr. Winston cocked his head as though listening for a faraway sound. "I don't hear it anymore. Strange, isn't it? The Ferris Wheel. The ornament of sorts meant to save the fair's finances. It's no longer running?" He leaned closer with an awareness in his eyes that told Fernando he was not stupid. "Curious. I thought I saw a pair of lovers sneak onto it, hand in hand. I swear it spun slowly. One lonely round."

Fernando shuddered, but ignored the gentle allusion to Clara. "There's still work to be done. It won't be open for a few weeks." The words felt lifeless. Practiced and hard.

A gilded sarcophagus stood in the center of Houdini's stage, easily three feet taller than the magician. Houdini gestured to the grand coffin and helped a man from the audience stroll inside before locking him in. The suits beside Fernando murmured to each other, words too low for anyone else to hear. They spilled their brandies over the edges of their tumblers. Heckles rose from the audience—jokes and laughter meant to jostle Houdini—but

Fernando watched as the magician's focus narrowed on the sarcophagus.

Each wooden slot of the door was tight around the man—all three panels perfectly in place. The head was the last to be covered, as though Houdini yearned to draw out the suspense. Fernando glanced sideways at Mr. Winston. The older man was immersed in the show, a long slow tap of fingers on the armrest of his chair indicative of his calm.

The roars of the crowd seemed to lessen as Fernando lost himself in thought. The firelight of Houdini's tent dimmed. Wild and thunderous applause shook the ground, and Fernando knew somehow the magician had pulled off his caper. But it didn't matter. Not when he was minutes away from being ordered to destroy the very real and scientific magic of the fair to repay his debt.

Or maybe not.

Fernando's hands tightened into fists. The rich men around him laughed harder at their own incredulity, shaking their heads as they gulped their brandies. Fernando hated them. Their easy lives and how they pulled the strings of those in Chicago not unlike the magician in front of them.

But there was something Fernando could do to make sure the castle of Chicago's finest all came tumbling down. If he did nothing—if he refused to abide by Mr. Winston's wishes, what would happen then?

"I could walk," he said, calling on all bravery inside him to reinforce his strength. "I could pay you back, bill for bill. Penny for penny. Or I could abandon ship. Work on a traveling show after this fair until I make enough money to get myself to California." Fernando stared at Winston's narrowed eyes. They glinted as they watched. "There's a lot of money to be made out west. I don't need you, Mr. Winston. I don't need to be involved in whatever scandal happened in Machinery Hall the night I went there on your behalf."

But if Winston ever caught Fernando's accusation—if Winston ever *knew* Fernando suspected he was involved in something ominous—there wasn't even as much as a blink to indicate so.

"Scandal at Machinery Hall? A ragamuffin group of vandals, surely, is what you saw. Nothing to do with me or mine, and you can ask anyone at The Cat's Whisker that. They'll verify it, boy. An initiation is set to occur into our world come sundown tonight, and these things take much preparation." The ghost of a smile on someone who'd long since forgotten how to do so properly graced Winston's lips, but though skepticism had found Fernando, he decided against questioning that. "As such, on Thursday night, I was quite busy."

More ferocious applause rattled the tent, and Mr. Winston stared solemnly at Fernando as he reached into his pocket, withdrawing what looked like a telegram.

"There is a way for you to stay in Chicago, Fernando. A way that would ensure it, certainly. A way that, if completed, would lead you to a life that would quench that hunger that longs for something you cannot name just yet." His voice was loud, like there was no conflict. And then, "A message from your mother."

For what felt like an eternity, Fernando stared at the bit of folded paper. The words rushed at him again in a way that said Winston had given Fernando's position much thought.

"My mother?" was all Fernando could manage. "She wouldn't have written me."

Unless it was something bigger than the family betrayal Fernando had left behind in Brooklyn.

Fernando saw his own fright reflected in the sheen of Mr. Winston's contented eyes. "Nothing to worry about. If it were something dire, she would have mentioned that." He left the truth open for interpretation in the silence that came next.

The crowd applauded again, but Fernando did not know what magic Houdini had accomplished this time. Nor did he care.

"Please, sir," Fernando said softly, reaching for the small bit of paper. "I'd like to read it." Because there was little chance this was a bluff. Not a powerful man like Rex Winston, who could turn the world on the pinky of his left hand with nothing more than a nudge.

Winston cocked his head as though internally questioning whether to oblige, and for a half second, Fernando expected Winston to pocket the folded paper, an unspoken order to follow through with sabotaging the fair before he'd get the chance to read a single word.

It didn't happen—Mr. Winston gave Fernando the telegram, and Fernando gripped it like it were a Gospel reading. A strange thing—only a bit of paper and ink, really, with an address typed at the top. This was not written in Imogen Carolan's own hand. The careful swoops and swirls of her cursive had not graced this correspondence. The bottom did carry her initials, but once he read the message, Fernando heard the cadence of her voice and the Irish inflection of her words.

> Second payment impossible now. My husband
> needs another month to replace our son on the site.
> We've already suffered enough.
> Have mercy, sir.
> I.C.

Fernando frowned. This message was not for him. He reread

the top of the telegram and saw whom it was meant for: **Mr. Rex Winston.**

"Your parents' construction company has lagged in recent months, isn't that true, Fernando?"

Fernando stared at the telegram.

"Owning fifty percent of Teaghlach Construction Ltd. offers me certain privileges. Books, accounting—these sorts of things. I have to make sure my investments are profitable, naturally. It would be an utter shame to have to withdraw my support. Or sell. After that terrible accident? I'm the only thing now keeping your family's livelihood afloat. Otherwise? Tsk, tsk. So much liability. So many lost jobs. So many men out of work."

Fernando's blood boiled as he imagined his father, one of the brightest men he'd ever known, sitting in the armchair in his living room and wondering how to buy tea for their dinners or jam for their breakfasts.

"It really wouldn't take much, truthfully. All that's been keeping me as a benefactor to Teaghlach Construction is loyalty."

A second payment? Fernando wracked his brain for something that would click, but only one thing did. Slowly, the pieces began to fall into place.

"They're still paying you for bringing me to Chicago." Shame warmed his skin. "I thought the envelope I gave you when I arrived was everything."

Mr. Winston's eyes bore into his. "Not nearly enough for a turn-of-the-century world's exposition and the cost of living that creates. Come on, dear boy. You must be smarter than that."

Fernando's shame turned to anger. "You said my debt would be forgiven."

"Yours, not theirs."

Fernando stared at Mr. Winston. Long enough that the entire Houdini show of magic vanished, melting into the crisp black suit on the old man's back. Fernando wondered if hatred could be felt on the same level as love—deeply inside the bones—and wished the entirety of it upon Mr. Winston. He imagined his mother at the telegram office, dictating one word at a time to send along to Chicago. A bitter part of him wanted to know what sort of humiliation Imogen Carolan had felt at such a moment. Fernando had wanted to hate them for the hardship that had fallen upon their family, but now, even more, he wanted to save his parents from this. And the longer Fernando stared Mr. Winston down, the fewer memories of this benefactor occupying his own childhood Fernando truly had.

It was Mr. Winston who broke the silence. "It'd be a real tragedy for them to face sheer destitution. Poor houses. I suppose we'll see how things turn out, though."

A warning. A curse. A threat.

A fire rose up inside Fernando. He wanted to seize Mr. Winston's crisp white collar and throw him across the row of rich men until the stink of brandy soiled his suit. But propriety kept Fernando in place. Propriety ensured he would be a willing participant in Mr. Winston's desire for sabotage. Even if it'd mean lowering himself to the same savage cruelty those who ran the world took part in.

"I don't think that will happen," Fernando replied calmly.

A message. A promise. A concession.

"You don't, now?"

"No." Fernando clenched his fists at his side. "Because people have a way of paying their debts in full." He yearned to ask *Why me? Why not some other fool you could con instead?* But he had no strength to utter those questions.

Or maybe he did—maybe Fernando had spoken without realizing it.

"Everybody has a purpose, Fernando, and if you'd only look past today, into the future, you'd see that yours is to be a hero. A savior of the fair. An emblem of Chicago, perhaps. Imagine what fortune awaits!"

Fernando remembered the soirée he'd interrupted on his first night in the city. Silk and liquor mere feet away from him and yet so much farther than he could ever reach on his own.

"People most certainly do have a way to give back to the world—don't call it a debt. But a *gift*." Winston reached for Fernando's hand and squeezed it in a firm handshake. His fingers were cold, and they chilled Fernando. Then Winston sat back in his chair, a cloud wafting over him as though this illusion of his were now past. "Enjoy the fair, Fernando. It promises to be a good day for us all."

The crowd burst into awed applause highlighted with cheers.

"Did you see that?"

"Houdini made that man disappear!"

The same suit from the Ferris Wheel appeared again. He gestured to the path. The cue was clear, and Fernando stood, following the suit out of the tent and onto the Midway. He touched his face as the fresh air cut through the stench of brandy. He wanted to remember how Clara had run her fingers down his cheeks when he'd pulled her into his arms on the Ferris Wheel, but instead, all he felt was the hollow of a face with no skin or flesh—only the chipped surface of a skull, as plain as day.

It didn't matter anymore. The road to a better future was paved with dishonorable intentions, ones Fernando was sure he could eventually live with.

He tore off down the Midway Plaisance toward Machinery Hall.

CHAPTER 23

FLASH

"Broken hearts slow the feet."

It was a strange expression Clara's mother had once told her, one conjured from a long line of old wives' tales trailing as far back as her family tree went, but it was only once Clara ran with Sally that she truly understood it. Because Fernando's cold words had finally stung in a way that had made her unable to move or breathe until Sally pulled her along.

"Come along, Clara." A kind and soothing order, like Sally had known there had been feelings blossoming in Clara's heart for the boy on the Midway, the boy who'd held her like he loved her atop the Ferris Wheel after a brush with death.

"You never made it to Marine Café, Sally," Clara said. "What happened? Why did you stay at the clubhouse?"

Sally's brown eyes gleamed with zeal. "I had an epiphany, and that epiphany needed time at Château Perle to develop into a moment of sheer eureka."

"Epiphany?" Clara questioned. "On Bynum Island! Don't you know how dangerous that was? I was worried sick, Sal! And who knows about the rest of the girls now!"

"Oh, don't you worry," Sally called back. "I've seen many of the girls since I got to the fairgrounds. All Alouettes accounted for. All but Marta and Lily, but everyone knows that's because they never finished their essays, and Headmistress made them stay at St. Joan's until every last word was written."

Clara whistled in a sympathizing tone and remembered how Kimiko had come to collect Lily and Marta from Château Perle. "Glad I finished mine last week."

"Me too," Sally replied. "Now they've missed the opening ceremonies, and Headmistress had to open St. Joan's on every-one's day off. I bet she's just as sore as they are."

They reached the Terminal, the first Alouettes to arrive at what Clara assumed was a meeting place. She tucked a dark tendril behind her ear. "Then what is all this? What did you find?"

Sally grinned. "Let me show you." She reached into the pocket of her school blazer and pulled out a bit of folded newsprint. Clara had thought it was strange to wear their uniform on a day off, but with the ease of pockets, it made sense. "Take a look at that." She shoved it into Clara's waiting hand.

"I'll spare you my disappointment for destroying the Alou-ettes' newspaper collection." Clara unfolded the newsprint and read the headline along the crease at the top. " 'Girl disappears from downtown Chicago late last night. Last seen at The Dog's Whimper.' " She frowned. "This is dated ten years ago."

"Yes, I found it at Château Perle this morning. Now this one." Another folded newsprint, yellower than the first.

Clara ran her finger along the headline. " 'Couple goes missing from Jackson Park while heading home from The Hen's Feather. June 1857.' "

Sally's eyes gleamed. "They fit with the spiral, Clara. These are connected. I've made such a stupid mistake—we'd only been looking at the disappearances from St. Joan's, but there were others. There *have been* others who vanished in exactly the same way, all immediately after at least one St. Joan's girl disappeared. Like our girls spurred on the rest. That note of yours never actually specified *solely* Bynum Island—what if?"

Clara shook her head in confusion. "How does that help us today?"

Sally glared in a way that suggested utter disbelief. "Come on, Clara. Use that smashing brain of yours. What do those headlines have in common?"

Clara flipped both stories between her fingers. "People have gone missing."

"No. Read again."

Clara focused on the headlines and the entire story to see if there were secrets in the inked words. The noise of the fair went silent.

"They were last seen in the vicinity of pubs. Both of them." Clara didn't know how that was important, but there was a similarity, not to mention a familiarity to the syntax of what had undoubtedly been seedy taverns.

"Yes. And how can we further connect that to the fair?"

Clara thought of the World's Columbian Exposition and all she knew of it: the lights and monsters who'd lit them, monsters who then evaporated through only a touch of a lightbulb and then the flash of a Kodak. Her skin held the sensation of Fernando's arms around her on the Ferris Wheel while the Midway Plaisance expanded ahead of her. She could smell the fair's sugary food, see dancers wearing colors she'd never glimpsed before other than in dreams or fairy tales. She gazed upon the peristyle with Lady Liberty standing in the clear waters of the Grand Basin, laureled and proud. The German Village stood beside them, where suits of armor and fencing swords were ever-present, quiet symbols of antiquity in a world itching for progress. Clara remembered her footsteps following Fernando's as curiosity had overcome her and brought her to another adventure instead of a tour of the fairgrounds.

Her father had told her stories about everything the newspapers knew nothing about. How his frustration with the lawsuit between Westinghouse and Edison was causing more headaches than excitement, enough that one night, he couldn't even finish the halibut he'd ordered at The Cat's Whisker, and—

Clara gasped. "A traveling pub for the elite." *Father*.

Sally lifted her chin in victory. "One that might be changing its name over the years, at that. Almost as though it were a clubhouse in its own right. But no one knows where The Cat's Whisker is. Do you think they dispense invitations to a pub for the wealthy to just anyone? Heaven forbid." She stepped closer. "But you, oddly enough, are the only Alouette who has ever visited it. Isn't that the most ironic thing you've ever heard, new money? We have to find The Cat's Whisker. I don't know what'll happen when we do, but whatever lies inside could be the answer."

A distant call stole Clara's attention away from Sally. Marta and Lily were ambling toward them from the Promenade, Marta calling Sally's name in a way that sounded unsure. From the Terminal, Clara could make out plates of hotcakes in their hands drenched in thick maple syrup.

"We have to tell the rest, Sally," Clara said. She wouldn't forget how she and Sally were descendants of girls who'd gone missing before them but pushed the very idea of it aside. "Every Alouette needs to know about this if we're going to stop it from happening again."

Sally considered Clara's words, a gamble for sure. The more Alouettes in the know about the quest to solve this mystery, the more dangerous it would inevitably become. But Sally nodded. "All right. Blood to bone."

"And bone to ash," Clara replied.

The pale yellow cakes on Marta and Lily's plates were nearly gone once they arrived, the sweetness a heaven Clara longed to taste. But once their gazes settled on Clara, their whispering came to a halt.

"You two look like the most serious girls ever to eat hotcakes," Sally chided. "Hurry up and give me some. We have to talk. Where are the rest?" Marta handed over her plate of syrupy hotcakes to Sally, who took a bite with divine intent.

"Yes, we need to talk," Lily agreed in a low voice. "But let us go first. Before anyone else arrives."

Clara had a hunch this wasn't going to be good.

"What is it?" She told herself to be strong and remembered she was now part of their sisterhood of unstoppable girls. Her chipped-bone finger still ached from the initiation at Château Perle, but it was an ache Clara now appreciated.

"Clara," Marta began in an unsure way. "Do you remember the other night? I was fiddling with the Kodak, and I came across you and…well."

Marta gestured in a knowing way, and Clara knew instantly Marta was referring to the night under the willow tree when Fernando had held her and nearly kissed her. The part of Clara that longed for propriety over desire flooded her with the command to look away, to feel the slightest bit of shame for putting her arms around a boy's neck and holding him close, but Clara refused it and lifted her chin high.

"Spit it out, Marta. You can say it. You'd found me on Bynum Island only minutes before curfew in the arms of a boy who did not belong there."

Lily's eyes widened at Clara's words, and Sally glanced twice at her, a newfound respect in her eyes to match her smile.

Marta's cheeks warmed, but not because of what Clara had said—as Clara watched, unabashed by the truth her sisters now knew, she could see Marta might have been more ashamed she'd found it improper to begin with.

"Right," Marta conceded. "Yes. Then."

"Clara Banks, the newest of new money at St. Joan's, spending unchaperoned evening hours with a boy?" Sally's eyes darted to Lily's. "One of yours from St. Francis, I assume."

Lily held up her hands in protest. "I'll have you know I haven't been there in weeks. *Well* since before Clara became an Alouette."

Clara gestured to Marta. "Go on then. What is it?"

Marta elbowed Lily gently. There were pockets in Lily's skirt, and from one, she fished out a twice-folded photograph. "You should see this."

"I developed the photographs, Clara," Marta added. "After Headmistress's ridiculous, nay, *unreasonable* scolding, I went to the classroom to collect them."

Clara unfolded the picture and stared at its crisp scalloped edges. A slow bit of horror blossomed from her chest. On the night in question, there'd been a flash of light. The Kodak. Marta. She had easily caught the tender moment when Clara's eyes and Fernando's had bound to one another, their hands caught in each other's hair, their lips drawing dangerously close. Clara had to acknowledge Marta's skills. Despite the darkness of twilight, the portrait was graceful and lovely.

But it wasn't this about the photograph that had stirred a sullen mood in Marta and Lily. It wasn't even the possibility of scandalous societal consequences should anyone outside of St. Joan's see it. Reputation was not at stake here.

There was a figure behind Clara and Fernando—just a glimpse of one. Long and shadowy and not exactly human, its limbs pressed against the willow tree in a way that suggested it had been trying to hide from Clara and Fernando.

Clara squinted at it. "What on earth is that?"

She looked closer. *No*—it hadn't been hiding. The positioning of the hands and the curl of the body was all wrong. It looked as though it had been readying.

As though it'd been moments away from striking.

Curiously, though, that attack seemed to be more aimed at the vicinity of Fernando than Clara. Or was that simply the angle at which Marta had taken the photograph? Clara felt her eyes widen the longer she stared. There'd been a rustle of leaves, yes. There'd been something else on the island, almost exactly where Marta had nearly been stolen away. Where girls vanished without a trace.

Clara's great-aunt, Miranda, one of them.

She or Fernando might have been only seconds from disappearing next.

Her eyes welled with hot stinging tears that clouded her vision, and the entire photograph faded. Her skin cooled with fright, and her body shook just as it had on the Ferris Wheel, hanging a hundred feet above ground.

Was nowhere safe?

Clara blinked several times, traitorous tears ribboning down her cheeks. She tried to see the shadow in the photograph as anything other than the skeletons that'd been fiddling with the bulbs at Machinery Hall, but somehow, she just couldn't manage it.

"I didn't see anything at the time, Clara," Marta added. "I swear. It was just you and—"

"Fernando," Clara said, and strangely, his name crossing her lips made it sound sad.

None of the Alouettes spoke.

Sally shoved Marta's syrupy plate back into her hands. "Seems like an odd time for hotcakes with news like this."

Marta ducked her head, mildly ashamed. "There was a kiosk on the way, Sal. Be reasonable." She sneaked another bite.

Clara stared at the two people embracing in the photograph and covered the shadowy monster with one hand. She had never seen an image of herself before, and now she considered how the world saw her. She wasn't sure she liked it. Her face was vulnerable and afraid. This had certainly been how she'd felt in that moment, but this wasn't the Clara she wanted to be.

"There's more," Marta said. She glanced at the crowds spilling around them, ensuring no one else was paying attention. "That boy. Fernando. Do you know why he's in Chicago?"

Something worrying ignited inside Clara. "No," she admitted. "Just that he can't go home."

Marta glanced at Lily in a way that said it was time for Clara to learn the truth. "Antoine, the foreman at the Ferris Wheel. He heard from Dodger. We meet up on Fridays sometimes on the Midway for booze and cards." Lily seemed to be searching for the kindest words to say. "One time Fernando joined us, and he'd had some whiskey. I don't think the boy can hold his own that well. He didn't get sick or anything, don't worry, but I doubt he remembers what he told Dodger. And Dodger and Antoine… they're nice. They know what it's like to be at the bottom, so I don't think they've brought it up—"

"Oh, spit it out, Lil," Marta said.

"I will!" Lily responded. "Apparently, Fernando's parents work in construction in New York." She paused there, letting each word sink in. "One day, last month. There was a freak accident. Three men died. Steel beams fell from an enormous height in a way they never should have. But it didn't matter. It was concluded to have been safety negligence, and…" Lily's eyes dropped to her black shoes. "Their family's business never recovered, but instead of…God knows what, Fernando got into a fight with his parents and stormed out. His mother disowned him, but the damage was already done. Fernando could never go home because of…" Lily snapped her fingers three times as she searched for the story. "That accident. Something strange. Something they couldn't explain once they…"

Clara felt a knot forming in her throat as she stepped forward, taking Lily's hand in hers. "Lil? Please."

Lily's eyes turned sad. "His father got him work somehow at the fair as a ticket out of Brooklyn, even after he vowed never to speak to them again. And so now he's here."

The tears Clara had let well up seemed all so inconsequential now. Her eyes burned with bitterness as she strove to keep her composure.

"I didn't know that," Clara said, lifting her chin. "But it doesn't matter."

"Clara," Sally said with a shake of her head. "This is the world we live in, and a story like that attached to a boy like him…" She touched the edge of the picture in Clara's hands. "It'd be a scandal, the daughter of Westinghouse's rags-to-riches liaison courting a boy with a tainted past. It could ruin you."

Clara was never going to risk her own future for a boy—that had been determined long ago. But now she stood firm. Not because of Fernando or the memory of being in his arms on the Ferris Wheel. But because now she was more determined than ever to know the truth about the fair and the monsters in Chicago.

Especially one who'd had the gull nearly to attack her with her back turned.

She tore up the photograph and tossed the pieces into a trash bin. Then she faced the Alouettes and gathered a divine bout of courage inside her.

"Let the world do whatever it will," she said. "We have work to do." She nodded at Sally. "Tell them, Sal."

Sally's eyes widened with awe at the discarded photograph, but her excitement soon vanished for their mission. "All right. Whatever's been taking the girls from St. Joan's is going to try again today. With all of us at the fair, I can't imagine it'd be anywhere else, even if the rest had been connected somehow to Bynum Island."

Clara considered that part of Sally's speech. *But we can't rule out St. Joan's entirely, can we?*

"We have to find The Cat's Whisker," Sally continued. "It's our best lead to finding out what sort of monster wanders Chicago. It's supposed to be today. I double-checked the math—*triple*-checked it. I swear it's today or it's not at all."

Marta's eyes fluttered. "The Cat's Whisker? You mean the pub? But no one knows where that is. On purpose. How on earth are we going to find it?"

"My father is a member," Clara replied. "The tricky bit is that The Cat's Whisker moves every few days. We have a lead as long as we can find Jonathan Banks. If not him, then we have to get to Machinery Hall." She nodded at Lily. "You know someone who works there."

Lily nodded back, a quick salute enunciating her answer.

Marta's smile was bold. "Look at Miss Clara Banks, daughter to old Westinghouse's liaison. You've been holding out on us, new money."

Clara continued. "We have the chance to solve the mystery of the century today, but I can't promise it won't be dangerous. I wouldn't ask anything of you that would lead down a path you cannot follow."

Then Clara paused as humility come over her.

"But, speaking honestly for myself, I would prefer my sisters by my side."

The girls smiled. Sally nudged Clara. "Then it's decided."

Clara blinked. "What is?"

"Look. They've finally arrived."

Clara glanced across the Court of Honor. President Cleveland's opening ceremony had long since ended, and the platform they'd built to switch on the official telegram nonsense had been disassembled and taken elsewhere. Machinery Hall was only a short skip away, and a part of Clara wanted to rebel and seek the truth herself, but the memory of that night—shadows and sparks of white light humming from them as five or six workers gazed upon their glow—filled Clara with sick dread.

Then the crowd parted for several dozen girls Clara recognized from school. She grinned as they approached, waving at Sally and Marta and Lily, lemonades in hand and pearl rings shiny on their fingers. For a moment, Clara watched them unite, the smiling faces of girls who would always be sisters, whispering and laughing with each other. She knew she had made the right choice in enlisting the help of the Alouettes.

Then a flash of light froze Clara just as it had the night on Bynum Island with Fernando, and she startled. Past the Alouettes, in front of the Grand Basin, where titans of Chicago strolled amongst the families who'd saved for months for this momentous day, there was a photographer. One with a real and true Kodak. He was setting up his tripod in another spot, possibly for a better view of the crystal-blue waters and the fountains that danced upon them. Then he ducked underneath a velvet curtain to snap candid shots of history in the making.

The flash went off loudly, crackling the air like the violence of thunder.

Clara remembered the same bright lights and how they'd revealed skulls in the middle of a dark room. "The lightbulbs," she whispered. Her eyes widened. "The lightbulbs."

Sally frowned. "Clara? What is it? You look sick."

Clara shook her head, the Alouettes staring as they waited to hear the next step in the plan. "I'm not sick," she said. "I'm enlightened." She gathered her wits about her. "Marine Café on Wooden Island," she told the newly-arrived Alouettes. "Look for Jonathan Banks—he can help you find The Cat's Whisker!"

Something magical dwelled inside the light of the electric bulbs. Magic that could reveal everything.

"Sally, Marta, Lily—come with me!" Clara called next as she ran toward the Midway Plaisance. She heard three sets of footsteps behind her, each telltale of the sisters she'd asked to join her. They'd stayed with Clara—they were by her side.

They needed something that would capture the monsters straight in their tracks. Sally had said Headmistress was at the school today, which meant St. Joan's was unlocked.

"Where are we going?" Lily called ahead.

Clara Banks had never been a wicked girl, but today she was willing to bend the rules if it meant saving Chicago from the evil that lurked there.

"Back to St. Joan's," Clara called back. "We need the Kodak."

CHAPTER 24

THE RED LIGHT

FERNANDO RACED TOWARD A STRETCH OF LAND COVERED IN Japanese cherry blossoms. He dashed through the delicate petals the air teased into flight around signs pointing to exhibitions from each of the American states—California's massive tower of oranges, the ritzy banquet hall of New York, the Liberty Bell of Pennsylvania.

Warm maple syrup scented the Court of Honor, intensifying Fernando's hunger, and parasols dotted the promenade, elongating the distance still to go. Sunlight cascaded upon the Ferris Wheel and told him in a whisper it was approximately one o'clock. Plenty of time before sundown, but the electric lights he needed to kill taunted him with their presence. They hummed and flickered as he raced past as though there were life in the electricity that knew he needed it dead. He set a sweaty palm against his neck as he passed the Grand Basin. Fernando knew he should be amazed by the sight of its dancing fountains, but a hunger was growing inside him, one he wasn't sure he understood. Stronger and stronger ever since he'd left Mr. Winston on the Midway.

No—ever since Machinery Hall that night. With Clara and the magic of a simple lightbulb.

One day, one moment in Fernando's life he'd always thought of as being Out Of The Ordinary. That moment had transformed into a hazy dream over the years, but now, as he looked out at the Grand Basin's waters—so boldly hued they reminded him of penny taffy—it was as clear as day.

Viggo's shop in Brooklyn had been a necessary pit stop on the way home from Holy Mass with Juan García Díaz. Eight-year-old Fernando had grown hungrier and hungrier the longer he'd stared at the taffy that hadn't been his. And then came the *clack, clack, clacking* of expensive shoes, and the voice of someone with ulterior intentions.

Just take it.

Fernando had glanced over at his father pointing to the editorial section in the newspaper. *They must have printed Papá's letter,* he'd thought as Viggo nodded along while Juan García Díaz spoke of unionizing for fairer wages and how his own grandfather, Eduardo, had done the same sort of rebellion as a teenager against those in power back in Barcelona.

A better opportunity would never come. Fernando's hand had snapped forward and clamped around two sticky pieces of taffy and stuffed them into his pocket. He'd smiled at the ease of it, but as he clutched his candy in its hidden spot, he'd frowned. His fingers had grown stiff. The same feeling as whenever he'd fall asleep with his hand under his pillow.

Fernando slowed in the middle of the Court of Honor.

Christ, he thought. *I've seen it all before.*

That day, a tightness had found the skin on his hands and pulled as though muscle would tear free of bone. As gasp after gasp escaped his lips, the skin had shucked itself from Fernando's shaking hands, leaving behind only bone. He'd dropped the taffy onto the floor, leaping away with a scream. His father had turned to the stolen candy, and his fury had been laced with unbearable disappointment. Fernando could never look Viggo in the face after that.

Several days later, Rex Winston had left New York for Chicago.

A group of boys bumped into Fernando outside Buffalo Bill's Wild West show. "Hey! Out of the way!"

Fernando was brushed aside, shaken by the old and strange thought that suddenly seemed so clear. The boys stared back at him as they kept walking, pointing and laughing and straightening their silk threads.

"Must be a clown. Do you know anyone else who would have that sort of rubbish on their eyelids?"

"Throw him a penny, Thomas. See if he'll dance for us."

Fernando rubbed his eyes. The stickiness of Antoine's kohl was mixing with the sweat from Fernando's brow, and he was certain he looked a sight. But that couldn't matter. He tugged his newsboy cap lower over his eyes and moved onward.

A suit paced in front of Machinery Hall. A crony to someone wealthy. Fernando hesitated when the deep-set gaze of the man —more stone than human—fell to his.

"You must be Fernando," the man said, his voice smooth like silk, but dangerous like fire. He opened the door. "You've been expected."

The door opened to a cacophony of madness. Fernando jumped at the sudden clashing of metal against metal, the grinding of iron teeth penetrating a space whose glass ceiling remained remarkably unshattered by all. Machinery Hall had looked different at night with starlight fallen over the space like it'd wanted to tell a secret in the quietest way.

Now everything was wild and unleashed.

No one was there, but Fernando chalked it up to the truth that to be inside any longer than five minutes would be utterly maddening. The constant thumps and scratches rang through his skull and made his teeth chatter.

Finally, Fernando came upon the switch board.

He took a deep breath. "Dodge," he called.

From the top of a platform, Dodger turned, like he'd been inside so long the sounds of the hall had vanished entirely.

"Well, look who it is." Dodger was wearing the same bowler cap Fernando knew well, and he flicked it up to see Fernando better, rolled up the white sleeves of his shirt, and then faced the switch board again.

Fernando could tell Dodger had dressed up—not just from the suspenders, but also the gray tie, as though headed to a countryside wedding in the spring. The first day of the World's Columbian Exposition was a day worthy of everyone's very best. But how much of it had really been for Lily?

"Who sent you? Last week, it was that really young kid— Jeremy or Jason or something. Said unless I abandoned ship here and raced to the Midway in the next five seconds, the entire Ferris Wheel was going to collapse and crush a thousand people. I might have believed it if the new foreman had sent a better liar. I'm guessing that's you?" Dodger slipped the pencil from behind his ear and chewed it as he studied his work. "What do they need now?"

No words came from Fernando.

A moment later, Dodger glanced over his shoulder. "Cat got your tongue, Fernando? Or cat got your whisker? Couldn't have found it today." He winked.

"No, Dodge. It was Winston. Mr. Winston sent me," Fernando began, figuring the truth would set him free, even as a nervous tremor clung to his voice. "The electric lights." He searched for the right explanation, anything to make Dodger believe him. "Word is they're dangerous, Dodge."

Dodger narrowed his eyes then laughed. "Dangerous? Ha—

bullshit. They're as safe as Christmas pudding. I rigged this whole board myself. *These* bulbs are, granted, a bit shittier than General Electric's, but nothing to be done about that now. You afraid or something?" He gestured to Machinery Hall's front door. "Get out of this circus of a building and go take a look. The fountain's in full swing, and the lights are already sprucing up the courtyard. You'll see 'em better once the sun sets. They'll brighten like stars. And they're a hell of a lot safer than gas and fire." Then, to himself, "Christ Almighty. He thinks this is *dangerous*."

The churning of levers and engines permeated the atmosphere, monsters of steel coming alive. A rise of courage found Fernando, and he stepped past Dodger for the switch board. "No, Dodge. You don't understand—"

"Whoa there," Dodger said, blocking Fernando's way. "Let's not do anything we might regret."

He could see in the glint in Dodger's eyes that no one was getting on that platform, least of all him.

"Nothing up there for you to get your hands on. I promise you that. Step down."

But time was running out. "You don't understand. Mr. Winston ordered the electricity off," Fernando tried.

"I don't work for Mr. Winston. And neither do you, come to think of it. The hell are you doing? You're turning into a marionette for the suits." Dodger studied Fernando, and then his eyes fell again. "Wait a second. The Ferris Wheel isn't operational yet. You aren't on the clock today. What are—"

"Enough," came another voice.

It wasn't Rex Winston, the suit from the Ferris Wheel, or even the brute guarding the door. It wasn't anyone Fernando knew. But still he recognized the type of man—silk tie, crisp white shirt with more dollars behind it than Fernando's own life was worth, black shoes polished so well Fernando could see the desperation in his reflection's eyes. This was one of the many crawling the fairgrounds who worked for Mr. Winston. Fernando could spot it through nothing more than the clear bulk of the man's frame. His shorn head and ugly mug were enough to assure Fernando he had no qualms about getting violent if there was a need for it.

"Begging your pardon, sir. Welcome to Machinery Hall. Are you looking for Mr. Tesla's exhibit?" Dodger asked in his politest voice. He removed his cap and smoothed out his hair, a habit common amongst the working class whenever the elite approached. It was something Fernando himself couldn't stop even if he tried, and as that thought crawled over him, he found his own newsboy cap tight in his hands.

The suit came closer. "Not today." His cold glance found Fernando. "I'm here to vet Mr. García Carolan's claims that the electricity is to be disconnected."

Fernando could see in Dodger a fight between well-bred obedience to superiors and none at all. Dodger shook his head. "I'd lose my job, sir."

"Your job is to ensure the fair is the very best the world has ever seen."

"No, sir, begging your pardon," Dodger continued, relentless. Fernando admired his ferocity. "But you folks up in your towers don't exactly know how things are run down here, and now if you please, sir, I'll have to ask you to leave so I *can* do my job. Which is to make sure there's electric light in Chicago today."

Fernando held his breath as the burly man stepped closer to Dodger.

"Is that so?" the suit demanded.

Dodger's voice trembled. "Yes, sir. No disrespect. I simply need to attend to the switch board."

The man side-eyed Fernando. "You stand by this, boy?"

Fernando knew Dodger was doing the right thing. Tonight, Chicago would see a spectacle those of days prior could only ever dream of, a bit of magic on an otherwise normal spring day. But there was something strange or secretive or ominous about Mr. Winston's request Fernando could no longer deny. Something wrong. Storybook monsters had always been wholly evil, determined as such by a turn of dialogue that would make it perfectly clear This Person Was Of No Good.

The real world was gray and about to be speckled with yellow lights, little wads of fresh butter brightening more and more once the sun dipped below the horizon. And Fernando had no choice but to deny Chicago the spectacle that awaited.

"It's not just a matter of superiority, Dodge," Fernando admitted as the suit watched. "I already told you—the safety of the lights." The lie was thick on his tongue.

Dodger's face twisted. "There were hundreds of hours put toward making sure everything would be all right. They'll work *perfectly*."

"You're wrong. That's why they've sent word to stop them."

Small red flashes scattering across the switchboard illuminated brightly like a candlestick's dying embers. Even now, Fernando was drawn to the color.

"Please, Dodge," he begged, wanting Dodger to run and be saved from all this.

With a final look at the man in the suit, Dodger conceded and led them up the platform, where he gauged the console indicating how and if currents of electricity were actively flowing. Fernando's heart pounded with anticipation. He was nearly at the end, and if all went according to plan, Fernando would soon be debt-free.

"Go ahead then, boy," the suit ordered.

But then Dodger caught sight of something and froze, and Fernando glanced over.

And likewise went still.

The suit's hand pressed against the switch board as he waited for Dodger to cut the electricity. His palm had fallen over a small bit of glass covering one of the red lights, and the brightness of it shone through.

But it wasn't skin that revealed who this suit really was.

It was bone.

Fernando's eyes snapped up. The suit's gaze fell to the console and the bones resting on the incandescent light. Just as quickly, he tore his hand away. He straightened his tie, and—sinew by sinew—each bone transformed back to flesh.

Dodger shuffled on the other side of Fernando, moving his weight from one foot to the other. The air was tense, the anarchy of Machinery Hall fading somehow.

"Say, mister," Fernando said. "Why didn't Mr. Winston have you do this yourself? Why have you follow me instead? I'm sure you could have eventually talked some sense into Dodge here without me."

The suit snarled. "Rex Winston said you were a traitorous outcast from a city crawling with them. It has to be your blood on the console instead of ours unless we want to collapse into dust."

The suit lunged for Fernando, big thick hands reaching to strangle him, but Fernando jerked away in time.

"Fernando!" Dodger yelled.

The suit turned to Dodger next, and he, against the console and its flashing red buttons, readied his fists in mid-air but couldn't throw a punch through his terror.

Fernando slipped through the bars separating the platform from the ground. He turned back. The suit grabbed Dodger's jaw before Dodger could stop him.

He cupped Dodger's jaw with both hands.

And snapped his neck.

Fernando flinched. The sound was sharp, a pitch unlike any other, and it sickened him. The slow slump of Dodger's body to the platform came next. Revulsion came over Fernando, and he backed away from what he was seeing—praying to his saints it was only his imagination, that it wasn't really happening, that in a moment, Dodger would wake, stand, and kick the suit where it counted.

The suit crouched before Dodger and set a palm to his forehead like he yearned to feel the warmth of life leave Dodger's skin. Fernando's palms chilled, drenched in sweat. His body shook, and Machinery Hall vanished for a nightmare. The suit leaned closer to Dodger's body, the outline of his white head turning the same gray as Dodger's deadening skin.

Fernando gulped. "Hey!" he strove to shout. It came out as a crackle. "Hey!" Fernando tried again, louder now. "You killed him! Wh-why would you *kill him?*" His breath raced. The hall slanted as his head went light. Everything was turning upside-down, and he couldn't see straight.

The suit ignored him. Instead, his skull loosened itself of any skin. Fernando balked at the transformation, but he couldn't peel his eyes away. The heft of the suit's body vanished, and then the muscle. But the power within him stayed put.

Then the suit gripped Dodger by the temples and *pulled*—there was no other word for it, none Fernando could think of in English or Spanish. The suit drew something from Dodger's body, and Fernando watched as Dodger's skin seemed to shrink to nothingness.

No, Fernando thought. *Not while I'm here.* He rose, his legs unstable. "Get the fuck away from him!" He stormed toward the thing, a suit no more, and slammed into the skeleton it had become. The impact was harsh, blunt, and it sent a lightning bolt of pain up Fernando's side. They both flew off what was left of Dodger and onto the platform, and Fernando's heels against concrete backed him away from the suit.

The suit stared at the ground, shaking like he might be dazed. His claw-like fingertips scratched at the floor as he clutched the side where Fernando had barreled into him. Fernando's eyes widened in horror. He'd slammed straight into the monster and dented his rib cage, the bones now caved in with fashionable threads settled on top. This wasn't a human being.

"Stupid and disobedient. Just like Eduardo."

Fernando frowned, taken aback by the name. It rang inside his mind. His father's grandfather: *Eduardo.* He hadn't truly thought of that name since the night in the tent on the Midway, when Antoine had told him a story of monsters in Paris and how the very same name had slipped past their lips.

The suit's eyes went wild, and Fernando knew the reaction on his face was a book the suit could read well. "A bastard of a man, and his grandson is no different. The taste of salt ocean still lingers on my tongue—the only thing I can taste now after Eduardo and his reckless gang sent us straight into the sea." He snarled. "But not this time. No—this time, your family, *your blood,* won't stop our reign."

Fernando's breath caught in his throat. He scrambled to put together the pieces of everything the suit had uttered, but it remained a puzzle.

"I could have turned him into one of us," the man in the suit growled in a low voice as his body suddenly lifted with power. He gestured to Dodger's lifeless form. "If the anchor satiates her hunger in time today, you could become one of us, too."

Anchor? Fernando trembled.

Now the suit was the same sort of creature Fernando had seen with Clara that night he'd flat-out refused to believe. Dark, empty eye holes and teeth went on for way too long. Vertebrae heightened, stained with dirt or mud or age itself. But then with a morbid shake of the man's head, everything shifted back into place, and Fernando was staring again at a person.

Fernando backed away from the platform. Away from the creature and the forgotten remains of Dodger, now unrecognizable in a slumped-over pile of clothing, bones, and wrinkled gray skin.

"He was good. He was good, and you killed him." Panic twisted Fernando's insides, and the desire to cry clenched them like a vice. He could only think of how *kill* was the wrong word, when *evaporate* was so much closer.

"You fear the dark, boy, but you should really fear the light. That's where the truth in this world really hides." The suit struggled to stand, but when he did, he stretched an entire foot taller than he had been before. With a twist and a growl, the caved-in ribcage pulled back to its normal spot, concave and proper. "But enough of this violence that only begets more violence. Let's be civilized." He refastened a set of bone cufflinks at his wrists in a manner that felt kingly. "Shall we?"

"No," Fernando whispered. "The world needs to know."

Fernando inched toward the edge of the platform, ready to make a break for the front doors of Machinery Hall. He swallowed. He didn't know where the boldness inside him had come from.

"It's the light that does it, right? You can hide in the daytime, but once the sun sets, you'll be discovered through the incandescent bulbs. That's why I'm supposed to sabotage the electricity." Another step.

"If you don't, you'll create a panic in the city. Do you really want to be responsible for that? *Think.* It'd be the wrong way to go about it. Instead, work *with* us. The world doesn't need to know we walk amongst them. There's so much good we can do from the darkness."

"Like what?" Fernando inched around the monster with the front doors in sight. "You just *killed* a man!"

"But there are so many more we can *save*. We control the power in the city. The chance to make the world a better place is in our grasp! Imagine hunger abolished. Poverty. Imagine saving your parents from financial ruin."

Fernando's heart dove at the memory of Mr. Winston's telegram. He couldn't afford to help his mother and father, two people he loved more than anyone, two people he'd told he never wanted to see again. Anger burned inside Fernando, but the need to save them from distress was an even hotter fire flickering through that rage.

"The strong will rise, Fernando. They always do. It's a matter of whether you choose the winning side. Make the right decision before it's too late." The man's voice turned to honey. His appearance was no longer the horrid snarl Fernando had seen earlier, but the carefully-postured face of a man anyone would trust: handsome with caring blue eyes and a face that could easily offer genuine smiles. As though by killing Dodger, this monster now embodied him. "The anchor will consume by the day's end —she *has* to. Before her time runs out. Then you'll have your chance. Join us, boy. Join those who run Chicago."

A life-changing opportunity.

"The lights will brighten at nightfall," Fernando said very clearly, so nothing could be mistaken for compliance. "I'm going to make sure they do. And if you can't touch them, you can't stop them."

The suit glowered, his contagious and charming smile vanishing for another scowl, like a glamour let him shift between all the personas he'd ever stolen.

"Wrong choice."

The suit's arm slammed straight into a pair of gas lamps to the side of the switch board, and the impact sent the lamps' white-hot flames across the platform. Fernando growled in pain as spots of light clouded his eyes and stole his sight. And then, once the fires died, Machinery Hall fell to darkness—a darkness that was dangerous.

Fernando stumbled toward the doors with heavy footsteps following him in the middle of a gale of noise. With a panicked heartbeat, he scrambled away from the switch board as quickly as he could.

Until his foot hit something in the middle of the floor. Fernando felt the curved steel of it. It was the arc light Jonathan Banks had carried the night he'd caught Fernando inside Machinery Hall.

I'm off the path, Fernando thought. *I could hide.*

"Fernando! You know it's inevitable, boy!"

The footsteps were persistent. It'd only be a matter of time before he'd be in the monster's clutches.

But something jogged Fernando's memory. He blinked to ease his vision back and recalled the workstation with the foreman's tools.

With a ragged breath, he yanked open the drawers and ran his fingers through the pencils and wood shavings until his hand fell upon something familiar.

Something cold and solid and made with the promise of danger. His eyes pulled into focus, and the Remington came into view.

"Thank you," Fernando whispered to his saints.

The footsteps were mere yards away.

Fernando lifted the gun. It wobbled in his shaky grasp.

He thumbed back the hammer.

And pulled the trigger.

CHAPTER 25

GRIEF

THE BULLET STRUCK THE SUIT IN THE SHOULDER. THE RECOIL threw him back a few yards. He growled and curled over from the impact.

Fernando didn't know how an injury of that sort would affect most. But he did know one thing. In the case of a bullet wound, there should be blood.

There was no blood.

He dropped the Remington, which clattered onto the floor of Machinery Hall, and ran out the door. When no footsteps followed, he basked in relief. He pushed past the fairgoers and pressed onward—as far away from the Court of Honor as he could get.

He'd known there'd be a price to pay for the luxury of a debt-free youth, especially so soon after the collapse of his family's business. He'd known once he agreed to sell his morality, there'd be consequences. This was the way of the world, after all.

But he hadn't expected firing a gun at someone who was most definitely *not* human would become part of his budding repertoire of corruption.

Or, *saints*, losing a friend as it happened.

Fernando ran from the building where Dodger once worked and the promise of electrical magic now sprang to life. He needed to find the fastest way out of the fair. Come hell or high water—or street lamps full of electricity—Fernando was never going to follow through with the wishes of Mr. Winston.

To hell with his debt.

To hell with seeking a stable future amongst the giants of this city.

To hell with the World's Columbian Exposition.

To hell with the very idea he might be without a home that very night.

Fernando García Carolan was leaving Chicago. *Now.*

But then another thought hit him, and the give of dirt beneath his feet kicked into the air as he stopped.

Clara.

The last time he'd seen that exuberant and exhilarating girl from the peristyle, he'd told her to leave. With the heavy presence of a suit behind him, he'd silently begged her to walk away. Better yet—*run*. Find another path, one that wouldn't tangle her up in the cobweb of Winston's plans. He'd turned his back on Clara, and when he'd finally gathered the strength to glance over his shoulder at her, she'd already left.

Now Fernando searched for her, as hopeless as it was in a sea of laughing, happy folks. Each red-lipped smile, each bounce of short dark curls, each girl standing as tall as she did—Fernando prayed he would find her.

But why? To convince her to leave Chicago? The only home she's ever known? You must be out of your mind.

"No," he whispered. Not leave. Fernando had to find her because if Chicago were in danger, the only person he could trust to do anything about it was Clara Banks.

Step after step brought Fernando to the Grand Basin, the

center of the World's Columbian Exposition and the best spot to see everything modern and indicative of progress. He hopped atop a white bench and gazed out into the crowd. Hundreds of thousands of people walked amongst him. They didn't know the lights come nightfall would reveal monsters. That danger lurked in the brightness of day. There were parasols and moustaches and the laughter of those enjoying the trivia and geography within the pavilions. He saw groups of boys and groups of girls, and when he saw the girls, he searched for one with a midnight-black ribbon around her neck and a look of determination in her eyes. Fernando searched for the red lips he'd imagined kissing more than once. He searched, but he was coming up empty.

A shiver ran down his spine at the danger in that. Perhaps Clara had been caught. He imagined her in the clutches of suits who wore the faces of ordinary people but weren't. He imagined terror in her eyes, her body shaking as they stole her away. He tried not to imagine them killing her the way the suit had Dodger by seizing the force of life that moves through everyone.

Fernando shook the thoughts from his head. "Stop. You're going to find her."

But the World's Columbian Exposition was no small matter. It'd been built as a nation of its own, and to see absolutely every-thing might take weeks. As he waded through the crowds, Fernando begged the saints that had helped him find that blessed Remington now to help him find Clara. He raced past the pavil-ions of Japan, Egypt, France, Colombia—even a great Viking ship—but there was no sign of Clara Banks.

Until, yes, there was.

She was racing toward the Midway with eureka-like zeal. A glow brightened her face, and ferocity narrowed her focus. Three girls followed—two from the Midway tent, and the third from the Ferris Wheel not long ago. They might not know why they'd followed Clara into a crowd, but he could see they trusted Clara enough to go along with her. They weren't too far off from where Fernando stood, but they were running fast.

Fernando's breath caught. Clara might be on her way back to the Ferris Wheel. To him. He couldn't help the smile that rose to his lips, but he was even more surprised to realize his whole self had yearned to know she was all right.

"Clara!" he called, dropping from the bench and squeezing through couples and families and children all Sunday-marching through the Court of Honor. "Clara!"

She halted when she heard her name and lit up with relief. That relief woke something inside Fernando. He hadn't realized the reserve of courage trapped inside his heart while he'd remained under the thumb of Rex Winston.

"Wait a moment," Clara said to her friends.

"Clara?" Marta said.

"What is it?" Lily said at the same time.

Clara ran toward him. Her hair bounced with her steps, a strange but sympathetic sadness rising to her face. She no longer carried bravery or determination or that same ferocity as before. Instead, it was grief that had grabbed hold of her.

Fernando knew grief well. He saw it staring back at him in the mirror every morning. Maybe Clara had already heard about Dodger somehow, but—no, that wasn't it. There was no chaos from the fallout of a missing switch board controller or the pile of bones lying beneath the whole contraption. This was something else.

A sadness not tinged with horror, but one that acknowledged loss. The sadness a person felt when there was nothing to be done about the truth of the past even if the present begged for relief from it.

As Clara drew closer, Fernando felt a chill. Like grief had suddenly turned contagious, and he'd managed to catch it from her. When it struck his chest, she was only inches away, and his hands shook from the memory of speaking with his mother on that last day. Losing his parents even though they were both still very much alive rang as closely to Fernando's heart as death did, and the horror of how close that felt to losing a friend grew too strong to keep to himself.

"It's Dodger," he blurted out, his gaze clamping on Lily's. She paled not just at the name Fernando had spoken but at the dread that drowned it. "Dodger," he said again.

Clara froze. Fernando longed for her to step closer, to embrace him, to comfort him like he had when everything had been upside-down on the Ferris Wheel. But she didn't speak or interrupt or even ask for an explanation. She waited.

Fernando's chest tightened. All he could do was stare at Lily's translucent eyes, wet with tears that declared she knew exactly what Fernando would confess but begged to be wrong.

"Whatever they are," he said. "I don't know. But Dodger. He's gone."

Sally and Marta echoed Fernando's look of horror and each turned to Lily, who crumpled against them, her hands cupping her mouth as she sobbed. Ferociously, she shook her head.

"I ran," Fernando said. "I couldn't save him."

The men on Papá's site that day. It'd been an accident. But careless, and stupid, and maybe if I had spent those extra few minutes making sure the railings had been stable…

If I'd done my job properly.

I was so scared.

Christ. They're dead because of me.

"I couldn't save him," he said again.

I couldn't save them.

Clara set her arms around Fernando's neck and held him closely. "I'm sorry," she whispered. "I'm so sorry."

Fernando's arms circled Clara's waist. He let out a long exhale, and with it came the agony that had taken a hold of him for weeks. Each Catholic prayer that had crossed his lips every night that begged for the same money, power, and status he'd seen in Mr. Winston, even though there'd always been a part of him that'd known it'd never be worthwhile if it couldn't be shared with family.

He couldn't stop the outpouring of moments that followed. He remembered the wrinkles that riveted from the corners of his father's eyes whenever Juan García Díaz laughed—some of Fernando's proudest moments were the times he could make his father smile. The smell of shortbread cookies on Christmas Eve and the touches of flour on Imogen Carolan's gray apron as she baked and philosophized with her son about Transubstantiation according to the Church.

The day he'd waved off his father's instruction to check the steel railings that had been about to rise into the sky.

The day three new widows had come to his parents' home wearing white gloves.

White, because women of good standing wore white gloves when they couldn't afford black ones.

The fight with his mother when Fernando had sworn he wouldn't descend with them into poverty.

The last time he saw New York City.

And Dodger.

"I'm so sorry," Clara said again.

Fernando shut his eyes, fighting the impulse to cry or scream. A long raspy breath cleared away his grief, but only for now—he'd give in to it eventually, but there was still danger at the fair. Danger in Chicago. He pulled away from Clara and offered a warm embrace to Lily, who cried gently in his arms. Sounds from the fair peppered around them, a mixture of string quartets and laughter.

After enough time, Lily drew away, like to cry any more would be too exhausting.

"I'm sorry," Fernando said again. He inclined his head toward Clara, so she'd know he meant her now. "I hated every second I spoke to you the way I did."

Clara shook her head. "I understand why you did it."

After a long pause, Fernando took a breath. "The lights." A lamp they stood beneath hummed softly. Fernando gathered his newfound courage, reached for Clara's hands, and held both tightly.

Clara's gray eyes found his. No more grief. Only understanding. "You meant to sabotage them, right? That night? In Machinery Hall when I found you with my father?"

Fernando nodded. He didn't trust himself to speak. He was thinking about the roses Dodger had wanted to buy for Lily. Flowers for a girl with a flower name.

"We have to stop them," Clara said. "I know you won't believe me, but there *were* monsters. Skeletons. *Something.* I know you're going to say my eyes were playing tricks that night, but they weren't. I know what I saw, Fernando, and though I can't explain it—"

"I saw them, too," he confessed. "That night. I saw them, too." The shame of his lie weighed on him.

Clara tilted her head in confusion. "You did? Why didn't you say anything? Why didn't you—"

"Because I didn't want to believe it. Because it'd mean I was just like them. If they weren't monsters, I couldn't become one either." He stretched his hand against hers and felt the bones in his fingers press against hers. But no skin disappeared this time— his flesh stayed put.

Clara dropped Fernando's hand. She stared her disappointment at him from beneath long lashes. "Anyone is capable of monstrosity, Fernando."

"I know," he said, exasperated. But how much monstrosity

did it take for a person truly to turn bad? "Now, though, I'm worried they'll find some other way to stop all of it."

"If that happens," Clara said, hope lingering on her voice, "there could be a chance to reveal them anyway."

"Other than the lights?"

"For the whole world to see, not just us. If there's something about the electric lights come sunset that reveals who they are, there's one way to make sure that moment is captured in time forever. Proof they exist."

Fernando felt a spring of hope in his chest. "How do we do that?"

Now Clara offered Fernando a small smile. "*We.* You're staying for this? You aren't running back to New York or somewhere else altogether?"

It was on the tip of his tongue to refuse such an idea. But the nuances and memories of New York were still there, beckoning him. The salty smell of the ocean, the Eastern European restaurants whose potato pastries Fernando would be tempted to box a nun for, the warm embrace of his mother tinged with rose soap, and the contagious laugh of his father at the best jokes he could tell.

Fernando had left that world behind, but a spool of thread was tied around his wrists, tugging him back to it. Back to a place he should never have run from. Back to the blood of family instead of the water of Chicago.

Clara waited for his answer.

"I ran before. I ran when things got hard," he admitted. "But you can't just run when that happens. You fight, even if it terrifies you." Fernando smiled, near-forgotten plans to California fading the longer he looked at Clara. Going with her would inevitably mean defaulting on the deal he'd made with Mr. Winston, and what would happen afterward to what was left of his parents' business, he didn't know.

There's always a way, he told himself. *Don't let him hold your parents' legacy over your head. There's no honor in that. There's always a way to make things right.*

Clara wove her fingers with his and held tightly. She offered a sad look to Lily. "I won't ask you to come."

Lily wiped at the tears streaking her face and shook her head in resolve. "They almost took Marta from us, and now they've killed Dodger? There's not a chance in hell I'm missing out on this."

Marta smoothed Lily's sleeve with her hand. "Are you sure? Maybe it's best you go somewhere safe until all of this—"

"No," Lily interrupted, strength in her voice so unlike that fun and light timbre that had greeted Fernando the night in the Midway tent. "Dodger would have done the same for me. You know this, Sally."

The girl named Sally nodded and set her arm around Lily's shoulder. "All right. We do this, then. For the girls who were lost before. And for Dodger."

"For Dodger," Lily repeated.

"Let's go then," Clara said, with a quick glance at the girls. "Let's go fight some monsters."

Clara's smile was hypnotizing, alluring, addicting, but it vanished once she dropped Fernando's hand, spun on her heel, and ran straight for the Midway Plaisance, the girls in tow.

"Wait—where are you going?" Fernando called, racing to catch up.

"Like I said! I have an idea!" she called back, and no one around paid any mind in the midst of the great World's Columbian Exposition. "We just happen to have access to an incandescent bulb back at our school. And this one doesn't require a switch board."

CHAPTER 26

THE SECRET AT ST. JOAN'S

PINES AND WILLOWS SPOTTED THE LAND SURROUNDING ST. JOAN'S Academy for Girls like rows of ready guards. They were everywhere Fernando looked, and in the wind ruffling the needles and leaves, there were memories, as though these trees had stood their ground for decades, facing every girl and the futures awaiting them. Up ahead from where they ran was the school, a brick structure so old and sun-kissed, it vanished straight into the woods, hidden by ivy walls with sparrow nests in the rooftops.

As they neared, Lily walked beside Fernando, staring in his direction. He did his best to ignore it until finally he could no more. He saw in her face no tears, no sadness, not even a sense of despair—simply curiosity.

"I didn't know him for that long," she stated plainly. *Dodge.* "I'd only met him through Antoine several weeks ago, when I'd been sneaking onto the fairgrounds. He was big and sullen and way too quiet for me, but I'd noticed how he'd steal glances of me whenever he thought I wasn't looking." She stared ahead. "I'm not stupid, you know. I can tell when a boy fancies me but is too frightened to do anything about it."

"I didn't think you were stupid. And he did fancy you. Very, very much."

Somewhere in Chicago, a florist would never sell a bouquet of roses to Dodger to give to Lily. Flowers for a girl with a flower name.

Clara, Sally, and Marta walked ahead of them, giving Fernando a quiet moment with Lily. The three girls were lost in a somber discussion with cautious eyes on every part of Bynum Island.

It was safe for Fernando and Lily to talk well out of earshot of the rest.

"I know," Lily replied, and her voice caught on a sob. "I could see it in his face every time he looked at me. Tell me a story, fair boy. A story about him. There are so many moments of Dodger's life I don't know and never will. Help me fill in those empty chapters."

Fernando wanted to tell her a happy memory, but all he could think of whenever he shut his eyes was losing Dodger on the platform in Machinery Hall. The horror of the suit sucking Dodger's life straight from his bones. The agony of it must have shown on Fernando's face, but Lily pressed again.

"Please, Fernando," she said in a small voice, trying out his name like it meant something important. "I cared for him more than he ever knew. I didn't have the chance to tell him. Please. Tell me a happy thing about Dodger. Even if it's a lie."

But actually there was a bit of truth Fernando could share. "Dodger gave a portion of his salary to his friends, ones who'd been left jobless or homeless after the Chicago fires. He never told me himself. I found out from a stranger." He shrugged. "I think it was because he didn't want to boast. Maybe he didn't want to look like a hero."

Lily's walk slowed, and Fernando watched her take in the

little tale, quiet tears on her cheeks. Drops of crystals the sun caught while fighting the overcast clouds. "Thank you."

The group reached the front door of St. Joan's, and Clara held a finger to her lips to ensure silence before she turned the knob. It wouldn't budge.

"Damn," Sally whispered. "Headmistress must have left once you two finished with your English essays. Or she kept the door locked just in case one of us decided to pay this place an unsolicited visit."

Marta scowled. "The way you say it, Sal, makes Lily and me sound like we're the worst sort of girls at this school, when you know full-well who completely forgot to write a philosophy paper on Descartes last semester."

Sally cut a quick glance at Marta. "Careful, dearest. You and I both know I was well-distracted that week."

Clara regarded the locked door and set her fists to her hips. "I have an idea." She fiddled with her curls until a hairpin pulled free. "Does anyone have a pocket knife, by chance?"

Fernando did. Old work habit from New York. He fished it out of his pocket and handed it to her, and Clara knelt in front of the door and set the hairpin inside the lock. The blade of Fernando's knife went next, and Clara finagled with it until she found a latch inside that clicked once and unlocked the door.

"I didn't know St. Joan's specialized in teaching such pragmatic life skills," Fernando quipped, only slightly joking.

Clara stood. "It becomes necessary when one of your roommates frequently steals your favorite burgundy coat."

Lily's eyes widened at the accusation. "I have *never*."

Clara glared at Lily. "Never?"

Lily conceded and held up two fingers. "*Twice*, Clara Banks, and you damn well know it." She crossed her arms, and that was that.

They stepped inside. The slick wood floors reminded

Fernando of the inside of a velvety-smooth pub, the walls chalk-white, doorway frames matching the floors. The classrooms would easily sit thirty students, each with her own desk and an ink well built into the oak.

"What are we doing here?" Fernando whispered, scanning each classroom in case a teacher waited just around the corner.

Clara smiled at him. "We are going to a room where a genuine Kodak awaits us. One with a flash. And that flash comes about from an incandescent bulb, like the ones our dear friend Mr. Westinghouse has strung up around the fairgrounds."

Fernando didn't understand what purpose the flash of a camera would have, unless— "You want to take a photograph of the monsters." No response. "Why?"

Clara cleared her throat in a way that suggested to Fernando she might be pretending she hadn't heard him.

"Clara." He stopped in the middle of the hallway. "This is a bad idea. You can't believe they wouldn't stop this. It'll draw attention to us. We could get killed!"

Clara turned. "We have to!" She gestured to her friends. "Whatever it was that killed Dodger—" Lily's face fell at his name, but Fernando saw how she refused to cry. "—is a part of all this. For all the girls whose memories everyone's forgotten, this will prove there had been monsters here all along! Besides, don't you want to know the truth?"

Fernando's heart raced. He didn't like how the hallways felt haunted, alive. "Clara. My God, Dodger died *because* of whatever the hell is happening in this city. Not ten minutes before I found you! You're trying to court death here!"

Clara shuddered as though there were a draft. Her white teeth sucked in a crimson lip, a nervous gesture Fernando had never noticed before. Sally stared at the shiny floor. Marta clutched Sally's hand and rested her head on Sally's shoulder.

And Lily paced beside Clara, like she trusted the hallways even less than Fernando did.

Fernando shook his head. "Don't play with any more lives. Let's find Exposition guards for help."

Clara lifted her chin in defiance. "No guards. This is going to be worth it."

"Worth being snatched away from whatever's been taking girls from this place?"

Sally blinked in surprise. "He knows about that? Nobody in this damn city knows about that." She lifted an eyebrow. "Well. Did you know it's supposed to happen today?"

"What?"

Clara stared off into the space ahead of her. "That's what all our research points to. Generations of girls, all vanishing one after the other. Then faster and faster. Until today. My mother's aunt, Miranda. Sally's great-aunt, Dora. Marta was almost seized only a week ago."

A chill ran down Fernando's spine, and with it came the emptiness of hunger. He told it to leave him. He hated how it'd become so prominent ever since arriving in Chicago. "No one has disappeared since you arrived here, though. Right?"

Marta shook her head. "None beyond the usual. Girls getting married and running off to South Africa for their honeymoons. The occasional spring illnesses stranding them in the countryside."

"Poor Stevie," Lily said.

"The sprite." Clara's eyes flashed open. A slick smile tugged at her lips. "That's it. That's what we've been forgetting. We're missing the sprite!"

"What?" Fernando asked. He wanted to leave this school.

Clara checked the hallways like she anticipated a monster. "You know about the missing girls. But have you ever heard of *The Traveling Demon and the Peasant Girl?*"

Lily looked aghast. "Clara, it's only the locals who know it."

Marta shrugged. "And even then, it's not like it's cherished like a family heirloom by everyone who lives in Chicago. Most people go out of their way to forget it once the literature unit has passed." She shrugged. "At least that's true for most."

"You never know," Clara protested.

Fernando laughed abruptly. "Anything with a title like that would have been stopped at my mother's Catholic door." He felt the urge to cross himself but resisted. "But yes, I've heard details."

Marta smiled sweetly. "See? *Barely*. I give that dinosaur of a folktale one more generation before it's forgotten entirely."

Fernando wasn't sure, but he thought he saw a want to fume at Marta in Clara's eyes.

"Nevertheless," she said forcefully before turning her attention back to Fernando. "It's the story of a girl who has to stand up to a demon that travels the world looking for souls to consume."

The words came faster and faster as her eyes faded from their fury and brightened with epiphany.

"She learns about him when she finds a sprite who lures people to their deaths. I suppose you'd say the sprite is chained to the demon and must feed off the souls of the captured to continue her existence, but this transforms her into a conduit for the demon and the others he's turned. They can live a little bit longer because of her. As long as she keeps feeding. The note I found was a warning, and without it, all this would have been an allegory pulled apart in an English class and left at that."

Fernando's head was spinning. "Slow down. I don't follow." But there was something uneasy about the word *feed*, and his hands shook uncontrollably at the sound of it—rattling bony things he prayed only he could hear and none of these girls.

"The shadow in Marta's photograph," Clara said to the rest

of them. "What if that hadn't been one of those…*things* at all, but something else?"

Fernando gripped the bridge of his nose with two fingers. The shaking stopped. His hands were his. "Photograph?"

Clara locked eyes with Sally and nodded, an unspoken truth passing between them but never uttered out loud.

Lily shook her head in disapproval. "Clara, you shouldn't have torn it up."

Clara sucked in a breath and tore down the hallway as the rest followed. "We'll just have to develop another photo then, Lily. The clues *were* in the story all along, Sally! Come on, girls. We have to hurry. What if that thing had been the sprite in the folktale?"

They reached a room whose door was closed, and Fernando couldn't tell who—or what—lay inside. Clara tucked her hair behind her ears as they slowed, not noticing when strands of it fell back immediately.

"What sprite?" Fernando asked. "What are you talking about?"

Each girl turned to Fernando, Clara last. She blinked. "In the story, she was initially a girl," she said. "A girl with a secret. Who'd become deathly jealous of other girls eons prior. Her hatred of them turned her into something soulless, and as she became the anchor for the demon, she vowed to have her revenge on the descendants of those girls." She shared a look of worry with Sally. "Yes. Descendants. It's ironic, isn't it, Sal? Without that story—without learning my mother's book had been sent to St. Joan's—I never would have asked my father for the transfer. And then I never would have known about the Alou-ettes. In fact, I never would have met Fernando on the peristyle that night."

Lily eyed Clara. "Fernando was the worker who helped you to the ground?" She set her fists to her hips. "There are only so many times you can omit scandalous details like that, Clara, before the entire world realizes you're pulling the wool over their eyes."

It struck Fernando instantly—so a hazing had brought Clara to the fairgrounds the night they'd met. "You're part of a club? All of you?"

Clara held out her left hand. Adorning her index finger was a pearl ring, a big cluster of shining stones. Sally reluctantly followed suit, lifting her own left hand with the same ring shining. Then Marta. Then Lily. Identical rings. But as Clara stared at her own hand, Fernando realized she wasn't showing it off. Her brows were drawn, and her eyes, pensive. A thousand miles away in thought, but no farther than the reach of a hand.

"Clara," Sally warned.

Clara yanked off the ring and held up her palm.

Marta leaned against a wall with a sigh. "I've never understood Pandora's Box as much as I do right now."

Fernando stared, unsure of what he was supposed to see. Until he did. The part of Clara's index finger, right before the knuckle—conveniently the same spot one would wear a ring—had been sliced into, as though someone had tried to carve free a bit of bone, and the red mark leftover was bright with dried blood.

"Holy Mother." Fernando grabbed her hand as tenderly as he could manage and caressed it. "Clara..." He blinked at the others—Sally was twirling her own ring around her finger, Marta had already crossed her arms and hidden hers, and Lily clasped her hands behind her back and took a step away. "You all have this mark?"

"Every Alouette does," Marta said. "It's a lifelong sisterhood, and with that privilege comes sacrifice."

Fernando was starting to hate the very walls of this school.

Clara's eyes were far away. "Stories can have strange meanings and even stranger origins. I'm new at St. Joan's. Maybe it was me, Sally, and not you who was supposed to disappear next. Maybe it would have been easier to have gotten rid of new money."

"Clara, you can't truly believe no one would notice if you were to just disappear," Lily said.

"No, not like that," Clara insisted. "But in a way that would nearly…hypnotize. Like being put under a spell from the shine of a flash. Like that Houdini fellow on the Midway. Maybe that's what it meant in the note: *hiding.* Maybe it really should have been *vanishing.* Sally, everyone forgets the girls after they've gone missing, isn't that right? Like they'd never existed to begin with? Unless someone had the good sense to report a disappearance to the newspapers right away?"

Sally nodded. "And keep those newspaper clippings in a clubhouse."

Lily looked as though she might cry. "We never should have come back here."

"Well," Clara said. "It's too late now." She stared at Fernando. "We're not leaving without the Kodak. It's the only chance we have at stopping this thing. This is our home, and nothing is going to take us from it."

The word *home* struck Fernando in a strange way. Home was far away. Home was lost. Home was an idea he was slowly forgetting the longer he stayed away from Brooklyn. Home was a family that was no longer his, and home was a world that now went days without knowing which lonely nights spurred on thoughts of anguish. Home wasn't a school or an island he'd only ever stepped foot onto twice now. But home could be something that moved about and changed as Fernando lived. A spark of belonging surprised him. Clara was talking to Fernando as much as she was talking to the Alouettes.

Guiding him there.

"Let's get the camera, then," Sally said.

Clara opened the classroom door with a slow push. It uttered a heavy creak, and they winced at the sound, but no one was inside. The four girls beelined straight to a corner, where Fernando saw a Kodak.

"It'll just be a moment," Clara said. "Marta and I can pack it up quickly." She pointed to the corner. "Sally, Lily. We'll need the flash, the lightbulbs, all the pieces. Use the burlap. Fernando, stand guard."

Fernando thanked his saints Clara wasn't going to make him fiddle with any pieces that looked a little too breakable for his comfort. Steel beams on the Ferris Wheel were one thing—a collection of small glass bits and ruddy cords was quite another.

"You're not at all concerned someone here might find the school's only Kodak missing?" Fernando asked as he studied the nuances of the room and paced in the door frame. "That thing must cost a fortune."

"Well, let's not cross that bridge until we're safely past the one that leads off this island," Sally quipped back as she and Lily filled a burlap sack.

Fernando lifted one shoulder in a defeated shrug and pushed away the anxiety building in his stomach. The best way to calm himself whenever feats on the Ferris Wheel or construction sites in New York became too much was by focusing on his surroundings. He glanced around the classroom—the blackboard, the set of chalk, the open windows with dragonflies resting on the sills. And then he felt himself drawn to a set of photographs framed on the wall. Arranged like a border. Soft sepia tones like spilt tea showcasing girls in that room, each year followed by the next. The smiles were subtle, and they stood proudly in rows, the teachers and the students ever changing with time. One after the other, Fernando studied them, until he came upon something strange.

A familiar face stared out from one of the more recent photographs, but, *no*—it was not a familiar face.

"Someone must have failed this class a few times," he called to the others. "I've seen the same girl in last year's class photo, the year before, and the year before that."

"What?" Clara ducked under the camera's curtain as Marta helped her fold the tripod.

Fernando glanced back to the wall and retraced his steps in photographic time. The girl was in the prior one as well.

She was in all of them.

But the camera's flash must have been turned off, because once he returned to the first photograph, he saw a different version of the same classroom. They were inside St. Joan's, but the windows were closed. A flash would be necessary with such poor light.

And in this photograph, the girl was there, but not, in a way.

She stared at the camera lens, inquisitive but bitter, her hair a russet waterfall around her cheeks. But what should have been flesh and skin had faded ever so slightly for something else. The flash had captured more than she'd expected, only truly noticeable if someone were to study the photograph intently.

Bone.

"That's not..." Fernando whispered, instantly famished and suddenly recognizing—

A creak on the floor startled him. He spun toward the door he was supposed to be guarding.

Standing there was the girl with russet hair, her dead eyes on his.

In a fraction of a second, she was inches away. Her speed was impossibly fast, and before he could react, her hands were squeezing at his throat. She appeared frail, but she was strong. Fernando fought her, his throat gargling as he gripped her arms in panic. The touch of her cold skin made him gasp. Her fingers were those of a skeleton with bits of flesh warring against their dull white sheen. In less than a second, the girl had Fernando kneeling.

"*They* do not have permission to touch the Kodak. And *you* do not belong here, boy," she said in a cool, even voice, red hair hiding her eyes.

"Fernando!" Sally shrieked.

Fear pricked at Fernando as the girl suddenly pulled him to his feet. She stared hatred at him until that hatred vanished for inquisitiveness. A frown. Fernando stilled. And then recognition in her dead stare, as clear as crystal. "Another anchor. To replace me. *To replace me?*"

She threw him straight into the wall with unimaginable strength. A loud smash sounded as several of the framed photographs tumbled to the floor, glass shattering into a thousand pieces.

Once he landed, Fernando braced himself. The girl moved to strike, but Clara and Sally's quick hands yanked her away. Her curtain of hair fell to the side, revealing the length of a skeleton neck piercing through the remnants of skin.

"Stevie!" Clara shouted.

Lily raced to Fernando's side, crouching before him as she grabbed his shoulder. "Oh God, Fernando. Are you all right?" Fear welled in her eyes just as quickly as it faded for resolve. "This is what killed him, isn't it? This is what killed Dodger? Something like her?"

Fernando couldn't answer. He could only nod. Nod and cough—something like ash spilling from his throat, a dryness that burrowed into his flesh and bones. A hunger that sprang forward next.

The girl Stevie spun and flung Sally off her. Sally fell against the wall and winced as her back hit the wood. Stevie tightened her grip around the strip of black ribbon circling Clara's throat until Clara's face went beet-red.

"You should have minded your own business, Clara Banks," Stevie said. "It could have been painless for you. But now I'm hungry. *Famished.* So much more than before—even more so than when I broke the neck of that Carveth girl. And time is running out."

Fernando could see the hunger the girl spoke of. It was not for food. Desperation left her eyes wild and her mouth gaping. Fatigue followed, like it took every bit of strength to stay in one piece. He knew her now. He recognized the want for something, the drive, the desire. He saw it every day in the mirror.

But it would not become him. Whatever this was.

Clara was choking. Her eyes ran tears, mixing with the dark kohl on her lashes.

Fernando rolled his shoulder until Lily dropped it. He stumbled toward Stevie and Clara through the pain threading his spine. "Drop her!" He yanked at Stevie's arms as Clara's eyes rolled into the back of her head.

Stevie swiped at Fernando's cheek, and the sting of four sharp nails scratched his skin. He winced but didn't falter. But before there was any chance to react, Lily burst past and slammed Stevie into a nearby desk. Stevie tripped backward at the sudden movement, and the back of her skull hit the blunt edge. Clara slumped to the floor, coughing. And Fernando fell back, watching as the girl Stevie lay dazed.

Lily stood and stared at what she'd done. "That's for Dodger, you horrible thing."

Fernando dropped beside Clara, cupping her cheeks as she forced herself to breathe. "All right?" he asked.

She nodded. "The camera." She pointed at the tripod beside her, ready with its flash, and glanced quickly at each of the Alouettes. "We have to go. Now."

Fernando and Marta raced for the Kodak, and together they lifted it, a heavy wooden thing with too many pieces he didn't understand. Marta helped Fernando set it against his shoulder, and he reached for Clara's hand. "Come on."

Marta slung Sally's arm over her shoulder as they followed.

But Lily remained in the middle of the room, two fists clenching angrily as she forced herself to breathe as Stevie hung off the desk. Stevie moaned as she inched her fingers toward the back of her head. An ugly spot of darkness blossomed from a crack there. Not blood—something else.

"Quickly," Clara said, pulling Fernando toward the door. "Lily, now! Forget Stevie!"

"She caused all of this, Clara! The sprite from the folktale!" Lily's voice broke as she cried angry tears. "Dodger's dead because of her!"

Stevie grinned a crimson smile. "Wrong. It was an army that did it. I'm simply hungry, sweet Lily."

Fernando tightened his grip on Clara's hand. "Come on," he said again. He eyed Stevie carefully, not trusting she was truly hurt.

Clara beckoned Lily again. "Lil, please!"

Lily gritted her teeth, and through tears of fury, she tore away from Stevie and raced after them. Fernando led Clara into the hallway fast enough that Stevie's echoing cries—*"You can't escape this island!"*—were fading fast.

Then something stalled Clara, and she gasped. Each of the Alouettes went still. Fernando wanted to ask, but then he heard it, too.

Footsteps.

He couldn't tell if it was one person or a thousand. All Fernando knew was they weren't alone, and suddenly the preposterous idea the suit from Machinery Hall had managed to follow them off the fairgrounds wasn't so preposterous after all.

A long shadow at the end of the hallway shortened with each step, and then an old woman appeared, tall with a gray chignon at the nape of her neck. Her eyes were all-knowing, and her disposition was one of grace.

Clara began to shake, but Fernando couldn't tell if it was from relief or fright. "Headmistress."

The woman's eyes found the Alouettes. "*Run,* girls."

Chapter 27

Flowers

THERE WAS SOMETHING ABOUT THE WAY HEADMISTRESS addressed the Alouettes—with Stevie wailing her agony inside the classroom and the Kodak settled against Fernando's shoulder —that told Clara whatever mystery they had been trying to solve had never once been lost upon Florence McGill, all this time.

Headmistress walked the hallway toward the group looking no different from whenever girls were tardy or truant or required counsel.

"*Now*, girls," she demanded. "*Run.*"

Only then did Clara's eyes drop to Headmistress's left hand, where the older woman wore not her usual black gloves but an old ring, one with polished stones embedded into a silver band. Humble compared to the rings circling the fingers of the Alouettes, but recognizable nonetheless. The polished stones weren't stones at all—but pearls, worn down from time and the life of a woman whom nuns had taught never to fear manual labor.

Headmistress set that hand atop Clara's shoulder as she stared into the Reporting classroom. "Blood to bone."

"And bone to ash," Clara whispered.

Headmistress walked inside the classroom, and Clara raced to the doorway. Fernando and Sally followed with Lily and Marta peeking over any shoulder they could.

"She told us to run," Fernando whispered.

Sally shook her head furiously. "Headmistress is an Alouette."

"We can't leave her," Clara added.

"We won't," Lily echoed.

Headmistress set her chin high as she regarded Stevie Graham bent over at an awkward angle on the desk as though her spine had snapped in two. Stevie's eyes were scarlet with anger or hurt or something else entirely, but when they settled on Headmistress, the girl only smiled.

"Florence," she said in a steady voice.

Headmistress inclined her head. "I've been searching for you. The sprite from Miranda's story, here in the flesh—no, not flesh. Not the right word, perhaps." She narrowed her eyes. "All these years after the time we spent studying together, you ended up as a student in my very own class. I couldn't have forgotten what you looked like—impossible. Was it the work of a glamour, Stevie? *Their eyes had missed glamours / Warnings failed to slip free?*"

Stevie lifted a shoulder in a slow shrug. "Perhaps it was rather convenient that your eyeglasses would become horribly smudged whenever I was near."

Headmistress ignored the retort. "Of course, a glamour would be the only way to hide on Bynum Island, especially since you are chained here. Poor little sprite. Miranda was wise to have hidden your story. Now I can stop you from taking another girl for that monster you serve."

Clara's heart quickened its pace. "Monster she serves?" *So there is another, then. Just like in the folktale. A traveling demon who controls all of this.*

Stevie straightened, arms limp at her side as she glared through tendrils of straight hair.

Headmistress cocked her head. Clara had seen that look before—whenever a girl lied to get out of trouble. "Do you really intend to hold onto that face now? We both know it's useless."

Clara shared worried glances with the Alouettes. A look of horror fell upon Fernando's face.

"What's happening?" he whispered.

Clara had a hunch. She hoped she was wrong.

Stevie glanced up at Headmistress with a look too far from human to be real. "All right. Since we were such dear friends during our schooldays here, maybe the next girl to disappear, dear Florence, should be you."

The skin and flesh and all that came with it vanished from Stevie's body, leaving behind jagged bones and shadows where there should be eyes. Clara screamed, and Fernando's hand slammed across her mouth. Sally and Marta shushed her instantly, and Lily frantically set a finger to her lips to mimic the order. But it was too late—Headmistress glanced over and saw them at the door.

Which let Stevie lunge forward, her fingers claws instead of nails, and when she found Headmistress's neck, she dug at the woman's skin.

Stevie's shadowy eyes found Clara next. Her skeletal hand quickly lifted, and the classroom door slammed shut between them.

"Stevie!" Clara yelled, yanking on the locked doorknob and pounding on the wood. "Headmistress!" Her throat was raw with her screams.

"What do we do?" yelled Marta, her hands cupping her mouth in horror. "Headmistress is locked in there!"

Sally put on a brave face. "Slip through the window. One has to be unlocked. If not, we can break the glass."

Clara shook her head. "That'll take too long!"

Fernando slammed his shoulder into the door again and

again, and Clara clutched at the window frame as Stevie sliced at Headmistress's hair and dress as the older woman fought back. Only for a moment did Clara catch Headmistress's eye.

"Run!" the woman ordered.

"We won't leave you!" Clara protested.

"We sure as hell will not!" Lily added as Fernando kicked the door again and again. She timed her own kick perfectly with his and the door splintered open, fragments of wood soaring across the room.

Marta screamed at the shock of it, but not Sally. As though she knew precisely what Lily meant to do, Sally reached to grab Lily's arm to stop her from storming straight into the classroom, but it was already too late.

"Lil!" Sally screamed.

"Lily!" Fernando shouted. "Don't!"

But Lily had already raced inside, the spirits of a thousand Alouettes strengthening her. She seized Stevie's hands from Headmistress's throat and peeled them off before sending an elbow straight into Stevie's stomach. Headmistress wheezed as her breathing returned, and Lily lowered her to the floor.

"Help me! We need to get her to safety!" Lily screamed to the Alouettes.

A grim look fell upon Sally's face. "Damn it all, Lil," she said, mostly to herself. "Come on!" she ordered the rest.

Clara raced to Headmistress's side, gripping her cold, shaking hand as she and Sally helped her to her feet. "Gracious, Headmistress," Clara said. There were scrapes on the woman's neck and wet blood streaked onto the collar of her dress and Clara's hand alike. "Are you all right?"

Headmistress slowed her breaths but nodded. "Run," she ordered, and this time, there was no room for discussion.

Clara nodded. "Lily," she said, eyeing Stevie curled in the

corner like a wolf readying to attack. "We have to go. Forget all this."

"Not likely," Lily answered as she stared at Stevie. She side-stepped toward the corner, where the school kept supplies for the classroom. Just in case the lights of the Kodak's flash were ever to break. "There's a special surprise greeting the fair tonight. Dodger told me all about it." Her voice wobbled but held strong.

Stevie narrowed her eyes. "There's nothing you can do to stop what's to come, you silly half-wit. Even if I go, someone else will follow. Someone else has already been chosen." She slid her gaze to Fernando, and Clara frowned at that.

Fernando took the weight of Headmistress's arm off Clara's shoulder. "Clara, please." Sally and Marta were already that much further out the doorway.

Clara shouted, "Lily! Now!"

The drive in Lily's eyes and the anger she bore transformed. Instead of determination, Clara saw hurt in Lily's gaze. Instead of anger, sacrifice.

It petrified Clara. *"Lily!"*

Lily swallowed and lifted a bulb with a long cord that would easily lead to a second power source. There was an entire box of bulbs. Incandescent. Born of the future, and certainly the progress the world was headed into.

"I always knew there was something haunting this damn island."

Clara watched in horror as Lily set the bulb to its rightful place to connect it. As Stevie soared toward her, readying to devour, a flash of light covered the entirety of the classroom, illuminating everything.

"Lily!" Clara shouted.

They all covered their eyes at the exhilarating light, and two screams loosened from the inside of the classroom.

One human. One not.

The brightness seemed to go on forever, and the cries even longer until everything seemed to slow.

And then shake.

Clara fought the light and searched the school as rumbles of pain sliced through her bones, splitting her head into halves. The ground was trembling—the walls, the glass windows.

Fernando tugged at the Kodak. "Something's happening. This isn't right."

Headmistress steadied herself enough to grab Clara's chin to seize her attention. "We are leaving this place *now*, Miss Banks!"

There was no choice.

Clara rallied the Alouettes with a look of despair at Lily. "Run!"

Together, they raced through the hallways whose shined wooden floorboards sprang free, the nails holding everything in place collapsing from the ceiling, from the walls, from the door frames. The light followed them from the classroom, too harsh to look at straight on, like the birth of a new sun. The screams were echoes or they were memories, and Clara wasn't sure she could tell the difference anymore, but she knew if they didn't get out of St. Joan's now, there was a good chance they never would.

Helping Headmistress along, they cleared the corner and ran toward the entrance of the school, grass and ivy and deep green willows in the distance—all signs of their freedom from Stevie and whatever horror had come from the bulb Lily had ignited. A beam of wood from the ceiling broke free, barely missing their heads, and they screamed their surprise. Clara pulled on Fernando's hand and ran around the wood until they were outside.

But the shaking didn't end.

It was an earthquake. It was the end of the world. It was a call of distress from a girl Clara had stumbled upon in the gardens, up to her neck in spirits with riddles spilling from her lips like silk ribbons from a magician's sleeve.

"The bridge!" Clara yelled, as Bynum Island rebelled and rebelled and rebelled.

They ran through the grass, each step heavier than the last as their breaths faltered and Headmistress's gait grew weary. Clara's feet ached and begged her to quit, but onward she ran. The foot bridge was a vision of paradise.

"Oh you horribly old and wonderful thing," Clara whispered as the dark brown wood, ancient against the freshness of grass and water, called to her to hurry. The green mildew on the beams made the wood slippery, but with the earth shaking beneath them, Clara couldn't risk slowing.

As they reached the middle of the bridge, a sound like the heavens splitting in two made Clara slam her hands over her ears with a shriek. Sally and Marta winced, squeezing their eyes shut like that could drown out the noise.

"Oh God," Fernando whispered beside Clara, and when she heard his footsteps slow to nothing, she turned back to St. Joan's Academy for Girls.

The shaking grew more vicious, more violent, more turbulent. Clara and Fernando gripped the bridge as they watched the ground break apart and swallow the school whole, like it was quicksand and St. Joan's had been unlucky to have found itself there.

Clara clasped her hands over her mouth. "No. Impossible. That's impossible."

The screams of Lily and Stevie warred against each other inside the school, and bits of bright and unnatural light spilled through the windows as the old bricks of St. Joan's collapsed into the ground. The world shook and shook and shook.

"Heaven save us," Headmistress prayed. She crossed herself three times in a frightened fashion Clara had never seen in her before.

Fernando rested a hand on Clara's shoulder, but there was no amount of comfort that could fix what Clara was seeing now. At first, all of this had been to learn the truth about Miranda Carveth. Her mother's aunt who'd vanished and left in her stead a folktale of Chicago that was less allegorical than Clara had realized. When Sally had told Clara about her great-aunt Dora, things hadn't changed—her desire to do something greater had never exactly *changed*—but there'd been a new softness where before, her determination had been rock solid.

But now Lily was gone. Lily, who'd protested ever returning to Bynum Island out of fear or practicality or perhaps a bit of both. And Clara had refused that.

"She saved us," Clara whispered, her eyes full of hot and angry tears.

Marta sank onto the bridge and covered her mouth, sobbing into her hands as Sally knelt beside her, wrapping herself around Marta and rocking to comfort them both.

"We love her," Sally said to Marta. "We've always loved her. We always will."

Clara felt her cheeks go wet with tears. "We never should have come back. This is all my fault."

Sally glanced sideways at Clara and offered no protest. "Now we have to make sure we didn't lose Lil for nothing." It was the most serious thing Sally had ever told her.

Clara shut her eyes. "How? How can we stop all this? There's no way to bring justice to our missing girls. Or even those of Chicago who disappeared thereafter. Or Dodger. Or Lily. We've already lost."

She hung her head in defeat, fingers fiddling with the pearl ring she didn't deserve to wear. Until another hand reached for hers and held it. One like crepe paper with long fingers that looked like those of a pianist. One that'd always been cloaked in black leather gloves. Clara stared at Headmistress's pearl ring and imagined how it would have been when Florence McGill had received her own initiation into the Alouettes. She could make out the jagged ending of a scar peeking out from underneath, but that was all.

"Your Great-Aunt Miranda and I were the same age when we began teaching at St. Joan's," Headmistress began. "She and I were each nineteen. I'd gone to St. Joan's myself after moving from Canada, but Miranda hadn't. In those first few months of teaching—wrangling classrooms of girls only a few years younger than we were—Miranda and I would sit together under that willow tree in the yard and eat apples as we complained about the students who wouldn't listen. The ones who spoke back to us and made us look like sheer imbeciles in our own classrooms."

Clara's fingers wrapped around Headmistress's hand as she listened. She could feel Fernando's presence on the other side of her. It was enough—simply sitting beside her when Lily could not was everything to Clara.

"It became a daily ritual for us, you know," Headmistress continued. "On that first day, I'd been looking for a quiet spot for my daily rosary, but instead, I found a friend. A kindred spirit. As we grew into our jobs—Miranda teaching history and me teaching literature—our routine continued. We sat beside each other. We ate apples. Then we started to hold hands. Every day."

Clara glanced up at Headmistress through her tears and saw the same sort of devastation that had always been peeking through Headmistress's quiet disposition. Now it was spilling freely.

"Until one day, Miranda was gone. Presumed home sick." Headmistress's eyes softened, like she was looking into the past and watching it all happen again. "And then slowly forgotten. Like girls on this island were of no importance in the greater scheme of things. But she was never truly forgotten." Headmistress reached into her pocket and withdrew a small leather-bound journal. Clara frowned and then gasped when Headmistress opened the journal to the first page, where in ink had been written, *The Traveling Demon and the Peasant Girl.*

Astonished, Clara looked at Headmistress.

"It's the first version of the folktale," Headmistress admitted. "And would eventually be printed by a small press as simply a story of Chicago. I'd never known about the missing girls until I'd found this book in Miranda's bedroom one day, weeks before she vanished. She'd been recording each girl's disappearance in a form of poetry before falling prey to the glamour that had fallen upon the city, and it fell to me to make sure Miranda's legacy would stay alive through the Alouettes. To pass on this story in hopes this mystery would one day be solved. Girls would vanish, Clara, and then they'd be forgotten." Headmistress's face fell into resolve. "But no more. Stevie Graham was amongst the first Alouettes, once only a girl who had been no more or less human than any of us. But she found herself in a place that turned her into the sprite in Miranda's story, and she'd hidden herself from me as I'd searched for her and a way to stop her from taking girls from this world." Headmistress dropped Clara's hand and used it to brush away some wayward strands of dark hair from her face. "Stevie might have been stopped, Miss Banks, but there are still monsters in this city. Miranda was brave and brilliant, and now so must you be."

Headmistress's words shook Clara as devastation caught up with her. With a nod, Clara stood and brushed any stubborn leaves or dirt from the skirt of her dress.

What seemed like a lifetime ago, Headmistress had told Clara she didn't look like her mother, as Clara had always thought, but someone else.

Great-Aunt Miranda Carveth.

Someone who'd been taken by Stevie for the sake of monsters.

And now that Lily had fallen, too, Clara was not going to stand for it anymore.

The last of St. Joan's dipped beneath the ground, like a eulogy that yearned to sleep with the dead instead of living for them. Then the world went still, and the grass stitched itself back up. The birds returned, their chirps not of larks or alouettes, but tiny songbirds that sang anthems lingering between sadness and hope. The horrible flash of light was gone, and in its place was the buttery sun of spring in Chicago, dusting its glow on the island now free of St. Joan's.

Like nothing had happened at all.

And St. Joan's had never been.

Clara loosened a breath and blinked. Her cheeks were wet with tears, and her breath was ragged.

Fernando lay a hand on her shoulder. "Lily did it to save us," he told her, speaking as though he understood her guilt. "It can't be for nothing."

Clara nodded, because Fernando was right. If she were to steal St. Joan's Kodak for the photograph of the millennium, it would not be done in vain. As the thought crossed her mind, the tree above her wilted its early spring buds, little white flowers that weren't lilies but reminded Clara of them tremendously.

"Flowers for a girl with a flower name," Fernando said as he watched them flutter.

"We love you, Lil," Clara whispered, catching one in her hand. "Once all of this is said and done, you will be remembered. By every Alouette. I promise."

ACT IV

CHAPTER 28

THE GRAND BASIN

It was a shock to see people smiling at the fair. Rejoicing on the first day of the biggest event in Chicago's history. Eating hotcakes with maple syrup and pointing at a list of the amazing exhibits inside the Horticulture Building. Chatting with one another about the ornate wine displays in the French Pavilion, or the art in the galleries on the north end, or even the giant clock tower in the Electricity Building. The world was still turning, and the fair was still as spectacular as it had been that morning, and no one seemed to know or care that a girl named Lily was now gone from it.

Even though Headmistress's touching words back at St. Joan's had ignited a newfound sense of determination inside Clara, weakness proved to be stronger. Clara knew she was likely hungry, probably thirsty, and definitely exhausted, but even more, a cloud of defeat loomed.

What if there was no way to ensure they'd all come out of this as victors?

What if Lily had died for nothing?

Fernando touched her arm. "Come on. Almost there."

Headmistress had left to send a telegram to the Garner family in Switzerland, and now, for Clara, it was as though Headmistress's words on the footbridge had never been spoken. As they walked onward, Marta in a fog and Sally even more so, Clara realized how unfinished her plan to photograph the monsters had always been. She couldn't believe no one had noticed the earthquake that had swallowed up St. Joan's—what sort of magical power had stopped Stevie? What had torn the world apart and sewn it back up?

They passed the Transportation Building, and in the distance was the familiarity of the Court of Honor. Clara didn't want to return there.

"Where should we set up the Kodak? The peristyle?" Fernando suggested, but then again, "Maybe not."

Clara hardened her gaze on the horizon. "There."

She pointed at the Grand Basin, in front of which stood a white granite bench. Couples adorned it, caught up in the romance of the day's end and the shy stars slowly peeking through a candy-pink sky. Clara knew they'd have to clear the crowd to set up the Kodak, but it would be the perfect spot. George Westinghouse's promise to the public would come to fruition at the same place that had greeted them that morning. Children perched on the grass beside the walkways, their feet tucked under their bodies as they eagerly waited. The fountains danced with the breeze Chicago knew well this time of year—a soft kiss of coolness leftover from winter and a bit of warmth from spring approaching. Hot and cold dancing in the middle.

Clara summoned the strength she knew Lily would have. She dropped Fernando's arm and jogged ahead. "Move!" she called to the young couples sprawling across the bench, nearly tripping over the wooden baseball bat of a mischievous child. "Fair patrol! We have permission from the Columbian Exposition to take the official photographs of the fairgrounds at sunset. Out of the way, folks, out of the way! Official business! We need this spot!" Her voice danced upon a line between order and anger, but she didn't care. Her foot hit the baseball bat, and she kicked it across the grass.

A girl with delicate brows and a proper chignon scowled. "We're not moving." She searched Clara. "And shouldn't you have permission of some sort if you work for the fair? Where is it?"

Knowing Clara's game, Sally set her hands to her hips and stared the girl down. "Move so we can take pictures of Mr. Westinghouse's grand event, or I'll find him myself so he can summon his security guards."

Marta rested an arm on Sally's shoulder. "How embarrassing it would be for everyone to see you being escorted away. What would they *say*?"

Clara knew never to underestimate the power of reputation in Chicago, and so she wasn't the least bit surprised at how quickly the crowd dispersed. The spot was bare in a split-second, though not without an array of dirty glances at the girls who had the nerve to order the world around.

Sally nodded at Clara and Marta. "For Lily."

"For Lil," Marta said.

"Lily," Clara added.

Fernando offered the Kodak to Clara, and she and Marta steadied the tripod into position. "We have to be careful," Fernando said. "We're out in the open. And those suits—they'll see this. They'll run the other way."

"Not if we catch them by surprise," Clara replied defiantly.

Skepticism fell upon Fernando like rainfall. "Clara."

Marta beckoned Sally to help her with the Kodak, and it left Clara and Fernando together.

"Don't give up on this now," Clara said. "These pictures will be proof for the entire world to see! Do you think my word is good enough for my own father to listen? Do you think he'd trust me if I walked up to him and told him there were monsters sabotaging his great fair?"

"Clara," he whispered again, a hesitant hand wrapping around her shoulder. She found herself leaning into his touch. "It wasn't your fault. I couldn't have known Dodger… and you couldn't have known Lily would—"

"All right, fine. But now I have to do something about it," Clara whispered back. A truth she knew as well as she knew her name. But she couldn't let those words spring free without seeing if the same truth lay in Fernando's eyes, too. "No one was supposed to die today. So I have to set things right. The best I can."

Clara loosened a breath as she waited for his reply. Fernando had beautiful brown eyes that seemed to carry the burdens of a thousand lives. The skin on his cheeks was rough, as though with his age approaching twenty, his beard would soon begin to grow in thicker. The way his cheekbones carried the dimming light was breathtaking. He watched her with a sadness that tried to understand. And then Fernando offered a small quirk of a smile —just one side of his mouth, really—and pressed his lips to her cheek in a kiss that was sweeter than any lemon cake she'd ever tasted.

"Whatever happens, you're not alone," he whispered against her skin.

Clara saw how Fernando was cautious in the way he took her hand, but she let him, a bitter peace finding her once their fingers laced into each other's.

"I'm glad you stayed in Chicago," Clara whispered back.

And then the sun dipped beneath the horizon.

"Nightfall!" called the children.

"Aha!" Sally declared as she presented the Kodak, propped up and magnificent. "Ready!"

Marta stood as she caught sight of the horizon. "Just in time, too."

Fernando swallowed, clutching Clara's hands with desperation she knew tilted closer to fear. In only seconds they'd know if the suits had dismantled the lights another way. Or if they'd failed through sheer pride or for fear of touching a single bulb themselves.

"They might not come. What if they don't?" Clara whispered. "They must know now you didn't dismantle the lights. What if…"

What if Lily died for nothing?

"No. They'll come," Fernando replied. "They think this world is theirs."

Clara knew Fernando had no reason to be in Chicago anymore. And yet he'd stayed. She was more than willing to put herself in danger for Lily and Miranda and Dora and any other girl who was supposed to have lived and thrived. But she hadn't expected anyone else to do the same.

Fernando stood with her. With the Alouettes. Ready to reveal monsters to the world.

"As soon as those lights brighten," Sally began.

"I'll take the photograph," Clara finished, bracing herself with courage as she reluctantly pulled away from Fernando. She gauged the sky, how twilight was making Chicago light and dark all at once. Her focus had changed—an instinct she couldn't place. There would be a time to mourn Lily, but it was not now. And as though Lily's spirit were with them, Clara felt the boldness of all Alouettes transcend her fear. She nodded to Marta. "I'm counting on you to give me the signal."

Marta nodded, and Clara glanced up at the stoic bulbs in their glass encasements, scheduled to brighten at any second.

Silence dawned as Chicago darkened from a rich blue that stretched with the fiery sky to steal any violet. The lights that hung beside them wobbled in the wind. Clara watched one. A second click was followed by a hum, a low note that buzzed. Clara held her breath. The spark of a red glow illuminated more brightly in the center of the incandescent bulb. With every second, it grew stronger and stronger until it turned yellow, and as the crowds gasped in awe of such a magical sight, the wires inside the bulb sprang to electric life and lit up the glass.

Fernando watched the splendor. "They're on. They've stayed on. Clara—they were never dismantled."

In another life, Clara would have yearned to watch the setting sun with the rest of Chicago. But in this life, the one with Fernando in it, she decided to shut out the world and admire him instead. Another click sounded, and Fernando's gaze flickered toward a nearby streetlamp. The glow of its bulb brightened. Science instead of fire, controlled and sophisticated instead of wild and predatory.

Chicago transformed. Those walking through the fairgrounds exuberant embodied the delight Westinghouse had surely intended for. The World's Fair was going to dazzle from that night onward. Nothing would be the same now that the thought of night had become drastically different. And they were lucky enough to witness it.

Fernando stepped closer to Clara in a way that pulled her into a dream. She felt like a photograph, frozen in time and wanting nothing more than to stay there forever. They stared at the scattered bits of luminescence, and Clara dared herself to try to tell the difference between these manmade lights and the stars shining beside them.

Until a sudden movement snapped her focus back into place.

"Fernando," she breathed, drawing him out of the lights' spell.

Fernando tensed, and she knew he saw it, too.

"Clara!" Sally called. "The Kodak!"

Suits stormed for them, but as soon as they fell into the same light as the rest, their faces changed. Skin peeled away for bone. Their eyes vanished into their sockets until they were forever gone. Their mouths sank deeper into their heads until all that was left were long jagged teeth.

Clara's eyes widened in horror. The shadow in the photograph on Bynum Island ambushed her mind like a thunderstorm. The group of skeletons huddled around the crate in Machinery Hall. Stevie readying to attack Lily, the bravest girl Clara had ever known.

All of it now stared Clara in the face.

She ducked under the Kodak's curtain, her hands shaking as she lifted the flash and clicked the camera's shutter. A burst of light followed, and the suits halted. Around them, patrons who'd been distracted by such sudden movement blinked and saw there were not men beside them, but skeletons.

Monsters.

The reaction on the promenade and the entire Court of Honor was quick. Screams cut into the atmosphere. Children clutched at their parents for repose. Several men loosened guns from their belts and raised them, firing shots into the breadth of skeletons. Not a single one fell, and Clara was horrified at the thought that whatever these things were might be stronger than ammunition.

The flash of the Kodak went faint, powder and a desperate hum piercing the air, but the damage had been done—the lights around the Court of Honor showed all. They tried to hide themselves, conceal their bones, drag the length of their sleeves or collars across any traitorous body part as shots rang futilely into the night.

More and more and more until the world had gone from stunning to thunderous in less than a handful of seconds.

Bullets flew clear through the suits, and the incandescent

lights burned brightly, sending a yellow shine across all of Chicago like stardust fallen until the truth of who the suits were —bone and grit and nothing else—could no longer be denied. Clara held her breath as they faced her, spying the camera and the flash she held high.

"Got them," she announced to Sally, to Marta, to Fernando —all frazzled by the burst of light. She yanked open the Kodak's canister and pulled out a black spool of film. "We've got them."

"Best it happened now and not later," Fernando whispered, a note of fear tainting each word. "With the initiation tonight, who knows how many would actually be on the fairgrounds if we'd waited any longer?"

Something in Clara's heart jumped. "Initiation?"

"Yeah," he said, glancing at her. "At The Cat's Whisker."

Clara's blood turned cold, but she couldn't place what had chilled her so.

"Now is definitely not the time for sweet nothings, you two!" Marta cried as Sally collapsed the Kodak back into its casing. "Run!"

Suits lunged toward them, long limbs made longer by their bones. The scowls on their faces might have been smiles in daylight, but here they were ghouls doing all in their power to stop a handful of girls and a fair worker from stealing all they'd built.

"Jesus, Mary, and Joseph," Fernando swore quietly as he reached for Clara's hand. "Where to now?"

A parade of frightened fairgoers cascaded the promenade like an exodus. With one quick hoist, the Kodak was on Marta's back, and the flash was with Sally, and both girls beckoned Clara and Fernando to join.

"We have to lose them!" Marta said. "If we don't, it'll all have been for nothing!"

Clara fell into step with Fernando, pushing against silk blazers and soft parasols as panic took over and Westinghouse's lights flickered down upon them.

Then, "Clara," came a sad, sad call.

Clara startled at the familiarity of the voice that spoke so clearly in the madness. For a moment, it sounded like her mother —laughter or lullabies—but the voice's timbre was low. The cadence, masculine. The world dulled to a hum, even as chaos escalated by the second.

She searched the crowd until she found a man no more than five yards away. One with eyes as crimson as the deepest sunset and skin clammy like he'd been taken by fever, but Clara knew better.

A suit stood on either side of Jonathan Banks, skeletal hands clamped like vices around his biceps. Banks barely noticed as his eyes searched Clara's like he might be caught between the memory of a whiskey tumbler and a promise he'd loathed himself to make.

"Clara, my sweet girl," he whispered. He'd never said her name with guilt before. "Please. Run."

Time slowed, and though Clara could feel Fernando's hand pulling at hers, she planted her feet and refused another step. "Father, what are you doing here? What are *they* doing?"

But she already knew. Fernando had already said. *An initiation.*

The peppering of stray bullets shocked Clara back into focus. The screams of frightened children, and the cries of babies following. The crowd was an ocean quickly becoming a hurricane. Through all the madness, Clara heard echoes of her question to Banks, and though her father's lips parted as he answered, the sound of it was swallowed by the fair.

Clara knew her father well, though. And she knew exactly how he'd respond.

"This way, you could have everything I couldn't give you. Not since Bethany."

Banks's eyes softened at what was to become of him. He tore away from Clara's gaze and nodded once at the suits.

"Fuck the initiation, I say," one of them declared through his skeletal grin. "The world's on fire, and this one's ready now."

And then they were sinking into him like shadows that wanted to lap up the darkness.

The anarchy of the promenade erupted more loudly, and Clara snapped to life. She could feel Fernando pulling her after him—she might have even heard her name once or twice—but that didn't matter.

Clara tore free and ran in the opposite direction.

"Clara! Wait!" Fernando called.

But onward she ran.

"Father!" Clara pushed against the crowd striving to escape. Suit after suit grasped at Clara's arms, her skirt, the heels of her shoes, like they knew she had taken the photograph just as Fernando had failed to sabotage the lights. She kicked and elbowed, meeting only bone on the other end as she gritted her teeth and fought to free herself. "Father!"

As Clara ran toward the two suits—their backs curled into dark wisps of shadows over a now much smaller figure—her foot hit something in the middle of the promenade.

The baseball bat she'd so eloquently kicked only moments before.

"Splendid." She seized it and ran as fast as she could across the promenade.

Only seconds later did she reach the suits. Without hesitation, Clara slammed the bat into the shadows hovering over her father. She could feel the wood hit bone in a way that was nauseating, but she hit nonetheless at ribs and collar bones and shoulders and skulls. Their screams were inhuman, and their empty eyes were haunting things. Clara clenched her teeth and forced her way through their silk linens and sinewy ligaments until she found her father. His eyes were shut, and his body was still, but as Clara yanked his arm around her shoulder, she could feel the slow beat of the pulse in his wrist.

Not dead, she thought. And not one of them. That was enough for now.

Clara tapped on Banks's lulling cheek. "It's all right. I'm here. You need to stand, Father. We have to get you out of this place!"

Banks cupped his daughter's cheek in return. "Bethany?"

Clara's eyes welled from heat and exhaustion—tears belonging to Lily and tears belonging to her mother. They mixed down Clara's cheeks with memories attached to each. The florals of a garden. The sweetness of lemon cake. "No. Please. Can't you see? It's me."

Banks's eyes softened in painful delight. "Clara. My Clara. Yes, that's right. I wanted to give you the world. St. Joan's, The Cat's Whisker, the endless nights away from you and your mother. It was all for you. I was such a fool." He curled against her and cried.

Clara held her father tightly. "Yes, you are a fool. A lovable, wonderful fool, but a fool nonetheless. You might have wanted to give me the world, but all I ever needed was my father."

CHAPTER 29

———————

MONSTERS

Fernando searched the crowd for Clara amongst movement, fear, lights, and skeletons, but she was gone.

"Clara!" he shouted. "Clara!"

Try as he might to plant his feet firmly into the granite path, the panic of the fairgoers was a hell of a lot stronger, now that monsters had been revealed. They pushed and shoved, a torrent whose dam had urgently cracked. Footsteps tipped too close to the edge of the Grand Basin, and shoulders slammed into the pristine white of the buildings and terminals. The entire world spilled out from the World's Columbian Exposition.

Lights hummed and buzzed, circumventing the grounds, and the world ran in the opposite direction. Away from the lights. Back into the darkness.

Fernando's heart pounded. "Clara!' he shouted again.

This time, too loudly.

Fernando's heart skipped a beat as the realization hit. Suits searched the thousands parading the promenade. They pulled apart arms and limbs and tossed them aside. They didn't care about fighting back—even against those with hot and fast pistols ready to blast bullets into their bodies. They were much more interested in finding someone who'd failed them. Someone who refused to let them hide in the daylight of yesterday.

The monsters' faces cocked toward his, and everything turned as clear as water. They wanted Fernando García Carolan. Now that the lights were on, they were searching for him.

Fernando's blood ran hot. "Fuck, what now?" he muttered.

"He's there," the suit at the front said, a low and strange voice that spurred wisps into the air like the curls of cigar smoke. Despite the bullets and screams, the suits pushed onward, brushing anyone aside like a swarm of mosquitoes. They were as slow as they were lanky and awkward, but they could speak. And the tallest one did.

"You owe Mr. Winston a great debt," he said as Fernando inched away from the newly-sparse crowd. "Now greater since you were unable to see your agreement through. What a disappointment, Mr. García Carolan." The suit tsked several times, shaking its head. As it spoke, the teeth in its skull stretched with every word, like vowels were as much of a problem as the idea of not wearing skin. "What an utter *disappointment*." And then the monster inclined its head and smiled. It looked like a shining gourd of a thing. "No wonder your parents ordered you out of their house."

Fernando's hands shook with rage. He steadied his hands into ready fists.

The skeleton stretched an ugly gray finger toward him. "Why fight this? There is so much you will gain. We didn't lose an anchor on that island today. We found ourselves a better one."

The shakes in Fernando's hands voyaged across his body like a fleet of vengeful ships. "I'd rather be ripped into a million pieces and fed to fat Brooklyn rats than become one of you."

The skeleton pressed its bony fingers together and cocked its head in the other direction. "Is that so? Well, I'm sure such a thing can be arranged."

Fernando frowned.

The skeleton nodded. At who, Fernando didn't see. Because a sack of black silk had suddenly fallen over Fernando's face.

And just as he tried to scream, a hand slapped over his mouth.

CHAPTER 30

———————

HOPE

THE PANIC IN CHICAGO DISORIENTED CLARA'S WALK FROM THE promenade toward the Midway. Her father's weight rested against her and Sally while Marta hauled the Kodak with the precious spool of film tight in her hand. Glowing lights, gardens of flowers, and streams so still Clara nearly mistook them for glass—it all felt like a dream as the noise of the world grew too loud to be noise at all. It transformed into an ear-ringing silence that shook her dreadfully.

"Come on," she whispered to her father, like to speak to him might mean he'd be all right. She couldn't hear his groans as he pulled to and from consciousness, but she felt their vibrations against her thudding heart. "Come on," she said again and caught Sally's worried eyes amidst the chaos. "We have to go—"

Where? St. Joan's was destroyed—gone forever with the memories of Lily and Stevie—and they were too far away from any of their homes.

"Downtown?" A panic rose in Clara's throat as she searched the fair and saw thousands of frightened people but no one to help. "Oh God, Sally. What do we do now?"

"Just keep going," Sally replied. "Keep walking. We're getting out of here."

A sharp cry startled all three girls as Banks halted. Clara gripped the crisp white collar of her father's shirt. "Father?" She patted the five o'clock shadow on his jaw, heat and sweat from astonishment and whiskey collecting on her hand. A fever, maybe. Or shock from what had nearly transpired. Clara didn't want to think about it until they were safe.

"Stop," Banks suddenly ordered. Clara and Sally let go.

He stepped away with a bout of heavy breathing, ambling for his necktie and loosening it like it had been strangling him. They were a good distance from the Court of Honor, but not quite yet on the Midway. Or far enough from danger that Clara could justify stopping.

"Father?" she asked again.

Banks found his way off the path and collapsed onto the grass, his knees pulled up so he could rest his elbows on them. His eyes fell shut as he steadied his heart with slow breaths. And then he shook his head. "I'm fine. Just a moment. Please."

Clara turned to Sally and Marta, who were staring at the black cylinder in Marta's hand.

Marta's lips pursed in thought. "What if the newspapers think it's fake? What if they don't believe us? What if it's easier to dismiss three girls than see the truth?"

Clara hadn't considered that. She'd always assumed her word would never be as strong as hard and tangible proof, but the Alouettes had a good point—it wasn't as though tricksters or con artists hadn't been fiddling with this new technology already. "My father could deliver it to *The Chicago Tribune*. Marta, yours works there, doesn't he? Wouldn't that make a difference?"

Marta lifted one shoulder in an uncertain shrug. "It might."

"It's the best chance we've got," Clara said. "Our city is being run by monsters, and these monsters have been stealing girls from

Bynum Island and others from Chicago to stay alive!" Her father's breathing had slowed to a relaxed pace. His lips moved like he was praying, something he'd never done since Clara's mother had died. "That's our plan. The work isn't done yet."

Sally nodded. "We have to put a stop to all of it."

Marta gripped her hand. "Tonight."

"We have to find their leader," Clara said, recalling Miranda's story about the traveling demon and how he was king of his own world. But then, "Where's Fernando?"

Sally searched the Midway. "I don't know."

"He was with us when the madness exploded on the promenade," Marta said. "Clara, he was holding your hand."

But Clara had dropped Fernando's hand to save her father. Fernando had called her name, but that was it. She'd run from him, left him alone in a crowd of fairgoers and monsters.

Monsters, the sprite said,
Are famished but eat none.
They lock to another
For eons to come.

"Oh God," Clara whispered as she sucked a nervous breath between her teeth. She raced to her father's side and knelt in front of him. "Father." She clutched his hand. "The Cat's Whisker. Where is it?"

It shocked Banks out of the prayer he was reciting, and his bright eyes found Clara's. "No." He shook his head furiously. "You're not going there. Not my daughter. We're going back to our house in the countryside, and we are taking the first train out of this godforsaken city—"

"Father," Clara said sternly. "I am not running away." Impatiently, Clara reached toward Marta for the spool of film and then gave it to Banks, closing it in his hand. "This is something the world needs to see. Please. Take it to the newspapers. And then I need you to trust me."

It came out as a plea, and Clara was unsure of whether her father would do this for her.

Banks pulled his daughter into a shaky embrace. "I lost my wife, Clara. I won't lose you, too."

"You won't," Clara promised. "I need to know where The Cat's Whisker is. Please," she said again. And then she let him see the eyes she'd inherited from her mother. "It's a traveling pub. Where is it now?"

Banks cupped his daughter's cheek and regarded her like her voice were a symphony loved long ago and only remembered now. His lips trembled as he fought back his fear, and then he slipped the spool into his pocket and withdrew something else: a business card. One that a Mr. Rex Winston had given to him at Marine Café. A bit of navy-colored card stock Banks had held tightly between a thumb and a finger like it could set the world on fire without warning. He gave the card to Clara.

She frowned. "There's nothing written here." And then, as her father waited, she turned the card until a bit of light caught its surface, seizing the faint lettering of a silver script, easily missed if one weren't looking too closely. "Mr. Rex Winston," Clara read in astonishment. "The Navy Pier."

"Where's the Navy Pier?" Sally asked.

Marta frowned. "It's over by the Viking ship. I took photographs of it last week."

The last stop. The great red X marked on a treasure map. But there would be no gold seized tonight when an army of monsters waited, maybe with Fernando in their clutches. Lily was gone. Dodger was gone. Sally's Great-Aunt Dora. And, of course, Great-Aunt Miranda.

No more would disappear. Not if the Alouettes could help it.

"All right," Clara said as she tucked the navy card in her pocket. "I have an idea. But it involves making a stop at the German Village first."

CHAPTER 31

THE CAT'S WHISKER

THE SUIT THAT HAD SLUNG FERNANDO OVER HIS SHOULDER MUST have felt the sting of a stray bullet during the chaos on the promenade—he emitted a painful grunt with each uneven step.

Fernando, on the other hand, was torn between thrashing and going completely still. Anything to stop himself from thinking of what would happen to someone who had failed an army of monsters.

Eventually, his patience wore down to nothing, and he smashed his palms against the suit's legs. "Put me down, you fucking bastard!" Silk bag over his head or not, he wasn't going down without a fight.

But the suit didn't as much as shudder, as though his bones were made of rock. He walked onward with only a stutter in his step.

And then they began to descend.

They descended several steps at a time until the air grew muggier and colder and wetter—like the lake might be within reach, but no cresting waves sounded in the vicinity. They were somewhere else. Heading underground, where there would likely be no lights.

The smell of liquor hit Fernando next.

It was whiskey, and it assaulted his sense of smell enough that he flinched, like someone had struck him in the face with all the spirits in his mother's Irish hometown.

Suddenly, the suit halted.

"It's him, then? You're sure?" came another voice. A familiar one.

At first, Fernando was elated a family friend was there and would surely fix this horrible misunderstanding. But then Fernando remembered why he'd been brought to Rex Winston.

This was no family friend.

"Drop him."

Fernando braced for the inevitable fall.

Thump came the drop, and when his shoulder slammed into rock, he winced at the hot pain of it. He had no idea where he was. There were no basements at the World's Columbian Exposition—but there were pubs. Secret ones that moved about.

Places like The Cat's Whisker.

"Take that wretched thing off his head. He'll meet my eyes like a man, and if I don't like what I hear, he'll die like one, too."

The silk bag whipped off Fernando's face. He blinked ferociously as his eyes adjusted to the lights. Incandescent ones, which surprised him, but perhaps it was now more convenient than the glow of candlelight or gas. There was a redness to the walls like it'd recently met fresh paint. Magnificent oak moldings held up the rock above them as though the idea of stalactites in Chicago created a pleasant amount of terror, or at least enough to forego a proper ceiling.

A crowd of men surrounded Fernando, but no—that wasn't right.

Because they were definitely not human.

Fernando remembered the night he'd caught a glance of a monster in his bedroom window. Dark shadows and white bone and painted with electric light. Staring straight at him from the safety of the rose bush outside his window despite having only deep-set sockets. The shock of that returned. His hands pressing against the ground were not skeletal but flesh and blood, human. That was something. That was a relief.

I am not one of them.

He wondered if choosing not to destroy the lights had saved him from such a fate.

"Looks years younger now that he's afraid," one of the monsters growled. "Just a boy! Trying to hide it with some ashy shit around the lids?"

A handful of suits stared down at Fernando. Some straightened and re-cuffed the links on their sleeves, settling against a luxurious oak-lined bar. They reached for sparkling tumblers. Cheers to them all, and then a handful took a drink.

Then, there was another. Sitting at the bar, crouched over a drink Fernando couldn't quite see. Clutching the glass was a hand with bony fingers and gray-white knuckles and a skull ring, like the joke had been on the whole world this entire time. A sharp movement forced Fernando's gaze upward to the face that had turned sideways, a silhouette eclipsing one of the lights.

There was no nose. And the teeth were too long.

"Welcome to The Cat's Whisker, Fernando García Carolan."

Rex Winston always greeted a colleague with their full name. As a boy, Fernando had never been granted the privilege of being called on in such a grown-up way. On the contrary, Winston, whenever visiting New York for business, had always referred to him as simply, *"Fernando."* Or at the very least, *"that boy of yours"* to Juan or Imogen.

In the most saccharinely endearing way possible.

Now Fernando hated how Winston addressed him, like all

three parts of him—his own name, his father's, and his mother's —were being mocked with every syllable.

Winston turned fully, and Fernando saw the extent to which his form shone through. The eyes were empty sockets, and the teeth revealed themselves in a gory smile. Cracks and dents served as natural imperfections along the jawline, like true skulls and bones were as unique as the people who wore them in life and carried their stories carved into the surface.

Fernando refused the impossibility this was the man who had once broken bread with his family.

But no, not quite. "You never ate my mother's beef stew. None of it. You sat there. You drank tea." He remembered the trays of cucumber sandwiches and lemon cakes from Mrs. Grant. All of these plates of decadent treats, untouched.

It was a strange thing to say at such a time, but Winston laughed in amusement, and through the echo that came from having fang-like teeth, it rang out as a sound Fernando could only describe as a heavy rattling of mismatched notes.

"You know what I've noticed about the human race in all these years, Fernando? As long as the conversation revolves around that which someone cares about most deeply, most *intently*, they'll never notice what you don't want them to see. I discussed American infrastructure with your father and the future of New York. With your mother, I talked about the tragedy of St. Monica devoting her life to praying for her sinner son. None of this was magic or power, Fernando. Indulging in someone's self-interest is the easiest way to create a glamour." A scoff. "Who has time for beef stew in situations like that?"

Winston straightened his bony fingers and wagged them in a row. Fernando watched as a pressed coin labeled *World's Columbian Exposition 1893, Chicago, Illinois* appeared on his right thumb like a turn of magic Fernando might have seen in Houdini's tent. He flicked it into the air only a few feet, and then reached to snatch it back. His hand fell into the shadow of another suit, where the skin of an old man appeared in the absence of electric light.

"Misdirection. Whatever you'd like to call it."

Winston pocketed the coin and lifted his own glass tumbler with whiskey, swirling it in his palm.

"No, we do not consume food anymore. Instead, we drink spirits. But it doesn't satiate us forever. That's why we keep feeding, with humanity's help. And the world gives it to us, Fernando. You wouldn't believe how many people say yes to the world of which I am king, even at the price I ask."

Winston—or at least, the creature Fernando had known to be Rex Winston—leaned forward, his cracking elbows settling nicely on knobby knees. Fernando had to lean away, and only then did he realize he was being held back by two suits. Their nails pressed painfully into his shoulders, and with a wince, Fernando sneaked a glance at the gray tips that spidered outward from each finger.

He forced his attention back to Winston. "Does my father know?"

Winston scoffed. "That fool from the old world? God, no. There'd be no reason to tell him. I could never turn someone with a heart that strong anyway."

Fernando shook. There was one more thing still left unasked. "My mother?"

Winston's dead eyes seemed to light up like onyx searching for sunshine. "Who do you think reminded Imogen Carolan of the parable of The Prodigal Son? Who gave her the prayer card of St. Monica that now sits facing away on her mantle?"

Fernando shook harder now. "She wouldn't have been fooled by someone like you."

"Correct. Your mother was too close to her faith to be of good use to me. And anyway, it'd been time to leave New York.

Chicago was a growing metropolis. A bustling city with warring men like Edison and Tesla. How could I refuse the opportunity to grow my family in such a place? A place where decades ago, I found a girl on a small island with an angry heart at that all-girls school whose jealousy for those around her provided me with a conduit—an *anchor*—into Chicago that gave us more strength than we could ever get on our own?" A pause, and then Winston cocked his skull-head loudly on his skeletal neck. "We had to lock her to the island, naturally. Though now, her time has come to an end. They only last for so long before they extinguish like a candle, but today the girl Stevie still had yet to fulfill one last feed before fading into oblivion, which means the era of a new anchor is on the horizon." As he spoke, his bones cracked in several spots. "You, Fernando. You have provided a serendipitous sort of opportunity for me. The failing business of your parents only helped. Your ambition was just what I needed to ensure my kind would remain secret from the world."

Fernando tried to shake free of the creatures' holds. But their fingers pressed more deeply into his flesh and muscle until an ache took up residence inside him. "Mr. Winston. Tell them to let go of me."

"Not so fast, boy. I was compassionate. I offered you the chance to repay me in action instead of money. Surely, a better choice for someone in your financial situation with eyes on the loftiest perch in society. All I asked for was a favor. And you couldn't even honor me with that."

"You wanted me to sabotage the fair."

"No. I wanted you to *save* the fair."

Fernando wretched his arms again. The monsters held more tightly. "You ordered me to destroy the lights."

Winston leaned back against the bar. He sighed. "Fernando, the world is not just. Some are born poor and die poor. Some are born rich and die richer. Much of it is a roll of the dice, and not as much as you think comes from hard work. As such, what you and I contribute to the world will always be seen as separate things. I have access to a great fortune. Centuries of living does that to an individual. Trust funds, marriages to the rich, escaping one city for another until you're too old to remember what the one you were born in actually looks like."

He laughed, and the shattering of it throughout the pub was enough to disturb the marrow in Fernando's bones.

"The decisions I make change the world. The wealth I could spread, oh, poets could write *sonnets*, Fernando. The opportunities—jobs, private schools—all of them come from a handful of men such as myself. I am not cruel. I want to continue living so I can do more good. If I were to be forced out of Chicago, well, surely you could see how that would affect the city as a whole. Surely, you could see how that might result in another tragic accident of sorts. A faulty steel beam hanging stories above Brooklyn loosened easily when Juan's boy was consistently negligent, daydreaming instead of champagne soirées with the rich."

Fernando froze. He would never forget the screams of the men who'd been crushed by steel. A ferocious anger heated his blood.

He'd been a marionette controlled by Winston all along.

"Surely," Winston continued, "you could see how a similar freak accident might happen to a girl named...*Clara.*"

"Stay away from Clara." A darkness inside Fernando freed itself with each heated word.

Winston continued, unthreatened, "You can see how very valuable I am to the growth of Chicago. Whereas you, with where you come from, your parents and their humble beginnings, you could never offer the same. Any good you do in the world, while still noble in intention, would affect only, perhaps, a handful of people at the very most. Don't you see, Fernando?

How important it was to ensure my secret was kept safe? It was for the good of the entire city, boy. *The world.*"

Fernando shook his head despite himself. "People like you—*monsters* like you—need to be stopped."

Winston didn't as much as flinch at the word. "What is a monster? The ones among us who've been loyal to me since the very beginning? The children they've cultivated themselves? My kind are simply trying to thrive."

"You're killing people to do it. That's a monster."

The pause that followed was loud. It rang in Fernando's ears like church bells. He couldn't see what lay inside the mind of Rex Winston. His black eyes were memories of what true eyes should look like. But the mannerisms hadn't changed. Winston tapped his fingers against his knee in thought, just as Fernando had always known him to do.

It sent shivers down Fernando's spine.

Winston leaned back in his chair. "Fernando. There's nothing down here that would protect you. Those who'd been shocked by Westinghouse's display of electrical lights have long since gone home, reminisced about their day as they've sunk into soft beds with feather pillows and down blankets. They've boiled milk for their children to drink. They've convinced themselves what they saw had been nothing more than a sheer illusion. A magician's trick. A good one, at that. Houdini, perhaps. Chicago will weave their stories into something believable. And come the start of next week, they'll talk to their friends about what it'd been, speculate as to whether the papers will report the same. They'll be certain they saw the edges of a mask when upon first glance it'd seemed like something else. And if not, they'll fool themselves, lie to themselves, trick themselves."

Fernando had one card left to play. "Clara took a photograph of the Court of Honor. Your monsters were there, captured by the flash. Soon the papers will know everything."

Winston shrugged. "A doctored illusion. Exactly like the moving pictures that old boy Edison unveiled today. What is more believable—a trick, a prank, a child's hoax? Or eternal beings who walk amongst the living appearing as they do? You cannot win, boy. I'm terribly sorry, but power trumps good intentions. Every time."

Fernando refused this. Furiously he screamed for help. As loudly as he could manage until he felt it in his bones. Something clicked free inside him that amplified the feeling—a sadness transformed into defiance. Against the world, against Chicago, against Winston, and against the skeletons piercing their claws into his flesh. Until all that was left of Fernando was an empty rawness.

"Scream, then. All you like! Scream until no one comes after you and your voice is hoarse like the scratch of steel wool! Scream, because in only a few moments, the debt you and your ancestors owe me will be paid, and you will become my next anchor."

Fernando's scream faltered. He struggled against the suits. *I won't, I won't, I won't.*

Winston stood, glass in hand as he reached over the counter to take the bottle and pour another drink. Neat. He drank until the glass was empty, amber droplets shining on the edges. And then he approached Fernando and stared him straight in the eyes.

"I, for one, am quite hungry."

As Winston's shadowy claw of a hand reached for Fernando's cheek, a slam shattered the silence. Winston jerked away. The skeletal monsters held Fernando tightly, but not enough that he couldn't turn toward the racket.

A burst of yellow light spilled from the door at the top of the stairs. There were shadows in the places of people storming down, and Fernando couldn't see who it was.

It was the footstep on the first stair that told him it was her. Strong, clacking—shoes he couldn't imagine running in.

Completely and utterly Clara Banks.

She and the girls following her stepped into the pub's thick light.

"Clara," Fernando managed. It was impossible she could be there, that she, Sally, and Marta could find him amid monsters in an underground pub that traveled this way and that across the fairgrounds. But they had, and when Clara saw him, her eyes swelled with a kind of courage he couldn't imagine in himself.

"I came for a drink, but I'm going to stay for the monsters." In her grip she held a thin sword, one Fernando recognized from the German Village on the Midway. He knew it was real and sharp, and in his amazement, he saw all of the other girls carried swords, too.

Sally pursed her lips as though about to blow a kiss, but instead of doing so, she whistled.

Fernando recognized the tune immediately from walking past his neighbors' home in Brooklyn, the ones who'd come from Lyon ten years prior.

Alouette, gentille alouette.

Alouette, je te plumerai.

He frowned, confused. But then behind Sally, more girls from St. Joan's spilled down the stairs. Five, ten, fifteen. Perhaps twenty-five. Clara stood in front of them, tall as she was brave, and she stared at Winston.

Winston grabbed Fernando's head—one cold and bony finger around his entire jaw. Fernando choked. Winston could easily snap his neck, and no one would be able to stop him.

"One more step, girl. Just try me," he growled.

But Clara would not be threatened. "You think I'm afraid of a dusty old man?" She pointed the bulk of the sword toward him.

"Let him go or I'll smash your pumpkin of a head against the wall."

CHAPTER 32

THE KING OF MONSTERS

It was probably unwise to infiltrate an army of monsters like Stevie: complicated and horrifying arrangements of marching bones, monstrous and immortal because of the evil they'd chosen instead of good.

Probably unwise.

But before that, the Alouettes had also had the even *less* unwise idea to return to the German Village, into which Clara had boldly followed Fernando a lifetime ago. Because inside were suits of armor. Weaponry.

Swords of all shapes and sizes.

Including those a girl could use to fight.

The sword Clara had liberally borrowed while the crowds at the fair dispersed in a maddening way was too archaic for any possible intimidation. But the very idea of a group of girls all wielding old-fashioned blades as they ambushed a secret traveling pub for Chicago's rich and powerful might be frightening enough.

For now.

"Stay strong," Sally whispered.

Clara lifted her chin high and remembered what Lily had taught her about ferocity with a blade. Everything came like a flood of orders as though Lily were there herself, reminding each girl of their plan.

"He is leaving with us." Clara pointed her sword at Fernando. She was elated to see him alive and well and in one piece, but cautious, too, because that could change in the quickest of split-seconds.

The monster who was undoubtedly the leader amongst the lot of skeletons stood taller at Clara's words. He was not a big man, but there was strength radiating from him, the same kind that comes whenever someone has garnered power, and Clara changed her mind about calling him a leader—he was more of a king, this traveling demon. She wondered what sort of face this man would wear if incandescent bulbs were not shining upon them all.

She wondered if she knew him.

"Dear girl," the king said, "you think you can threaten me? You can hardly hold that weapon."

The way he said it was not to mock or to tease but out of confusion by the presence of Clara and the Alouettes. The monsters laughed, and Clara felt anger rise up inside her, hot lava scalding her veins.

She couldn't even demand the respect of monsters.

But she dug her heel into the ground nonetheless. "This is our home. Leave Chicago. Now."

The king burst into a deep bout of laughter with the rest. Clara shrank back into herself as she studied the horrid things they were. Skulls of the dead, bobbing against their skeletal shoulders, and skulls of the evil, turning Clara's threat into a joke.

When the laughter fell quiet, the king pointed a bony finger. "Kill her first."

Suddenly the steel in Clara's hands was not strong enough, and she sucked in a terrified breath.

Fernando shook against the monsters' grips. "Clara, run!"

"No." Clara had run before, and Lily had died.

One of the monsters was suddenly inches from her, and Clara's blade shook from her fright. Its cold dead hands swiped recklessly at her skin—nothing like the other one on Bynum Island, but new to this undead existence—and Clara swung, smashing the edge of the sword against its jawline. As the steel hit the skull, shards of bone went flying with cigar smoke and the stench of brandy. The monster slammed into the wall and collapsed to the floor.

All went silent.

Then chaos broke out between Alouettes and monsters.

"Leave not a single one alive!" the king shouted, ordering skeleton after skeleton upon the girls with angry waves of his hand.

Sally stepped forward, her sword aimed at the perfect angle for sparring. "Lily would show no mercy, Alouettes. Do her memory proud!" And then she charged forward, straight into the skeletons as the Alouettes followed.

A big burly monster seized Clara's wrist and twisted her arm so his bony fingers could curl around the edge of her blade. She gritted her teeth and fought back, but he slammed her into the stone wall, pinning her so she couldn't move.

"Horrible girl," he growled, ash and whiskey against her skin. "Learn your place."

Clara glowered with the fire of a thousand infernos. "My place is right here," she retorted. "Making sure monsters get what's coming to them." With a swift move, she sent her knee into the bones across his stomach, and he tore away with a pained cry. Clara freed her sword and slammed it into the monster's burly chest.

Splintered bone rained upon her as the shuddering blade pulled free, and Clara forced herself not to think of what that meant.

Around her, monsters howled as they ambled forward. The Alouettes crashed the steel of their blades against them, slicing at arms or legs. The fight grew bloody, dark, quick. Sally and Marta garnered a pile of bones at their feet, close enough to the stairwell and ready for the inevitable escape.

The Alouettes were winning, but it was only a matter of seconds before the monsters would have to change their tactics. One by one, the suits slammed their skeletal fists into the fixtures on the wall, bursting every bubble of electric light and granting them the safety of darkness.

"Don't let them break the lights!" Clara shouted. "They want to hide who they are."

Across the room, Fernando's neck was tucked between the king's bony hands, fingers edging close to his jaw. With one fast twist and a snap, Fernando's neck would be broken.

Clara wasn't going to let that happen.

A scream slowly built in her throat and released as she ran. It caught the king off-guard, and he loosened his hold on Fernando's throat enough that a great skull-topped ring slipped from his finger. Clara's sword smashed against his head, but it didn't crack the bone like it'd done to the others, those who were much younger than the rest.

On the contrary, this king of monsters remained without a scratch from her blade and seemed more interested in his fumbling ring than the fact Fernando was now free. Another monster reached and caught it before the ring could hit the floor. Inches above the ground, it floated for only a moment. A split-second later, and the ornate skull might have shattered into pieces.

Clara froze. Symbols carried power to men like these. She considered the pearl ring on her own finger.

Fernando raced to her side. "Clara, he can't die."

Another fixture on the wall came crashing down with the sharp sound of breaking glass, and a second section of The Cat's Whisker went dark. It gave Clara an idea. "I don't think that's true."

The king rose again and scowled like a gargoyle. "*Die?* The older I get, the stronger I become. Did you really think a blade of pitiful steel was going to destroy me? I've had rifles shot straight through my heart in Georgia, cannons blasted at me in Pennsylvania." He stormed toward her. "The more I convince fools to join me, the longer I stay amongst you. What I offer the world is irresistible, and now my skeleton is turning to iron instead of bone. *Indestructible.*"

Fernando shot in front of Clara, his arms outstretched. The king seized Fernando by the collar and tossed him aside, black eyes straight on Clara. He towered over her.

"I knew you when your mother passed, Clara, dear. You have the same shape of eyes, the same dark curl of hair. And then your pathetic father—driven to the drink, but still full of love for you. You remind him of her, and dear God, I must agree—the resemblance is there."

Clara was sickened by the idea of this thing knowing such personal memories. "Who are you when there are no lights to be found?" She had to know.

"I am the reason Jonathan Banks has become anything important in this world," he replied. He snatched her throat before she could stop him, and Clara dropped her sword. The king slammed Clara into the side of the wall, cold from the rock spiraling up her back.

Clara's hands instinctively flew to her throat as though it could make any difference. She wondered if she would be courting death in these next few moments, if this monster would turn her into one of his walking skeletons, if she'd come back like Stevie. She wondered if that would be better than the darkness flooding her eyes—to have an immoral existence instead of none at all.

Clara Banks was a Protestant but not a very good one, and right then, the idea of any afterlife seemed bleak.

As the king pressed his sharp thumbs into her throat, drawing blood, Clara's blackening eyes found the shine of the skull on his finger. The room was spinning, and her chest was collapsing.

Fernando raced to grab the king's hands, pulling futilely at them.

"Fernando!" she managed, her throat sharp as her voice tried its mightiest. "Let go!"

Time slowed. Fernando's dark eyes with the smears of kohl lining them stared into hers, and she willed him to understand, to know all of this could come to an end if only he would let her save herself. It was a risk.

But Clara suspected there was one way to stop this king of monsters.

With the slight quiver of a lip, Fernando dropped his grip as Clara felt the beginnings of suffocation. She pulled herself free of the king's hand with all her strength. She set her gaze toward the dark ceiling and another light fixture, and with one swift swing, she hooked the king's hand with its ring onto the fixture and pulled. The ring caught on the steel, and the fixture came off the wall easily, the lightbulb inside falling with the case. With gritted teeth, Clara smashed the whole lot of it onto the king's head—glass shattering into an explosion of dust and wires, the bulb with it.

But it didn't just disorient the king—it did more.

It was a symbol of the future in Chicago, and it sent a foul dent into the king's skull. His blackened eyes widened with horror as the electricity still alive and flowing caught on his entire skeleton and lit up the room. A sharp sound like a scream of defeat rang throughout The Cat's Whisker, and the Alouettes and Fernando covered their ears. All of the monsters sank to their knees, sickening gurgles spilling free from their ugly jaws.

The king gasped—his mouth too wide to be human—and dropped Clara.

She fell beside Fernando, and he drew her against him, lifting her face as she sucked air into her lungs. She stared into his dark eyes, terrified and fierce, and nodded.

"I'm all right," she said, her fingers pressing against the bleeding scratches at her throat. "I swear to you, I am."

Fernando slowly shook his head side-to-side, like to see Clara now was nothing short of unbelievable. His hand fell into hers, and she inhaled sharply as she came alive with his touch. Had she caught the electricity, too? Was she dying just as the king surely was?

Fernando brushed a thumb across her cheek. "That's twice now you've saved me."

Clara tried to breathe, but it was impossible. "Please don't let there be a third," she whispered.

Fernando smiled, and then despite war and electric light, monsters and Alouettes, his dark eyes dropped to Clara's lips and he leaned closer, closer, closer, until his mouth could brush against hers. They tensed ever so slightly at the sweet kiss it was. He was warm against her, and Clara knew without any shadow of a doubt that if there ever were to be a third time she'd have to save Fernando from death, it would most certainly be worth it.

The kiss ended, and they smiled—but there was a strange taste of sadness on Clara's lips she didn't understand.

Then the world shook them free of each other. The king's shrill gasp was never-ending. It flooded the space around them with a fog, like something had been released from the new cracks forming on his skull. Then, one at a time, the monsters began to crumble. Their bones lifted and turned into sand that held its place for a mere second before falling apart. The screams they gave as their bodies unraveled were a mix of hell and song, an orchestra of undoing amplified. Fernando helped Clara to her feet, and together they watched, hand-in-hand.

"It's killing them," Fernando said, amazed.

Clara swallowed. It was true, what Fernando said, but not entirely. Some of the livelier skeletons collapsed into dust, ones whose bony faces were brighter than the rest. Newer. Younger. The king paced the room, his bony hands clutching his skull like he was desperate to hold himself together.

"Wretched girl!" he shouted. "I've lost my army! I've lost the ones they've created themselves!"

Fernando picked up Clara's sword. "How does your iron skeleton like this pitiful blade of steel now?"

He lifted the sword higher.

This time, when Fernando struck, a chunk of skull flew from the monster's face straight into the wall.

CHAPTER 33

AT THE EDGE OF THE LAKE

THE CEILING ABOVE THEM SHOOK—GRIT AND GRIME AND STONE
and earth. It rattled. Dirt tumbled into Clara's hair and eyes, and
she rubbed it away. It was an earthquake following a musical
score, just like the one on Bynum Island that had swallowed St.
Joan's. A call of thunder new to iambic pentameter. The Alouettes shrieked at each interval, and Clara clutched Fernando's
hand to steady herself. The lights flickered but stayed on. Bless-
edly so. Because Clara feared the darkness now that she knew the
incandescent bulbs showed the true faces of these suits.

"Get above ground!" Clara ordered the Alouettes. "If any girl
is hurt, help her up the stairs!"

Together, they ran. Girls with broken arms, girls with gashes
across their cheeks, girls with the strength that came when a sister
needed help, and girls who were unlucky enough to have all of it.

The last to reach the steps, Clara searched for the king in the
flickering darkness. As the bulbs burnt out one by one with each
tremor in the ground, she saw the king's face shift from skull to
man. A man whose face she recognized. Bright eyes and white
hair styled in a debonair silhouette. The illusion was alarming,

330

but Clara turned away not in fear but disgust, ashamed of the moments earlier that day when she'd been utterly charmed by Rex Winston.

"Clara," Fernando said. "What about the rest?"

But Clara refused to look back. "Let the earth bury them."

They fought their way up the shaking stairs. Above ground, the world was shockingly calm. Empty of fairgoers, though not of monsters. The World's Columbian Exposition, illuminated by Westinghouse's miraculous lights, had transformed into a gala for the hundreds of skeletons that now walked Chicago. Bright beams shone into their bone faces, but they ignored Clara and Fernando and the Alouettes.

They marched east, toward the lake.

Sally ran amongst them, testing the skeletons' vision by waving her hand in front of their faces and finding only emptiness. "They can't see us, Clara. What are they doing?" She threw a fierce punch into one's jaw, but her hand slid straight through. "We can't even fight them anymore."

Clara recognized so many as they fell in and out of the bulbs' glow. She saw women she knew from sweet shops she'd visit on her birthday—when her father would take her to get vanilla cake with snow-white frosting—who'd gossip about their patrons between custard slices. Folks on Easter Sunday who'd inevitably offer their prayers but never their coins to those outside churches. Bankers in the downtown of Chicago good enough at math to know how to lie about it well.

These were faces they'd worn in this city, and now these skeletons marched through the empty fairgrounds toward the capped waves crashing against the shore. They waded into the icy water, sloshing deeply into it, crisp shirts and formal wear and cravats and parasols be damned. They disappeared beneath the waves as Clara and Fernando and all the rest ran to the pier and watched.

Every single skeleton submerged itself, like sinking into the lake could very well be the fastest way out of Chicago.

Another girl came with them, one with russet hair and the memory of a Kodak in hand.

"Stevie!" Clara called. It was impossible, and yet there she was.

The girl turned to Clara, and her face was the worst of all. The eyes were gone—blistered and blackened and looking as though a giant had put out a pair of candles in her sockets while the rest of her fought the ashes that longed to become skin—but still Stevie managed to stare straight through Clara. The wet clothing she wore dripped lake water off her frame, and there was a long pause as though Stevie wanted to say something.

Clara wondered how Stevie had become Winston's sprite while living as an Alouette, a St. Joan's student, a girl who loved bitter chocolate cake and the bubbles of champagne. But Clara's only peace now came from knowing the creature Stevie Graham would never again cause the disappearance of another girl. The Alouettes could move forward in life and remember those who'd been lost to Stevie and the evil Rex Winston had set upon Chicago.

Sally could mourn Dora with her grandmother, Clara could mourn Miranda, and together, the Alouettes could love and cry and remember dear brave Lily. And one day, peace could be found.

Go, Stevie. Clara told herself to say the words out loud, to shout them into the wind. For Lily and Dodger, and for all the rest. But Clara couldn't speak. She searched wildly amongst the skeletons for a girl named Dora, a young teacher named Miranda. She had no idea what either had even looked like, but in that moment Clara hoped against hope she'd somehow know. If she saw them. If there truly was hope. If Dora and Miranda or any of the missing girls had survived.

But there was no one.

Stevie sank beneath the black waters, and then she was gone.

When all of the skeletons had vanished, Fernando glanced at Clara. "He is still here. Somewhere."

An unsettling weight sank any hope inside Clara. Fernando was right. She scanned the fairgrounds. And then a clicking sound drew her attention toward The Cat's Whisker at the Navy Pier.

"Look," Clara said, pointing.

The careful walk of a man who might have spent years in the spotlight of society came into the shadows. Rex Winston, who indeed had been instrumental in ensuring Clara's father had gotten the connection to Westinghouse and promised Clara a bright future, was now a shadow of who he'd truly been. No longer did he carry the power he'd boasted before. Now he was hunched over, like the burden of his own existence and that of his other monsters was too much to carry. The chipping at his jawline had hurt him horribly, but where the bone had shattered, now there was only emptiness.

He approached the waters, just before the pier.

Fernando tensed. "You don't deserve the chance to escape!"

Winston laughed. It rang through the night sky as a short growl of pain mixed with dark humor. "It doesn't matter. You might have weakened me as your grandfather did, but that's all you've done. As long as there are people, there I shall be, Fernando García Carolan, Clara Banks."

Clara held all the more tightly to Fernando's hand.

"Now I'll find another city," Winston said. "Another home. I'll gather my strength, and then I'll start again. Perhaps I'll return to Chicago one day. When your grandchildren are your age."

Clara's heart stopped from the threat in those words.

"Or," Winston added. "Perhaps it'll be in another city all

together. I hear St. Louis is quite the place to be." Then Winston marched straight into Lake Michigan, the last of his army. When the waves crested over the top of his skull, all went quiet.

Clara and Fernando stood together on the pier, looking over the fairgrounds and the lake beside it. Other than Sally and Marta, there was no one to verify what they'd seen.

Clara loosened a breath. "It's over." She shut her eyes and squeezed Fernando's hand. He was so warm, and the desire to embrace him overcame Clara like a stampede.

"Clara."

Her eyes opened slowly, catching sight of Lake Michigan, its tugging and releasing waves. But that wasn't what Clara focused on. She glanced up. At the stars.

The same stars she'd see if she were in Chicago. Or New York.

A sob caught in her throat, and she sucked in a breath to hide it. Beside her, Fernando turned ever so slightly. He released her hand, and Clara's skin chilled with the Chicago night. As soon as he'd said her name, she'd known. Her eyes welled, and she could no longer stop their slow fall onto her cold cheeks.

Fernando wrapped his arms around her shoulders and pulled her close. She wanted to breathe him in and out all at once—remember him forever and forget he'd ever been in her life. She didn't know which was worse, and then she cast aside her loud and persistent thoughts in favor of feeling his body against hers.

Not yet, she begged. *Please, not yet.*

Fernando didn't speak again, but he pulled back so he could press his lips to her forehead. His hands cradled her face, and she smiled as he did so.

It would be all right. One day. Home had a way of bringing peace, and if nothing else, Clara told herself to be happy Fernando would soon have that.

He smiled and stepped away. Though she wanted to go with

him, Clara did not move. Fernando tapped up his newsboy cap at her and the Alouettes, and then with a quick look at the night sky, he turned on his heel and walked back toward the promenade with his eyes on the lake and beyond, like he was sending a prayer to the place he'd soon return to.

Sally touched Clara's arm. "It's going to be okay, new money."

Clara nodded. "Yes. I know." She wiped the tears from her cheeks. "The photograph. My father will take it to the newspapers. All of Chicago will see what those monsters were."

Marta clutched Sally's arm. "Does it really matter? They said they'd come back!"

"But for now, they're gone," Clara assured her.

"We'll be ready if they ever return," Sally said.

Clara smiled. "Absolutely. Now come on, Alouettes. The world is about to change, and we need to be there for it."

THE END

Author's Note

There is a danger in approaching a period of history for storytelling—especially an American period of history. Details change because of artistic license, facts are skewed in favor of plot, and what comes from that is a tale some might consider factual, when it is far from such a descriptor.

Of course, the magic in this story isn't real, but at the 1893 World Columbian Exposition in Chicago, Illinois, there were real people—from the city, the outskirts, the rest of the United States, the entire world—who came together for a great, glorious event. There was also worker exploitation, greed beyond all measure, and racism.

Although Bynum Island is a real place in Illinois, St. Joan's Academy for Girls did not exist. In writing this story, I imagined a world where students of all races and ethnicities could come together to tinker with a Kodak camera, create a bit of mischief in the middle of the night, and solve a mystery at the World's Fair.

Sally and Marta exist in these pages only. Please do not take from this book that 1893 was a time of equality and that both girls represent those who would have enjoyed the same opportunities as Clara and Lily. To imply such an idea as truth would be incredibly irresponsible of me. It was absolutely not the case, and to suggest otherwise is to suggest we erase the racist history of America.

American history has always valued white voices above all

others: a disgraceful truth. It doesn't have to remain that way. We can lift the voices of People of Color, many whose stories and histories have been ignored and forgotten to the past, nothing short of a tragedy.

We must continue to push harder for inclusive platforms through which Authors of Color can share their stories with the world. We must consider how best to prioritize stories of those who lived through significant—and not so significant—times, told by those whose shared cultures with their heroes and heroines have shaped them into the storytellers they are today. And finally, we must always remember that white voices are not the right ones to tell some stories; instead, we must make room at the table for those who are.

Thank you for reading, and please check out hashtags such as #OwnVoices and #WeNeedDiverseBooks to find your next book.

Enjoy the adventures awaiting you!

Acknowledgments

I decided to release this book—one of the books of my heart—after so much change had occurred in my life.

I won't bore you with the details.

Safe to say, I want to first acknowledge my sister Sarah, to whom this book is dedicated. You're one of the very best people I know, and my life is so much better with you in it. A thousand people would agree with me. I truly think our birth order got mixed up somehow, and you were always meant to be my older and much-wiser sister, but whatever happened that made me the eldest, I love you dearly, and I thank you from the bottom of my heart for everything you've done for me.

I also want to thank the love of my life, Leland. My darling, I am so thankful for your strength, support, honesty, love—and so much more. Every day I am over-the-moon joyful and thankful that we found each other, and every day I know neither of us takes such gratitude for granted. We truly are the dreamiest of all dream teams, and I cannot wait for all the adventures to come in our life together. Thank you, my darling. I love you five all of the evers!

A special thank-you to my wife from another life, my forever Doode, and my perpetual mind-twin: Carla, we must have known each other for a thousand lifetimes by now, and you won't get rid of me just yet. I'm so proud of us for maintaining such a strong friendship even when there was 3,000 miles between us and a pandemic-related world lockdown that prevented us from seeing each other in person for four years. I love you with all my heart, and I couldn't ask for a better best friend.

I've also received so much love, support, and encouragement over the years from family, friends, colleagues, students, readers, and fellow writers. Your check-ins with me about my writing have pushed me to continue, even when this wild world of publishing feels like a mountain I'm not sure I can climb. I'm honored when you ask about my stories, and I hope I do you proud. Special shout-outs go to Nico for helping me with the French and Cesar for helping me with the Spanish.

Lastly, I want to acknowledge my mother, Roseanne, who passed away suddenly in August 2023.

Mom: You read the first chapter of this book almost ten years ago. That chapter has since changed into something better (I hope). I know it's hard to get objective artistic feedback from one's mother, but you loved it and wanted more. I have to reiterate something I mentioned in the first set of acknowledgments I was privileged to write for my debut: You never cared that I was never going to become a doctor, lawyer, an engineer, or anything else many parents wish for their children. You supported my love of the arts—always—and not everyone in life gets that kind of support. I don't take it for granted.

Thank you. I miss you. I wish I'd told you how the story ends while you were still with us.

But I'm glad you and Dad are together again.

Love,

Kathryn

About the Author

Kathryn Rose was born in Toronto, Canada, and grew up in the Kitchener-Waterloo region of Southern Ontario. After graduating with honours from York University, where she studied literature and philosophy, she relocated to Los Angeles, California. She lives on the west coast with her partner Leland and their two cats.

Kathryn is also the author of the METAL & LACE series, an Arthurian legend retelling with a steampunk twist, from Flux Books. In 2024, she founded Château Boho Books, an imprint for her fantasy novels.

Scan the QR code below to sign up for Kathryn's newsletter, and please leave a review wherever you buy your books!

Château Boho Books, LLC
Los Angeles, California, United States of America
www.chateaubohobooks.com